DELIRIOUS

RISE OF THE CHARIOTEER
BOOK FOUR

SUSAN LASPE

Top of the Hill
PUBLISHING

First Printing, 2025

ISBN 978-1-7377188-6-4

Cover Art, Design, & Layout by: Susan Laspe

Year of the Frog Publishing, LLC

6209 Mid Rivers Mall Dr. Ste 202

St. Charles, MO 63304

http://susanlaspe.com

ALSO BY SUSAN LASPE

CAST OF CHARACTERS

ABBOT CARADOC: abbot, monk at Valle Crucis Abbey

AETERNAE: ancient wolf-creature with horn protrusions all over its body; predator

AERON DREFAN: former knight of Chaddesden, son of Janus

ASINIA: dryad (tree nymph) from Cataractonium, warrior maiden

BRYNWEN MASSON: healer and midwife-in-training, twin of Talfryn

CIRCE: Roman goddess, sorceress, relative of Padric

CORNELIA: dryad (tree nymph) from Cataractonium, warrior maiden

ELIVA: dryad (tree nymph) from Cataractonium, warrior maiden

FAUNUS: Roman god of flora and fauna, a faun

GARRICK DE CLIFTON: Captain of knight corps in Derby, father of Padric

GREGORIO FIORI / TELEGONUS: tutor in Chaddesden, Derby / immortal son of Circe and Ulysses

HELIUS: Roman god of the sun, ancient charioteer, father of Circe

HERBERT HERRINGTON: Sheriff of Nottingham

HOWELL: monk at Valle Crucis Abbey

IDAISE: dryad (tree nymph) from Cataractonium, warrior maiden

JANUS: two-faced Roman god of time, one face sees the future, the other the past.

KETT: carpenter's apprentice from Chaddesden, descendent of Vulcan

LUCILIANA: dryad (tree nymph) from Cataractonium, warrior maiden

MEDEA: witch, allied with Janus, immortal

MISER: red squirrel from the Yorkshire Dales

NALINI: dryad (tree nymph) from Cataractonium, warrior maiden

PADRIC DE CLIFTON: knight of Chaddesden, descendent and heir of Helius

PAYLA: daughter of Pasiphae, priestess of Mithras, immortal

RANULF RAWLINS: knight of Chaddesden, has a knack for invisibility, godly parentage unknown

SEIA: dryad (tree nymph) from Cataractonium, warrior maiden

SHADOW DRUID: an ancient, cursed Druid, underling of Janus

TALFRYN MASSON: farmer, twin of Brynwen

ULYSSES: peryton (half-stag, half-bird), relative of Padric

WARIN INGRAM: knight of Nottingham, has Herculean strength, descendent of Helius and Jupiter

The Roman Gods & their Greek form

Apollo

Circe

Diana (Artemis)

Dionysus (Bacchus)

Faunus

Helius (Helios)

Juno (Hera)

Jupiter (Zeus)

Mars (Ares)

Mercury (Hades)

Minerva (Athena)

Neptune (Poseidon)

Pasiphae

Pluto (Hades)
Proserpina (Persephone)
Venus (Aphrodite)
Vesta (Hestia)
Vulcan (Hephaestus)

For you, reader

"Fear not; rise, He is calling you."
—Mark 10:49

"O haggard queen! To Athens dost thou guide
Thy glowing chariot, steeped in kindred gore;
Or seek to hide they damned parricide
Where peace and justice dwell for evermore?"
—*Euripides, from the tragedy cf "Medea"*

PART I
JOUST

"No man or woman born, coward or brave, can shun his destiny."

— Homer, *The Iliad*

PROLOGUE

September, AD 1356

"*I* will kill you."

Aeron awoke with a jolt, the scream dying on his lips. *No! I almost had him!* He tried to raise his hand to bash it on the cot in frustration, but it refused to yield to his will. Instead, it merely twitched. A terrible stitch in his side made him groan.

"Nay, I must finish him." His throat was parched and sounded scratchy to his own ears.

"*Soon, child. Soon, you shall have your revenge on de Clifton and his friends.*" The Shadow's grating voice sounded as though it came from inside Aeron's head, instead of the man himself. It was something he'd never fully get used to.

The Shadow's translucent hand hovered over his arm, radiating a chill that flowed into his bones. Aeron almost gasped at the sensation. "*But first, you must heal.*"

Heal? The memory of Padric's sword slicing through the flesh of his side returned, and he spat obscenities. His chest was covered in pink lines, and a bandage covered his abdomen. "Heal me now, so I may finish him."

"Already have Medea and I saved your life with enough magic to fill a trough. Now, your body must do the rest."

Aeron raised a skeptical eyebrow at him.

"If you wish retribution against your nemesis, you will follow my every word."

It took much patience for Aeron to bite back the retort he wished to make. He lacked the strength to carry out the threat, anyway.

Instead of stewing on his lust for revenge, he decided to go the more practical route. "Where are we? How long have I been asleep?" He did not recognize this place with raised ceiling and shuttered windows. From what else he could see without moving his head much, the room contained the single bed where he lay, two wooden chairs, a wash basin, and a long table with bowls, cups, and the smells of flowers, herbs, and blood. It turned his stomach.

"As you were on death's door, it has been over three weeks. Autumn is nigh upon us. After you were injured, we brought you to your father and Mistress Medea. You have not been here before."

"Three weeks?" Bile rose in Aeron's throat as he realized just how much he had missed in that time. The end of summer planting had passed and the autumn harvest was upon the people from his home. The handful of beauteous maidens he'd courted for the autumnal harvest ball would have new beaus.

No more "Sir Aeron." He had relinquished that title the moment he'd betrayed everything that knighthood meant to those who had sworn the oath. To him, the oath was a joke, something to laugh about in trying times. A mere title to impress the people of Derbyshire, namely Eudo Drefan, the insufferable man who had raised him but who had no love for the youngest of his six sons.

All of these things had been rejected from his life. All because of one worthless knight who thought he was better than the rest: Padric de Clifton.

"Medea has contributed much to your improvement," the Shadow went on.

"Has she?" *After Padric, she is the last person I wish to be beholden to.* "What of my father?"

"The lord Janus has come many times to look after your health. He is working on the next phase of our plan."

The door slammed open. "Ah, at last, my patient is awake." Medea glided into the room, her long raven hair bouncing in her wake. She looked as beautiful and deadly as ever, her sickly sweet floral scent making his nose crinkle in contempt.

Oh, he loathed her.

"Medea," Aeron said warily. *I should have known she would return.*

"Ah, back to your perky self, I see." Her ringing laughter grated on his nerves. "Here. I require you to drink this." She picked up a goblet from the table and poured dark red liquid from a white gourd.

"And if I refuse?"

The scent of juniper swept into the room as Janus, the god of time, strode through the door. He had two faces on his head, one facing forward toward the future, the other behind him to the past. Separating the faces was smooth black hair. When looking straight on, no one would ever guess there was a face on the other side. The past and future faces were identical—with the exception of the future face boasting a black goatee while the past's face was clean-shaven—yet each had their own unique personality.

After a cursory glance at Aeron, Janus headed straight to Medea, his eyes hungry for her only. Grabbing her waist, he kissed her neck. She laughed, her voice ringing throughout the room, then she turned into him. They kissed with a deep passion, seemingly forgetting there were others present.

It was the most awkward thing to watch. Aeron was glad his stomach was empty, else he would have lost his latest meal. Apparently, nothing had changed while he slept.

When at last their lips unlocked, Janus and Medea gazed at each other and...

Oh no, no, no.

Aeron loudly cleared his throat.

Startled out of whatever his intentions had been, Janus's future face

5

jerked toward him. He recovered quite fast. "Excellent, Aeron. You are awake." His eyes sparked as he approached the bed.

"Father." Aeron tried to sit up, but his side stung fiercely. The Shadow's cold fingers touched his bare chest to push him back down.

"Let me see him, brother," said the voice in the back of Janus's head—his past self.

"Oh, very well." The forward-facing head turned enough so that his past-seeing face could look at Aeron.

Janus's past's face, usually melancholic and quiet, brightened upon beholding his son. "How do you feel, Aeron?"

"I've been better." He couldn't keep the bitterness from his voice.

"You have gone through so much. But you look quite well. Mayhap we can take you outside for some fresh air."

"Not now," Janus the Future cut in. "There is too much to do."

"Yes, brother. I only meant well."

"Yes, yes." He waved him off. "Now, Aeron, you must get well so we may continue with our next course of action. Are you up for a task?"

"But he is not yet healed, brother."

The future face ignored the past. "Well?"

"Of course, Father."

Medea rolled her eyes, plopping herself onto the edge of the herb table. She tapped her foot. "Really, Janus, he only awoke a few moments ago. He will need at least a week more of healing."

Janus contemplated Medea's diagnosis. "Then I will find someone else. Shadow, find that upstart—what was his name?"

Bolting upright, Aeron screamed in silence, sure his wound had ripped open. "I can do it," he ground out. "I know where to find Drogo the huntsman." That was, if he still resided in the same area.

"Get up."

Aeron started. "What?"

"If you can stand, you can go."

"But brother, he needs rest," Janus the past protested.

Is this a test? Aeron wondered. Had his failure in killing Padric come to this—from his own father?

Steeling himself, Aeron swung his bare legs over the edge of the bed, every inch of movement excruciating. With the will of a lion, he rose to his feet, holding in his grimace as the skin around his wound pulled taut. Sweat beaded on his brow, and black spots filled his vision. *Don't pass out, don't pass out.*

"Excellent." The two-faced god clapped his hands together once. "You will leave on the morrow to find this Drogo and give him his next instruction."

The Shadow's hooded head popped up. "But my lord, that is too soon."

"What if he will not come?" Medea asked.

The god ignored them, his intense gaze resting on Aeron only. "On the morrow." He swiveled on his golden-sandaled heel and closed the door behind him.

Aeron collapsed onto the bed. Breath wouldn't come. To calm himself, he thought about all the ways in which Padric would pay for what he had done.

"Foolish lad." Medea poked around the table of herbs until she found what she was looking for: the clawed foot of a raven and a powdery red substance. "If you are to leave on the morrow, you will need a better healing regimen. Shadow, I need..."

Sleep overtook Aeron, with blissful dreams of Padric's demise dancing through his mind.

CHAPTER 1

September, AD 1356
Derbyshire, England

Talfryn grinned at Roger the miller with confidence. "I'm excellent with boats."

"Yeah?" Roger squinted at him in the torchlight. "I thought you were a farmer."

"I dabble on my days off. Loads of dabbling, in fact." He picked up the oar from the tied up cobble rowboat at his foot. The other end of the boat, treading water, dipped next to its fellow watercraft near the red mill, the water wheel spinning as though it had no notion of what nefarious deeds its owner meant to perform with it that day. He didn't understand how Roger could enjoy boating down the river in the dark.

Come on, come on, come on, Talfryn urged. *Take the bait!*

"You've been down to Repton, then, have you?"

"Well, no..." Heart picking up pace, Talfryn feared the old miller-turned-smuggler would decline. And then where would he be?

Fingers rubbing his bearded chin, Roger considered Talfryn's proposal. "That's a shame. Well, we are short a hand—Bran's sick. Five shillings're in it for you, the same as Bran's pay should he of come."

"Seven, and we've got a deal." Talfryn put out his hand. *Yes, yes, yes, yes, yes!*

"Six, and that's my final offer."

"Sold."

"If you don't sink the boat, there's a mug of ale with your name on it at the end."

"Huzzah." Had Talfryn been an actual expert boatsman, he might have been offended by Roger's remark. However, he didn't know the first thing about boats. Heck, he didn't even know the last thing about boats or which way they were supposed to point in the river. A drink did sound mighty nice on his parched throat right now, though.

It was all Talfryn could do not to search the surrounding area for his hidden friends. The breeze flipped his hair, and Talfryn thought he heard a soft, mocking laugh carried on it.

Roger and Talfryn were shaking hands when a group of seven men came around the corner. They ranged in age from about seventeen to forty, all manner of laboring men in plain, rough tunics. Talfryn held his breath as they rounded the corner of the mill, praying none of them recognized him. Thankfully, Talfryn had only seen a few of them in town but hadn't ever met them, so they might not know who he was.

When everyone had assembled, Talfryn was listening to Roger give everyone instructions when he spied two stragglers rounding the mill.

Drat! It was Duran and Devon Evers, helpers on the farm two properties over from his family's. The brothers were a couple of years older than him, somewhat more acquainted with his older brother Samuel than with Talfryn. The Massons had never really trusted the Evers brothers, especially after a few of their chickens had gone missing and the thief—or thieves—was never caught.

Trying to look inconspicuous, Talfryn ducked behind another smuggler. Just when he'd thought he might be safe, the smuggler's weight shifted to the other leg, giving the brothers a full-on view of Talfryn.

"Talfryn Masson," Duran said with raised brow. "Didn't expect to see you here."

Devon snickered beside him. "Yeah, shouldn't you be out on another adventure by now?"

"Oh, yeah, well." Thick beads of sweat dripped down the back of Talfryn's neck. "I thought this'd be a great adventure. You know, sailing into the unknown with smuggled goods and whatnot..."

"We're going to Repton," Devon said. "It's only nine miles away."

Ignoring him, Talfryn continued. "Making new friends."

"Nah, that ain't it." Duran's eyebrows knit together in thought.

"The ale, then?" *This isn't going well.*

"Wait...ain't you working for the knights or something? Under Captain de Clifton?"

Roger did a double-take. "What?"

"Yeah, that's right," Devon agreed. "Come to think of it, Sam mentioned it just last week, didn't he?"

Talfryn snorted. "Ha ha, good ol' Sam, always making jokes." *Bad Sam! Bad! Older brothers are supposed to help their little brothers, not get them into trouble...*

"I seen you too," one of the men said. "You're friends with the cap'n's son, the lieutenant in Chaddesden."

Well, darn the luck.

Red in the face, Roger glared at Talfryn. "Is this so, Masson?"

"I...got fired?" Talfryn hesitated, raising his free hand. He'd almost forgotten the paddle in his other hand as he smacked his thigh with it and dropped it onto the grass with two thuds.

Roger placed his fists on his hips. "You don't really dabble in boats, do you?"

"What if I said I liked the *idea* of boats?"

Talfryn thought Roger's head would explode as he cried out, "Get him!"

"Any time now," Talfryn shouted with uncertainty. He spared a glance into the distance to look for his friends. That was a mistake.

Because the miller's fist came smashing into Talfryn's face.

This could have gone better. Talfryn stumbled back, his cheek throbbing. He spit blood onto the grass. *Yep, definitely could've gone better.*

In good news, Padric, Rawlins, and the others emerged from their hiding spots.

Recovering quickly, Talfryn sent a fist into the miller's rotund stomach. The man waddled backward and put up his fists again. "You're not getting me or my wares. I'll fight you for 'em."

"Isn't that what we're doing right now?"

The man blinked. Realizing his verbal blunder, his cheeks and nose reddened in unbecoming blotches.

Thanks to the distraction, Talfryn laid in a couple more hits to his ample abdomen and kidney in quick succession. What he didn't see was the scrawny fellow sneaking up behind him.

Somehow, Talfryn ended up flat on his back, all the air squeezed from his lungs. Face smug, the scrawny fellow sat on Talfryn's chest, feet on Talfryn's left, fists pumping in victory.

Unable to expand his diaphragm, Talfryn gasped for breath. Frantically, his hands searched the ground for a weapon. Unfortunately, Padric had taken his hatchet before sending him on the mission, so he was unarmed against the mob standing over him with snarling faces.

Before they could reach down and tear him to pieces, though, he heard a couple of grunts followed by thuds on the ground. A commotion rose within the group at the sudden interruption.

Hope rose in Talfryn's chest.

A second hope came when his fingers closed around the arm of the fallen paddle. Good timing, as those pesky black dots were swirling around in his vision and making him lightheaded. Gripping the paddle tightly in his left hand, he flicked his arm up. The flat part of the paddle caught the unassuming chest-sitter under the chin, and the man's legs came up over his head in a comical way as he flailed onto the shore.

Blessed air sucked into Talfryn's lungs in an instant. Rolling over, he launched to his feet and nearly tipped over into a fist fight between his friend Rawlins and Devon. Talfryn almost felt sorry for Devon, having to fight the brawny, stoic Rawlins. It wouldn't end well for the scrawnier Devon. Rare was the time when Rawlins hadn't won a fist fight—even before he'd acquired his uncanny ability of invisibility.

Devon flung his hands around in a cocky manor and taunted the deadly knight—he who didn't take taunts very well—while the knight feinted and socked the farmhand in the eye. Head jerking back, Devon went down like a sack of flour.

Padric, Rawlins, Serill, Byron, and the other knights from Chaddesden fought bravely against the rest.

Caught up in the excitement and still trying to recover his breath, Talfryn happened to spy a pudgy profile on one of the crate-laden boats. Roger cursed as he struggled to unwind the boat from its mooring, but the rope had gotten twisted.

Bad for you, good for me! "Oy, Master Miller, sir," Talfryn called after him.

Startled, Roger glanced up for a second before continuing his fruitless unknotting.

"Where d'you think you're going with that fine sailing vessel?"

"Just gotta deliver this one load," he muttered under his breath.

Talfryn placed his foot on the top of the short piling and placed his elbow on his knee. "How about, instead of a long, sweaty ride down river, why not stay at a nice suite in the city gaol? I hear it's been redecorated with a fresh coat of paint. There's a lovely vista through an enormous window"—for a squirrel—"into the very exciting alleyway. Oh, and the food's much improved." He nodded encouragingly, as though he believed his own words.

"As enticing as that all sounds, I'd best be on my way. Now, be a good lad and untie the mooring, will you?"

A sigh escaped Talfryn's mouth. "Well, can't say I didn't try." Removing his foot, he bent down and untwisted the rope from the piling. "Good luck and all. I'll give your crew your respects."

Roger tried to hide his surprise at Talfryn's easy manor. "Much appreciated. Tell them no hard feelings and all. It's just business."

"Course." He tossed the end of the rope to Roger. "Good luck and all," he repeated.

Roger gave a salute, which was more like a half-hearted wave, and tucked the rope into the boat. When he sat down on the seat, his body displaced a splash of water.

"What the…"

Talfryn waved it off. "That's probably from the weight of the crates. You'd better be off now, or Sir Padric'll catch you."

"Yer right...Bye." Roger hauled up the oars and paddled toward the center of the river. He only got about five feet when he began to panic. "The water...it's getting higher!"

"It is?" Talfryn feigned innocence. He snapped his finger and thumb together. "Oh, yeah. Forgot to warn ya—you see, my friends and I got up early and poked some holes in each boat. The moment anyone steps inside one, the boat'll sink just enough that water comes in through the holes. Ingenious—but I can't take the credit. Well, have a nice trip!"

Wide-eyed, Roger looked at the soggy interior of the boat, water creeping up the tarps covering the crates. A huge bubble gurgled to the top and gave a loud *pop!* In seconds, the boat began to sink in earnest. With his hands, Roger tried to scoop the water out of the row boat. But with each splash of water that left the boat, two more entered. Soon, only an inch of the boat could be seen above water.

Roger panicked in earnest. "I...I can't swim."

"Then you should get talking. Who's your contact in Repton?" Padric asked, coming up beside Talfryn.

"I'm about to drown, and all you'll do is ask me questions?"

"Yep."

Murder crossed the miller's face.

"I'd say you have less than thirty heartbeats left before your boat sinks, sir."

"Fine, fine, fine. It's Elbert the Miller."

Padric walked up beside Talfryn and grinned at the unfortunate miller. "Ah, a thieving ring of millers. How appropriate. Does your miller ring operate all up and down the River Trent?"

Talfryn glanced behind him. All of the miscreants had been captured or lay unconscious.

"I'll never tell."

"Five heartbeats left, Roger."

"Yes! For heaven's sake, YES! Get me outta here *now*!"

Talfryn rolled his eyes. "Sheesh, a little *please* would have sufficed."

Now all that could be seen of the miller was from the chest up and what crates of his stolen goods could float.

"Aren't you going to help me?" He slapped frantically at the water.

"Yeah, yeah, stop yelling." Talfryn stepped into the river. The chilly water sent shivers up his spine, but he crept forward one step at a time.

All of Roger's fitful movements shifted the heavy crates under the tarp. In another moment, the boat began to list to the left. River water rushed over the top. Roger's cries of dread could have awoken the dead as he and the remaining crates plopped into the water with a splash.

He looked like a large, drowning rat as he flailed his arms and legs. "I'm drowning!"

Talfryn and Padric shared a look. It was difficult to keep their faces under control as they watched him flounder for another few heartbeats. Then Padric cleared his throat.

"Try standing up," Padric offered. He clamped his mouth shut to stop the chuckle that wanted to force its way out.

"But...but..."

"Just try it."

Composing himself, Roger set his feet down. His face brightened when he realized he wouldn't drown after all but could stand in chest-high water. It clouded again as he realized what that meant.

Serill came up on Talfryn's other side. "He didn't know how shallow his own part of the river was? How sad."

Together, Talfryn and Padric waded into the chilly shallow water to retrieve the drenched criminal, each taking an arm.

The defeated miller looked up at Talfryn. "Would you've saved me if I was going to drown?"

"Uh, not me. I can't swim either." He winked at Padric.

The miller's face turned whiter than the flour he milled.

The time a few months ago, when the river near Manchester had swept him away to his doom, loomed in Talfryn's mind. Padric and Ulysses had rescued him from drowning that day. Worse, they'd thought Brynwen had already drowned in it. He shook his head to dislodge the awful memory. Opening his mouth for another quip, he froze when a haunting laugh came from behind him. The hairs on the back of his neck stood on end. The laugh began as a quiet growl, then grew, deep and throaty and awful.

He spun, but nothing was there.

"Count yourself lucky it was shallow." This time, Padric released a light snicker. Nothing like the growl Talfryn had just heard. "Come on, Master Miller, it is time to take you and your merry band to your luxurious suite in the Derby gaol." He winked at Talfryn, then clapped him on the shoulder. "Well done, Tal, on capturing your first villain."

The creepy laughter forgotten, Talfryn beamed, so happy he hadn't messed it up completely. "Are all these kinda tasks this easy?"

Padric's eyebrow raised in amusement. "Ask me that next time."

A few minutes later, the prisoners were assembled into a line and marched away by the knights. Talfryn waved at them as they passed by. "Duran, Devon. By the way, stealing is *bad*."

Roger the Miller, the last prisoner, gave him the dirtiest look, then pressed on, head held high.

CHAPTER 2

*A*fter dropping Roger the Miller and his gang of miscreants off at the gaol in Derby, and the knights' report was given to Padric's father, Captain Garrick de Clifton, all of those who had participated in the raid met at the Brown Bear Inn for a celebratory pint.

Everyone cheered and patted Talfryn on the back as he entered the tavern. A wide grin spread over his face as he sat on the bench at their table beside Padric and Byron. He picked up the pint of golden ale, just now realizing how thirsty he was. He downed it in no time.

Byron thunked his mug against Serill's, their ale sloshing without spilling. "Good thing we put holes in those boats when we did."

"Oy, his face when he realized he wasn't drowning." Serill duplicated the miller's reaction, then laughed and took a long swig of ale. With his sleeve, he wiped the froth from his mouth. "Never seen so much animosity toward anyone. Quick thinking, there, Talfryn." He shoved his arm jovially.

"For an old squire." Byron nudged Talfryn's arm with his elbow. Everyone burst into laughter, including Talfryn. It was their joke, with him being the oldest squire ever to start training at seventeen. But he didn't mind. Finally, he felt like he belonged somewhere.

He had worked and fought beside a handful of these knights during their captivity in Cataractonium. Under the dark influence of Janus, Helius had forced his daughter, the goddess Circe, to kidnap young people to build a massive temple that nearly used the power of the sun to destroy the world. They had worked together again to bring down the Shadow Druid's plan of stealing a valuable relic from the Minotaur in the Labyrinth below the underground city of Rellea.

Shortly after their return from Rellea at the beginning of August, Padric had presented his recommendation of Talfryn as squire to Captain Garrick. Afterward, the captain had granted Talfryn an interview. Talfryn had been a wreck leading up to the one-on-one meeting with the captain, but Padric's father had been fair and asked formal questions regarding why Talfryn thought he was a good fit and what fighting skills he had. After Talfryn's explanation and examples, the older knight had seemed surprised at all of his accomplishments, and after a stunning review from five knights and townsfolk who'd been at Cataractonium, he had declared, "If Padric and the others have faith in you, lad, then I am willing to give you a chance."

And now, here he was. On his way to becoming a knight of Chaddesden and Derbyshire.

Still chuckling, Talfryn had just raised the mug to his parched lips when he heard something that didn't sound right. Pausing, he strained his ears to hear over his table mates. The noise reduced to a low din before he heard it again, this time unmistakable.

A low growl.

Heart rate increasing, Talfryn dropped his mug on the table. *No. No, no, no, it can't be here.* His body broke out in a cold sweat while at the same time the hairs on the back of his neck stood on end.

He could practically feel the monster's foul breath on his neck, drool dripping down his back. Its huge body and mottled fur, its partially chewed ear, and the hatchet sticking out of its back.

In an instant, he relived the day when he and his cousin Leowyn had fought the wolficorn—er, *aeternae*—on top of Helius's temple in Cataractonium. The giant wolf charged. Leo dove right while Talfryn dove left—but not in time. The sharp horn protruding out of the center of the beast's head like a unicorn sliced through Talfryn's thigh, and he sprawled on the tiles in pain. His hatchet slipped out of his hand. Leowyn continued to fight valiantly, but the wolficorn snuffed out his life like a piece of meat on a skewer.

"Leo." His breath hitched. The ache in Talfryn's leg returned, even after it had healed months ago.

The growl had come from the front window to his left. He dared not move toward it, not *look*. Maybe the monster hadn't seen him. Maybe it was just passing through on its way to somewhere else—anywhere else.

He gritted his teeth as the ache in his leg turned into throbbing.

"Tal?" Worry lines creased Padric's forehead as he regarded Talfryn.

Everyone, in fact, stared at him. That is, except for Rawlins, who regarded him thoughtfully as he slowly sipped his ale.

"Uh, I, uh..." Talfryn mumbled. He sent the barest glance out the window. Nothing. No wolficorn, or aeternae, as Helius had called it, but a dark shadow on the side that quickly disappeared. *Did I imagine it, or is it really lurking outside?* Lately, he'd had a hard time being able to tell the difference. But would it dare to be around so many people? All at once, it felt really hot inside the inn. "I gotta go."

Without waiting for anyone to respond, he extricated himself from the bench and bolted for the back door with a heavy limp. He half expected the wolficorn to burst through the front door and dive after him to finish what it had started back in Cataractonium.

Through the empty corridor in the back, he lunged at the door, but his hand paused on the latch. His heart pounded so loud in his ears, he'd never be able to hear the wolficorn coming. Taking a shaky breath, he gripped his hatchet and turned the latch.

Pressure gripped his shoulder.

Startled, Talfryn whipped around, raising his hatchet to kill the beast once and for all. He anticipated the wolficorn's claws ripping right through him.

"Tal!"

Through his fear and frenzy, Talfryn barely registered his friend's voice. In the next instant, the frenzied instinct vanished, and Padric stood in front of him, eyes wide and gritting his teeth.

"Pa...Padric?" It was then that he noticed his friend gripping the hatchet's handle in self-defense. He released his grip and slumped against the door. "Padric...I'm—I'm so sorry. I dunno what happened." As Padric lowered the hatchet, Talfryn thought he'd be sick. *I almost killed my best friend. What's wrong with me?*

The knight took deep breaths, his face pale after his brush with death. "Remind me never to sneak up on you ever again."

"Yeah, ya may need some pointers from Rawlins on that one."

Padric chuckled. "Aye, that I do." An awkward silence ensued before Padric spoke again. "Here, you left this." He raised up Talfryn's squire cap. It was red with a black rim, announcing to the world that he was in training to become a knight of Chaddesden. After seeing his cousin Leowyn being dubbed a knight a little over a year ago, Talfryn had secretly wanted to become one too. So secret, he hadn't even realized his longing for it until only a few short weeks ago. Part of him wanted to fill the role Leo had left open, and a big part of him wanted to leave farming behind. He'd discovered he could hold his own in a fight and had finally found his path. But the nightmares...

Talfryn gulped and shook his head. *Will I ever be ready?*

No.

The urge to flea overtook him, and he shoved off the door and grabbed up the cap. "Thanks. Seriously, though, I gotta go."

"Tal, if you want to talk—"

But Talfryn was already out the door. Without any pauses, his feet took him all the way home. Not to the barracks, where all his things were, but *home*. The farm. He needed the one person who could calm him down. Well, the one person and four animals who could calm him down the way no one else could.

In the yard, the white goats Hay and Stack were terrorizing the dog, Finn, per their usual routine. Talfryn's grin was a thin one, but his hands didn't stop shaking until he heard the humming of his sister's new favorite tune through the open cottage window. Out of said window popped Miser, the wily little red squirrel he'd found in the Yorkshire Moors and adopted. He scurried around Talfryn's legs, then climbed up to his shoulder, chittering in excitement and tickling Talfryn's chin with a swish of his red tail.

"Good to see you, too, buddy. And yes, we caught the smugglers."

The tightness in his chest calmed down closer to its normal rate.

"Sis," he called out, a smile reaching up his cheeks, "d'you have any fresh chamomile tea lying about, by chance?"

"Talfryn?" She stuck her auburn head out the window. Her braid fell off her shoulder to swing like a pendulum. "What are you doing home so soon? Did you catch the smugglers?"

"We did. And am I ever thirsty."

"That is great news! Come inside, the tea is almost finished brewing."

When her head ducked out of the window, the instantaneous fear of being alone gripped Talfryn's lungs like a vise. Miser must have sensed his terror or else felt his heart rate increase. Either way, he chittered and leapt all over Talfryn's shoulders, flicking his red tail in his face again. The action jolted Talfryn out of his stupor.

"Thanks, buddy." He patted him on the head.

Lurching for the door, he set his trembling hand on the latch. It occurred to him that he should tell his sister about what was going on with him. How his nightmares of the wolficorn seemed to be projecting into broad daylight. He and Brynwen had always shared everything growing up, so this wasn't any different, right? However, he couldn't really pinpoint when it had started. It had begun as nightmares, then during the day a nagging feeling would creep up on him, and all of a sudden today it had bloomed into what it was now.

Yes, I'll tell her.

When at last he opened the door, Brynwen was leaning over the little pot hanging from the large fireplace, scooping tea leaves and spices into the steaming wooden mug he'd always used when he'd lived here. It lightened his heart somewhat.

"There you are." Her cheerfulness warmed him further. "I thought mayhap you had decided to go back to your quarters after all. Grandfather and Sam should be back from the village soon." She dumped a spoonful of honey and added a pinch of nutmeg into it, stirred with the spoon, then tapped the utensil on the edge of the mug to get every last drop off of it. "They will be happy to see you. I know you just saw Sam yesterday, but he'll be pleased just the same."

21

Talfryn's chest compressed as the wolficorn's laugh surrounded him again the moment Brynwen looked up. He couldn't breathe. Without hesitation, he scooped her into a hug.

"Woah, Talfryn." Brynwen laughed, steadying the mug without spilling a drop. "I missed you, too."

Close to tears, he dug his head into her shoulder.

Brynwen tensed. "Tal, are you all right?" She patted his back.

He took a deep breath. Soaked in her strength and resilience. Something he needed right now in droves.

Miser told him to tell her what was wrong. The squirrel spoke so fast, per usual, that Talfryn nearly missed what he was saying. If only it were as easy to communicate with his goats, Hay and Stack—they mostly spoke with their stomachs.

Tell her, Talfryn told himself. *Tell her everything. Right now.*

But if you do that, she'll think you're going crazy.

"*Indeed,*" the wolficorn's deep voice concurred. "*Go ahead. Tell her everything.*"

Raising his head in alarm, he opened his mouth, then shut it. Swallowed. "Aye," he said at last with more calmness than he'd thought possible. "I just missed you is all. And your tea, of course." Breaking away, he grabbed up the mug from her hand, raised it to her health with a quick nod, and swallowed the refreshing beverage in two gulps. The calming chamomile soothed his aching throat like a balm.

Her eyebrow quirked a tad. "I missed you too. Are you sure everything is all right?" She took the mug to refill it, not taking her eyes off of him.

He shrugged with what he hoped was nonchalance. "Of course. I mean, the captain's getting antsy about the upcoming tourney with Nottingham. Everybody's excited about it and getting their gear together. But until Grandfather and Sam return, tell me about what you've been up to. And Finn, Hay, and Stack—are they behaving themselves?" He pulled out a chair from beside the table and sat.

Brynwen laughed. The happiest sound in the world. All the tension released from his shoulders as though it had never been there in the first place.

CHAPTER 3

*T*he sun peeked a minuscule slice above the hillside, its red-gold rays welcoming the dawn. The goat-man, or faun, stretched and yawned. His wisened face peered up into the rising sunlight. His lean, bare muscles stretched out the tiredness of sleep. Little horns stuck up out of his brown curls. A touch of gray sprouted from just above his ears, with gray hairs littered throughout. Not ten feet away, a creek trickled with fresh water, partly shaded in the early morning light by an overhanging spruce tree. Sitting up, he smiled down at the hare lying beside him in the plush grass, its eyes cracking opening with bleary intent.

"It will be a marvelous day." The faun took a deep breath of the crisp morning air, his favorite time of the day.

The hare blinked in rapid succession and peered up at the faun, into his kind, deep-brown eyes.

Then, all around them, other woodland animals awoke with the dawn. They shook out their fur and tails, removing any dew that covered them, and moved about, ready for the day ahead.

In short order, the faun scooped up some water into a shallow clay bowl and started a fire. He boiled vegetables and herbs with ingredients growing nearby. A hare brought him a carrot from his little garden.

"Thank you, my friend." The faun plopped the carrot into the boiling pot.

23

After his meal, the faun tended to his garden, plucking out the weeds as he whistled a jaunty tune. That accomplished, he left his hill and roamed around the vicinity, checking on the trees and the plants and greeting the animals living there.

The peace of the place was heaven on earth.

When at last the faun made it home to his hillside, filled his pot, made a fire, and began making a fresh vegetable stew, the sun had begun to set into thin red and purple strips. He had just dipped a few leaves of cabbage into the pot when his hand hesitated.

Head popping up, he looked straight ahead and gave his warmest smile. "Hello, Talfryn," he said. "I have been waiting to meet to you for some time."

Talfryn startled awake and shot up in his cot. Sweat poured down his face and neck as he breathed harder than a run up the highest hill in Chaddesden.

Taking in his surroundings, he found himself in a line of cots in the garrison, alongside the other knights and squires sleeping under blankets.

"Did-did that…" He gulped, running his hands through his auburn hair. "Did he just speak to me? In a dream?"

Talfryn had been following the faun in his dreams for a long time. Every night for the last few months, each appearance slightly different. But this was the first time his dream had ever spoken *to him.*

It took several aching and confused minutes to get his heart to normalize as he tried to figure it out. In the meantime, no one else in the barracks had awoken, especially not the snorers. "Am I still dreaming?" he wondered aloud.

Byron snorted in his sleep before rolling over, to commence his loud snoring.

Nope, can't dream that.

After a few more minutes, though, exhaustion took over, and he laid back onto the thin mattress and drifted off to sleep.

But not before the monstrous wolf's maniacal laughter filled the garrison…

FOR PERHAPS THE fiftieth time that afternoon, Padric worried the ring in his palm as he waited in the field for the recruits to show up. Earlier in the week, he had picked up the shining piece of jewelry from the blacksmith, and all week, he had brainstormed the perfect place to ask Brynwen the question which had been on his mind for weeks—*months, really*. Near the forest where they'd first met? At the spring where they'd met for the second time? After the tournament if he won an important match?

He also needed to figure out a way to tell his parents his plan, get Eduard Masson's blessing, and—

"Padric."

Startled, Padric jumped and fumbled with the ring before swiping it out of the air. Safe in his clutches. He let out a breath of relief that the trinket hadn't fallen in the grass, only to get lost in the sea of green, perhaps forever. The one-of-a-kind ring with little flowers carved into it—or so the blacksmith had claimed—would not be easy to come by again. Quickly, he stuffed it into his pocket.

"Captain," Padric said once he recovered. "Father, what is it?"

Ever since Padric's parents and sister had stumbled upon him and his friends in the de Clifton orchard—with Padric in his centaur form, bull's horns protruding from Payla's head, Ulysses the peryton with his graceful white wings unfurled, and Gregorio looking nearly forty years younger than normal—things between his family had changed. Stammering out the details, the picnickers, who had also included the twins and Rawlins, had related their adventures with the Roman gods and monsters and their newfound abilities.

Padric was proud of his mother Tabitha. Although she had looked about ready to faint from the moment she'd stepped foot in the orchard, she'd had the fortitude to never lose consciousness. Drinking the chamomile tea Brynwen had poured for her had helped considerably. It was Chelsea who'd recovered the quickest—having a child's vivid imagination despite her fifteen years—and she'd asked dozens of questions with wide eyes and flailing arms, while Garrick had either spluttered or gaped in confusion.

When they'd finished their tale, Garrick had regarded them all in silence for a long time. At last, he'd asked a few stammering questions. Obtaining the answers, he'd then dragged his wife and daughter out of the orchard toward their home, hearing none of Chelsea's protests.

The captain had become distant for several days afterward, trying to come to terms with what he'd seen and the new information he'd gleaned about his son and his friends.

Slowly, though, Garrick had warmed up to Padric's shape-changing abilities and would even ask about it. Once, when they were alone, Padric had demonstrated each of the forms he could make: faun, centaur, and goat. Sometimes, Padric would spy Garrick conferring with Gregorio or Rawlins about something relating to mythology. Other times, Padric saw his father's eyes wandering toward any cluster of trees, and Padric knew Garrick was searching for Ulysses.

Today, his father regarded him with something akin to curiosity instead of wariness. But how long would his mood last?

"May I sit?" Garrick asked. Padric nodded, and the man sidled onto the worn tree stump. "We must speak of the tournament."

Padric sighed. What was there to say? "Everything is under control. I shan't have an issue with turning into an animal—I have not relapsed in weeks. Gregorio is a great teacher, and I have learned much from him. He has been changing his appearance for many years, as you may recall."

"Yes, yes, but one slip up could cause confusion and chaos. We can't have that, not with Nottingham hosting this year." He ran a hand through his graying black hair, a trait Padric had adopted as one of his own nervous ticks. More gray strands had protruded from Garrick's well-trimmed beard and hair since Padric had disappeared nearly five months ago when escorting his friend Miriel Wilmot to her sister's home. Cursed by Circe, Padric had not returned until the end of June when he had freed Helius's prisoners from Cataractonium in northern Yorkshire.

The tournament with Nottingham was the affair of the year. Whichever city's knights and squires won the most games got bragging rights until the following year's tourney. The competition was fierce, each knight and squire vying to win for their city.

In truth, Padric was excited about the tourney and his rematch with

Warin Ingram. Their match to prove who deserved Helius's title of heir had been interrupted by a raving manticore. Having survived the deadly brawl, they'd vowed to resolve the fight they had begun at the tourney.

"I will not let you down, sir. You have my word."

"What about Rawlins and his...ability?"

Padric held in a laugh at the way his father tried and failed at subtlety. "He promises not to disappear during any matches." He was about to say more on the subject, but noticed his father's expression. "That is not all that worries you, though. What is it?"

The older man pressed his lips together. "Oh it is just the musings of an old man."

"You are hardly that old, sir." Padric grinned. "Tell me."

"Fine, if you must know...I am considering entering the tournament."

"You what?" Padric launched to his feet. "The last time you entered was..."

"A while ago, yes, I know."

"I was a page, and Rawlins's father was still alive." Five years between tournaments was a long time for a knight. Folding his arms across his chest, Padric cocked a smirk at his father. "I know. Rumor has it that Nottingham's Captain Costane is entering this year. You two are around the same age—are you planning on squaring off with him, then?"

"I might," his father rumbled. Bending over to fix his boot, Padric didn't miss the scarlet blotching his cheeks.

"You should. You have been practicing enough with your broadsword. I have the bruises and cuts to show for it." He rubbed his sore upper arm to prove the point. Some of their father-son sparring matches had been particularly brutal the more they got into the groove. Now he knew why, of late, his father had been more driven in fighting and at other times more distracted. "I think it will be good for you to get into the thick of it again, sir. Show the young ones you've still got it."

Garrick rubbed his chin, a grin forming. "Yes, that would show them a thing or two, wouldn't it? Why are you frowning now?"

"I just realized that the lads and I shall be your punching bags for the next couple of weeks, won't we?"

A twinkle kindled in the captain's eye. "Aye lad, you will. And my first victim—I mean sparring partner—will be your clumsy squire, Talfryn."

Grinning, Padric was beginning to feel sorry for his friend. "Oh, he will be thrilled, sir. Just thrilled..."

He only prayed that Talfryn did not have one of the strange lapses which he'd suffered of late while sparring with the captain.

"One more question," Garrick said, bestowing Padric with one of his more authoritarian stares.

"What is it?"

"When are you going to ask that nice young maiden Brynwen for her hand?"

Sweat broke out on Padric's face as he looked at his father in shock.

Garrick broke into laugher, doubling over with the force of his mirth. "Oh, dear son, it is obvious you are smitten over the lass every time you are with her or speak of her." Seeing Padric still at a loss, he continued. "Brynwen is a fine maiden, and I have no doubt she would make you a most worthy wife."

"Do you...really think so, Father?"

"Aye, son. Also, I've spied you fumbling with that ring all week. So, tell me, when do you plan to propose?"

"Well, I was thinking..." Taking a deep breath, he spilled his whole plan to his father, who listened with rapt attention, a knowing smile on his face.

CHAPTER 4

a s every other dawn, Talfryn watched as the faun stretched and yawned as the sun peeked over the hillside.

"Another perfect morning, my friends." The faun sighed happily.

Like all the days before, the other animals surrounding the faun on the little hillside shook out the sleep and dew from their fur and whiskers.

Gathering water and kindling for a small fire, the faun hummed a cheerful tune. As his vegetables and herbs boiled, he peered up, straight ahead as he had the day before. "Ah, Talfryn, welcome back." A genuine smile showed straight white teeth, and he waved Talfryn forward.

A strange sensation came over him as his body transitioned from incorporeal to corporeal within a heartbeat. He dropped to the ground the last foot and landed with a stumble and a huff of surprise.

"Whew!" Talfryn gathered his wits and straightened his shoulders. He brushed his hair out of his eyes. "How'd you do that?"

The faun waved a dismissive hand. "Oh, a little trick I learned once. Please, sit and join in the morning repast."

Talfryn's stomach rumbled. *When was the last time I ate? Wait, was the last meal in real time or dream time?*

Shrugging because it didn't really matter, Talfryn gladly dropped onto his knees and took the proffered bowl of savory smelling soup. He ate every last drop, feeling traitorous for eating food that outstripped Brynwen's own cooking skills. *But*, he rationalized, *she doesn't need to know, does she? Besides, it's dream food.*

As he slurped up the last dregs of the tasty soup, wishing there was more in the pot, he glanced up to find the faun looking at him in thoughtful contemplation.

"Umm, thank you for the stew, sir. It was amazing. I should really get this recipe to my sister. And the cooks in the garrison. They need some new recipes badly."

The faun laughed. A merry sound that drew Talfryn to the faun even more than he already had been.

"I am glad to hear it, Talfryn Masson. Having only cooked for myself these last seven hundred years, I hardly know what great skill cooking tastes like anymore."

Not sure what to say, Talfryn gave a quick nod. "If I may, sir...who are you?"

"I am called Faunus. Some call me Pan. Although we share many similarities, we are quite different. He is the god of the wild, shepherds and flocks, and wild nature of mountains. I, however, watch over live-stock, fields, forests, and dreams. Come, allow me to show you around."

Dreams, eh? Talfryn scratched his neck, feeling the flush turn his cheeks crimson like his uniform. "Well, Sir Faunus, you see, I've kinda been following you around for months. I think I've seen everything by now."

"Please, Faunus will do. And nay, you have not yet seen everything. Follow me."

For some reason, Talfryn didn't quite feel like leaving the tranquility of the hill, but curiosity got the better of him. "Sure. But..."

Faunus chuckled and placed a gentle hand on Talfryn's shoulder. "We will return to this hill before you wake so you may begin your duties on time."

Talfryn's shoulders relaxed. "Thanks, appreciate it."

They walked along the creek for a bit, Talfryn taking in the beautiful scenery as though for the first time. Birds chirped and animals skittered around them, only pausing to pay their respects to Faunus, then continuing on their way. He couldn't help but think how much Miser would love this place.

"Where are we?" Talfryn asked in amazement. The place looked like it could be in the English countryside, but he hadn't been anywhere else resembling this to know for certain. Besides, it was a dream, so it could be anywhere.

"We are not so far from where you live."

"Really? Then why haven't you visited me?"

Faunus chuckled. The skin around his eyes crinkled when he did so. "You were not yet ready to meet me. Although, if my dreams are true, we may meet very soon."

"Yeah?" Talfryn found himself walking faster in excitement, although he had no idea where they were going. "Can I come here again? I'd love for you to meet Bryn—I could bring her next time." Elation built up in his chest at the prospect. "Miser and Padric would love to meet you, too. And Gregorio—er, I mean Telegonus…"

"Talfryn." The older immortal placed a calming hand on Talfryn's shoulder. "One thing at a time."

"Oh, yeah, right. Sorry."

Faunus smiled, and Talfryn returned it, delight bubbling up inside him. It was the best he'd felt in ages.

"We are nearly there. Think you can make it?" He cocked his head in question, though Talfryn could see the humor in his eyes.

"I'll try to manage. Lead on, good sir."

Soon, Talfryn heard running water. "Is that what I think it is?"

As they crested the hill, the water became almost deafening, and he spotted its source. His stomach dropped with the water. It flowed from a river off to the right and dumped down a ravine. The wondrous vista gave him pleasant chills.

"This…this is more amazing than the Gordale Scar in the Yorkshire Dells."

"I knew you would like it."

"What I wouldn't give to see this view every day. If only in my dreams, right?" Talfryn chuckled.

The faun's expression grew dour. "Not every problem can be solved by dreams, lad. Nor can one's darkest dreams be ignored forever."

An icy wind brushed Talfryn's skin. *Does he really know about my nightmares?*

Faunus looked into the bright, clear water at the bottom of the fall. "I think that is enough for one day. Come, it is time to leave."

"Already?" Talfryn whined. "But we just arrived." Darkest dreams were the last thing he wanted to talk about or return to.

"Mayhap you can return on the morrow."

Faunus led the way back, but Talfryn didn't remember much of it.

The next thing he knew, he awoke in his cot in the garrison. The half moon waned, indicating the second half of the night. A sadness engulfed him at how much he already missed Faunus and his home, the hills, the animals, and the waterfall. Maybe he'd see them tomorrow in his dreams.

As he was drifting off, a light scratching came at the window. Startled, he looked up, but no one was there. But a few seconds after he'd gotten comfy again, the growling laughter began...

...and didn't stop until dawn.

CHAPTER 5

Two weeks later, October 15, AD 1356

*A*rms so full of equipment he could barely see over the top, Talfryn shuffled behind Padric on their way to the cluster of colorful striped tents used by the Derby knights. Their barracks at Chaddesden were too far away for the participating knights and squires to prepare for each match efficiently, so they stayed in tents. Rawlins, Byron, Serill, and their squires were likely already there. Talfryn and Padric were running late because Talfryn couldn't find Padric's baldric which had somehow gotten kicked under the far corner beneath his cot. Miser was too small to pull it out, so Talfryn had to shine a candle under the cot to see it. *How could this long belt end up under here?* he'd wondered as he'd lugged the baldric out from beneath the bed.

Talfryn had checked and double checked that each piece of Padric's armor was polished and that he could see his face in its reflection. The knight only wore full armor once or twice a year, so it was in desperate need of a good cleaning.

His new scarlet and black uniform chafed at his neck, but Talfryn tried to ignore it as he dodged through the packed crowd. In contrast,

Padric, with arms less burdened, sailed through the throng with an ease Talfryn could only hope to one day emulate.

Two young lads in dingy brown tunics zipped past them. One nearly collided with Talfryn's arm, but he deftly pulled it out of harm's way.

As he righted himself, a gorgeous, smiling woman in a royal blue cloak and wavy raven hair tripped and bumped into him. As they touched, the scent of flowers wafted to him. The act pushed him into Padric's back, and together they lost their footing, Talfryn falling against two noblemen. The older nobleman's goblet spilled red wine all down his cream colored brocade tunic with gold trim. It also splattered onto the clothes of the young man at his side wearing rich-but-not-quite-as-rich attire of dark blue with white trim.

Having dropped the gear on the ground, Talfryn spun to see if the woman in the royal blue cloak was all right, but she was gone. "Where'd she go?"

"Oh, dear." The older man frowned at the maroon stains dripping down his clothes. His hair was graying and his stomach protruded between his buttons.

Deep crimson flew to Talfryn's cheeks. "I'm so sor—" Before he could apologize further, though, the nobleman's young companion threw his own bronze goblet on the ground with a *thunk* at Talfryn's feet. Its maroon contents splattered all over his newly-shined black boots. The man's dark blue cap shifted on his slicked back, dark brown hair.

Turning on his heel, Padric took in the situation, hand on pommel, and looked with concern from Talfryn to the two dripping men.

Everyone in the vicinity stopped what they were doing, and Talfryn heard a few gasps at the scene he'd just caused.

Talfryn's first thought was, *Seriously, why are you wearing such a nice tunic to a crowded and dirty old tournament in the first place?* But he wisely held his tongue as the younger man cursed Talfryn's ancestry and future descendants, which led into questioning his parentage in the first place, without seeming to take a single breath. *That's some talent right there!* Oddly enough, all sense of apology left him.

Padric stepped up beside Talfryn and gave a respectful bow when at last the man paused to take a breath. "My good sir, please forgive my squire. The crowd is anxious to see the games, and we are in haste to make our tent for preparations. Please allow me to find a servant to clean your tunics."

"Who do you think you are, you young upstart? Your servant here should be groveling at my lord's feet and begging his forgiveness. Do you know who he is?"

"Daniel..." the older man said in a warning tone.

Daniel's irate behavior was beginning to grate on Talfryn's nerves. Besides, Padric wasn't that much younger than him. Talfryn was about to give a sarcastic retort when Padric made a sign to stay silent.

"Unfortunately, sir," Padric said, "I must beg ignorance of your lord's personage. I am Sir Padric de Clifton of Derbyshire, and this is my squire, Talfryn Masson." He bowed again.

Talfryn bowed too, more out of respect for Padric and the kind older gentleman.

Daniel's nostrils flared and his hawkish nose raised in disgust and sniffed.

The older man's eyes twinkled, and he opened his mouth to reply, but Daniel cut him off.

"Of course you're from Derby. Only a rapscallion from Derby would not know who we are. You have the pleasure of an audience with Vernon Perry, Earl of York. And I am *Lord* Daniel Lambert."

"My lords, please excuse my ignorance." Padric bowed a second time. As he rose, he raised an eyebrow at Talfryn.

Talfryn hastily made another awkward bow over the pile of equipment he still held. A greave slid from the middle. In an attempt to shift and catch it, one of the two vambraces rolled off the top. "Ugh, I just polished that!" *How important is it to re-buff shin and forearm guards only for Padric to dirty them up again?*

Lord Daniel didn't even notice him. "You would do well to remember it, peasant."

The earl rolled his eyes to heaven. "Daniel, Daniel, let these poor men go. It was a pure accident, and these young men have much to do for the tournament and our entertainment." He turned his attention to

Padric and Talfryn. "Please excuse my nephew, he laments the loss of a good wine."

"Uncle!" Daniel's eyes flashed in embarrassment.

"My aunt declares that wine is a terrible thing to waste," Padric replied with a grin. "She prefers—"

"Ah, de Clifton, isn't it?" Daniel's chest puffed out in an attempt to look bigger than his scrawny body could emulate. "What my dear uncle is trying to say is that you shall clean us up presently, or I shall see your superior for your insolence toward my distinguished uncle and myself."

The earl's lips pressed together in growing irritation.

"As you wish, m'lord." Padric's voice evened out in equally growing irritation. "We will send someone to clean your attire regardless."

"Uh, Padric—*Sir* Padric, that is, mayhap we should, you know, go?" Talfryn whispered. He didn't like the mischief in Daniel's expression, and now they were even *more* late.

"Presently," Padric replied. "Where are you staying, m'lord?"

Before Daniel could respond, the earl gave the name of the Peregrine Inn and when they would be there to change clothes. His valet would meet the laundress there.

"That was pretty terrible," Talfryn said once they were out of earshot. "I mean, the earl was great, but his nephew...whew! Let him spend a day in the garrison and see if he survives."

Padric laughed, dispelling the cloud that had formed above their heads. "Yes, I very much doubt he would deign to complain to a soldier ever again. But first, before we invite him to the garrison, we should see about the laundress."

"Is she far?"

"She is on the way to the tent. In fact"—the crowd parted and he waved—"there she is now. Lotty!" The matron wearing a simple white woolen blouse, skirt, once-white apron, and veil made her way over, and Padric weighed the small purse tied to his belt and sighed.

"What's wrong?" Talfryn asked.

"Based on the clientele of her newest customers, she is going to require most of this. I was hoping to buy Brynwen a gift from the vendors, but..."

"Take it out of my wages," Talfryn offered. "It was my fault, after all. Me an' my big elbows."

"You do have large elbows."

"Hey!"

Padric grinned, then sobered as Lotty walked up.

She smiled, the laugh lines around her eyes and mouth a welcome sight after their latest run in. "Sir Padric, there you are. I've set your fresh linen in yer tent, all ready to go. Is there anything else I can do fer you?"

"Miss Lotty, my thanks for your expert and efficient services. Please forgive me for adding more to your load, but, you see, I have a special project for you…"

CHAPTER 6

*D*odging his opponent's overhead swing toward his head, Padric lunged his broadsword at the armor-clad knight's mail breastplate. The knight, Sir Peter Petrival of Nottingham, pivoted so Padric's weapon slid along the armor's links without damage.

"Ha, ha, de Clifton," Sir Peter crowed. "Can't catch me off guard."

"It is still early, Petrival," Padric replied in kind. He smiled as his opponent danced away. With a trained eye, he studied the knight's movements and planned his next attack. So as not to look bored or too contemplative, Padric twirled his sword and arced it into the air.

Sir Peter's foot lurched out, catching Padric's shin with a loud metallic clash. Padric landed on his shoulder, the pauldron digging through the padded gambeson right into his shoulder, doing little to cushion his fall. His shoulder smarted, but he rolled once to avoid Peter's broadsword to the chest as he stumbled.

For the briefest moment, Padric thought to transform into a faun, but knew that would not go well for either himself or his father's appraising eye. Plus, he had no idea how his faun legs would mesh with his armor.

Abandoning that idea, he raised himself to his knee and ducked

Peter's next strike. The knight overextended, and Padric batted him on the back.

"Ugh!" Unbalanced, Peter sprawled on the ground.

By the time Peter shimmied himself onto his hands and knees, Padric's sword was at his neck.

"Do you surrender, Peter?"

Seeing no way out—literally, as his helmet had somehow been knocked askew so his eye holes were on the side of his head—Peter nodded. "Yes, I surrender," his muffled voice said. Blindly, he held out his hand and Padric took it to hoist him up.

"Here, let me help you with your helmet," Padric offered.

"You are too kind. But I will get you next time, Padric."

Padric held in his laugh. "Oh, I have no doubt."

PURE BLISS MET Padric's senses as he removed his stifling, sweaty helmet and coif, sweet air hitting his face. In spite of the cool October with its fickle winds, he was hot after the joust. He breathed in the welcome scents of food and sweets from the vendors until human sweat wafted his way in the next step.

Along with the smells, Padric's ears could better pick up the noise of the crowd now that he had removed his helmet. Waving at the revelers, he could tell the Derby supporters from the Nottingham supporters without any difficulty. He made a quick scan of the crowd for Brynwen, his family, and his friends. Almost giving up, he finally spotted his mother and sister Chelsea's golden tresses and Brynwen's auburn hair. Eyes bright, she clapped for him heartily, and his stomach leapt. She shouted something at him, but he could not hear over the great din. If time permitted, he would have bounded over the wall and into the stands toward her—but, alas, the next match was about to begin, and he had to clear out of the exit closest to him.

Talfryn met him under the green awning of the northwest exit. Padric could not wait to get out of his hot, sticky, smelly armor to take a bath.

"Well done!" Talfryn clapped Padric's gardbrace. "Only one more win to secure your position in the third round. I thought for sure when Sir Peter tripped that you were done for."

"Ha, so did I. But then he left his right side wide open—how could I not take advantage of that? I could hardly believe my good fortune."

"Good fortune is right. This calls for a celebration!"

"If we are to celebrate every victory, we will be but a veritable pile of rags by the end."

"Ah, come on, Padric! You didn't best a manticore, the Druid fellow, or a bunch of rogue *cobali* to forego a little celebration every now and then. Why, my grandfather once—"

"Ah, de Clifton, what are you doing here?" called a strong voice from behind.

Startled, Padric spun around. He grimaced as the sweaty garments beneath his armor clung to his skin. What he wouldn't give for a nice soak in Cataractonium's bathhouse.

Hands on his hips, the tall and muscled form of Sir Warin Ingram of Nottingham stood without blinking or a smile. His friend Herman and a handful of other familiar knights stood behind him.

Warin sniffed. "Shouldn't you be running around a pen instead of gawping about drinks?"

Padric's eyebrow rose. "Should I not be asking you the same thing, Warin? Shall I order an extra helping of vittles from the closest sty for your supper?"

The two glared at each other for a moment, then Warin extended his hand. When their hands clasped, both knights laughed, pounding each other on the arm. Padric held in the wince from his friend's enthusiastic blow—he just hoped it would not hinder his swordplay later.

"That was impressive work. Sir Peter Petrival is one of our fastest knights, and you bested him fairly quickly, considering."

It warmed Padric that Warin, who had until recently been his greatest nemesis, had given him a compliment. At the previous year's tourney, he and the Nottingham knight would have come to blows amongst the tents had their captains not appeared to intervene. Then in June, when they competed to be claimed as the the sun god Helius's heir at Cataractonium, a mutual understanding had occurred, one Padric could never have foreseen: together, they had fought and defeated the manticore. Padric had pushed Warin out of harm's way from one of the manticore's venomous spikes, an act which had very nearly cost Padric his life. A bond of friendship had been borne between them that day.

"I must admit, it was a close match." Padric had no desire to give Warin any insight into his strategy and fighting mindset. "I see we are slotted to battle on the last day at noon, should the stars align."

Warin nodded eagerly, showing his white teeth. "We shall finally see who is the better fighter."

"My money's on Warin," Herman said with a smug cock to his head.

"Yeah, well, mine's on Padric," Talfryn countered.

Herman leaned in toward Talfryn. "Double the wager?"

"Uh"—Talfryn's cheeks paled—"isn't that against the law?"

"Not if you know who to go to."

"Oh." He looked to Padric for guidance. "Well, I should really be helping Padric with his armor."

"Just one teensy wager? Come on." A mischievous grin swept over Herman's features as he put an arm around Talfryn's shoulders and spun the squire back into the crowd. "Perfect. Let's find the money dealer and—"

Chuckling, Padric watched the two for a moment before turning back to Warin. "Is he always so…"

"Low on coin?" Warin snorted. "Always." Rocking on his heels, his booming laugh could be heard clear to the center of Nottingham.

Warin's laughter was infectious, and Padric had to wipe his eyes from both sweat and tears of mirth. "Poor Talfryn, then, for he has been saving up for a new saddle. I hope Herman does not plan on making him bid on every knight yet to fight." When he saw Warin's blank expression, though, he blanched. "You cannot be serious."

"With Herman, anything goes. Comes with being the son of Mercury, I suppose." He sighed and tapped the pommel of his sheathed broadsword. "I'd best see he doesn't sucker Masson into the debt house, then. Care to meet us for the evening meal? I know a great place in

Nottingham, the Swan & Gables. Best ale in the county. Bring your friends along."

"We would be delighted. I shall bring Brynwen as well. She shall be glad to see you."

Warin's expression brightened. "Perfect, I look forward to it. See you at eight bells." He returned to the games and began whistling a tune.

Padric stared after him with a tightening in his chest. *Is it just me or is Warin a little too eager to see Brynwen?* He shook his head, hoping he had imagined the expression. Part of him had a desire to decline Warin's invitation, but knew it would be impolite. The other half had to trust in giving the knight the benefit of the doubt.

Before he could ponder it more, however, a familiar face appeared.

Garrick flashed his son a proud smile. "Ah, Padric, there you are. Well done, lad. Well done." He clapped his son on the arm. "Winning both of your games on the first day without seeming to break a sweat."

"If only it were that easy."

"Where is your squire?"

Padric felt uneasy, not wishing to get his friend into trouble. "He is on an errand," he said carefully.

Garrick nodded. "Nothing to be done about that, I suppose. Come, let me help you with your armor until he returns."

A flood of anticipated relief flooded through Padric, especially since the breeze had died down several minutes before. Any longer and the armor would slip off of him of its own accord. "Thank you. While we are at it, you can tell me about how the other knights are doing."

CHAPTER 7

*P*adric's intention of arriving early to choose his and Brynwen's seats at the Swan & Gables was dashed as everyone else was already seated when they arrived. All that remained was a seat for one on the bench between Warin and Serill, and a final seat between Herman and another Nottingham man.

Upon seeing them, Warin hastened to his feet. His height and broad shoulders overshadowed Brynwen. He took her hand in his and gazed at her with an intensity that made Padric seethe.

"Ah, Brynwen, so lovely to see you."

"Warin." She gave him a smile and slight curtsy.

The knight kissed her hand, then turned a nod to Padric. "Padric, so glad you made it. Come, drinks have been ordered for all."

To Padric's dismay, Warin tucked Brynwen's hand under his arm and led her to the table. Brynwen's eyes sparkled in merriment at Padric, and she gave an apologetic shrug. When Warin sat her next to him, Padric felt he might implode. All of his friends—Talfryn, Serill, Rawlins, and Byron—grew quiet when they witnessed the exchange, and their eyes slid to Padric. Talfryn stood up, his attention wavering nervously from his sister and Warin to Padric, uncertain what to do. A couple of

Nottingham knights began to shift in their seats, but Warin raised his eyebrow at them, and they stopped and shrugged.

Where was the chivalry?

Plastering a smile on his face, Padric rounded the table and sat between the two Nottingham men. He nodded a greeting to his friends but said not a word until after having drunk over half his mug of ale. Then he turned to Herman on his lefthand side, who was enjoying laughing at his neighbor's jokes and downing his own ale.

"Herman." Padric tried very hard not to make it come out as a growl, but he was not sure he succeeded. "Were you able to mend your winged shoes?" As the son of the Roman god Mercury, he had received a pair of wondrous shoes from his godly father. Each shoe boasted two wings that could raise the wearer into the sky and take him anywhere. However, during the first trial in Cataractonium, in his attempt to win, Warin had demanded to wear them until his overlarge feet had damaged them quite thoroughly.

Mention of the shoes made Herman's face fall. "Not as such. My godly father is vexed that I not only allowed another to use them, but that I didn't take care of his gift. He says it serves me right that they are broken. Who knows if he'll ever fix them." He shot a heated glance in Warin's direction, but the knight was too busy speaking to Brynwen to notice.

Seeing the pair, Padric's insides reignited. He had a momentary daydream about choking the life out of his new friend. Then Brynwen glanced up and gave him her scolding glare. Taken aback, Padric sobered. *Of course I trust her. It is Warin whom I worry about.* He then remembered Herman, who was drowning his sorrows in his cups, and continued. "That is a shame, for they are a marvelous creation, exactly how I had always imagined them in the mythology. How did you acquire them?"

Herman looked heavenward and sighed. "Aren't they? Mercury gave them to me when he learned I was in the trial. It was the first time he actually spoke to me, and he was happy to have a son in such a competition. He said it was rare these days to have an offspring in such a delightful undertaking."

"I can imagine. However, I am not certain that being a breath away from becoming the meal of a giant fish, deadly infant snakes, and carnivorous plants is a 'delightful undertaking.'"

"Exactly! Makes me wonder what he considers difficult."

I could think of a number of things. Downing the rest of his ale, Padric set the mug on the table with a thunk. "The next round is on me." He stood to go to the bar, when a fine-clothed body stepped in his way.

"Ah, peasant," Daniel goaded. Today he wore a different blue tunic with silver trim. It gave Padric the distinct impression that he was trying to look more regal than he really was. Unfortunately, his more agreeable uncle, the earl, was not in sight to subdue him. "I see you were able to get away from the games. Have you ruined any more of our fine countrymen's clothing this day? Although, I dare say there is yet more time for such careless acts to occur."

Pressing his lips together, Padric could not find the courtesy in himself to make even the slightest bow of respect. Since yesterday, he had discovered that Daniel Lambert was the son of a minor lord, nothing more. It was, in fact, the same situation with Padric's father being the second son of a lord, thus Garrick's brother had inherited the title. Yet this had never bothered Garrick in the slightest. "Not today, I am afraid, Master Lambert. I trust your clothes were cleaned and left with your valet to your satisfaction? And you might refer to me as 'sir' and not 'peasant.'"

Daniel's eyes sparked at the lack of his lordly title, but he recovered quickly. "Indeed, they were cleaned, but not to my satisfaction. Only my laundry staff know the proper cleansing technique for the silks and brocades of my impeccable wardrobe."

Padric felt compelled to show Daniel a different type of technique, this one with a fist.

Daniel continued, "You would do well to fire that laundry woman of yours and hire one with more skill. You will thank me for it later."

"My thanks for your suggestion," Padric said through gritted teeth, "but I am quite satisfied with our laundress's work. She is thorough and meticulous with my men's clothes. There is no better laundress in all of Derbyshire."

A snort exited Daniel's pompous lips. "I suppose you fight better than you bestow manners on your betters."

"I see no one better here. Only a youth who does not know how to conduct a civil conversation."

It was then that Padric noticed all other noises in the tavern had stopped. Everyone's attention was drawn to Padric's escalating discourse with Daniel.

Daniel's eyes grew wide, and Padric thought he saw steam emitting from his nostrils. "How dare you, you worthless piece of—"

"Mind your language, *Lord Daniel*, a lady is present."

That quieted him. Gaze searching behind Padric for the lady in question, Daniel's mouth twisted into something feral. His lingering scrutiny over Brynwen's person made her shift uncomfortably in her seat. "Well, well, such a pretty little thing. What are you doing with a group of brutes such as this?" He made to move toward her, but Padric barred his way.

Fists clenched and only one more insult away from finding the lordling's face, he gritted out, "That is quite enough. You would do well to leave, sir, before I throw you out personally."

First Rawlins, next Warin, then all of the other men at the table stood to back him up.

Daniel snarled. "You cannot speak to me like that, you foul wretch. You call yourself a knight—a sham, I say! I will see your superior, and you shall be barred from the rest of the tournament, Nottingham, and your current employment, for the rest of your days. You shall grovel at my feet the next time I see you."

Incensed beyond measure, Padric set his hand on the pommel of his sword. "I am about ready to take that chance. Do not tempt me to draw my blade."

The young man opened his mouth to spout some final cutting remark, but after a quick look at Padric's sword and his muscled friends, snapped it shut. In one move, he straightened his tunic, frowned disapprovingly at Padric, sniffed, raised his shoulders, and walked out the front door as though he were the most important person leaving the room.

Once the horrible man had left, all of Padric's bluster deflated. He barely remembered sitting down and grabbing up his mug, which was still empty.

A cacophony of excited voices filled the tavern and several hands clapped him on the back, nearly knocking the mug from his hand.

Warin's laugh drowned out the rest of the room. "Well, well, de Clifton, I never thought you had it in you. 'I am about ready to take that chance. Do not tempt me to draw my blade,'" he mimicked in a lower voice. "Never have I heard a better quip. Bartender—another round!"

Truth be told, Padric had not thought he had it in him, either. He knew not what had come over him. But when his gaze met Brynwen's, he was met with a look somewhere between thanks, shame, and horror.

When a new mug of ale landed in front of him, though, he thought to down it right quick to drown out the mixture of emotions he felt.

CHAPTER 8

During the previous two weeks, Talfryn had met up with Faunus every night in his dreams. He always alluded that his hilltop was close to where Talfryn was, but never gave the exact location. It was so vexing.

Sadly, Faunus never brought him back to the waterfall. Nor did they speak of things Talfryn didn't want to talk about. Instead, they discussed animal husbandry and plants and crops and a bit about the Roman gods.

It was on one such day, in the wee hours of the night—although it was daylight where Faunus was—that the horrible thing happened.

Faunus had agreed to take him back to the waterfall. Talfryn had only nagged him once or twice or maybe twenty times about it. It was hard to place his finger on why, but it struck him as the most serene place in the world. He felt that not even his most beastly nightmares could reach him there.

On their daily walk, Talfryn fidgeted and hooked his thumbs into and out of his trouser band.

Faunus didn't slow his pace as he raised an eyebrow at Talfryn. "Whatever is the matter, lad? You are more agitated than a new swan chick on his first day of flight."

"Well, sir," he began and swallowed. "Do you know why I come here in my dreams?"

A smile widened Faunus's cheeks. "Why do you think you come here?"

"Hey." Talfryn folded his arms over his chest. "No fair flipping the question back on me."

Faunus laughed, crinkles forming around his eyes.

When Faunus didn't respond, Talfryn grew quiet and thought about it. "Well, I guess I feel drawn to you."

"Why?"

"Because you've got the best vegetable stew in all of the world?"

"I doubt it would muster against your sister's."

Talfryn's eyes grew wide. "Wait, wait, wait. .you've had my sister's stew? When?"

"Now who is flipping the questions?"

"Fine, fine, fine." Talfryn huffed a breath, the action blowing his wavy hair off his forehead. "We both like animals?"

"What else?"

Seriously? What kind of game are we playing?

Talfryn ducked under the leafy branch of a low-hanging tree. Peering up, he saw two squirrels happily scurrying from one branch to another. "I feel comfortable around you. Like I did with my father." A lump grew in the pit of his stomach. His father had been a wonderful man, who had taught Talfryn everything he knew about farming and the animals they kept. He had allowed Talfryn to pick out his goats, Hay and Stack, from a group of kids when their old goat was about to die. Together, Talfryn and his father had built his mother a brilliant hearth for cooking. When the plague took both his father and mother, he had been devastated. Each passing year, he felt he'd lost a little more of his father. After nine years, he'd forgotten what he looked like, except that Samuel supposedly looked just like him.

Talfryn's throat went dry. "Wait, you're not really my father, are you?" The thought of betrayal and sense of being lied to overtook him, and he thought he'd be sick. He glared at the faun.

Faunus did not laugh. "I am not, nor could I ever take the place of your father. But I have been watching you for another reason. You are my—"

"Let me guess. I'm your great-great-great-great..." He stopped to count on his fingers, then quickly gave up. "Many-great-grandson? Like how Padric's related to Helius and Gregorio—er, Telegonus? And Bryn to Aesculapius?" Without losing step, he leapt over a fallen log. "I guess I'm related to Aesculapius as well."

Faunus glided over the same log. "Indeed you are."

"Am I also related to Padric?"

With the shake of his head, Faunus clasped his hands behind his back. "Different line. My descendants have worked the land from the onset of our creation. Tell me, your father had premonitions, did he not?"

Talfryn paused to think. "Come to think of it, he had a few. And they mostly came true." This time, the pit fell all the way to his heels. "He knew just when the crops were ready to harvest; and predicted when Samuel or I would come home with a busted lip or skinned knee. He knew the plague was in Derby, didn't he?" he asked with a shudder. His mother had insisted that her husband come with her into Derby that fateful morning, but he didn't want to. When she'd threatened to go by herself, in the end, he'd relented and had gone along with her. Talfryn and the rest of his family never saw them again.

A nod. "He certainly knew something bad would happen that day. But tell me. Have *you* foreseen anything of late?"

Cold, red eyes and the menacing laugh that belonged to them permeated his thoughts, and he thought his knees would give out. Swallowing, he shoved the vision away, calming his shaky breaths.

It's not real. Like this, it's just a dream. Right?

Talfryn tapped his chin. "Not that I can think of."

"Have you ever had a sudden hankering to buy something at the market, and it turns out your sister was in need of it? Or have you ever carried an extra weapon to training sessions for when someone breaks theirs?"

"Well, I may have once or twice." He thought about it, surprised that

Faunus had known about those. But he'd said he'd been watching over Talfryn. *Have I been having premonitions all the time?*

Not wishing to be questioned more on the subject, Talfryn rushed into his next question. "There is one more thing. Is there the slightest hint you can give me as to your location? It's nagging at me something awful."

"Well, is that all?" Faunus chuckled. He paused, expression thoughtful. "Should the need arise, it may be a good idea. For now, I will give you one hint. It is south and east of—"

A flurry of sound emanated behind them. Birds, squirrels, deer, and every other animal that lived in the vicinity of Faunus's home cried out in distress, hundreds of voices bearing down on Talfryn's ears. Reaching for his weapons, his hands slapped only his sides. Apparently, dream Talfryn didn't wear weapons. He'd think about changing that later.

From over Faunus's peaceful hill, the animals scurried away in terror. Talfryn thought he heard the animals screaming something about "the blue lady," but didn't know what that meant.

Faunus frowned. "I thought we would have more time."

Talfryn shooed the curious animals away from the disturbance. "Is there anywhere you can hide in safety? I'll keep them at bay." *Me and my bare hands.* Talfryn wondered how well he could fight without any weapons at all against whoever was coming over that hill. He reached for Faunus, but the immortal drew away.

"Nay, son. I am afraid you cannot stay here. My friends and I will face them."

"But I can help. Please." This time, when Talfryn swiped for Faunus's arm, he didn't pull away. However, Talfryn blanched when his hand went through it.

"What?" He raised his hand up in front of his face. It looked normal. "What's wrong with me?"

Forehead creasing, Faunus looked pained. "Alas, only your mind is here while your body slumbers in your cot in the tent. You never touched me or anyone before. Not once."

Talfryn was taken aback. He hadn't realized that he'd never touched

Faunus or the animals or really anything whenever he came here. Except that he'd eaten his food—*was that all in my mind too?*

The animals continued to scream as they streamed past them, the wind they made whipping at Faunus's hair and vest. Peering down, Talfryn's clothes remained just as if he were still sleeping on a still night with all the windows shuttered.

Seeing Faunus's look of regret, Talfryn tried one more time. "Come on. Let me try."

"I am afraid not." The phrase was final and so forceful, it raised Talfryn off the ground. Faunus raised his voice. "There is more I needed to impart to you but did not feel you were ready. I was wrong." He smiled at Talfryn's disorientation. "Fear not, my many great-grandson, we shall meet again. Soon." Weightless, Talfryn's body tripped over the animals, until he looked down on the burly, bellowing warriors below. They shouted their oaths, and Talfryn understood why the animals fled.

Leading the charge was a woman in a blue cloak. Her head was cowled, but he spied black strands of hair sticking out. The hand held out before her sparked out a couple of yards and made a horrendous sound. Behind her rushed a couple dozen men.

No, no, no. "Faunus! Run!"

All Talfryn could do was watch as the lady in blue and her force surrounded Faunus. The lady's voice rose over the shouts and fleeing animals, but Talfryn still couldn't hear what she said. The fight was over in seconds as Faunus put up no struggle, and they bound his hands behind him.

Without looking up, Faunus's voice reached Talfryn. *"You must go. Now."*

"I won't leave you—"

"Listen to my voice when I call you. Come to this place whenever you are troubled, even if I am not here."

"But..." A great pressure seized Talfryn's chest, legs, and arms, as though a great boulder were crushing him. "Faunus? *Faunus!*"

TALFRYN AWOKE, gasping for air. Heaving in great breaths, he shot up to a sitting position. There, in the dark, the shadows of the tent sought to move in and consume him. Swallow him up. The army of the blue lady and wolficorn, bent on his destruction. His hand groped the head of the cot for a weapon.

A groggy groan emanated from the next cot, its dark form shifting under the blanket. "What's going on?" The voice of Rawlins calmed Talfryn's quaking heart. It was just him and Padric with the rugs, armor, and chests filled with weapons. Not the wolficorn hunting him. "Shouting in yer sleep again. I'm about to request a change in bunk assignments."

Normally, Talfryn would've had a witty response to that, but his nerves refused to allow him much thought beyond survival.

Faunus's capture still on his mind, Talfryn had the brazen thought to go after him. The only thing stopping him was the realization that he had no idea where he was being taken or who had taken him.

"A'right." Rawlins growled. He hauled his legs over the edge of his bed, one side of him illuminated by the three-quarter moon, looking about ready to throttle Talfryn so he could get back to sleep. "Somethin's wrong—yer too quiet. Spill."

Talfryn had no idea where to start. But he didn't have to reveal everything, did he? So, in a quiet, quick tale, he explained about his daily dream visits to Faunus followed by the god's capture and being forcefully thrust out of the dream.

"That sounds troubling," a voice said from behind.

Talfryn leapt out of his cot and spun about in fighting stance.

But it was only Padric, propped up on his elbow. "Forgive me for overhearing, but I could not help it—you two whisper quite loudly, you know. Tell me, did you say Faunus as in the god who protects livestock, fields, and forests?"

"Aye," Talfryn responded. "My many-great grandfather."

Padric rubbed his forefinger and thumb against his jaw. "That is indeed troubling. I believe Gregorio should hear this."

"How can we rescue him?" Talfryn asked.

Half of Padric's frown was hidden by shadow. "I know not. Unless we know his location, we can be of little help. Unfortunately, with the tourney in full swing, our absence would be noticed."

Dawning of what day it was hit Talfryn like a pile of building stones. His heart sank, wondering what horrible things were being done to Faunus.

"We can send Ulysses out to search," Rawlins offered.

Talfryn perked at that. "That is a splendid idea."

"We'll find him at first light."

Despite the slim amount of hope, Talfryn's dreams were fitful, filled with the wolficorn mauling everyone in its path, and Faunus being tortured by the blue lady.

CHAPTER 9

On the fourth morning of the tournament, Talfryn stayed busy enough that his thoughts didn't wander to Faunus and his kidnapping. At a knock on the outside tent pole, he opened the cloth flap to be greeted by a young man holding a pristine jousting lance.

"Kett! You're just in time."

Miser chittered a cheery hello from Talfryn's shoulder.

The young man, apprentice to the Chaddesden carpenter, smiled. His brown skin and black, coarse, close-cropped hair, contrasted with the bright sun. He proudly wore a badge with Chaddesden's red and black colors pinned to his tunic, on which Talfryn spied specs of wood shavings. Around his middle, he wore an apron with several deep pockets bursting with tools of his trade.

Talfryn had known him a little before they both wound up in Cataractonium as builders on Helius's temple. There, Kett had shown his growing ability at carpentry and even masonry, building faster and better than just about anyone else, even though he was only sixteen. Only two other people there had been bestowed with a similar gift.

"Good morning, Talfryn. Miser. I finished fixing Sir Padric's lance last night." He handed Talfryn the wooden lance, complete with a fresh coat of black and red checkered paint as its decoration. A full twelve feet long, the pole never seemed to get any lighter after each joust. Lances shattered upon impact so as not to gravely injure the knights, but somehow Kett was able to fit all the pieces back together. It saved on wood and gave the carpenter a self-imposed challenge.

"Is this really the same lance Padric broke yesterday?" Talfryn couldn't spot a single flaw. *Amazing.*

"It sure is. Oh, and this is also for him." Kett handed Talfryn a sealed letter.

Padric's name was written on the letter in a delicate script. He didn't recognize the blue wax seal with a curled-up snake on it, but that didn't mean much here in Nottingham. Loads of strangers sent the knights letters with their own fancy seals. Invitations to dine, hunt, target practice, and so on.

"Who's this from?"

Kett shrugged. "Dunno. It was waiting in the captain's tent when I came to deliver his new lance, and his assistant told me to deliver it straight away. 'Orders are orders,' he told me."

"Aye, orders are orders. Thanks, Kett. See you later—probably to ask you to fix this lance again."

Kett laughed. "I'll save time to fix it."

Talfryn balanced the lance in its wooden holder—also crafted by Kett—outside the tent opening. Talfryn let the tent flap fall as he studied the letter further. A floral aroma wafted off of it, which he couldn't quite place, but he thought he'd smelled it before somewhere. In the recesses of his mind, he wondered if his sister would know what flower it came from.

A few minutes later, a shadow appeared at the tent flap, and Padric's voice carried from the other side.

"Oh, good, Kett fixed the lance. I would never have guessed that it had ever broken into more than fifty pieces."

"I can't believe it myself." The second voice belonged to Talfryn's twin sister.

"Oh, good." Talfryn scooped up the letter and opened the tent flap to find Padric and Brynwen appreciating the fixed lance. "Kett just brought it by a few minutes ago." Turning to Padric, he held out the folded paper. "Letter for ya, Sir Knight. Smells real nice, too—seems you've got yourself an admirer." He batted his eyes at Padric, then chortled at his own joke.

"An admirer, eh?" Padric eyed the letter, removing his hand from within his gray-blue cloak to grab it up. Studying the seal, his eyebrows furrowed. "I do not recognize this seal. It has an interesting scent, too." He ripped the edges from the blue wax holding the paper together and read the short message within. His brows rose in surprise.

Brynwen leaned over and sniffed. "It smells like calla lily. Who is it from, Padric?"

"Strange, it doesn't say."

Talfryn frowned for his sister's sake. "A *secret* admirer, eh?" He knew Padric would never cheat on Brynwen.

"Not quite? But it appears to be a woman's hand and sounds quite urgent.

"Sir Padric,

Please do not think me too forward, but I am in pressing need of your aid, and only you can help. Would that I could regale to you my plight in this letter, but I cannot risk the words in writing lest they fall into the wrong hands. It is in regards to your dear relations up north. I beg of you to meet me at the Blazing Dragon Inn immediately upon reading this missive. Pray hurry—

A Friend."

"THAT'S all it's signed as, 'A Friend'?" Talfryn asked.

"Could it be from Roana?" Brynwen wondered.

Talfryn scrunched his nose. Of all the people they might see in Nottingham, Roana was the last he wished to run into. He was having enough fun trying to handle squire duties without having to go save the world again thanks to the Sibylline Oracle. She'd already given both Padric and Brynwen prophecies—he didn't want to be the recipient of one as well. It'd been almost two months since the whole business in the Labyrinth had occurred—maybe by now Janus had given up the whole thing.

Ha!

"I doubt it," Padric said. "I am sure she or Hamon would have come personally. Whoever it is, though, she refers to my "relations up north" and must know something of Circe and Helius, or even another relation. She must be in danger if she could not explain her problem in the letter. She could even be someone who was at Cataractonium with us. I should find her at once."

Brynwen's eyebrow quirked. "Is that wise? What if she's a..." she blushed, but Talfryn knew she meant 'a succubus' like the one named Lilith who they'd encountered a few months earlier in the ruined ancient Roman fortress called Mamucium. Using her power of seduction, Lilith had nearly succeeded in having him and Padric fight each other to the death. If Brynwen hadn't found them and thrown holy water on her, it would've been disastrous. Just thinking about Lilith gave Talfryn the shivers. "It could be a trick, you know. Mayhap I should come with you."

"Nay, Bryn, fret not. I shall be on my guard, I promise."

"You'd better hurry. Your bout with Warin's in a couple of hours."

Padric kissed her on the head and then hurried away from the tent, his blue-gray cloak swirling about him.

"Tal, won't you go with him?"

Talfryn smirked. "He is a big lad, you know, sis. 'Sides, I have to get his armor ready for his big match with Warin in those couple of hours."

"It's just"—she twirled her braid around her finger—"I don't know why, but I have a bad feeling."

Talfryn thought to make a joke, but the look on her face changed his mind. "I'm sure he'll be fine. Here, in the meantime, you can help me with the really exciting chore of polishing Padric's helmet." He led the way inside the tent.

Taking up Padric's hauberk and a clean cloth, Brynwen grinned and set to work. "Nothing says love like polishing your swain's helmet just so he can get it dirty again."

Talfryn laughed. "Hear, hear."

CHAPTER 10

*B*ut after more than an hour had passed, Padric hadn't returned, and his fight was in under an hour. Even if Padric returned right this minute, he would barely have time to assemble into his shining gear and get to the field on the other side of the tent city in time.

Feeling the tension in the room, Miser paced on Talfryn's shoulder, muttering how humans got lost so easily without trees. In the forest, you always knew where you were.

"I don't think moving to the forest'll help, buddy."

"Tal…" Brynwen began.

"I know, I know, I'll go look for him. Stay here."

He barely waited for her nod before rushing out of the tent. He hadn't gone five steps before he ran into Rawlins.

"Rawlins, have you seen Padric?"

"Nah, I was coming to look for him. What's the matter?"

"He's hasn't returned, and he's fighting Warin in a few minutes." He gave a quick explanation of the letter and Padric's decision to find the writer at the Blazing Dragon Inn.

Rawlins's eyebrows furrowed at the news. "Let's find him, then."

Racing around Nottingham was harder than Talfryn had expected.

Rawlins knew it a little better, after coming every other year for tourneys, but he usually went to all the same places. Even after visiting the city for a week, they still only knew a portion of it—a couple of taverns and supply shops. They should have tried to grab one of Warin's friends on the way out of the tourney tents to act as a guide.

When at last Talfryn made it to the bursting Blazing Dragon Inn, Padric was nowhere in sight. He scanned the boisterous crowd inside and out for his friend's golden curls and green tunic, but spied only a couple of men with similar hair color and frames. Rawlins scanned everyone and shook his head. For a second, Talfryn panicked that perhaps Padric had gotten overwhelmed and became a hunger-crazed goat once again and was terrorizing the streets in his pursuit of a snack. But he pushed the fear down. Padric hadn't had an episode in months. But still, where was he?

"Afternoon." Talfryn greeted the barkeep of the Blazing Dragon and placed a hand on the long, worn counter. Nicks on the wood indicated many long years of use. "Might you have seen a young man come in a bit ago, with golden curls and wearing a green tunic and knightly looks? Might have little horns on his head."

"Eh? Horns?"

"Uh, forget about the horns. Have you seen him, by chance?"

"Can't say that I have, but it's been swamped e'er since the tourney began. I near ran out o' ale three nights in a row.'

"I can believe it. Well, thanks anyway."

Exiting the inn in defeat, they searched the street, trying to figure out where to go next.

"Let's split up," Rawlins suggested. "You go east, an' I'll go west. Meet back up here in a few minutes."

"Right. See you soon—hopefully with Padric."

As soon as Rawlins set out, the din of the pedestrians and peddlers picked up. Talfryn was about to go to the right when he heard a sound. The hairs on the back of his neck prickled up as the volume of the low, snarling growl ground through his ears and nerves like daggers. Memories of the creature's sharp claws, teeth, horns on its head and bones jutting out all over its body flashed at him. His cousin Leowyn dying horribly in front of him over and over again. The creature's horn ripping into Talfryn's leg. He almost collapsed where he stood.

His breath hitched. *No, not again. How'd it find me here with all these people around?*

Sweat built up on his brow and neck as his muddled brain tried to figure out what to do. The rational part of his brain knew he should draw his weapon, move away slowly, and find a hiding place. And yet, his hands and feet refused to move but shook instead. Every part of him refused to cooperate.

Clamping his eyes shut, he prayed the wolficorn wouldn't see him, that it'd just go away and find a nice woodland somewhere on the other side of the world.

Finally, the growling stopped.

When at last he opened his eyes and they adjusted to the midday sun, a familiar set of violet eyes with a mop of curls sticking out of a cream colored cap peered up at him. In her arms she held a squirming light yellow bundle. Inside the bundled blanket he spied a small face with a button nose and dark curls like hers. Those weren't violet eyes that looked up at him, though.

"Roana?" Joy flooded through Talfryn at her not being a deadly animal. "I'm so glad you're here. Have you seen..." He was so relieved at seeing a familiar face, he nearly forgot about her oracular gift and what it meant. "Oooh, no. No, no, no, no, no. I know why you're here. Go away."

She smirked, her violet eyes flashing in mirth. "Talfryn, I live here."

"You know what I mean."

Roana opened her mouth to reply.

In a flash, Talfryn raised a finger into the air between them. "Stop it, don't say another word. Trying to soften me up by bringing an adorable baby won't help, you know. I'm baby-resistant."

"It works on his father. If you would just hold him for a minute—"

"Nope, no way. Padric's missing and I gotta go find him. Maybe another time."

Before he could take a step, Roana moved as quick as lightning and placed the bundled baby into Talfryn's shaking arms.

Talfryn might've balked if the cute little human inside the blankets hadn't looked up at him with such doleful brown eyes and made the cutest gurgles he'd ever heard besides those from his baby cousin Amalia. All of his protests deflated, all anxiety subsided. Then he noticed the huge bulge of her stomach. "Umm, Roana, you didn't steal a random baby just to butter me up, did you?"

"Of course not. I stole—borrowed—my sister's baby. Now—"

"There are more of you?"

"She luckily doesn't bear the gift of the Sibylline. Now, will you listen to me?" Roana had placed her hands on her hips, her head cocked in expectation.

Weighing his options, Talfryn finally acquiesced. "Fine. But I'm not going to like this, am I?"

"It isn't very likely."

"'Isn't very likely,' as in a little likely, as though I'm going to need to pay off Herman's gambling debts for the next couple of years; or really likely, like I'm going to be going off on a very dangerous quest and it's uncertain if I'll return alive, likely?"

Roana pursed her lips as though deciding what to say.

"Never mind, I don't want to know. Here, have your sister's baby back."

"Talfryn." She stepped back so he couldn't return the baby. "Eral and I aren't leaving until you've heard the prophecy."

"His name's Eral?"

"Don't change the subject. You may wish to sit down for this. There is a crate you can sit on in the alleyway behind you."

"You prepared for this, I see." Excuses ran through Talfryn's brain. Then he remembered the first time he had met Roana at her tavern, and he scrunched his eyes. As a Sibylline Oracle, Roana was impelled to give the prophecy to the recipient or else the consequences for both her and possibly for the recipient could be dire.

With a loud sigh, he hooked his arms more securely around the gurgling baby and withdrew into the alley. Low and behold, a crate, its sturdiness most questionable, rested about halfway down. Next to it he found a basket large enough to settle the baby into.

Trying to tamp down his nerves, he set Eral into the basket and fussed with his blanket to make sure he was comfortable. "Well, little guy, it looks like you're gonna have to get used to these prophecies from your auntie at some point. Might as well learn now, eh?"

"Hurry, Talfryn, there isn't much time."

Seeing the worry in Roana's face, Talfryn promptly plopped down on the groaning crate and waited. He wondered if he should move the baby further away when Roana's body stiffened, her violet eyes clouded over into orbs of fathomless ebony.

Talfryn gulped, wondering if it would hurt, if he'd get visions like Padric had, or pass out like Bryn.

The moment the Oracle's mouth opened, Talfryn's head ripped apart.

CHAPTER 11

*D*oubled over in agony, Talfryn gripped his head with both hands. Large, red and gold letters seared through his closed eyes with each syllable Roana recited, each letter more painful than the last. There was nothing Talfryn could do but try not to pass out as the text sped across his vision at dizzying speed. If it didn't stop soon, he'd lose his meal.

> *O tu fili domini*
> *Faunae atque somnii*
> *Hostis tibi obeundus*
> *Est sub occidente tuus.*
> *Eius Sancti virtute*
> *Lucis bonitatisque*
> *Quaere illam semitam*
> *Per noctem obscurissimam.*
> *Qui est Auriga libere*
> *Donum debet iam sumere*
> *In alata quadriga*
> *Sub luna lucidissima.*

Ad monstrum illum obiendum
Est tibi forti attendendum
Ne Olympus praematurum
Ipse obeat terminum.

Thou son of the lord
Of fauna and dream
Must face thine foe
By westering.
By the Saint of
Goodness and light
Seek the path
Through darkest night.
The Charioteer must
Take up the boon
Upon wing-ed carriage
At brightest moon.
In facing the monster
Thou must attend
Lest Olympus
Meets an early end.

The words slowed down, and he thought the worst had passed. Then descended upon him a light so bright, it blinded him even more than the prophecy had. Talfryn would have flinched, but then the silhouette of a person walked out of the light source. The being moved slowly, as in a dream, and Talfryn couldn't see much more than the darkened shape of a man with crooked legs and hoofs, his features drowned out by the brightness behind him.

"*Talfryn,*" the deep male voice said.

"*Faunus?*"

"*You must find me.*"

"*Where are you? Where did they take you?*"

"*Talfryn.*"

Talfryn startled awake. Calming his racing heart, the red and gold text of the prophecy flitted across his closed eyelids in rapid succession. It was quite distracting as he tried to remember what had happened.

"Talfryn?" Roana sounded worried.

Ah, that's right, the prophecy. Cautiously opening his eyes, he stared up into the worried face of Roana. Crinkles at the edges of her eyes revealed the stress he hadn't noticed before. She'd picked up the fussing baby from the basket and was patting his back to shush him.

Talfryn was lying on his back on the ground.

"That was fun," Talfryn croaked. "Let's do that again, never."

With a snort, Roana patted Talfryn's shoulder. "Back to your old self, I see, praise be. You had me worried there for a minute."

Sitting up, it felt like he was fighting against a pile of bricks or like he'd slept for a week. Except that he didn't feel rested at all, and the words of the Oracle's prophecy swirled around in his head, at times obscuring her face. The way she gazed at him and pursed her lips made the pit of his stomach drop. He swallowed hard, not looking forward to what she'd say. "So, uh, what happened?"

"Once I was myself again, your eyes…clouded over. Very white—the opposite of mine. It was like you were in some sort of a trance. When you didn't come out of it right away, I feared you'd been lost for good. But then, finally, your eyes cleared and you crumpled to the ground and fainted for a few seconds. What did you see?"

Talfryn regarded her, trying to remember the details. Slowly, he said, "There was a bright light and Faunus. He wants me to find him. And— wait, I can't stay here, I'm looking for Padric."

Roana shook her head impatiently. "Padric is fine, well, nearly fine, and will be at his tent by the time you get there. Now, this Faunus—"

"Talfryn, where the devil are you?" Rawlins stalked past the alley's entrance then doubled back. When he spotted Talfryn and Roana, he glared between the two of them. "Have you been here the whole time?"

"Yes. She wanted to show me something." Talfryn had considered lying but knew better.

Rawlins's eyes turned to slits. "I didn't see Padric anywhere."

"Roana says he's back at the tent."

Rawlins gave a glaring nod of thanks to the Sibylline Oracle and baby, then looked back to Talfryn.

Stepping forward, Roana held out a hand to Talfryn.

"Not now, Roana." Talfryn launched to his feet, a renewed energy zipping through his limbs. "Padric's going to be late for his fight."

The Oracle peered at him skeptically but at last relented. "I think I know who you saw. There is trouble ahead for you."

"There always is," Talfryn said distractedly, ready to be off.

"Talfryn." Roana's voice carried authority.

He jerked, startled by her tone. He imagined it would be used many times on little Eral and her own baby when she was born.

"Tell Padric good luck. And to your journey, God speed, lads."

"Thanks. Wait, *journey?*"

Rawlins grabbed his arm. Without looking back, he and Talfryn dashed out of the city toward the knights' tents.

"What was that all about with you and Roana and a journey?" Rawlins asked. "She didn't give you a prophecy or anything, did she?"

Talfryn nearly swallowed his tongue. He really didn't want to talk about it, at least not now. "Later."

Rawlins shrugged. "Suit yourself." He nearly left Talfryn in the dust in his hurry to reach their tent.

THE PROPHECY STILL ON, and literally in, his mind, Talfryn stopped in front of the tent just in time to allow Rawlins's stormy entrance through the flap. Even though they were now friends, prudence warned him to keep out of the dangerous knight's way when he was in a mood.

Coming up behind the knight, Talfryn spied Padric sitting inside just before the red and white striped tent flap fell in his face. He deliberated over whether or not he should tell Padric about the prophecy now or later. Rawlins had only asked if he'd received a prophecy and that was it. Talfryn had been grateful, as his head still reeled from the flaming words swirling around it. It had been enough of a struggle to keep up with the knight without falling flat on his face, which had nearly happened more than once.

"Where've you been?" Rawlins asked Padric in annoyance.

"I…" Padric said, his voice quiet. "I am not sure."

"What d'you mean?"

Batting the flap away, Talfryn stepped into the tent. Padric was sitting on his cot, head in his hands, looking worse for the wear. Standing a few paces away from him, Brynwen twisted her finger in her braid, her eyebrows furrowed in concern. "Did you make it to the Blazing Dragon Inn?"

Padric ran his shaking hands through his dark blond curls. "I did. At least, I meant to. I have no recollection of going inside, though."

All thoughts of telling Padric about the prophecy sizzled to nothing as he gaped at his friend.

With a gentle movement, Brynwen placed her hand on Padric's arm. "What do you remember? Start from the beginning—from when you left here."

The gesture seemed to calm Padric, for his muscles relaxed somewhat. Closing his eyes, he took a deep breath before answering. "After leaving here, I made my way straight to the Blazing Dragon. When I was about there, the crowd became very condensed, and I was nearly thrown to the ground. Then, without warning, the crowd thinned out, and I found myself at the inn's door. I became disoriented. Then…the next thing I knew, I was standing in front of this tent." He scratched his head in confusion. "That is everything I remember."

Rawlins's arms were folded over his chest, his face unreadable per usual. "Did someone in the crowd knock you on the head?"

"You saw no one you knew?" Brynwen asked.

A shake of the head. "Nay. Although"—he paused, his face scrunching in thought—"there was someone who looked vaguely familiar. A maiden in a dark blue cloak. I know I've seen her recently, but cannot place where."

Talfryn started. "A woman in a dark blue cloak, you say?" Likewise, a memory came upon the edge of Talfryn's mind. Sure, there might have been hundreds of girls wearing cloaks in the autumn. And yet, he couldn't shake the feeling that he should know what Padric was talking about.

The sound of trumpets carried to them.

"You're next, Padric." Talfryn shook his head. They'd have to sort it out later. And then he'd tell them about his run-in with Roana. "Sorry, but I've got to get you ready. Bryn?"

"Yes." Try as she might to hide it, Talfryn could see her disappointment in leaving before getting more answers about Padric's disappearance. She leaned over to peck a kiss on Padric's cheek, squeezing his arm for good measure. "Good luck, Padric. I know you will do well."

Padric grabbed up her hand and kissed it gently, their eyes meeting in mutual regard.

She smiled, then exited the tent.

In an instant, Talfryn switched his demeanor into that of a squire, shoving aside all thoughts of Roana and prophecies. All that mattered for the next hour was Padric's match with Warin Ingram. "All right, stand up and strip." Without waiting for Padric to comply, he rushed over to the armor laid out neatly on a table, a task he had spent much time perfecting over the last few weeks once he knew he'd be Padric's squire at the tourney. He handed Rawlins the wool leggings, then in order the gambeson for padding under his armor, chainmail, the breastplate, then the gorget around his throat. Pouldrons, vambraces, and gauntlets on his shoulders, arms, and hands.

It took a considerably shorter amount of time with two people strapping on his gear. They were just finishing tying the final fasteners, and Talfryn thought of quickly telling Padric about his encounter with Roana, when the tent flap opened, and Captain Garrick poked his head inside. "Padric, what is the hold up? Everyone is waiting for you."

By now, one wouldn't have known anything amiss had happened to Padric only a short time ago. Based on his expression, his mind was already getting set for the fight to come. "I am on my way, sir."

"Yep," Talfryn replied. "Just adjusting Sir Padric's vambrace...and"—he tugged on the buckle for good measure—"there. Go show Sir Warin who's the better jouster! Put some hoof into it, so they say."

The captain's face blanched as he stared at Talfryn in horror.

A grin raised Padric's mouth and he laughed.

There we go! Much better!

"Padric, seriously, this is no laughing matter."

"But, sir, it is. I have come to learn that, despite what life throws at us, there is almost always a time for laughter." He snickered again. "Come on, Talfryn, Rawlins. Captain."

CHAPTER 12

*L*imping, Brynwen found her seat on the spectator's bench between Gregorio and her grandfather Eduard. Her older brother, Samuel, and his new wife, Edina, sat on the other side of Eduard, thoroughly enjoying the show. In front of them sat Padric's mother, Tabitha, and his sister, Chelsea.

Ever chivalrous, Gregorio, clad in his persona of graying hair, worn red cloak, and studious wrinkles, beamed and rose as Brynwen approached. His Italian accent was back, as well. "Ah, there you are, Brynwen. We were beginning to worry about you. You left a while ago with Sir Padric." Seeing her limp, though, he quickly caught her hand to help lower her onto her seat spread with the quilt her grandmother had made when she and Eduard had first wed. "Good heavens! What has happened to your foot?"

Scarlet flamed her cheeks. "Oh, it was the most stupid thing. All week, I was very careful to step around the tent rope spikes. And then, the first moment I took my attention elsewhere, I tripped! Twisted my ankle." She huffed in annoyance. "I would have fallen into a great mud puddle had the rope not been there." She hadn't been paying attention to where she was going because of what had happened to Padric. Her chest constricted when she thought of telling him about the mysterious letter and Padric's short disappearance. But this wasn't the time or place to speak of it.

Gregorio patted her hand. "I am glad it was not worse."

"Me too."

She scanned beyond the arena, happily spotting the antlers of Gregorio's father, Ulysses, peeking over the top of a tall guard post on stilts. Ulysses was the hero from Homer's story *The Odyssey*, who after being mortally wounded by Gregorio-Telegonus's venomous spear, had been rescued from death by Circe. In doing so, she had been forced to turn him into a *peryton*—a creature that was half stag, half bird. He had made it to every event at the tourney where Padric, Talfryn, and Rawlins competed.

"Is your cousin coming as well for the last day tomorrow?" she asked Gregorio.

The immortal frowned. "Alas, Payla contacted me last evening to say that she was unable to come after all. Her matron needs her there."

"I am sorry to hear that. She would have enjoyed it." Payla had been an integral part of their adventure into the Labyrinth below the underground city of Rellea, and Brynwen had been looking forward to seeing her again. Being an immortal priestess to the god Mithras and the secret twin sister to Asterion the Minotaur, Payla was called upon to do many chores and rituals and rarely had free time to visit family or friends. Despite this, she kept in constant contact with her cousin Gregorio-Telegonus, and now with Brynwen, Padric, and the rest of their party from their time in the Labyrinth.

"Speaking of Sir Padric, where is he?" her grandfather Eduard asked. He focused on the arena.

Brynwen followed his gaze into the arena and spied Sir Warin Ingram in full armor, his squire and horse by his side. The long, blue caparison on his steed hung down to its knees. A white lion and a heart were stitched onto the fabric and white embroidery circled the edges. Resplendent in shining chain mail and plate, Warin held himself erect, every bit the image of Hercules, smiling and waving at the cheering crowd. Girls swooned whenever his white-toothed smile flashed their way. Despite his boastful manner, Brynwen had come to like him during their encounters in Cataractonium and Nottingham.

"He's on his way." Her finger wrapped itself through her braid in worry. Having limped all the way from his tent, she'd prayed that with both Talfryn and Rawlins to help don Padric in his armor, it would be a quick task and that he would already be in the jousting field, prepared to face off with Warin. Alas, this was not the case.

She needn't worry long, however. Less than five minutes later, the *chink chink* of chainmail announced the presence of Padric moments before he sauntered into the field in his armor and upon his horse Firminus whose caparison portrayed the de Clifton coat of arms: a rose and seahorse. At his side strode Talfryn, wearing Derby squire black with a red and black checkered sash, holding Padric's broadsword, ten-foot jousting lance pointing heavenward, and a shield hooked onto his back.

Every time he came out in his chain mail and metal plate armor during the tourney, Padric made a dashing figure. Nowhere near the size of Warin with his bulging muscles inside his mail, Padric's figure was broad shouldered and all lithe, lean muscle. Unfortunately, Brynwen had missed the fight between the two knights in Cataractonium, when they had squared off for the final trial to determine which would be Helius's heir. Now, she felt both excitement and trepidation for the outcome.

Padric waved at the crowd. When he looked at Brynwen, butterflies flew around in her stomach. She noticed the green sash tied around his wrist—the one she had given him when the tourney had started four days earlier as a good luck token. Having heard that other girls did this with their knightly sweethearts, she couldn't resist bestowing him with her favorite green sash which matched his eyes. In a sweet gesture, he had held it to his heart and said, "I will cherish this gift all my days." The moment had filled her heart with such a deep warmth that she'd felt elated all the rest of that day and the next.

A trumpet blasted on the sidelines, and as one, the two knights donned their helmets over their coifs. Each squire handed the lance to their knight, and hurried out of the way to the sidelines. The knights walked their mounts into position on opposite ends of the arena, the tilt —a simple piece of white fabric—the only barrier keeping them on their respective sides.

The trumpet sounded again, this time a short blast, to initiate the match.

As usual, when Padric's matches began, Brynwen's stomach tied up into knots. She had made sure to bring all of her salves and of course the Miracle Mix in case Padric or any of the other knights were injured. Thankfully, so far only a few knights on either side had needed medical attention, but nothing more serious than sprained ankles, bruised ribs, and a few deep cuts on their arms.

Brynwen and everyone in the stands released a premature gasp as each knight lunged his lance at his opponent, but swiped only air. Several disappointed sighs and a few heckling remarks emanated from the stands. "My mother could'a hit that," and "You can buy a fine pair o' spect'cles from my cousin Fred right 'round the corner!"

Undaunted, the two knights circled back to their opening places. Again, the short trumpet blast sounded, and they dashed toward the center along the tilt.

This time, lances connected with bodies. Brynwen cringed at the crunch of the wooden lances against metal armor. The breath froze in her lungs as both Padric and Warin toppled from their mounts and landed with a metallic crash onto the packed earth. Great clouds of dust rose into the air.

No!

Launching to her feet, Brynwen searched for the quickest way down into the arena. Dozens of spectators trapped her in, and once she got to the aisle, she would have to drop down into the arena to attend to Padric and Warin.

A hand yanked her arm and pulled her down on her bottom.

"Sit down, my dear." Gregorio said and released her hand.

She glared incredulously at the tutor. "But Signore—"

"But nothing. Look, they are getting up." He pointed a thin arm down toward the center of the arena where the two knights had rolled over onto their hands and knees. By the time Padric made it to his feet,

Talfryn was at his side, handing him the broadsword and shield. Warin's squire did the same. Padric and Warin were ready with their broadswords and shields at the same time. They stepped with purpose to the center.

They circled each other, their heads bobbing as though conversing. Then, before the crowd became too restless, their exchange transferred to that of shining steel upon steel. At first, they lunged at each other half heartedly to get the other's measure. It wasn't long, though, before they came to true blows.

Brynwen's heart constricted with each clang of steel, each movement of feet, each slip or ring of a sword, each near miss. Certainly, Warin was the stronger fighter, his arcs full of power. She had no doubt that he could split a human in twain should he really try. On the other hand, Padric was more nimble. He could dodge many blows and strike with precision.

Chelsea was really into the proceedings while Tabitha winced with every blow made against her son.

Gregorio clapped and shouted encouragement along with everyone else. But then his body tensed, hands frozen mid-clap.

"*Signore?* What's wrong?" She touched his arm, which seemed to release his stupor.

The tutor shrunk in on himself, not taking his eyes off of whatever he was staring at. "Do you see that woman across the way? Over there." He dropped his accent.

Brynwen laughed. "There are many women over there, *Signore.*"

But Gregorio didn't laugh. "Look again. In a dark blue cloak—you cannot miss her."

Furrowing her brows in confusion, Brynwen searched the crowd on the opposite side. Everyone cheered for the two people flailing swords at each other. All except one.

She was beautiful, with a veil hiding most of her wavy raven-black locks. A royal blue cloak adorned her shoulders. Back ramrod straight, she seemed to own the wooden bench where she sat, her perfect lips set in a smile—or was that a smirk? The smile reminded her of someone, but for the moment she couldn't think who. The woman neither cheered nor clapped, but she placed her full attention on the two knights locked in battle.

A commotion broke out at the contender's entrance into the arena from the far side. Eight men in full armor sans helmets strode into the space despite the ongoing match. The fighters were so intent on each other that they didn't notice the armored men's approach. Undaunted, the man in the lead raised an arm and called for silence. When Padric and Warin didn't stop, the leader signaled to the trumpeter, who released a quick blast.

At last, the dueling knights halted their strikes and regarded the approaching men.

"What's the meaning of this?" Warin's voice rang out over the arena. Removing his helmet, he breathed heavily from the ordeal he had just been through. He wiped sweat from his glistening brow and frowned at the approaching men. "Can't it wait until after the match?"

"I am afraid not," the leader announced. He had long hair tied back with a black ribbon and the same colors of blue and white adorned the tunic over his armor, yet it had a different checkered pattern than what Warin and his fellow knights wore.

"Who is that?" Brynwen asked Gregorio.

"That is the Sheriff of Nottingham, Sir Herbert Herrington. Beside him is the Horse Master."

"Why would the sheriff interrupt the match?"

"Mayhap someone made an illegal move? I saw nothing obvious, though."

The next moment, Captain Garrick de Clifton emerged with purpose from the other contender's entrance to meet the group in the center, followed closely by Talfryn. Unfortunately, Brynwen couldn't hear the following exchange that transpired, but it was pretty evident they weren't sharing greetings of peace and comments upon the weather. Garrick's face turned first white, then bright red. Padric, having removed his helmet when the Sheriff of Nottingham began speaking, faced away from Brynwen, so she couldn't see his expression, but his shoulders seemed to tense despite the armor covering them. Talfryn's brows furrowed in worry and confusion.

"What are they saying?" Eduard asked.

Annoyed at her grandfather's question while she was trying to hear, Brynwen could only catch one part of the discussion. That one part, however, was enough. "...Padric de Clifton, you are under arrest for the murder of Daniel Lambert of Nottingham, nephew of Vernon Perry, Earl of York."

Tabitha spun in her seat, her eyes wide. "Did they say murder?"

Chelsea's jaw dropped. "It can't be true."

A wave of nausea rose in Brynwen's stomach. *Why would they think Padric capable of murder?* Again, she tried to launch to her feet, but Gregorio shoved her back down, this time with more force than his scrawny muscles seemed capable of.

She watched in helplessness as Padric surrendered his shield and sword to one of the sheriff's deputies. As one, the soldiers surrounded the unarmed knight and led him through the same place they had entered. Sir Garrick, Warin, and Talfryn followed behind them.

The moment they left, the crowd was abuzz. Derby people exclaimed their shock, while several Nottingham folk clucked their disapproval for "unruly Derby knights who clearly can't follow the rules."

Brynwen sat in a stupor. She couldn't comprehend it. It was like a very bad dream, one she hoped to waken from at any instant.

But the way Gregorio's hand was clamped over her forearm didn't feel like a dream. However, his gaze wasn't on the the space where they'd seen Padric being led away. It had returned to the direction of the woman with the ebony hair. But when Brynwen looked in the same spot, she was gone.

"Who is she?" Brynwen knew they should go after Padric, but the crowd was too riled to even think of moving. Besides, Gregorio's behavior about the veiled woman made her warily curious.

His eyes turned to slits, but he didn't look at Brynwen when he spoke. "Someone whom I had hoped would have plunged herself into a fissure eons ago." The venom in his voice was so unlike him, it took Brynwen aback. "Who doesn't deserve the immortality that has been graced upon her."

Now his grip was crushing her arm. She clawed at his fingers to pry them loose, but he wouldn't budge. "Signore, please."

Abruptly, the hardness in Gregorio's face dissipated, and he looked at Brynwen with utter horror. Releasing his grip, he quickly pulled his hands to his chest in contriteness. "Forgive me, Brynwen, I do not know what has come over me. Unfortunately, my cousin has that effect on me. It shall not happen again."

"I doubt it will." Brynwen rubbed feeling back into her forearm. "Why would she be here? Your cousin?"

"Medea." His nose scrunched as he said her name, as though it left a bitter taste in his mouth. "She shouldn't be here, nor anywhere nearby. She's been banished by the gods, and especially my family, ever since the day she made some unforgivable choices."

Medea. The name sounded familiar to Brynwen, but she couldn't place it. However, thoughts of Padric's fate with the Sheriff of Nottingham took over any worry she should have over a banished member of Gregorio's family.

"Come, Brynwen," Gregorio said, "we should find out what ill fate has befallen Padric. I see his mother and sister are making their way out, too." He rose to his feet and began moving toward the exit. A couple of clowns entered the arena to placate the crowd until the next set of knights were ready.

Brynwen sent her grandfather, brother, and sister-in-law a quick goodbye, then scampered after the de Clifton women and Gregorio's thin, determined form. Her ankle still bothered her, but there was nothing for it as she caught up with her friend. "I don't like the way you said 'ill fate.'" She'd never believed in fate, as it belonged to the pagan gods and their myths. But as more and more of the myths came to life, she wasn't so sure anymore.

Gregorio sounded weary. "Yes, well, whenever gods and immortals are involved, you can most assuredly count on it."

CHAPTER 13

Still surrounded by Lord Herbert Herrington, Sheriff of Nottingham, and his guards, Padric was guided through the crowded streets of Nottingham toward the city gaol. The protests he had proclaimed while in the jousting arena had fallen on deaf ears. It seemed the Sheriff had already made up his mind as to Padric's guilt, but he offered no clue as to why. Up front beside the sheriff strode his father and Warin. Following in the rear, picking up the guards' dust, Talfryn kept pace, still holding Padric's helmet. Passersby gaped at the spectacle, and Padric could hear loud whispers passing among them, though not every word. He could only guess at their meaning. In no time, word would spread throughout all of Nottingham.

Nothing his father said had any effect, either, even though the two men were old friends.

"But where is the proof?" Garrick had asked.

"Every person at the Swan & Gables heard their quarrel. It seems Daniel was a bit soused. Mayhap he began the unsavory discourse, but it appears that Padric ended it."

"That is unfair."

The sheriff shook his head. "Come see for yourself."

A dreadful feeling came over Padric. Try as he might, he still could recall nothing from the time he stood in front of the Blazing Dragon Inn and when he returned to his striped tent. The first thing he remembered was feeling groggy and opening the tent flap and finding Brynwen within, sitting on a chair worrying her hands. He had blinked at her, not sure how he had gotten there. The errand that was to have taken no more than half an hour at most had lasted twice that time.

Worse was learning how much time he was missing. Where had he been? *Could I have killed Daniel? But why?* Their quarrel was nothing but two men having a spat—was that so unusual?

It is when one of them ends up dead. Padric grimaced inwardly.

At last, they made it to the Nottingham City Gaol, a newer two-story white-stone affair with iron bars in each window and newly painted shutters of blue to match the sheriff's uniform. The old structure had burned down ten years previously, and a new, better gaol had been constructed in its place. His shoulders drooped. Leaving this place would be near to impossible.

When they entered the building, the first thing Padric noticed was the wide desk on the right side. A plush chair fit for a king or upper nobleman sat behind it. All the other wooden chairs in the establishment seemed drab in comparison. Buckets of chains and shelves of books and charts stood against the walls surrounding the desk, and another table stood by the barred window on the left. Straight ahead was a door which Padric guessed led to the cells.

The very sight of it made his chest constrict. Once he passed that door, he might very well never see the other side except for his own hearing and execution.

The sheriff rounded his desk and, instead of plopping down in his chair, remained standing. "Come here, de Clifton."

Silently, the guards parted so Padric could approach the desk. Upon it, Padric spotted two stacks of documents, each weighted down with a lead weight in the shape of a man riding a horse. A jar of black ink and an eagle feather quill within a holder rested in the corner. The center was what drew Padric's eye, however. A white handkerchief covered something long and thin.

Lord Herbert regarded Padric, likely trying to gauge his expression.

"Do you know what we shall find beneath this handkerchief, Sir Padric?"

"I have not the faintest idea, my lord."

The frown which the sheriff gave on him sent the temperature in the room plummeting. "It appears you wish to play games. I had hoped, being the son of an esteemed colleague and friend, that you would cooperate, Sir Padric. Very well, I shall play along with your little game of cat and mouse." He placed his gloved knuckles on the desk and leaned forward, all pretense of "games" long gone. "Where were you this morning between dawn and noon?"

It was difficult to calm his heart enough to speak clearly. "This morning, I dined with my family and Miss Brynwen Masson, then headed to my tent to ready for my match with Sir Warin. My squire, Talfryn Masson, met me there." He indicated behind him to where Talfryn stood at attention near the door. "Once there, I received an urgent missive to help someone in need. I was—"

"Who were you to meet?"

"The missive gave no name, nor did I recognize the seal. I was to meet this person at the Blazing Dragon and hastened to the task which I believed to take but half an hour. However..."

"However?"

Padric was unsure how to proceed without sounding guilty. "However, I have no recollection of what occurred after I arrived at the Blazing Dragon Inn. The next thing I remember, I was back at my tent, more than an hour later. Miss Masson was there, and Talfryn and Sir Rawlins were mere minutes behind."

"Are you saying you do not know what happened between arriving at the Blazing Dragon and your tent?"

Padric set his jaw and rounded his shoulders. "Yes, sir."

"And that you have no clue as to who wrote you the letter?"

"None at all."

The sheriff scowled. "You expect me to believe this?"

"I do not, sir. Yet it is the truth."

Pursing his lips, Lord Herbert brought his hands behind his back. "No one else saw you?"

Padric shook his head, wishing it was the exact opposite. "I have no idea. There were all sorts of people in the streets on my way there, but no one I could say I recognized."

"What, then, do you make of this?" In one fluid motion, Lord Herbert plucked the corner of the white handkerchief off the desk. The metal item it had concealed caught the light from the window.

The moment Padric saw it, he understood. All the blood drained from his face. A dagger of fine quality and binding, the dried blood on the blade defacing its beauty was revealed. But that wasn't what shocked him. The embossed gold shield with a seahorse and rose in opposite corners—the de Clifton family crest—proved it was his stolen dagger.

Beside him, Garrick gasped.

"Well? What have you to say to this?" Lord Herbert asked with a smug smile.

Throat suddenly parched, Padric tried to swallow. "It is mine," he admitted. It took another moment for him to completely comprehend what lay before him. He made brief eye contact with Talfryn, who looked just as stricken, before turning back to the desk. "I lost this dagger in June. And I cannot explain how it ended up in Daniel Lambert's heart this day."

"Your losing it four months ago seems a little convenient, does it not? When I have two witnesses who say you had it on you this morning on your way to the location where the murder took place."

"What?" Padric and Garrick said.

"That isn't true," Talfryn burst out.

All eyes turned to him, and Padric inwardly groaned. Apparently, after two months of squire training, his friend still could not learn to keep his mouth shut when it mattered most.

Talfryn clenched his fists. "It isn't. He lost it in June like he said. Sir Padric lent it to my sister for protection when we were on the road, and we were attacked by a group of huntsmen. The leader Drogo took it from her." Indeed, the huntsmen were in league with the traitorous Sir Aeron, who had disguised himself within Padric's own green cloak. The woodsmen's leader, Drogo, had confiscated the dagger from Brynwen when he had captured her. Padric had not hoped to see the weapon ever again. Now, he vehemently wished it had remained at large indefinitely.

A thought occurred to him that if the dagger were here, that meant Drogo might be nearby, too. Did he kill Daniel and try to cast the blame on its owner? Yet what disagreement could he have had with the dead man?

"A maiden wielding a dagger?" The sheriff looked horrified. "Absurd! I ought to have you arrested as well for contempt, squire."

To his credit, Talfryn stood his ground, although Padric could feel the mortification of what he had admitted oozing from him. And now Brynwen might be in danger of the sheriff's scrutiny as well.

Warin cleared his throat softly. "If I may, my lord. I encountered Sir Padric in June, and he had no such dagger on his person at the time. It could very well be the truth that he lost it." If it were not for the direness of the situation, Padric might have smiled at his friend's slyness. When they had encountered one another at Circe's lair, the dagger had already been lost, but it would have been confiscated by Circe and her dryads regardless.

Garrick spoke up, but Padric could tell his father strained to keep his composure. "Lord Herbert, I know my son, and if he said he did not murder this man, then I believe him. Were there no other clues?"

"There are none other than that of the receding foot marks leading to the knights' tents. Just because he is your son, Sir Garrick, doesn't mean beyond all doubt that he is innocent. Enough of this." He slammed his palms on his oaken desk. The impact stirred the papers under the weight to fluttering and the quill rotated in its holder. "Sir Padric, why did you murder Daniel Lambert?" The man looked about to burst a blood vessel in his temple.

Padric's blood began to seethe. "I have killed no one. Our exchange at the inn the other day was but a spat, nothing more, and certainly not enough for murder or a duel. I had thought little of the whole affair until now." *At least, not in my right mind.*

Lord Herbert released a deep sigh, momentary defeat plain on his face. He waved a hand at the Nottingham knights. "Guards, take this man away. Mayhap a few days in a cell will change his mind and we will get to the truth at last."

Before another word could be said, the guard on his left clamped a hand on Padric's arm and led him through the door to the cells, each step further and further away from freedom. And with each step, further and further from any hope of a misunderstanding.

CHAPTER 14

Together with Gregorio, Talfryn paced back and forth in the tent he shared with Rawlins and Padric, but there wasn't much room for the restless action, as the rest of the space was filled with Captain Garrick, Brynwen, Rawlins, Warin, Serill, and Byron. Rawlins withdrew from his next match, which might very well disqualify him from the entire tourney. Captain Garrick had strongly suggested that Brynwen go to her family while they sorted things out, but she would have none of it. She insisted on staying and could be of better use here. Besides, she *was* with her family—Talfryn was there.

The tent had already been ransacked by the Sheriff of Nottingham's men. All of their weapons had been confiscated—another concession to Rawlins's withdrawal—as well as some of Padric's other random personal belongings and an extra pair of boots. Except for the boots, which might have left foot marks around the dead man's body, none of these items seemed to pertain to the case at all.

They never found the mysterious letter. Padric had taken it with him to the Blazing Dragon Inn, but it didn't return with him.

"It's just petty," Byron said as he looked around the mess.

"They could have at least put everything back in its place," Brynwen muttered. She sat on the floor, trying to tidy up Padric's papers and maps, knowing he'd want them returned to their respective order when he returned.

If he returned.

Standing against the center tent pole with arms folded across his chest, Rawlins rolled his eyes. "Is now a good time for housekeeping?"

"What else can I do?" Brynwen sniffled. "The sheriff won't allow me to see him."

Garrick huffed and jabbed his hands on his hips. "Lord Herbert is a stubborn man when he wants to be. Apparently, that is today. He would not allow me to speak with Padric for more than a few seconds."

"It's not right," Talfryn lamented. He knew they'd wear a hole in the rugs with all of their pacing, but couldn't bring himself to stop. He had to do *something*.

"If only we had some proof of his innocence," Gregorio said. He wrung his hands so hard, Talfryn was sure they'd chafe the skin right off. "If Medea and Drogo are both here, it would make sense they'd be working together, yes?"

Three succinct knocks came from the pole outside the tent.

Everyone froze to stare at the tent flap, then their gazes flew to Talfryn.

"Who is it?" Talfryn removed his hatchet from his belt. Everyone else put their hands on their hilts. With a gulp, Talfryn realized that if Medea was anywhere near as good at magic as Circe was, they wouldn't stand a chance.

"It's Kett," said the familiar voice. "I've repaired Sir Padric's lance."

Belatedly, Talfryn did remember that it had been damaged during the shortened fight with Warin. He looked to the captain for guidance.

Garrick nodded toward the tent flap.

Opening the flap a sliver, Talfryn looked outside. Sure enough, it was Kett, holding Padric's painted lance. "Hello, Kett. What's Padric's favorite color?"

Miser asked him where to find the best oak trees.

"Uhh, what?" Kett's brows furrowed.

"For heavens sake, just let him in," Rawlins grumbled. He shoved

Talfryn aside, opened the flap and clutched Kett's tunic in one movement, then pulled him inside.

"Woah!" Kett cried out, dropping the lance. He cut his cry short when he saw all the people crammed inside the tent. Rawlins released his tunic.

Garrick jerked forward. "Whatever are you doing, Rawlins?"

"He's one of us, sir. He can help us."

The two knights glared at each other. Talfryn shuffled from foot to foot.

Brynwen broke the tension by smiling and limping forward. "Kett, we are so glad to see you."

"What's going on?" Reaching down, Kett picked up the fallen lance and dragged it inside. It filled the whole tent. "Is this a meeting about Sir Padric?"

"Very astute, young man," Garrick said.

"News spread quickly—everyone knows. I can't believe it." He frowned and shook his head.

"We can't either," Warin said. "He did not do it, though."

"Worse," Kett continued, "the Nottingham people want justice soon or they might riot."

Gregorio began to pace again. "The huntsman Drogo stole the dagger months ago. The question is, did he do the murder or did Medea take it from him and do the deed herself? Or did they have someone else do it?"

"Could Medea be here for another purpose?" Talfryn asked.

"Hardly."

Slamming one fist into the other, the captain huffed. "I don't like so many unknowns."

Brynwen's hands balled into fists, anger welling in her expression. She had taken the first brunt of Drogo's brutality, and Talfryn had taken the second. He'd never forget what the violent huntsman had done to them. And now he was back in their lives, whether he'd actually plunged the knife into Daniel Lambert or not.

"And we still don't have evidence of either of them doing it."

"However, I fear even if we did find this evidence," Gregorio said,

"Medea will have some hand in negating it. I did sense some magical residue when you exited the gaol, and although I had not seen her in a few centuries before today, I would know it anywhere." His nose scrunched up, likely recalling whatever she'd done to him.

Garrick's back straightened at the word "magical." After the last couple of months of living with the fact that his own son and several members of the community had powers or special abilities, he was still uncomfortable with the term "magic."

But something that Gregorio had said made the captain stop in his pacing. "What kind of magical residue did you detect?"

"A ripple, like someone tossing a pebble into a stream. Also, the scent which wafted from the gaol alarmed me. A particular flower."

In the midst of thumbing through papers, Brynwen froze. "A flower? Do you mean something like a calla lily?"

Gregorio's gaze shot to her. "That is correct. But how did you know?"

"The letter Padric received smelled like calla lilies," Talfryn replied.

"She needed a scapegoat," Rawlins finished. His eyes turned to slits, and Talfryn could almost see the hate radiating off his body. If they ever had the chance to corner Medea, he had no doubt Rawlins could tear her to shreds. That is, if she didn't cheat her way out, like some of the immortals he'd met so far did.

Foregoing the paper organization, Brynwen stood up from the rug and and brushed off her skirts. "Gregorio, what can you tell us about Medea? What terrible things has she done?"

"Who, exactly, is this Medea person?" Garrick asked. The question made him seem like a small child trying to comprehend what his elders were discussing.

"Oh"—Gregorio shuddered—"my cousin has many sins to her name. Medea is a sorceress, a dealer in black magic. It began when she was quite young and met a demigod named Jason. He was the crown prince of a land called Thessaly. In order to gain the throne from his usurping uncle Pelias, he was sent on a quest to obtain the much coveted Golden Fleece in the far-off land of Colchis."

Talfryn stopped pacing and picked up Padric's discarded hauberk to polish it. What else could he do with his hands? Miser, also agitated by Padric's arrest, helped by scrubbing it with his red tail. "Was the fleece also really soft and warm for cold winters? Because that would make it even more valuable." By the teacher's glare, he figured the answer was no. "All right, then, why'd he want it so badly?"

"The Fleece was said to have belonged to his family from ancient times. Jason hired a renowned boat builder named Argus to craft him a special ship he dubbed the *Argo*. He and his demigod friends, known as the Argonauts, had many adventures, and eventually found their way to Medea's home of Colchis. Her father, King Æetes, sent Jason on three impossible quests, and if they succeeded all three, they would win the Fleece."

"There's always a quest, isn't there?" Rawlins asked dryly.

"Always," Gregorio agreed. "He promised Jason marriage to his daughter Medea, and as they stood before the altar of the goddess Hecate, Medea furnished a charm which would aid Jason in overcoming his trials. With it, he obtained the Fleece with little difficulty. But instead of giving it to King Æetes, he fled with it, his friends, and Medea to the *Argo* before King Æetes could stop them. In her haste to escape, Medea killed her brother, Absyrtus."

Brynwen gasped. "Her own brother?"

Gregorio nodded gravely. "Indeed, and seemingly with little remorse. Soon after they returned to Thessaly and Jason and his father reclaimed the throne, Medea used her sorcery to kill his usurping uncle Pelias before he could try to retake it. For this act, Jason and Medea were exiled from Thessaly and fled in our grandfather Helius's sun chariot."

Talfryn rolled his eyes. "Obviously."

"Downtrodden, Jason found a small place for them in Corinth, where they lived in near-poverty and had two sons. Not long after, Jason had the idea to set Medea aside and marry the king of Corinth's daughter. In retribution, Medea killed her own children and the princess, and then she set fire to the palace. She fled on the chariot and married another king, where she continued to do nefarious things." By now, Gregorio was seething, and Talfryn was pretty sure he saw smoke coming out of his nose like a dragon.

"How awful," Brynwen exclaimed. She looked completely horrified.

Kett gulped. "She did all that? And she's here, now?" His dark face turned ashen.

Ignoring the blazing, swirling letters floating around in his brain, Talfryn finished polishing Padric's hauberk with a flourish. "So, in other words, you're not happy to see her."

Gregorio's eyes rose to the heavens and he muttered some mix of Latin and what Talfryn assumed to be Italian.

Garrick grunted and rubbed his chin. "It all sounds like an incredible story."

"I wish it were." The tutor sighed.

"So." Rawlins rubbed his chin, his other hand on the hilt of his sword. "We have both a huntsman and a sorceress on our hands who're no strangers to murder. But why'd Medea want to blame it on Padric? What's he got to do with her? And has it got anything to do with the prophecy Talfryn got this morning?"

The papers Brynwen had just ordered and neatly arranged slipped from her fingers. "What prophecy? Tal?" She looked at him expectantly.

"Uh, yeah." Heat soared up the back of Talfryn's neck, and he scrubbed at the already polished helmet. "So, I saw Roana today. She says 'hi' and has the cutest infant nephew."

"Talfryn Francis, do *not* change the subject!" Brynwen hissed.

Oh, dear, she's used the middle name. Now I'm in deep trouble! "Well, I was a tad more worried over Padric's disappearing predicament and getting him to his match on time than these words floating around in my head, thanks a lot." He tossed the hauberk on the pile of armor. "I was going to tell you eventually."

Standing up, Garrick's eyebrows furrowed as he studied Talfryn. "Are these prophecies, well, common amongst you people? Padric told me he had received one from this woman—Roana, was it? And then Brynwen. And now you, Talfryn?"

Talfryn gripped the table in consternation. "Aye, captain. The same kind." It wasn't like he'd asked for it or anything.

Then, a compulsion overtook him to recite the prophecy. Without a moment's delay, he spouted the words in perfect order, just as he'd heard it earlier in the day.

> *Thou son of the lord of fauna and dream*
> *Must face thine foe by westering.*
> *By the Saint of goodness and light*
> *Seek the path through darkest night.*
> *The Charioteer must take up the boon*
> *Upon wing-ed carriage at brightest moon.*
> *In facing the monster thou must attend*
> *Lest Olympus meets an early end.*

At the last word, a bout of lightheadedness hit Talfryn, and he didn't remember sitting down when reciting the prophecy. His leg began to throb. Having skipped the afternoon meal, he sat with his head in his hands, eyes scrunched shut as dark spots and exploding stars emerged from the corners.

A pressure touched his shoulder.

Upon opening his eyes, he peered up. He opened his mouth to scream, but nothing came out. The huge wolficorn stood before him, its blood-red eyes staring into his own, its gray fur as mottled as ever. Sharp horns sticking out of the top of its head and body. The deadly, toothy grin as big as Talfryn's head, not six inches from his face, stopped his heart.

Just as everything was becoming dark, a kindly voice called to him from far away. *"Talfryn."*

"Faunus?"

"Be at peace."

§

"TALFRYN!" Heart lurching, Brynwen lunged forward as Talfryn's shoulders sagged and his body began to pitch forward. However, already there, Warin caught his arms and kept him upright.

"What did you do to him?" Rawlins asked.

"I dunno what happened." Warin shot a hand up in defense. "I barely touched him." After reciting the prophecy, Warin had touched Talfryn, who had stared at him like he was the devil for several seconds, then fainted.

A groan escaped Talfryn's lips. He mumbled something. A moment later, eyes fluttering open, his head shot up. Seeing everyone staring at him, his back straightened like a pole. "I didn't mumble the prophecy, did I? 'Cause that would be embarrassing."

Captain Garrick, who had been gaping at the spectacle, cleared his throat. "Are you all right, son?"

"I…I think so." Talfryn rubbed his temples, his eyes drooping.

"Tal." Brynwen placed one hand on his arm and the other on his cheek to raise his head so she could verify that he was all right. "What happened? What frightened you so? And did you speak of Faunus just now?"

"Umm, I don't remember." He cast his gaze to his feet. She knew he was hiding something. "But Faunus did speak to me right before I passed out. He said something like, 'be at peace.'"

Rawlins snorted.

"A nice sentiment," Warin said wryly.

"Really?" Gregorio said it not as a question, but as a fascinating observation. "I wonder…" From his blue satchel, he retrieved his communication orb and fiddled with it.

Captain Garrick released a grimace and placed his hands on his hips. "This is all very interesting, but what are we going to do about Padric? And how do we capture Medea to prove his innocence? She could be miles away by now."

A spark of impatience came over Brynwen, and she tapped her foot. "What about the prophecy? What does it mean? It has everything to do with what's going on, doesn't it, mentioning 'the Charioteer'?"

"You are right, Brynwen," Gregorio agreed before the captain could retort. "I glean from the prophecy that Padric, and Talfryn as the prophecy bearer, must go west. However, I cannot yet tell what '*by the*

Saint of goodness and light' means, but 'darkest night' and 'brightest moon' could mean nighttime at—"

"The full moon is October 28." Talfryn interjected. "The prophecy." He pointed at his head to emphasize where the knowledge came from when Captain Garrick looked at him skeptically.

"That is only nine days from now." A sigh came from Gregorio, and he returned the orb to his satchel. "This is all so much. I cannot get a hold of my mother to verify, but, believe it or not, I think that the prophecy has everything to do with Padric being framed. Somehow, Medea—and I must surmise she is working with Janus now—knew of Padric's involvement with the prophecy and the events that are to come."

"Before the prophecy was even revealed to him?" Brynwen asked.

"Yes. He *is* capable of seeing into the future, after all. He doesn't always need Aeron to spy on us."

"I won't argue with that," Rawlins replied. "Not with all I've seen. This Medea person's got to know that Padric's at the center of this or she wouldn't've gone through all these lengths to stop him."

"Why not just kill Padric, then?" Warin asked. "It would be so much easier."

Gregorio's sharp laugh startled Brynwen. "But where would be the thrill in that? My cousin is not one to take vengeance too quickly. Since her first murders, she has come to delight in the long game."

"I bet that Shadow Druid isn't far away, either," Talfryn said in disgust. He got his wobbly legs under him and leaned against the tent pole. "He's not the giving up sorta guy."

Sir Garrick grimaced. "Is that the dangerous magical fellow who worked with Aeron?" Saying Aeron's name seemed to add years to the captain's already strained face. Padric had told Brynwen how awful the captain had felt once he'd learned of the ebony haired knight's murderous deeds. His face had blanched and then soured, afraid he couldn't trust his own judgment for some time after that.

"Yes." Brynwen rubbed her arm where the horrible Druid had touched her wrist. It had been so cold, it burned.

Now it was Warin's turn to show surprise. "You mean to say that Sir Aeron betrayed you?"

"Most cruelly." Brynwen's hands dug into her skirts. Never would she be able to remove his evil, laughing face or his vile threats from her memory. Even knowing Padric had mortally wounded him in the Labyrinth didn't help. Aeron's compatriot, the Shadow Druid, had escaped with Aeron, but there was little chance the former knight had survived such a grievous wound.

"Thus," Gregorio continued, as though not having been interrupted, "we must break Padric out of gaol. The prophecy is as much about Padric as it is Talfryn. The sheriff will not aid us—Medea has seen to that. So"—he turned to Garrick—"how can we free him, Captain?"

Nostrils flaring, Garrick huffed. "My job is to place criminals *in* gaol, *not* to break them out."

Anger coursed through Brynwen's veins. She shot to her feet, hardly noticing her satchel crashing to the ornate rug. "But he is your son! He is innocent of this crime, and you know it."

She winced as Garrick patted a tentative hand on her shoulder. "Aye, lass. Aye." Overcome by weariness, he sat down heavily on a wooden chair by Padric's cot, planting his face in his hands. "For my son and the fate of the world, I shall break him out. But how?"

"Excuse me, Captain"—Kett had been so quiet that Brynwen, and presumably everyone else, had forgotten he was there—"but I think I know of a way."

"You do?" Gregorio asked hopefully.

Kett picked up a hammer and chisel from his tool belt. "Yes. But I'll need some supplies, first."

CHAPTER 15

*W*hen the moon was past its zenith and the night guards of the gaol had been stationed long enough that they should've become sleepy, Talfryn stood in nervous agitation. He waited in an alley one block away from the gaol with Brynwen, Warin, Rawlins, and the other knights, Captain Garrick, and Gregorio. With only a tiny candle and the moon as his light, Kett made the finishing touches to the contraption he'd fashioned out of wood.

A handful of nails sticking out of his mouth, Kett somehow managed to saw and hammer quickly and with so little noise that not even a cat would mark it as significant. It was like sorcery.

"Have you made one of these before, Kett?" Talfryn asked, enthralled by his friend's impressive skill.

Careful not to drop the nails, the carpenter's answer came out as a muffled, "no."

In no time, Kett had finished and held up the contraption in triumph, bright eyes shining in the moonlight.

Talfryn couldn't have explained its likeness if he'd tried. But it had many sides, and a long "neck" with a pointed end resembling something like a goose. For all he knew, in the daylight, it might've looked completely different.

"Ah," a couple of the knights said, trying to sound like they knew exactly what it was. But Talfryn knew they had just as much knowledge about it as he did.

Garrick looked at it with skepticism, but Gregorio regarded it with excitement.

"Yes." The tutor rubbed his hands together. "Yes, I think this will work. Well done, Master Kett."

"At least Gregorio is confident about it," Brynwen whispered in Talfryn's ear.

Kett gave a small smile. "We've yet to see if it works."

"Then let us proceed," Garrick said. "Byron, Serill?"

The two knights raised their bottles of ale.

Nodding, Garrick held up his hand and made a circle with his index finger, indicating everyone was to get into place.

Talfryn's stomach twisted as he and Kett followed Rawlins behind the next building, to spill out into the alley beside the gaol.

Rawlins had already scouted the gaol before in his incognito form—that is, his uncanny ability to become invisible, thanks to being the descendent of an unknown Roman god—so he knew which cell Padric was in from the outside. He looked in the tiny window then ducked down again.

"He's there. Let's go."

Rawlins took hold of Kett's arm, and before they disappeared, Talfryn clutched at Kett's other arm. Now invisible, they rounded the corner, Kett's nervous breaths coming fast.

"Slow breaths, Kett," Talfryn suggested. "Like a stroll in the orchard."

"A stroll in the orchard." The carpenter repeated it a couple of times in the barest of whispers. When they neared the front door of the gaol, he became silent, thank goodness.

Down the lane, Byron and Serill sang loud and waved their bottles in the air. They stumbled up the steps to the gaol, peered left at where Talfryn, Rawlins, and Kett were hidden, then barged on the door.

"Open up!" Byron bellowed. "We want to see the lieutenant. He's innocent."

"Innocent," Serill repeated in slurred speech. "Quite innocent. Let us in so we may prove it."

A chair slid along the floor followed by the patter of boots on boards. "Go away. Come back in the morning." The footsteps receded.

Byron banged on the door again. "But good sir! This evidence cannot wait."

"Too bad. Now go home, we're closed."

"Would the sheriff not be pleased if *you* presented this indisputable evidence to him?"

"Mayhap get a nice, fat promotion?" Serill added.

The footsteps stopped. Creaked the floorboards. Returned.

A key slid through a lock noisily, and the door slid open two inches. "How 'indisputable' is the evidence?"

"Quite. Let me show you." Together, Byron and Serill attempted to push the door open, but they stumbled over each other and fell into the door. The guard jumped back quick enough to avoid a collision, allowing the door to swing open, and the knights crashed to the ground. When they picked themselves up, Byron's elbow knocked the door open wider.

"Oy, get outta here," the guard demanded. He was an older man, his hand on the pommel of his sword, ready to draw it should there be any trouble.

Oh, what trouble there will be!

As the guard moved inside, avoiding the "drunk" knights, Rawlins tugged on Talfryn and Kett, and they rushed inside before the guard could close the door in their faces. Talfryn held his breath as they slunk past him. A sort of scared whimper came from Kett, but the guard didn't seem to notice as he yelled at the two troublemakers.

Still wary of being caught, they inched to the door to the cells and waited until the two "inebriated" knights dragged the guard toward his desk. Byron pulled out a folded piece of paper from the breast of his tunic, and loudly voiced his so-called evidence.

Not wasting any more time, Kett set his invisible wooden contraption against the lock on the door. Alas, being invisible didn't allow

Talfryn to see what exactly Kett did with it. But in seconds, the door unlocked and they were inside, keeping the door open just a crack.

Rawlins released the invisibility and stumbled toward the cell.

Padric was already on his feet, hands gripping the bars. "What are you doing?" he whispered. "You will get caught and thrown in with me."

"Not if we can help it," Rawlins replied.

"It's a gaol break," Talfryn explained with a wide grin. "Kett?"

"But if I break out, they will be even more convinced of my guilt."

The red and gold prophetic text swirled around Talfryn's vision. He shook his head to clear it. "If we wait, worse things could happen."

Padric's eyebrows furrowed. "What do you mean?"

"Let's get you out first, then I'll tell you."

Padric nodded gravely.

Face set in determination, Kett set to work on the cell lock by inserting a pin attached to the long neck into the keyhole. After a few turns and jiggles of the wooden thing, the lock unlatched with a loud thunk.

Everyone stood silent for several heartbeats expecting the guard to rush in and catch them at any moment.

When nothing happened, Rawlins waved Padric out of the cell. "Come on, let's go. Byron and Serill can only convince the guard of your innocence for so long."

With no more hesitation, Padric joined them, closing the cell door behind him, and they exited the cell block as invisible entities again. Rawlins took the lead with Padric, sneaking across the floor of the front room. They had just gotten to the closed door when Kett tripped and knocked into Talfryn. Rawlins and Padric crashed into the door, and their invisibility failed.

Talfryn could see everyone again.

And so could everyone else.

Rawlins had enough time to glare at Kett and Talfryn before the guard's head whipped toward them in surprise. It took a whole three seconds of gaping at them before he found his voice. "Halt, you! Escape! The prisoner—"

He was quieted as both Serill and Byron drew their swords and pointed them at the guard's chest.

"Go," Byron directed. "You too, Serill."

Serill shook his head. "I'm staying. Get going, Padric."

Without any more prompting, Rawlins flung the door open and shoved Padric out before he could protest. He clutched Padric's arm, forcing him to run, Talfryn and Kett following close behind.

Candles blazed to life in windows along the street.

"I think they've discovered you're gone," Talfryn said drily.

A few guards and knights from Nottingham gave chase, but Rawlins drew them into the shadows of a building and then made them invisible again. They ran until they were out of breath at the agreed-upon meeting place outside of the city.

THE THIN RED ribbons of dawn were already beginning to break when they burst out into the forest. Padric's heart swelled to find Brynwen, Gregorio, Garrick, all of the Chaddesden knights, as well as Warin, Herman, and some of the Nottingham knights he was familiar with waiting, all donning cloaks but no armor. His breath caught when his mother and sister darted from the group after Brynwen.

"Padric!" Smiling with relief, Brynwen rushed to Padric and became engulfed in his embrace. He breathed in her scent of honey and lavender, and some of his worry rolled off his shoulders.

"I knew they would rescue you," his sister Chelsea cried, hugging the couple.

Padric's mother, Tabitha, squeezed his other arm and shoulder. "Praise the Lord you are safe." In spite of her smile, her eyes glistened with fear for him. In her arm was his gray-blue cloak, clutched to her bosom like a lifeline. "Here, Padric, you will need this on your journey." She placed it in his arms and squeezed his hand.

Worrying the cloth in his hands, his brain finally caught up to the situation. "But why did you break me out of gaol in the first place? Will they not believe more heavily in my guilt now? And you are all accomplices in my escape, if not the deed itself."

Rawlins's head jerked to peer over his shoulder. "They won't be far behind us." He picked up a brown bag from the ground and flung it over his shoulder.

"Father?" Padric gaped at his parent and friends who stood before him. "Do not tell me you all planned this?"

"Fine," Talfryn smirked. "We won't tell you."

Garrick clapped Padric on the shoulder. "We could not let you stay in prison, and clearing your name would take too long. Your mission is of greater importance."

Padric's eyebrows furrowed in suspicion. "What mission do you mean?"

"Let me deal with Lord Herbert."

Gregorio came forward and clasped Padric on the shoulder, then shoved a small metal object into his hand. "Talfryn received a visit from Roana this morning. We will tell you all about it while we are on the road."

Understanding alighted on Padric, then he narrowed his gaze on his youthful many-great grandfather. "I see. And where has Roana suggested we go?"

"'Westering' was the word she used."

"That sounds very specific."

Clutching the metallic item, Padric knew without looking that it was the amulet of obsidian, a gold ring with an obsidian stone. He had gone through great lengths to obtain it a few months ago. It may have looked like an ordinary piece of jewelry, but the magic within it had saved his life once against Janus. And now Gregorio insisted he bear it again. *This does not bode well.*

"Might I propose you go to Valle Crucis Abbey in Wales?" Herman suggested. "I know it is a fair distance, but my cousin Howell is a monk there and will vouch for you. Besides, the Sheriff will never think to look for you there."

"It is a sound plan," Garrick agreed.

Padric nodded. He had heard of the abbey but had never visited it. "Thank you, Herman."

Gregorio shouldered his blue bag. "And along the way, we can better discern the matter of Roana's warning."

"And make Padric a chariot," Talfryn added.

Now Padric was truly intrigued, but the sounds of shouts and dogs could be heard.

Garrick drew his sword as did several of the knights. "You must go now. May the Lord be with you all."

"Nay," Padric said. "You cannot stay here, nor can I permit you all to get into trouble on my account. Poor Byron and Serill are already paying the price."

"We will bar the sheriff's men as long as we are able. Isn't that right, men?"

"Yes, sir," the men cried, raising their swords.

Garrick smiled. "George, take m'lady de Clifton and Chelsea to the inn so they are not implicated in this."

"But father!" Chelsea clenched her fists at her sides.

"No 'buts,' child. George?"

"Aye, sir." George saluted and ushered the two women from the scene, but not before they gave Padric quick hugs and kisses on his cheeks, wet with tears. They hugged Brynwen, too.

A tic stabbed at Padric's chest as his mother and sister retreated ahead of George. He raised his sword in likewise salute. "God speed, and my thanks to you all. May we see each other soon. Captain, friends, take care of yourselves." Padric donned the now-rumpled cloak, its warmth around his shoulders a stark contrast to the chilly October night.

Garrick nodded. "We will. Herbert and his men will get in their sparring practice today whether they like it or not! Stop this Janus fellow's nefarious plot. Now *go*."

The shouts and barking drew ever closer, and Padric knew, with a heavy heart, that it was time to depart. To his delight, Firminus waited for him, his tail swishing in anticipation. Padric took a moment to rub his long nose before mounting. Once everyone was mounted atop their horses, he headed north up the road, followed by Brynwen, Talfryn,

Warin, Kett, Gregorio, and Rawlins. Padric knew better than to advise them to return home, for he knew they would not listen. He only prayed they did not pay the ultimate price for it.

The others had not been out of sight for more than a minute before a creature stepped into the road. It's antlers reached to the sky like fingers in an intricate pattern and white wings unfurled to block the road on both sides.

"Ulysses!" Padric exclaimed with warmth. "I wondered if you might join us."

The creature nodded, his eyes sparking with mischievous delight.

"*Pater*," Gregorio said in greeting to his peryton father. "He says he will keep the sheriff and his men busy while we ride the other way."

"Ulysses, you are a godsend. I am confident they will never catch you. Stay safe."

"To Valle Crucis Abbey, then."

ᚠ

AERON'S MEN had left the dead man lying in a puddle of his own blood. Daniel Lambert had been taken by complete surprise, not believing anyone would have the gall to murder him without cause. Not even when Drogo plunged Padric's own dagger into his heart did he begin to understand.

The poor, delusional fool.

Little did he know there *was* cause for it.

The corners of Aeron's lips slipped upward as he dreamed of Padric's head on a platter. His only wish was that he would have the chance to put it there himself.

"Watch yer step," one of the huntsmen grumbled.

Aeron's smile faded as he came back to himself. His horse side-stepped into an ankle-deep hole in the ground.

Drogo brandished his long knife, gazing at it as though at a long lost love. "What is the rush, Medea, if de Clifton is out of the way? We have plenty of time until the full moon."

"Tut, tut, young pup. Let us just say that there is much to do, and I have a premonition that Padric de Clifton will make his way to us, regardless of any guilt the ninny of a sheriff believes him to have."

Aeron grumbled like his companion. "We should have killed them both, not drugged him and returned him to his friends." *My former friends.* Padric would never know how close Aeron had come to strangling or stabbing him in the heart this day. Possibly both, if Medea hadn't kept him at bay. Shifting on his horse, Aeron grimaced, and touched the place where Padric had stabbed him in the Labyrinth. It still ached as though it were fresh, as a reminder of his failure to kill his enemy. *Nay, let him stew and hang like he deserves.*

Soon, Janus's plan would come to fruition, and he'd never have to worry about his former unit ever again. And Padric would be very, very dead.

Closing his eyes, Aeron savored the daydream of Padric's grisly execution by his hand, over and over in his mind.

Yes, soon.

CHAPTER 16

Two days later

*W*ith Miser gliding through the autumn trees and chittering with his fellow squirrels, Talfryn took his turn as guard at the back of their caravan. Ulysses must have been successful in leading Lord Herbert away from them, as after two days of hard travel on horseback, they hadn't heard the sounds of other humans or horses. Ulysses had returned after leading them northeast for several miles. Having him join them raised their spirits. At times, Talfryn almost forgot about the reason they'd fled Nottingham. And, miraculously, he almost forgot about the wolficorn hounding him day and night.

Almost.

Nights were still awful.

After a bit, it occurred to Talfryn that something was missing. He peered all around, but saw only trees and the sounds of wildlife.

"Hey, Kett, you see Miser anywhere?"

Kett raised an eyebrow. "Well, if you must know..." He gave a big show of looking in every direction. "I see trees and...ooo, look, *more* trees. And every animal sounds like one another to me. Sorry," he added.

He peered backward to check on the makeshift wooden cart he'd carved over an afternoon, filled with the half finished product of Padric's Grand Chariot. Talfryn had created the name, but no one seemed to care for it.

"I'd better find him before he gets himself lost."

"I don't think the little bugger could get lost. Not with that bulging food pack of yours. He can probably smell it ten miles off."

"You're hilarious. But right," Talfryn muttered. He spun his steed around to choose a direction. "There's a slight animal commotion to the north. You know how Miser loves drama. Be right back."

"Tal, wait. We need to stay together. Aww heck." With a sigh, Kett eyed their friends, of whom only Rawlins noted their departure, and turned his horse to follow Talfryn.

A short distance away, Talfryn thought he heard his little red-tailed friend's voice. The branches were lower here, so he had to dismount, otherwise his head would have more bruises than a toad has warts. The last thing he needed was for his sister to rebuke him for bashing his head over and over again. "Miser, come on, buddy. Where are you?"

"Are you sure he came this way?" Kett asked.

Talfryn swept his gaze among the high and medium branches again. "I thought I heard him." Raising his voice, he called again, "Miser, if we get lost, I'm not giving you any treats after our next meal. Honestly," he lowered his voice to normal again, "that squirrel is part dog."

Kett chuckled. "No joke. He's just like my father's—" A branch snapped. "Did you hear that?"

"Yeah." Talfryn unhooked his hatchet from his belt.

Miser leaped out of the tree directly above and alighted gracefully on Talfryn's shoulder. "Good grief, Miser, you nearly gave us heart attacks! Get some good exercise, friend?"

Unfazed by Talfryn's rebuke, the squirrel dashed from shoulder to shoulder and chittered in delight over his new squirrel friends' treasure-tree hole filled with all sorts of nuts and berries. He was in proverbial squirrel heaven.

"That's just great, buddy." Sighing, he rubbed the squirrel's back and propped him again on his shoulder. He hadn't moved his foot more than an inch before the swift shaft of an arrow whizzed past his nose and lodged itself into the tree next to Kett.

Mesmerized by the arrow's closeness, Kett gaped, frozen in place.

On the other hand, Talfryn's fight or flight reaction took over. Without thinking, he grabbed his friend's arm and yanked him to the ground as another arrow planted itself into the tree right above their heads. Miser squeaked in surprise. The horses whinnied in fright.

When Kett's knees struck the ground, he snapped back into focus. "Who's shooting at us?"

"Dunno." Hunched on hands and knees, Talfryn buried his distress deep down and scanned the area for a hidden enemy.

"Get behind cover," Talfryn instructed, shoving Kett to their right. "Hurry!"

Kett didn't need to be told a second time. He dove behind some low shrubs and scrambled behind a tree. Talfryn followed, heart pounding in his ears, hands and knees scraping against the rough ground and shrubs until he ducked behind his own tree. Knight school lesson number one: swords and hatchets weren't very good against arrows.

Grabbing a shaking Miser from his shoulder, Talfryn patted his head a couple of times to calm him. If only it had the same effect on himself. Under his breath, he whispered, "Miser, we need your help. Find Padric and bring him an' the others back here. Be swift."

Miser nodded and bounded out of Talfryn's hands and onto the ground, heading west and south.

No sooner had he stood up than a shadow emerged. Talfryn got his sword up just in time to deflect his attacker's blow. The man was about Talfryn's height but thinner in build compared to Talfryn's physique, created through years of laboring on the farm. However, he had the advantage of surprise on his side. Muscles straining, Talfryn shoved the man off him. As the assailant stumbled back, Talfryn glanced at where he'd left Kett by a tree and spotted a shadow coming up behind him.

"Look out!" Talfryn shouted as his own assailant recovered and renewed his advance. He and Talfryn clashed swords, avoiding tree trunks and low branches. The huntsman was quick and light on his feet, while Talfryn grimaced at his own stomping boots. Talfryn tripped over a jagged root, landing on his ribs on another thick, protruding tree root. Pain lanced up his side.

A few feet away, Kett was trying to defend himself against his own attacker. Mainly ducking behind trees and weaving away from the man's grasp. He didn't even try to use the wooden sword he'd made.

"*Use* the sword," Talfryn instructed. It was better than nothing until Talfryn could get to him.

Kett looked at him like he was crazy.

Talfryn's attention swung back to his own huntsman who laughed as he towered over him. "Give up. The mistress wants—gah!"

An arrow whizzed over Talfryn's head. His gaze followed the arrow that had imbedded itself into the man's bicep.

Is that Padric?

Seeing his opportunity, Talfryn bounded to his feet, ignoring the ache in his side and sliced upward. The sword carved into the man's stomach and chest. Eyes widening in a startled expression, he keeled over.

"I had him, Padric." Talfryn huffed.

"Sure you did."

Startled by the feminine voice, Talfryn spun around. A girl with red hair and green skin wearing layers of green and brown skirts bounded up to him. When she stopped, her braids and loose curly locks settled around her shoulders, one hand clutching a bow, her free hand on her hip. Light filtered through the trees to glint off a plain, shiny copper bangle around her wrist. A quiver of turquoise-fletched arrows was slung over her shoulder. His heart jumped into this throat at the sight of the dryad.

"Eliva?" he squeaked. "What're you doing here? And what happened to your hair?" He winced at his own poor choice of words and more than half expected her to strike him down with the bow. With reluctance, he did think her fiery red-orange hair pretty, though. It suited her much better than the brown shade ever had.

Eliva shrugged. "We heard you lot were in trouble. It seems we were correct." She didn't elaborate on her hair. Nor did she move to beat him with her bow, for which he was relieved.

Another green nymph bounded up beside Eliva wearing a similar outfit. All of the dryads from Cataractonium wore attire of more or less the same style and earthy colors. All of their outfits showing way more skin than any English girl would wear, for certain. He didn't know her name, but thought he might've seen her before in Circe's home.

"The other archer has been disposed of." The second dryad gave a triumphant smile.

An awkward silence followed as Talfryn tried and failed to come up with something witty to say until Kett's shout rescued him. *Oh, right, Kett!*

Talfryn loped over to where the carpenter's apprentice was struggling to jab at the huntsman with burly muscles, dark hair, and a short beard. The man looked familiar, his name right on the tip of Talfryn's tongue. *Where've I seen him before?*

As Kett made another pitiful attempt at jabbing, the huntsman's hatchet barely touched the wooden sword and it flew out of Kett's grasp.

Talfryn clutched at the man's green jerkin and spun him around. Now he knew where he'd seen him. "Jeffrey! I thought it was you." He was one of Drogo's huntsmen. A few months back, they'd kidnapped Gregorio and had tried to kill Padric, Brynwen, and Talfryn on their way to Cataractonium.

The man looked so surprised, he almost didn't block Talfryn's swing. In another moment, he recovered his composure and attacked Talfryn in earnest.

"Care for another go at hand-to-hand?" Talfryn offered. He'd bested the young huntsman a few months before. That time, Talfryn had only beaten him by sheer blind luck, literally. "Mayhap you'll beat me this time."

Calculations ran behind Jeffrey's eyes, and Talfryn hoped the huntsman didn't remember how lucky the previous knockout blow had been.

"Why not?" Stepping back, he flung his hatchet to the side. Talfryn did likewise.

"Talfryn," Eliva snapped. She and Kett stood with the other dryad. "What are you doing? We must go."

"It is a re-match," Jeffrey responded, as though that answered everything.

Eliva didn't seem one bit impressed and only pounded her hands against her hips in impatience.

It was similar to their last conversation, which hadn't gone very well. The youngest of the dryads in Circe's home, a wild little girl with short, uneven hair called Thimble, had been lonely and needed a friend. In exchange for friendship, she was to give him important information to stop Janus's first plot. But when an incident angered the little girl, Eliva was the one to inform him that Thimble didn't want to see him anymore. She'd seemed too happy to deliver her warning, and it had broken his heart. And now, here she was, the same as ever.

In another second, Talfryn and Jeffrey faced off. They grappled and punched. Talfryn wound up a swing to the face when something whistled past his ear. The object thunked against Jeffrey's forehead and bounced off. Jeffrey's eyes rolled up into his lids, and he crumpled to the ground. A huge, red welt formed on his forehead. Beside him lay a dagger. Kett's dagger.

Talfryn spun around, ready to fight. But it was only Kett and the dryads.

Both Kett and the other dryad gaped at Eliva, who stalked over and picked up the dagger, its hilt having knocked Jeffrey out cold with ease.

"Hey, why'd you do that?" Talfryn fumed.

"I told you, we must go. Now." Eliva shoved Talfryn by the tunic in the direction where their friends should be. "Your friends may be in danger too."

Talfryn's eyes widened. "What?" *I shoulda thought of that.* Talfryn tried to keep the worry out of his voice as he turned to his friend. "You all right, Kett?"

"Y-yes. I just need to...to..." Fingers shaking, he tried a couple of times to slide the wooden broadsword into its makeshift sheath, but the tip kept hitting just shy of the opening. "Get this darned thing to work."

With one final shove, the weapon slid into the sheath and stopped at the end with a *thunk*.

That done, Talfryn spun in the direction the others were headed. "Come on, we should hurry."

"Lead the way, Luciliana," Eliva said to her companion.

In the distance, he could hear the ring of clashing steel and raised voices.

The trees opened just wide enough to fit Padric's and Rawlins's jousting tent into. But instead of a tent, he saw a chariot drawn by two large, golden snakes with white scaled wings landing on the ground. *Kind of like dragons.* A picture of the same golden winged snakes were painted on the side of the contraption.

"Dracones," Luciliana hissed.

Inside the chariot stood a beautiful woman with wavy, raven locks, wearing a stunning black overdress with red embroidery and white under dress. The royal blue cloak she wore was made of quality material. Material he'd seen before.

"You," he said. His heart pounded in triple time as he recognized her. "You bumped into me at the tourney." And because of that instance, Daniel Lambert was dead and Padric had been blamed for it.

"Medea." Eliva's eyes radiated a hatred Talfryn hadn't ever seen, nor wished to ever see upon his own person. He barely saw her hands move to withdraw the bow from her back, nock an arrow, and aim at Medea's heart. Luciliana followed suit, her quick movements the twin of Eliva's.

Talfryn might have thought it a neat trick if it weren't for the girl standing before him. Or should he say woman at least two or three times over...

And just like that, all of Talfryn's hope flickered out like the stump of a candle.

CHAPTER 17

"Talfryn & Kett have been gone a while. Should I go after them, d'you think?" Rawlins asked Padric.

Lips pressing together, Padric sighed. "Miser must have wandered off again. That wily squirrel will be the death of him. Yes, go, and be quick. I do not like the air here and wish to be past it as soon as possible."

"Same here." Rawlins skirted his horse around a tree to follow the squire and carpenter-in-training.

"I must have a stern talking-to with that squirrel." Brynwen huffed. "Although I know it will only go in one ear and out the other."

"Mayhap if we stuff up one ear with wax, he will have no choice but to listen to you," Padric suggested.

She rubbed her hands together. "All right, I'll let you stuff his tiny ear with wax and then go from there."

Padric laughed. "Deal."

He had no sooner said this than a screaming man leaped at them from the trees, a dagger glinting in his hand.

Padric ducked just in time as the blade flashed past his eye. It clipped his hair, a few blond strands shucking into the air. Momentum pulling him to the side, he flicked his bow into the assailant's backside. The man went sprawling to the ground.

Taking Brynwen's arm, he nodded to a yew tree. "Bryn, get to that tree."

Padric's assailant launched to his feet and swiped at him again. Dropping his bow, Padric ducked and released his broadsword from its sheath. As he faced off with the young man, he thought he looked familiar—rather, his outfit did. A smattering of browns and greens on his tunic and leggings with soft leather boots. Casting a quick glance around, the others fought men in similar garb.

"You are a huntsman," he said. "With Drogo, I presume." The man whom his former friend and colleague, Aeron, had paid to waylay and take the amulet of obsidian from Padric, Talfryn, and Brynwen between Mamucium and York. The same Drogo who had nearly choked the life out of Talfryn with his huge, bare hands.

The man sneered. "Mayhap Drogo's with me." He hacked downward and Padric parried easily.

"Where is your gallant leader?"

"Right here."

Padric heard the speaker's footfall and leaped aside. A broadsword descended where his head had been, clipping his arm instead. A sharp sting flared through his bicep as he rounded on the tall, bearded leader.

"We meet again," Padric said. Blood gushed from the gash on his arm at an alarming rate. His stomach twinged as he changed into a faun, his hoofs ready to bound at a moment's notice. Both Drogo and his henchman made a slow circle with Padric, each gauging who would strike first.

Drogo grinned, his bearish stature and wild brown beard making him look twice the size of a normal man. "Not too soon, I hope."

"Not at all. It is not everyday one finds the man responsible for framing him for murder." Padric made the guess. At worst, the man would deny it.

"Well"—Drogo shrugged—"when one has the opportunity and the means, make a meat pie."

Padric scrunched his nose at the distasteful metaphor. "I do not think Daniel Lambert would agree."

"Who? Oh, the dead man. Yes, well—*Devin!*"

It was the eager protégé who lunged first. He attacked with a vigor known mostly in overeager subordinates trying to prove their worth to their leaders. Their steel clashed for a few seconds before Padric feinted, and Devin went reeling forward with mouth agape.

No time to take a breath, Drogo charged in with full force. His blows struck hard, their force almost as strong as Warin's. Or, he imagined, Hercules. He had just pushed back a heavy blow when a snarling Devin returned.

Devin's sword would have pierced Padric in the side had a maiden with skin of green not stepped in and slammed her polearm into his blade. She took on Devin, and they fought head to head, leaving Padric with Drogo.

"Nalini?" *Where did she come from?* The last time he had seen her was in Cataractonium during the second trial where she had disguised herself as Brynwen and attempted to seduce him in a test of loyalty and duty. Ultimately, he had passed the trial. And now, here she was.

"Well met, Padric!" Nalini blocked and jabbed with her polearm while Devin desperately tried to find a weakness.

A quick glance around revealed more dryads fighting off huntsmen.

Great, Padric thought. His wounded arm leaked a worrisome amount of blood and was weakening.

"Drogo, you will surrender and turn yourself in to the Nottingham authorities," Padric said.

Drogo barked a howling laugh. "I hardly think so, *abomination.*"

Padric reeled back in shock.

"Do you think for a second I'd have any remorse in framing a four-legged atrocity such as yourself? 'T'ain't natural nor proper. Better to let you rot and die than continue to breathe."

Heaving a breath to steady himself, Padric caught his assailant's blade on his. He heard the metal of his sword chip with the heavy blow, holding it inches from his face. It moaned with the effort. The ache in his arm was excruciating. A small voice in the back of his head urged him to fall down and rest.

"I shall not yield to you, huntsman."

Then a thought entered his mind. So small a thing that he almost laughed.

Drogo must have seen the amusement in Padric's eyes, as his narrowed. "What's so funny?"

"Your offer of deliverance. On second thought, I reconsider my answer. And…"

The moment he released his grip against Drogo's mighty strength, Padric fell as a dead weight, prone. Surprise overtook the big man. With no leverage against his own strength, he cried out and fumbled forward, tripping over his foe's chest. He fell head over heels.

Brynwen's scream rent the air.

Chest clenching, Padric launched to his feet, ignoring a kick to his ribs from the giant.

Pivoting to find her, the swoosh of arrows flew past his nose. His breath caught as three shafts lodged themselves into a large oak, not a foot from where Brynwen stood.

She gaped in horror, her eyes darting from Padric to someone beyond him, where the arrows had originated.

Padric spun in time to spy the sulking glare of the last person he had expected to see. He clenched his teeth in anger and betrayal—one Aeron Drefan, former knight of Chaddesden. Traitor to him and the crown.

Who had tried to kill Padric and his friends thrice over.

"Nay, you should be dead," Padric muttered. The last he had seen Aeron, they had fought to the death, and Padric had plunged his sword quite deep through Aeron's side, just under his rib. The Druid had fled into the shadows with the dying knight in tow. How could Aeron have survived such a grievous, mortal wound? Did the Druid or Medea save him? For he doubted they had a healing *caladrius. Or do they?*

Aeron nocked another arrow, pulled back the bow, and aimed at Padric. From behind him, a huntsman shouted something at him. Howling in frustration, Aeron lessened the tension. Before spinning on his heel, he gave Padric the most seething glare.

Despite the loss of blood—along with the shock of seeing his nemesis alive and well—new vigor shot through Padric's veins. He had determined to follow Aeron, to end this, when Brynwen cried out again.

Drogo had gotten to his feet and sprinted toward her.

CHAPTER 18

"*A*h, my children."

Talfryn squirmed as the lovely, soft words emanated from Medea's pert, smiling lips. It was easy to see and hear the resemblance to her aunts Circe and Pasiphae.

Medea glided from the chariot as though from the steps of a royal palace. She was, after all, a former queen, Talfryn remembered.

An Evil Queen.

Who'd killed her own children.

Who'd killed her own brother.

And several others had died under her bloodied thumb.

Yep, an all around first-class citizen.

Thus, he tried his hardest to keep Kett and Luciliana—although he trusted the dryad could take care of herself—behind him. Eliva stubbornly remained on his left.

"We are *not* your children, enchantress," Eliva spat. She'd drawn her bow and arrow before the immortal could land her chariot. "You killed your own, remember?"

"Eliva," Talfryn said so only she could hear. "That's no way to be polite to a witchy lady visiting in a chariot. I know from experience."

The green warrior girl's eyes flicked to Talfryn in annoyance, then returned to the immortal. "What do you want, Medea?" This time, Eliva kept her attitude more measured, although her elbow twitched like she was ready to shoot the bolt. Likewise, Luciliana inched out from behind Talfryn and held her bow at the ready.

The sweet smile Medea proffered slid into a thin, dangerous line. The fingers of her immaculate long fingertips twitched and sparked.

Oooh, this is going so well.

"You will put down those weapons," Medea said evenly.

"Or what?"

"I don't think she's going to reward us with afternoon tea." Talfryn's stomach rumbled. Right, they'd skipped that ever so important meal in his daily regimen. Even though Medea was by herself, if she were anywhere near as powerful as Circe, they could be in serious trouble.

Medea twisted her hand. In it, a corked vial filled with a pinkish liquid appeared. "Courtesy of the Shadow. He would have delighted in this little get together, but he has another task." In a flash, she unstoppered the liquid and flung its contents at the group.

Eliva and Luciliana had the foresight to duck back, but Talfryn and Kett weren't so lucky.

The moment the pink liquid touched their skin, Medea chanted a verse in Latin, her lips twisting in triumph.

Tuum corpus est mihi imperatum.
Tuum corpus est mihi imperatum.
Tuum corpus est mihi imperatum.

Your body is mine to control.
Your body is mine to control.
Your body is mine to control.

WITHOUT WARNING, Talfryn's muscles grew taut, and he couldn't move an inch. "Uh, this isn't good." The force of its grip was so painful, he thought his chest and appendages would burst. The next thing he knew, he was on his hands and knees, panting.

He recalled Padric's telling of the first time Circe had cast a spell on him, how his whole body had been locked up, as though bound by invisible rope. Had Medea learned that trick from Circe?

Eliva stepped back up beside Talfryn, rage evident on her face as she prepared to loose her arrow.

Abruptly, Talfryn's body twisted and lunged for her. Shocked by his own body's betrayal, he barely shouted a warning before he grabbed Eliva's bow and tugged it out of her hand, his other clenching her forearm.

Eyes wide, Eliva struggled in his grasp. "Talfryn...what are you doing?" Her face contorted in confusion and hurt.

"It's not me! Well, it *is* me, but I'm not trying to. I—"

"Stop talking," she said.

Flames flicking up his cheeks, Talfryn shut his mouth. Instead, he concentrated on *not* killing Eliva.

Which was very, very hard, because his body didn't seem to want to agree with his head one bit.

Eliva used all her strength to push him, but he gripped her forearm all the harder, his muscles developed from years of hard labor on the farm no match for her smaller frame.

Until she twisted her wrist free. And falling on her side, kicked his leg out from beneath him.

Talfryn landed on his back, the air slamming out of his lungs. "Good one," he wheezed, and coughed.

Meanwhile, Kett grappled with Luciliana. Her petite, lithe body could not compete with his big muscles, but she was quick and dodged his hold. She struck him a couple of times in the chest in key spots. Staggering backward, he clutched his chest and gave her a quizzical stare.

Eliva lunged to her knees and tried to hold Talfryn's arms down. "You were supposed to duck out of the way of the potion."

As his lungs regained air, the prophecy forced its way back in. *Danger. Charioteer. Beast.* "I...I'm trying..." Another sharp jab of pain struck from within his chest, causing an agony he'd never felt before, choking out his breaths. Every ounce of effort was draining his strength. Yet, he watched in dread as his own hand struck Eliva's face.

"I'm so sorry."

She glowered at him, determined not to show if it hurt or not. "Are you, really?"

"Yes!"

"Finish them, quick," Medea instructed. She glanced behind her to where a battle could be heard. "Then you must climb into the chariot. *Este celeres!*"

Why is she doing this? Because of the prophecy?

Talfryn's body obeyed her without question as he lunged for Eliva's throat. She went down under his weight as he straddled her to keep her legs from kicking him again.

Kett, struggling just as much against Medea's spell, held Luciliana in his arms as though hugging her, but her expression was anything but desiring of a hug.

As Talfryn began to squeeze the dryad's throat, his brain screamed at his arms to stop. A distant memory of someone else choking him made his blood run cold. He didn't wish this end for Eliva, but couldn't help himself.

Teeth clenched, Eliva's fingers clawed at his. The scratches she left bled, but still he couldn't stop. Her other hand reached out wide, searching desperately for a way of escape.

"Stop this, please, Medea," Talfryn begged. Eliva's eyes bulged and tiny wheezes escaped her lips.

"The only good nymph is a dead nymph," Medea said matter-of-factly. Then she shrugged with indifference. "But I suppose they are subdued enough. Now, both of you, Talfryn, Kett, get inside the chariot."

Talfryn cheered inwardly as his fingers released from around Eliva's throat. But then his legs jarred him up onto his feet, and he and Kett trudged to the smirking witch in her chariot. He could feel his will being pulled from him.

"*Fight.*" The voice from his dreams came to him. Faunus! "*You must fight, Talfryn. You cannot go with her, or all is lost.*"

"Where were you a couple of minutes ago?" he asked, but the space where the voice had been was gone. He forced his neck to turn just enough to see Eliva and Luciliana still on the ground. No help from there.

"Fight it, Kett," Talfryn said, hoping he could trust his godly grandparent.

Kett only gave him a worried look, sweat beading on his forehead. "Trying. What'll she do with us?"

"I haven't the slightest idea." Talfryn made a futile effort to veer off Medea's course, one leg at a time, but her power was too strong. All the same, he tried one more time. He borrowed the concentration Padric used when transforming into a faun, centaur, or goat. *Pull from your center. Concentrate on that.*

Straining all his nerves and muscles, he forced his foot to stop. It stopped. He began to congratulate himself when it moved again of its own accord. *Come on!* Trying again, he got it to stop where it was, mid-air. It wasn't hard to imagine how goofy he looked, but little did he care if it meant escaping from Medea.

Unfortunately, Kett wasn't so lucky, and he was rapidly approaching the chariot.

Putting a pause on his plan, Talfryn allowed Medea's power to flow through him again and rushed to the stolen chariot. Kett had already placed a hand on the gold of the flying box on wheels.

"See?" Medea said. "It is not so bad. We shall have a grand time together."

"Oh, I'm sure." Talfryn hoped the voice was right and practiced his body-stopping tactic again. With the greatest effort, he placed a hand on Kett's arm. "Don't get on."

Medea's frown sent a shiver down his spine. Magic swirled around her arm as she began to chant another spell.

"Leave them be, Medea!" Eliva rasped. Her throat ached, but both she and Luciliana had arrows nocked, ready to fly at the witch. If Medea captured Talfryn and Kett, they'd never be seen again—at least not alive. Circe, Nalini, and some of the other dryads had lived through Medea's early years when she had left so much carnage behind like fallen leaves in autumn. Very few people deserved that fate.

Interrupted, Medea's chant faltered.

"Now," Luciliana cried.

As drilled, they simultaneously released their arrows.

With startlingly swift reflexes, the witch turned, opened her hand before her, and blew a gray powder at the arrows. They veered to the left—directly at Talfryn and Kett.

No!

Kett cried out, blood spurting from his arm. The very next instant, Talfryn's head jerked, his whole body whipping around. Stumbling, he touched his temple. As he drew his hand away, blood dripped from his fingers.

"Nay! You fools." Medea chanted a quick, singsong phrase in Latin and flung another vial at Luciliana and Eliva. They dove out of the way. It smashed against a tree trunk spewing a fizzy white substance that ate at the bark.

Talfryn crumpled to the ground in a heap.

"Talfryn," Eliva cried. *Please don't be dead.* She didn't want to have to explain to Nalini that she'd accidentally gotten him and Kett killed.

A shadow emerged from above the tree line, and Eliva glimpsed a brown and white blur swoop down and over them. It whipped their clothes and hair around in every direction, then zipping at Medea, who dove onto the ground to avoid it. The winged snakes hissed nervously but didn't fly off.

Ulysses.

The peryton landed the moment Medea climbed into the chariot, his white wings unfurled wide and intimidating. Grabbing up the reins, she directed the dracones to flee. Eliva and Luciliana ran around Ulysses, but the creatures already had the chariot off the ground, and their arrows only struck the contraption.

Eliva scowled in frustration. "We had her, Ulysses."

The peryton merely eyed her. And Medea was long gone.

"Won't you go after her?" Luciliana asked.

He shook his head. *No*, Eliva thought, *he is a protector*. He would not leave the vulnerable. Instead, he moved to Talfryn's side to nudge his head.

Remembering the young men, Eliva and Luciliana ran to their sides. Kett clutched his arm, small trails of blood trickling down his fingers. Half of Talfryn's face was covered in blood. Eliva thought him dead until his head shifted and lips emitted a low groan.

"He lives," Luciliana cheered.

A red squirrel came out of nowhere and jumped up and down on Talfryn's chest, chittering with the greatest excitement and brushing its tail in his face. Talfryn's eyes popped open. He seemed to listen to the creature, nodding absently. "Good job, Miser," he said. "You deserve a great handful of..." Then his eyes closed, head lolling to the side. He lay still.

Eliva's heart stopped. "Talfryn?" *You can't die.*

After their first encounter, Eliva had been convinced that Talfryn was a bumbling buffoon and would only make things worse for everyone in Cataractonium. The last thing she had said to him had been mean and unkind. *I said those things to protect my sister.* But something unexpected had happened. The anguish on his face had been genuine. And he had helped to save them all from Janus's first plot. Now all she felt was guilt.

"He's breathing." Kett leaned forward. "The arrow grazed the side of his head." He patted his pockets, pulled out a kerchief, and pressed it against the wound on Talfryn's head.

"Allow Eliva to do that," Luciliana said. "Come here and let me tend to your arm, lad."

"Nay," Eliva cried, horrified. She bounded to her feet. "I—I must watch for intruders."

Luciliana gave her a reproachful glance and held out her hand for the cloth. "As you can see, there are none at the moment, and this young man needs tending. *Kerchief.*"

Nervous gaze sliding from Luciliana to Eliva and back, Kett surrendered the bloody kerchief to Luciliana. The older nymph took the proffered piece of cloth and held it out to Eliva. "Unless you prefer that he bleed out all over the forest floor?"

Eliva recoiled at the soiled cloth. Not because of the blood. Blood she could stand. As a huntress, seeing the blood that had been spilled in Cataractonium had been no issue. However, to become part of the Hunt, Diana had four strict rules for initiates. Few exceptions could be made:

- *Step one: Never speak to a man outside of your family.*
- *Step two: Never touch a man outside of a family member.*
- *Step three: Remain a chaste virgin all your days.*
- *Step four: Devote your life to the Hunt.*

Unfortunately, she had spoken to Talfryn on a number of occasions already, so step one was already out. And now, step two.

Luciliana shook the kerchief, drops of blood flicking off onto the grass.

"Fine, give it to me." Eliva swiped the cloth out of the dryad's hand and plopped unceremoniously by Talfryn's side.

The squirrel became quite agitated, nipping at her when she tried to reach for Talfryn's head.

"I am only trying to help, silly squirrel. His wound needs attention."

Kett gave the squirrel a stern look. "Miser."

Miser stopped mid-squeak to glare at Kett in return. But it must have done the trick, for he settled down, not taking his eyes off her.

At last.

Holding the kerchief against the gash on Talfryn's temple, she attempted to wipe off his face, but only managed to smear the blood around all the more. It made him look like he'd been in a massacre. She watched his chest rise and fall; his fine nose and full lips. Absently, she brushed a hand across his bloody brow. Then jerked it back. *Why did I do that? Did anyone see? Would Diana know I did that?* But both Luciliana and the young man called Kett were busy with his wound.

She released an inward sigh.

Just then, feet came crashing through the forest. Ulysses whipped his head around. Grabbing up her bow, she nocked an arrow and took aim in the direction of the intruders.

CHAPTER 19

*B*rynwen couldn't believe it. Aeron Drefan, the traitor, was still alive. Anger coursed through her veins.

The arrow Aeron shot at Padric narrowly missed and almost hit her instead. Then he fled like the coward he was.

But her worries weren't over. Drogo got up and rushed after her. She whipped forth her dagger—this time, promising herself not to lose it—and readied herself in the protective stance both Padric and Payla had taught her.

"Stay back," Brynwen warned. She prayed her voice sounded more intimidating than she felt and that he didn't noice her shaking hands.

Her heart beat irregularly with each step the giant huntsman took. The last time she'd seen him, he had tugged her hair so hard, it had left a bruise on her scalp.

Now here he was, the man who had probably stabbed Daniel Lambert to death in Nottingham with Padric's stolen dagger.

"Come here, my sweet. Last time didn't go to plan. But this time"—he twisted the long dagger in his hand, and made a frightening face—"we won't be interrupted."

Nerves frayed from all the huntsmen zipping by and this horrible man being impossible, Brynwen did the last thing she'd ever deign as smart.

She charged him.

The action took him by such surprise, he froze, eyebrows raised. It took another half-heartbeat for him to realize he should get his dagger ready.

Their steel clashed, and Brynwen's stomach filled with the thrill of the action. For once, it didn't frighten her. She felt almost in control.

Until he got his full attention back into the tiff and pushed back. Hard.

Muscles threatening to seize, Brynwen struggled to slide her dagger off his without gaining a scratch. *A miracle!* The extra lessons she'd had after their Labyrinth adventure hadn't completely gone to waste.

But soon she found her back against a tree.

Where is Padric? she thought frantically. This wasn't going as well as she'd planned in her mind.

Drogo leered forward, the dagger glinting between them, when suddenly, a blob of reddish-brown fur obscured his face. His scream filled the forest, a much higher pitch than she'd have expected from the burly man. He grabbed for Miser, but the squirrel was too wiry for him. "Get it off, get it off, get it off!"

"Great job, Miser." Brynwen kept her knife aloft, just in case Drogo recovered.

"Bryn!" Padric bounded toward her with determination, blood seeping from his arm.

She grew nervous when Drogo got a hand around Miser. The squirrel shrieked and wriggled around in his hand.

"You blighty little bugger, you. I'll—"

But before he could say what he'd do, Warin came crashing in and bashed Drogo in the face with his fist.

Drogo didn't know what had hit him. His face struck the tree, and he went down. Miser flew from his hand into Brynwen's arms, his tail a hair from being sliced off by her dagger.

Warin heaved as he glared at the downed huntsman and hiked up his sleeves, ready for another go. "Get up, you wild man."

Padric came bounding up n faun form and halted beside Warin, weapon in hand, his lips pressing flat, giving his friend the side-eye. *What is that about?* He helped Brynwen to her feet and took up her hands. "Are you well? Did he hurt you?"

"I am fine"—her gaze fell to his arm—"but you are not."

Warin's chest puffed out. "The wild man never got a chance to touch her."

"I would have called him a 'barbarian,'" Padric said drily.

Warin's eyes shifted to Padric, smiling quite wide, all of his teeth gleaming.

Sensing some sort of tension going on between the two knights, Brynwen looked from one to the other. "I thank you both for coming to my aid."

That must have had the desired effect, because the tension between the young men melted, and they smiled and bowed at her. Which was most embarrassing.

Just then, Miser chittered and jittered in her hands. She could tell he had something urgent to divest, and she wished she could communicate with him like Talfryn did.

"What is it, Miser?" Padric asked.

The squirrel leaped easily onto Padric's outstretched hand and chittered with great animation, pointing his head and tail to the northwest. Padric's eyebrows furrowed in concentration. "Slow down, you are speaking too fast." Shortly after their return from Rellea, Padric had discovered that he could speak with Miser and other animals when he was in goat form. But Miser's excited state didn't allow time for him to transform into a goat.

"Is it Talfryn?"

Miser jumped up and down and scurried up Padric's injured arm and down the other, then stopped on his hands again. Wincing a tad, Padric looked at his friends, a frown marring his features. "Ulysses," he called. "We need you."

In moments, the peryton arrived overhead, his wings batting their clothing and hair.

"Ulysses, Talfryn and Kett are in trouble. Miser knows where they are. We will follow behind you."

"Please hurry," Brynwen urged.

With the slightest nod as Miser leapt onto his back, Ulysses took to the air and headed northwest.

Brynwen's chest constricted as she gazed at Padric. "Let's go," she said, breathless with worry.

"What about the huntsman?" Warin asked. "Isn't he the one who took your dagger?" Although he had never met Drogo, he'd been given his description before their journey began. By now, Drogo's huntsmen had either been taken down or run off, thanks to the dryads.

"Leave him for now," Padric said. "We must aid Talfryn and Kett."

They had not gone ten paces before Rawlins and Nalini materialized beside them.

"Nalini tells me that Eliva and Luciliana went after them." Rawlins's expression was cold as death. A splatter of blood graced his sleeve.

Nalini came up on Brynwen's other side. "It is true. They did go after Talfryn. Come on." She kicked up the pace, and Brynwen was hard-pressed to keep up.

"Nalini? Why are you here?" She was grateful that the dryads had come in time to help them, but why'd it have to be Nalini? Brynwen still fumed over the dryad's actions in Cataractonium, betraying her trust by lacing her tea with a strong sleeping draught so she could try to seduce Padric.

"We hunt the aeternae. For months, it has alluded our grasp. A little bit ago,"—she leapt over a fallen tree trunk—"we spied the huntsmen and Medea." She brushed aside a hanging branch. "We decided to follow them, until they came to attack you."

Brynwen mostly missed the swinging branch, but it swiped the top of her shorter head, snarling in her hair as it whipped past.

They followed the peryton and squirrel for almost a quarter of a mile. Brynwen braced herself, knife at the ready to help her brother defeat whoever had come to harm him. Praying they weren't too late. Praying she didn't collapse from all this dreadful running.

They lost sight of Ulysses for a couple of minutes, but between Nalini, Padric, and Rawlins, they kept to the route.

When at last she spotted Ulysses again, separated by perhaps twenty trees, he had already landed. Some of the tension in her shoulders relaxed. If he wasn't fighting, everything must be all right.

Until she spotted her brother lying on the ground.

"Talfryn." Her racing heart barreled her forward. Bypassing Ulysses and Eliva, she fell to her knees beside her brother's head. There was blood everywhere. Miser jumped up and down beside her.

Hooking her bow on her back, Eliva dropped to the ground and picked up a bloody kerchief to place against a gash on Talfryn's head.

Kett, and a dryad whom she assumed to be Luciliana, sat on the other side of Talfryn. Luciliana was putting a paste on Kett's bloody arm. It smelled of herbs she could easily find in the forest, comfrey leaf and willow bark.

"What happened?" Brynwen's voice shook.

"Medea was here," Luciliana explained. "She attacked, and Eliva and I shot a couple of arrows but the witch deflected them." Her gaze drifted to Kett and Talfryn. "Ulysses chased her away." Seeing Brynwen's terrified face, Luciliana quickly added, "Your brother's head was only grazed by the arrow, but it bled so much because it is a head wound."

Brynwen bit her lip on a demeaning retort, but swallowed it down. Luciliana meant well and had lived much longer than herself. She likely knew what she was talking about.

Brynwen began to breathe easier when she saw Talfryn's chest rising and falling in an even rhythm, despite his face being so pale from the loss of blood.

Notwithstanding the great desire to help her brother right away, Brynwen took another breath and turned to Kett. "How is your arm?"

"It hurts, but Luciliana said it isn't too bad." Turning his injured arm toward her, he winced.

"That is good. Thank you for caring for him, Luciliana. I have a bandage for it when you are finished."

Kett nodded his thanks.

Brynwen set to work removing the supplies from her new green satchel. It had been a thoughtful birthday present from Padric, so much better than her poor brown one which had been all but destroyed in the Labyrinth. The best part? It had pockets! She cherished it every time she looked at it, knowing it had been given out of love and thoughtfulness.

Nalini had stopped by Ulysses. Rawlins and Warin stood guard in case Medea or her friends returned.

Eliva was still pressing the bloody cloth against Talfryn's temple.

"Thank you for your help, Eliva," Brynwen said. She gathered a salve to put on his head until she could look at it better. "I will help Talfryn from here."

"As you wish." Eliva's voice was cold, her expression even colder. It contrasted with her bright red hair. She removed the bloody cloth and shot to her feet, body rigid. "Now I must go find the rest of my arrows." Without another word, she dashed into the forest.

Nalini pardoned herself and went after the green maiden.

After that, Brynwen didn't have time to think about the strange dryad maiden who would send Talfryn into a panic whenever she was around. What had he though when she'd shown up here?

Pouring some water from her pigskin onto two clean pieces of linen from her satchel, she washed Talfryn's face and put a salve on it. Intermittently, Padric and Warin questioned Luciliana and Kett about what had transpired.

Brynwen listened as she patted Talfryn's wound with the wet cloth. Once it was cleaned, she examined it and determined it was indeed a shallow wound. Talfryn would be fine as long as he kept it clean. With a swipe, she wiped it dry and lathered some Miracle Mix onto it with a prayer of thanksgiving to the good Lord that neither her brother nor any of her friends were seriously injured in the battle. Then, she inspected Kett's and Padric's arm wounds, pleased with Luciliana's paste. *Why do they always insist on getting themselves hurt?* "I'm sorry, Kett, but this will need stitches."

The apprentice's dark skin paled to gray.

"I will try to make it as painless as possible, I promise."

"She is very gentle," Padric assured him. "Brynwen has stitched me and Talfryn up too many times to count."

As she reached for the white bandages, Talfryn's eyes fluttered. Then his eyes popped open. "Ohhhh," he groaned. "My head." He reached for his head but Brynwen swatted his hand away.

"Don't let your dirty hands touch your wound. I just cleaned it."

"Bryn?" He tried to sit up, but Padric pushed him back down. Disturbed from his slumber after his harrowing afternoon, Miser began chittering in an angry, high-pitched tone. Talfryn unconsciously scooped up the squirrel and patted his head. This seemed to calm the squirrel down somewhat. "Padric...where did you...what happened?"

"Do you remember Medea coming?"

Kett cringed. "I'll never forget."

"I remember...wait, did Eliva and Luciliana *shoot us?*" He gave his friend an incredulous look.

"Not on purpose," Kett said. "Medea blew that magic powder stuff at them, then the arrows changed direction and hit us."

"Did she say why she wanted you two?" Padric asked.

"Nay." Kett shook his head. "But her magic is strong. Talfryn was able to fight it a bit, but I wasn't."

"It's because my brother is stubborn," Brynwen said matter-of-factly.

"We should go." Nalini appeared at the edge of the forest, Eliva and Gregorio behind her. "They will regroup and return."

"Not tonight, surely?" Warin asked.

Nalini shook her head and squeezed her polearm. "There is always the chance. We must be on our guard."

Gregorio stepped forward, his hands twitching in agitation. "Ah, we have another complication. It seems they found the chariot and, well, I fear it is no longer suitable for anything other than kindling."

"All that work," Brynwen lamented. Kett had almost been done with it.

Nalini's lips pressed together. "Kett, you must rebuild the chariot as soon as you can."

He shifted the shoulder of his wounded arm. "Don't worry, Nalini, I'll get it done. We'll need more wood, though."

"I know you all love more problems, so here's another," Talfryn said. He raised haunted eyes to Brynwen. The same look she'd seen on him numerous times in the last few months, although he'd never spoken about it aloud. "The aeternae is close, and he's coming for us."

"Then we had better make haste to the abbey," Warin said.

"We will come with you," Nalini offered.

Brynwen bit her lip, willing Padric and Warin to tell her thanks, but no thanks.

Padric looked thoughtful before replying. "Your aid to us during the ambush was a godsend, and we are grateful for you all. Yet, we could not possibly ask you to risk more for our sakes."

Nalini tamped her polearm on the ground. "And as I stated before, we have come to help. Until the task is complete. Janus is as much a threat to us as to you. No matter what you may think of us, we will not abandon you."

Brynwen snorted in disbelief, twisting her finger in her hair until it yanked.

The dryad's head whipped around to peer at Brynwen with a most stern gaze. "You do not agree, Brynwen?"

A choking feeling of being caught—trapped—overcame her. Now she understood. Part of Nalini's reason for coming was guilt in her part of the deception in Cataractonium. She knew Nalini had been forced to do it, but it still felt like such a betrayal of trust. As opposed to Aeron who did it out of hate.

"Circe and Helius are in trouble too, aren't they? That's why you're really here," she guessed.

Emotion swept through Nalini's eyes so fast, Brynwen thought she'd imagined it. All the dryads, in fact, shared the emotion. "Yes. They were summoned to Olympus to a meeting with Jupiter and never returned. Our communication orbs have not been working properly, so we only found out this afternoon that they never came home. Other gods are missing as well."

"Including Faunus." Talfryn's eyes clouded over in another sort of pain.

"Including Faunus," Padric repeated with a grim frown. "It seems the task is meant for us all."

"Then let's go save them." Talfryn attempted to stand but fell back down onto his haunches and groaned. "After there stops being two of each of you, that is."

❧

AERON SHOOK WITH RAGE. The very sight of Medea had set his blood to boiling. He gripped the arrow that had been meant for de Clifton's heart so tight, the shaft began to splinter. "Why did you pull us from our hunt? We would have killed them all in another minute." *And my father would have looked at me with pride instead of down his nose in dissatisfaction. If I were in charge, this would all be over.*

The other huntsmen, many wounded, had walked or limped ahead. Face scarred with dozens of red scratches, Drogo was enraged and bellowed the early demise of anyone who came too close to him.

"We need the lad, or have you forgotten?" Medea seethed in aggravation. "Besides, you failed to accomplish *your* oath of killing the charioteer." The sweet voice Medea used around his father was gone, replaced by a grating, annoying caterwaul, severing Aeron's last nerve. Medea's chariot plodded along in the tall grass, the green stalks seeming to droop with the passing she made over them. "I had him in my grasp until that blight with wings ruined everything. But where were you? Out for a stroll. Again." She clenched her fists, and sparks of magic flew off them to disappear harmlessly inches away.

Out for a stroll? Aeron seethed, this close to stabbing the arrow into her eye. "I *will* kill him. I swear it. You gave us no time—"

"He swears it now." Medea's head flew back in laughter, then she bent her gaze at the Shadow who had thus far remained silent for the entire exchange. Observing their behavior, no doubt. Returning her dark blue gaze to Aeron, she poked her long-nailed finger into his chest. "He had better be dead before Janus and I control all of Olympus. Or there will be a reckoning."

Always with the threats. Aeron still couldn't understand why his father had chosen the witch over him. After all the years he had spent as a double agent, he still wasn't good enough. So far, Medea had accomplished nothing but pushing a divide between them. And here they were.

The Shadow's voice grated in Aeron's head. *"By my reckoning, the aeternae should rip them to shreds within the next few days. We have already destroyed their chariot. Why do we stay here if the creature will do the killing for us? Does not Janus require our haste?"*

Mention of the aeternae kicked Aeron's heart into running a foot race. When he had released it from Helius's cavern-filled monster collection in Cataractonium, the beast had nearly killed him where he stood. One of its horns had sliced his forehead open, and he had fallen unconscious. With blood covering his face, the monster had stood over him with the perfect opportunity to gore him. Instead, it had escaped its prison and gored a dozen other people. Aeron was smart enough to know that the aeternae hadn't spared him because it was grateful that he had released it. Not in the slightest. It had simply seen its window of opportunity and had taken it. He might have done the same thing in its place.

Smart creature. Too smart. He did not relish being on the receiving end of the beast's deadly horns nor its teeth. Sometimes, the sliver of a scar remaining on his forehead pained him, and his dreams of late had been troubled with eerie laughing that left him in a cold sweat when he awoke.

Aeron narrowed his eyes at Medea, but she was too busy fidgeting with the necklace made of teeth that she wore to take notice. She always fiddled with it when agitated. What was its significance?

Medea bristled. "All the more reason to stay. To ensure they die."

PART II
ABBEY

"For a friend with an understanding heart is worth no less than a brother."

— Homer, *The Odyssey*

CHAPTER 20

*W*hile Padric, Brynwen, and Rawlins entered the city of Llangollen to procure appropriate attire for the seven dryads, Nalini and Kett worked on creating amulets to make the dryads' skin and hair color look human. They would need real English-made clothes in case someone bumped into them. An illusion charm wouldn't hide the fact that they wore thin dresses underneath.

Talfryn watched in fascination as Kett carved the small amulets with symbols out of wood based on Nalini's specific instructions. The carpenter then poked a hole in each one so a thin leather cord could pass through to act as a necklace.

When finished, Nalini studied each one for accuracy. Picking up the third one, she shook her head. "This is not quite right. I will show you." With a stick, she drew the design she wanted in the dirt. Talfryn couldn't really tell the difference from the one Kett had carved, but Kett nodded and made a slight adjustment.

"Perfect," she said, then moved on to the next one. After confirming they were all complete, she unstoppered the vial filled with a creamy white substance, resembling one of Brynwen's salves. Dumping the substance in her hand, it glittered as it caught the light. She rubbed it into every cranny of each amulet, chanting in Latin under her breath all the while.

"They are done." She held them up, then handed them to each of the dryads.

"Don't you get one, too?" Talfryn asked.

"I have one already." She pulled out a similar necklace on a leather cord, but the amulet was made of a smooth blue-gray stone.

When they placed the amulets around their necks, the dryads' appearance changed in a blink. Talfryn couldn't believe his eyes. They looked completely different, even though their facial features and hair length and styles remained the same. Still great beauties in every respect. Despite this, they still looked exotic, but that could also have been because of their nymph clothes.

Seia had a deep tan with dark blonde hair like Padric's. The brown hair of Asinia, though, made her frown. "It looks just like before!" Cornelia's strawberry blonde hair was a slight shade darker than her sister Luciliana's. Raven hair adorned Idaise's head. Nalini's deep auburn hair had glints of red in the sunlight.

Last, he saw a redhead, and wondered if she'd wandered into their camp from the village. Braids swirled around her head like a crown, then trailed down her back among her curling hair. Brown freckles adorned her nose, her eyes as green as new spring grass. Something weird happened with his stomach. "Hey, who is that?"

"You're gaping." Warin smirked at Talfryn, arms folded over his chest.

Talfryn's cheeks burned. "That's *Eliva*?" he asked under his breath. "She looks so, so..."

"Human?" Warin snorted and quirked his eyebrow in a knowing look. "*Beautiful*, even?"

"Whaaat?" Talfryn shook his head with great vehemence. No, no, no. Eliva, who, despite her petite stature, had defeated him in battle, whose every loathing glance in his direction stated that she'd annihilate him one day. *Perhaps today, even.* "Don't go there, pal." He shoved Warin's face away. The knight only snorted again with humor.

The redheaded dryad-turned-human met Talfryn's gaze for a couple of seconds before a scowl marred her pretty features, and unhooking the bow from her back, she stomped off in the opposite direction with all the elegance of an incredibly graceful, irked human.

"Yep, that's Eliva." And yet, he couldn't get past how much more radiant her fiery red-orange hair looked against her fair skin.

A couple of the dryads giggled, and Talfryn realized their mirth was directed at him. A desire for his sister and friends to return and distract everyone came over him, and he had no more interest in amulets and magic and nymphs.

He slunk off in the opposite direction, Miser making huge eyes and laughing at his reaction to Eliva the entire time.

THE MIDDAY SUN snuggled behind a cloud, making the gray day look later than it was, as Padric marveled at the structure before him. Twice before when he was younger, he had gone with his family to visit Darley Abbey in Derbyshire. It was a grand place, originally an Augustinian priory, with a wide church and steeples nearly as high as the clouds—or so his young mind had believed. But this, with its high steeples and Romanesque windows, took his breath away. He looked forward to going inside the Cistercian Valle Crucis Abbey—meaning "Valley of the Cross" in Latin—and viewing the splendor of the church. His only trepidation was how to deal with the dryads, and how they might act amongst the brothers. He had overheard Gregorio explaining a few important details about the monks, particularly about their celibacy and strict prayer lives.

Padric raised the iron lion knocker on the front door at the visitors' entrance twice and waited. Behind him stood the others in nervous anticipation. The dryads fidgeted in their new dresses and slippers, which had taken the majority of the party's collective purses. Half of them tried to act like the clothes didn't bother them, but Eliva glared daggers at him and especially at Talfryn, seemingly at every opportunity —which was all of the time. Talfryn tried to keep Miser inside his shirt, but the wily squirrel's tail kept peeking out of his collar.

Ulysses had to stay outside the abbey walls. He was to also search for Medea, Aeron, Drogo, and the Shadow Druid—who had yet to show his face—and report back on their whereabouts, all without being seen by the enemy.

After a few minutes, the tall abbey door creaked open and a young brother with dark brown hair in the white robe of the Cistercian monk, white rope around his middle, and long sleeves past his first knuckles greeted him with a smile. "The Lord be with you." He gave them a slight bow, then rose. "How may I help you?" He regarded all of the party then returned his gaze to Padric.

"And with your spirit," Padric reciprocated, bowing his head in return. "My name is Padric de Clifton. My companions and I are traveling west and would request a roof over our heads if it is no trouble. We can pay for room and board, of course."

"It would be our pleasure to grant you lodging, but payment will not be necessary. Please, come in." Stepping back, he opened the door wide to allow the entrants to pass. As he did so, his brown hair, so dark it seemed almost black, hit the afternoon sun. "I am Brother Ambrose."

Once they were inside, Padric spoke again. "Well met, Brother Ambrose. A member of your clergy, Brother Howell, is the cousin of a friend of ours, Sir Herman Wherring."

The young man's face brightened and he clapped his hands together. "Ah, yes, Brother Howell. He is a most agreeable brother and a true follower of Christ. I shall tell him of your arrival. Also, I shall inform the abbot, who will come when he is able. Please, make yourselves comfortable." He spread his wide sleeve out to indicate a long bench on either side of the door for weary travelers. After four days of tournaments, three hard days on the road, and one attack, Padric felt as weary as though he'd taken a journey of half a year.

The dryads looked panicked as they were led into the building, and Padric recalled that they were used to the openness of nature, not closeted up within stone walls. He could not imagine what their thoughts were about this prospect.

As Brother Ambrose closed the front door and departed, Brynwen clasped Padric's hand and lowered her voice. "Do you think we will be safe here? What if Medea followed us?"

Nalini and the dryads heard her, for they snorted in derision.

The dryad leader's shoulders went taut. "I will have you know, we have hidden our trail so well, not even a squirrel could find it." Her gaze flitted to Miser who had climbed up on Talfryn's shoulder.

Brynwen's eyes sparked. "Forgive me, Nalini. I meant no offense. It's just that, well, Aeron Drefan is relentless, and I fear he will stop at nothing to follow us. I can only fear the same of Medea. After all, she ensured Padric was framed for murder. There's a reason she doesn't want him on this mission. And she wants Talfryn and Kett for something."

That seemed to mollify Nalini somewhat, for her muscles relaxed. "Yes, well." She waved a hand in nonchalance, almost like an aristocrat. "It is true of Medea. She is persistent once she has her mind set on something. A lesson some of us learned too late." Idaise and Cornelia frowned in agreement.

A few minutes later, Brother Ambrose returned leading an older man with receding gray hair and a portly exterior, whom Padric assumed to be the abbot, with a much younger man with blond hair around the age of five-and-twenty directly behind him.

As they drew closer, the blond man's head drew up in surprise when he made eye contact with Padric and Warin. His gaze slid up, eyeing something beyond Padric's head. Then a wide grin enveloped his face, and his steps quickened. When he drew even with the abbot, though, he seemed to remember his station and fell back a couple of steps.

Do I know him? Padric wondered. *He looks familiar.*

"The Lord be with you, and welcome to Valle Crucis Abbey," the abbot said with a warm smile that did not quite reach his eyes. He spoke with a thick Welsh accent. "I am Abbot Caradoc. Brother Ambrose tells me that Brother Howell's cousin from Nottingham is an acquaintance of yours." He indicated the young blond man. Padric recognized his likeness to that of his cousin, Herman, with the winged shoes.

Brother Howell bowed his greeting.

Padric was unsure if the abbot's unease was caused by having to walk a great distance, or that he was not expecting visitors. Regardless, Padric bowed his head and returned the abbot's greeting. "Thank you, Abbot Caradoc. I am Sir Padric de Clifton of Chaddesden." He introduced everyone in the party. They had discussed using false names, but in the end had decided to keep their names but change their story. "We are lately from Nottingham and are escorting these maidens to Leicester. Herman Wherring spoke so highly of your abbey's beauty and hospitality that we knew we must make this a stop for a few days."

"Splendid." The abbot clasped his hands together. "All are welcome here. Presently, rooms are in preparation and should be ready very soon. Brother Howell, why don't you show these fine travelers to the refectory for a light refreshment? They look famished. Their rooms should be ready by the time they finish, then you can lead them there directly."

Padric nodded his head as did everyone but the dryads. "Thank you, Father Abbot, you are too kind."

Brother Howell bent at the waist and cast his gaze to his sandaled feet. "As you wish, Father Abbot."

"It was pleasant to meet you all, and I will see you at supper, after Vespers." The abbot said a few more parting words, then he and Brother Ambrose retreated through the same door they had entered.

Brother Howell's gaze drew upward to the wall again. Padric was about to turn to look when Brynwen gasped.

"B-Brother Howell, who is that?" She pointed to the tapestry directly behind where Padric was standing.

Padric followed everyone else's gazes to the tapestry. When he looked at it, he started. It was a large tapestry, larger than any in John and Miriel Wilmot's manor in Chaddesden. The cloth was old but in grand condition, considering. The tapestry was of a gallant young knight in shining armor fighting a giant dragon. They fought on a hill covered in tall grasses and small trees. Around the border were swooping vines, leaves, and flowers of every variety and color. What struck Padric most, though, was the young man's head, covered in golden, curly hair. He had a hearty smile and strongly resembled—

"That is Saint George defeating the dragon,' Howell explained, eyes shining. "The tapestry is over two hundred years old."

Gregorio approached it, scrutinizing every detail. "It is amazing. What a great *coincidence*." He turned from the tapestry to Padric, then back again in admiration. "I never realized the similarity before."

Everyone else did the same.

Pricks of self-consciousness made Padric feel like a young school child being scrutinized by his elders. All semblance of authority flew from his mind.

A stomach rumbled. All eyes swiveled away from the tapestry—finally—to Talfryn, who gave a nervous laugh and patted his belly.

"Well said, Talfryn," Warin bellowed, "I too, am famished." Not to be outdone, his stomach repeated the plea for a meal, somehow as loud as the knight himself. He clapped a hand on Padric's shoulder.

Padric's mouth quirked up, and he nodded his thanks.

"Of course," the monk said, trying and failing to wipe his grin. "This way, if you please."

Brother Howell led them through a long deserted corridor and began to chat excitedly. "I say, Sir Padric and Sir Warin. I had not expected to ever see you two again. But I must say, you sparked a great deal of respect in everyone at"—he glanced around to make sure there were no eavesdroppers about—"*m'lady's residence up north*. I shall never forget it. You are legends to so many people. And my own cousin Herman helped in the battle, at that."

Padric exchanged a look with Warin.

Warin responded first. "It was our duty as knights to protect those in our charge."

"We did nothing more than any knight in our position would do," Padric agreed. "And we had the help of friends, your cousin Herman included."

"Well, I am more thankful for it," Howell responded.

"If you live here in Wales, however did you end up there in the first place?" Warin asked.

Howell grimaced. "Now that was poor timing. I came home to Nottingham when my father became ill with a fever which my mother thought would kill him. But he soon recovered, praise be God. After a few more days of visiting, I set out for the abbey. Not ten steps outside of Derby, m'lady Circe accosted me and brought me up north."

"Ooh." Talfryn looked intently at Howell. "I remember you now. You were the turtle, right?"

The monk's lips pursed. "That was me."

They reached the refectory, much to Howell's apparent relief, and he showed them to a long table with equally long benches. The room was large enough to hold all the monks and guests. Candelabras lined the room, along with sconces along the walls and small candelabras on the tables. A handful of other visitors were eating a light meal, still in traveling clothes. Serving staff and monks in white walked about on their business.

"I am sorry you just missed the main meal, but cook will have a light repast for you."

"Thank you. While we sup," Padric said, "you can regale us with what we need to know of the grounds, history, and security of this place."

"Of course, Sir Padric. I think you will be especially interested in the relic room." Howell grinned knowingly.

Gregorio perked up while Warin's eyes rolled to the top of his head.

Padric held in a chuckle. "You don't need to listen, Warin."

"Well, *I'm* interested," Brynwen said.

Warin sidled up next to her. "Then so am I."

Brynwen grinned up at him, and he returned her smile, gracing the too-cheerful action on Padric when she took her seat, completely oblivious of the men's exchange.

Padric narrowed his eyes at his friend in warning, but the knight merely snorted and smirked in challenge.

"He's just trying to get you riled up," Rawlins muttered in Padric's ear.

"Why would you think..." He stopped, knowing Rawlins would never believe the lie that was on the tip of his tongue. A sigh spilled from his lips. "It is working."

After their light refreshment of tea, cheese, biscuits, and information, Brother Howell was informed that their rooms were ready.

Exhausted, Padric looked forward to taking a bath and an afternoon nap on a soft bed to rest his weary bones. The forest floor did not make for the softest bedding.

"Before we part, brother Howell, who might we speak to about joining the evening guard during our stay? We would be pleased to help in any way we can as thanks for our lodging." His main objective was extra vigilance against another encounter with Medea and Aeron.

⁑

IN THE EVENING, while the men dined with the brothers and abbot, Brynwen and the disguised dryads supped in a separate refectory served by women. Their maid, Mildred, a plain little waif of perhaps fourteen, served them round flatbread trenchers as the first course of simple pottage arrived.

Nalini squared her shoulders and made eye contact with the maid. "Maid Mildred, are there any private gardens where we sisters might make use of upturning the soil and send beneficent prayers heavenward to our deity?"

The young maiden peered at Nalini quizzically.

Brynwen turned to Mildred and grinned apologetically. "She means a quiet place to pray to the Lord. My friends love the outdoors and gardening is their favorite pastime. Idle hands are the devil's work, so they say. Isn't that right, Sister Nalini?" She turned to the dryad in expectation.

Nalini narrowed her eyes. "That is quite correct, *Sister* Brynwen."

"Oh," the maid said with a smile, "yes, m'lady. I see. We do in fact have two gardens which could use some attention."

"They sound perfect." Nalini nodded.

"But..."

"But?"

Mildred twisted her hand in her apron. "Well...forget it. M'hap you shouldn't go there a'tall."

Brynwen raised an eyebrow. "Why ever not?" She scooped some of the delicious-smelling pottage onto her round flatbread trencher.

147

Face turning pale, the maid looked around her on both sides, then returned her gaze to them. "The reason no one goes to them's because they're supposedly...uhh."

"Out with it," Nalini said with stern voice.

"Haunted," the maid squeaked.

Brynwen sat, stunned.

"Do you mean specters and wraiths?" Cornelia asked.

Mildred's slow nod confirmed Cornelia's suspicions.

A trill of fear zipped up Brynwen's spine. "Have you...have you seen these specters?"

"I haven't, but some of the brothers have. It scares them to death, so they won't go near it!"

Nalini leaned back and folded her arms, unconvinced.

"If that'll be all, I've got to go back to my duties," Mildred said in a hurry, curtsied, and scurried away like a frightened mouse, ears down.

"What do you think, Nalini?" Eliva asked.

Tapping her chin, Nalini hummed. "I know not, but I, for one, wish to find out."

Brynwen gaped. "You're not afraid of ghosts?" Everyone in Chaddesden was terrified of them. If the wind blew wrong, they believed the ghosts of murdered people had come to take their revenge on anyone in their way.

"Not in the slightest." Nalini shook her head and her lip quirked up. "It sounds perfect for 'prayer and gardening.'"

The nymphs all snickered except Eliva, who ducked her head and fidgeted with her trencher. For a brief moment, Eliva's eyes met Brynwen's own but then lowered again. Brynwen frowned, feeling left out of the joke. Was playing with ghosts a part of a dryad's pastime? She supposed she'd find out soon enough.

CHAPTER 21

The following morning was bright and unseasonably warm, so they all took their breakfast outside on the lawn in a secluded spot on abbey property. As Talfryn absently fiddled his morning biscuit with shaking fingers, a yawn overtook him. He could feel the bags drooping under his eyes, but didn't know what to do about them. It'd been a miserable night, overrun with the usual nightmares. This time, he'd been soaring high above the ground in Helius's chariot, enjoying the breeze and the sights. To his right in the next carriage over, was his cousin Leowyn. To his left, Brynwen occupied another. Other friends filled the surrounding chariots. That was when the low growl began. When he turned, neck hairs on edge, he saw it—the wolficorn, red eyes gleaming. It licked its chops and then attacked not only him, but killed his cousin Leo a dozen times over, and then moved on to everyone else he cared for. Ulysses, Grandfather, Samuel, Bryn, Padric, and all of his friends at the barracks. It had been a massacre and no one could stop it—least of all, him.

Each time he woke from these nightmares, the prophecy filled his vision, making it a welcome boon against the dreams of night. That was, until exhaustion brought him under sleep's domain again, and the nightmares started all over.

His groggy, addled mind was just trying to remember what his first chore should be when he heard soft footfalls approaching in the grass. Peering up, he found Nalini passing with her fellow dryads, including Eliva. When he spotted her, the impassive look on her face relaxed and she gave him a soft smile. The gesture made her seem almost human, even as she wore her enchanted necklace to make her blend in.

"Ah, Talfryn. Just the person I wished to see this morning."

Something about her smile and greeting warmed his chest. He nearly forgot about his latest nightmare. Nearly. To be polite, he tried for his cheery grin. "Nalini. Morning. What're you and your merry band up to today?"

Padric and Brynwen joined them, their fingers locked together. "Nalini. Talfryn," Padric said. "Fine morning we are having."

Not this again. I'm too tired for pleasantries right now.

Nalini nodded her greeting. "My warrior maids and I are in need of our morning sparring practice and wondered if you and your men would care to practice with us. You are most welcome to join us, Brynwen."

Brynwen laughed. "I thank you, Nalini, but I don't think I'm quite... up to your standards just yet. Likely, your maids will get bored with me very fast."

"Be that as it may, you are welcome to join us. Mayhap you can get a few pointers."

"Mayhap I will. Later."

A huge lump landed in the pit of Talfryn's stomach. *Nalini wants me to spar with Eliva and the warrior maidens? No thank you!* The last time he'd sparred with Eliva, it hadn't gone well. His back still carried some of the scars from the carnivorous bramble bush she'd pushed him into, and which might have successfully eaten him alive had Padric not rescued him in time. That, and her un-charming manner toward him.

However, Miser had other ideas. He chittered away at how much Talfryn needed to practice so he'd be just as good as the others. "D'you have a bet going on with the other squirrels at home to see which squires fight the best?" When the red squirrel concurred, and admitted that he hadn't ever bet on *him*, Talfryn gasped. "Traitor," he accused.

Miser stuck his tongue out at him, then proceeded to chide him some more.

A few feet away, Eliva detached herself from among the other dryads and called to Nalini. Her fair skin, freckles, and deep red hair still caught him off guard.

The moment Nalini turned, Talfryn slunk over to where Gregorio munched on his morning gruel. He really hoped his friend couldn't see his distress.

"Gregorio, d'you need any help in the infirmary?" Talfryn asked, trying every little bit to keep his tone neutral. Happy, even.

Gregorio quirked an eyebrow. "Did I not just overhear that you have sparring practice this morning?"

"Well, yeah, but, you know." Somehow, his hand made its way to his neck. He brought it down quickly. "Just thought you might need an extra hand or two." He waved his hands as an example.

"There are few in the infirmary at this time. Brynwen and I are mainly helping with inventory and making new medicinal concoctions."

Why isn't he getting the hint?

"Tal." Brynwen came up to them. "Padric's waiting for you to go out to the 'haunted garden.'"

"Oh, is he?" he said with nonchalance. "Guess I'd better go, then." Spotting Padric speaking with Rawlins, he headed that way.

"Tal, don't you need your sword?"

"And your hatchet?" Gregorio raised the weapon from the picnic blanket.

Taking a deep breath to call on patience, Talfryn spun around with a grin plastered on his face. "Yep, yep, definitely need those to spar with the maidens of death."

"*Try* not to maim any of them." Brynwen sighed.

"Trust me, I won't be the one maiming anybody."

Once he swiped up his blade and hatchet, he trailed behind the others as Brother Howell led them to the haunted garden Maid Mildred had told them about. When they arrived, the brother led them to a red-brick wall inundated by vines. Tall trees ascended from inside the tall wall. Brother Howell pushed open a worn wooden door obscured by the vines. The door had once been painted green like the plants, but it had since mostly chipped away revealing ancient oak beneath.

Talfryn was the last inside and whistled as he entered. A canopy of tall trees covered the top, with vines growing everywhere. The plants, which had at one time been planted in neat rows, had overgrown their beds. However, the place was wide, and probably only required a small amount of cutting away overgrowth before they could begin to practice. It was the perfect location for their party to exercise and for the dryads to shed their human personas for a while.

Had Brynwen followed them, she'd've had a fit and begun gardening at once.

Removing the amulets from around their necks, the dryads returned to green and began to untie their dresses when Padric put a quick stop to it. "Might you maidens care to change into something more suitable over in those trees yonder?"

Talfryn thought he heard Warin groan in dismay.

Except for Eliva, who had already darted to the trees as though her life depended on it, the other dryads stared at Padric like he had grown a second head. At last, Nalini seemed to understand and ushered the remaining nymphs toward the trees.

While they changed, the men worked on clearing out some of the fallen foliage to make space.

"Hey"—Talfryn hauled off a dead branch—"has anyone checked for carnivorous bramble bushes, by chance?"

"Why? Are you planning on falling in one?" Eliva asked, coming out of the trees. She wore her normal green and brown flowing dress and was shoeless.

His eye caught the glint from the top of her polearm, likely the same one she'd used to thrash him before. Throat choking on an answer, he found himself mumbling something *really intelligent* and picked up his pace. His heart didn't stop until he reached Padric, Warin, Rawlins, and a fidgeting Kett. The carpenter's apprentice held a real borrowed broadsword out as far from his body as possible, as though it were a snake seeking to chomp on him.

"It only bites if you let it," he confided in Kett.

"Then I won't let it."

"Attaboy!" Talfryn patted him on the back.

"Pick a partner," Warin instructed. "The warrior maidens may choose their partners."

Talfryn spun around, mouth agape. "But Warin, I was planning on showing Kett some moves."

The knight chuckled. "You can do that in a later session. For now, let the maidens decide."

Miffed at his dilemma, he stared helplessly as the eager group of dryads congregated before the men. In the middle of the pack, Eliva tried to make her way to Padric, but Nalini arrived first. Then she shuffled to Warin, but was rebuffed by one of her friends. By the time she turned to the others, they were all taken—except for Talfryn. Two of the dryads, seeing that the three best and the one most pliable choices were taken, decided on each other.

Talfryn and Eliva gaped at each other for two excruciating heartbeats before she sprinted to where Nalini stood next to Padric and pulled her aside. Her face scrunched in fury as she spoke in rapid-fire Latin, arms flailing, her polearm somehow not impaling anyone as it moved about. Having none of it—whatever it was—Nalini retorted in like Latin. Meanwhile, it was clear that Padric tried not to overhear, but couldn't help wincing every so often.

At last, Nalini had the final word, and Eliva stormed off. She had cleared half of the garden before stopping. With a dramatic grunt, she spun around and marched toward Talfryn, face intent, steam practically pitching out of her green ears. When she was only five paces away, he felt sure she was going to ram right through him. It took all of his resolve not to flee and cry like a baby. She made an abrupt halt not two feet away. The charged air that emanated from her rushed through Talfryn and took his breath away. On the tail end of it, he thought he heard a wolffish laugh.

"We are partners." She stalked away, calling over her shoulder, "I promised Nalini not to maim you. Too much."

"Oh, gosh, you don't know how relieved I feel right now," Talfryn said. *I'm not gonna survive the day, am I?*

Kett, standing next to the dryad Luciliana, leaned close to Talfryn. "She always like that?"

"Just never offer her boots." She loathed footwear of any kind, and would just as likely throw them to the lions.

Leaving Kett in a puddle of confusion, Talfryn hoisted his hatchet onto his shoulder and trudged after the green maiden whom he'd been fated to spar with.

🍃

"YOU'RE DOING IT ALL WRONG," Eliva snarled.

For the last several months of training with the knights, Talfryn had learned more about a sword than he'd ever dreamed possible. All the ways to handle it, the ways to defend with it, the ways to kill with it.

In all that time, though, he'd never expected to dig a hole with it.

Oooh, Rawlins'll skin me alive if he finds out what I'm doing to my sword.

"Then *you* dig the hole," Talfryn retorted. "It's not my fault that my sword chopped off the heads of those pretty flowers." She had parried too fast for him, and he'd over-swiped, decapitating two purple flowers. Eliva had become livid and had demanded him to fix the situation.

"Asters."

Talfryn finished wiping off his sword from the flower carnage. "Whatever. Better their heads than mine."

"I wouldn't be so sure about that." In slow motion, she slid her finger along the bladed edge of her polearm without drawing blood, her gaze never faltering from his.

A chill ran down Talfryn's spine. In the greatest effort not to lose his cool, he grinned. "Just saying, but I don't think they'll be too happy if we return with only one head between the two of us."

"That remains to be seen. Hurry and finish planting the poor, defenseless seeds into the ground so we may continue."

Continue the slaughter, he thought miserably.

When at last he'd dug a hole deep enough for the seeds, he covered them up with the discarded dirt and patted it down with his hands. "There. You'd almost never know it happened." *Almost.* Except that one could clearly see the chopped off stalks not two feet from the small mound of dirt.

Eliva eyed him, and he wheeled around before he could squirm under her scrutiny. Why did she disdain him so?

"Now that we're done gardening, shall we?" He might have relished her wince as he wiped his dirt-covered sword off on a thick bush. With a huff, she dropped her polearm to pick up a short sword of her own.

They circled each other, Eliva's eyes shifting, likely trying to find Talfryn's weaknesses. In kind, Talfryn regarded her, although he could see absolutely no weaknesses on her. *Not fair. She should have at least one!*

She looked much too young to be so angsty.

Suddenly, he wondered how old she was. She looked sixteen or seventeen, but Circe and her family were quite old. His young dryad friend Thimble was older than she looked. He knew Nalini had been around for a very long time, much longer than the eighteen or nineteen years she so resembled, possibly even as long as Gregorio.

Eliva made the first move, and Talfryn barely had time to block it. She was merciless in her blows, and Talfryn had a heck of a time just trying to stay alive. Most of the blood drawn was his own, but he got a couple of hits in.

Then Eliva's foot hit a tree root. She stumbled backward. Seeing his chance, Talfryn made to strike and disarm her. As he brought the sword forward, the howl of his nightmares echoed in the distance.

The hot blaze of the prophecy and the stab of terror rent through him like a knife.

Blinded and gasping, Talfryn stumbled, his blade slicing a wide arc in the air. Something hard struck his head.

The next thing he knew, he was on the ground. His chest felt about to burst, his head throbbed from its impact with the hard earth, his leg likewise throbbed, and something cool touched his neck. Gasping, he opened his eyes, his vision spinning enough he thought he'd be sick. All he saw was green and dark red swirling around him.

"Pathetic," the green swirl said. At least, he *thought* it was the green swirl. "How you defeated the aeternae and the Shadow Druid's *cobali*, I shall never know."

"Sheer luck?" Talfryn offered. At last, the spinning slowed to a stop, and he stared at the angry glare of Eliva, kneeling beside him. Somehow, despite her blade being so near to drawing blood, her scowl and gray-blue eyes made her look almost comical and pretty, and the blade was cool after a hard workout, and...

Oh, no, I must've hit my head harder than I thought. Snap out of it!

"Stop groaning and get up. If we are to defeat the aeternae and Janus, Talfryn Masson, we must be prepared."

Talfryn sat up in agony. "What did you hit me with? A rock?"

"Better. The flat of my short sword. Handy, huh?" She held out the "handy" weapon, twisting and twirling it in a professional manner that any knight would be proud of.

Rubbing his head, he grumbled. "'Handy' isn't the word I'd choose."

"Too bad," she said. "I have already chosen it."

Talfryn was about to retort on how silly her statement was when his stomach rumbled. Loudly. "On that note, I'm headed to the afternoon meal. My sister's helping in the kitchen today, and she promised me the most tender mutton I've ever had. But continue training with that tree over there, if you'd like—looks to me like it needs a good beating."

"Till the morrow, then," she said, polishing her sword.

Talfryn tried not to wince as he touched a tender rib. "Yeah, I'm really looking forward to it."

AFTER VESPERS, during which Padric thought the dryads did quite well sitting and acting as though in prayer, considering their pagan background, Brother Howell met them in the empty kitchen to discuss prophecy matters. The kitchen staff would not return for another couple of hours to prepare the bread for the following day. Absent were Talfryn and Kett, who were working on the new chariot in the stable, and the maidens took an early night.

Nearing the completion of their meeting, in which they had gleaned nothing new, Brother Howell yawned, his teeth glinting in the candlelight.

"Past your bedtime, brother?" Padric asked with a grin.

"Just about. I had to get up extra early this morning to deal with the new brothers."

"Not gett'in along with the others?" Rawlins asked.

"Partly," Howell admitted. "And partly due to oversleeping. At least half of them don't seem to wish to attend morning prayers with the rest of us. Say their prayers in their sleep, so they claim. Nor do they remember to fast on Fridays. Brother Antony had a stern speaking with them, in which they seemed somewhat mollified. For a time."

"Where are they from?" Warin asked.

"Bordesley Abbey, southeast of here. Their superior sent them to Wales on a mission of peace." His voice lowered. "But it seems more like a mission of freedom to me."

Gregorio rubbed his chin. "Peace with whom?"

Brother Howell pursed his lips. "You know, I don't think they ever said. But their abbot is good friends with ours."

"Sounds like the brothers are just letting off some steam." Warin shrugged.

"Could be."

"Did they attend vespers tonight?" Padric asked.

"They did but sat huddled in the back. Mostly, they keep to themselves."

A scowl crept over Rawlins's mouth. "The fellas with their hoods down low, right? I noticed 'em whispering and carrying on."

"That was them."

Not a very prayerful group, Padric mused.

"With luck, they will only be here another few days, then they will move on and cast their nets of peace elsewhere."

"I am sure they will."

"I wonder, Brother Howell, where is your library?" Gregorio asked.

Howell closed his eyes as though in pain. "In the west wing. However," he said when Gregorio's eyes brightened, "it's closed for repairs. The new brothers are to be working on it as part of their keep."

"That is a shame." Gregorio frowned. "I have been seeking a specific volume of Pliny the Elder's *Naturalis Historia* for some time and wondered if it resided here. Can we not go in during their rest period?"

"Afraid not. The abbot's pretty strict about it. But I can introduce you to the chief librarian, Brother Edgar. If we have it, he would most certainly know."

Gregorio heartened. "Splendid."

Something about these traveling monks did not settle well with Padric. "I will come with you. I have some questions of my own for his ears."

CHAPTER 22

That night, Aeron had just filled his trencher with roast chicken and vegetables, its delicious spices wafting up to him, when he spotted his father pacing on the far end of the room. A dark cloud seemed to have dampened the two-faced god's mood this night. The idea to leave his father be so he could enjoy his meal came foremost, but then a speck of conscience hit him. He grunted, displeased with his dratted conscience. Perhaps he could persuade his father to join him in the meal. After all, they hadn't dined together in well over a fortnight. They could further their plans together.

Taking up his trencher, he rose and walked by his father's side. "Good evening, Father. Have you eaten yet? The cook has outdone himself this time."

Janus waved him off. "No time. There is much on my mind."

Aeron could tell the god of time was not telling him something. "Pray, sir, what is the matter?" For weeks, he had tried to get closer to his godly father, but the man was always too preoccupied with his quest for world domination. It was rare that his past self got to speak, either.

"It is none of your concern," Janus said, with another flutter of the wrist.

Stewing at his father's dismissal, Aeron was about to return to his seat, but it had been filled by one of the huntsmen he liked least, Laster. His father cleared his throat, stopping him in his tracks.

"On second thought, Aeron"—glancing around to ensure no one was listening in, Janus leaned close to Aeron's ear—"can you keep a secret?"

Nostrils flaring, it was almost impossible for Aeron not to shout to the rafters how he had kept his clandestine activities behind the backs of everyone in Derby for four long years. Instead, he took a breath, counted to three, and replied, "Of course, Father." It surprised him how calm he sounded, in spite of his racing heart.

"Good. Come with me, there is something I must tell you."

Aeron's gaze shifted as he scanned the room, then eagerly followed his father out of the door.

Only once before had he been in his father's room, to summon him for one of Medea's mad schemes, and it had been as clean and immaculate then as it was now. A narrow bed covered in white silk sheets and pillows. An ink-stained writing desk with a neat stack of papers, a quill, and a bottle of ink. A single chair. A stack of books on a small shelf in the corner. And in the other corner, a large trunk with scratches and stains that looked to be at least a thousand years old.

Waiting for his father to break the silence and stop his endless pacing, Aeron contemplated eating his trencher. He began to wonder if his father had forgotten he was there.

Janus halted his pacing and looked dead-on at his son. "I know no other way to say it, so here it is. My other half and I believe that my life might be in danger in the near future."

Aeron raised an eyebrow at that. "How so? Can you not see your own future, Father?"

"At times it is more clear than at others. This is one of those times where I receive an inkling—a feeling creeping up on me that something will happen."

Medea was his first thought. She was an anomaly whom he had never fully trusted, always on the edge of madness. It made Aeron wonder when she would break, when everything would end up the way it always did around her—with everyone dead.

But he had to hope for the best and trust in his father.

"Your premonitions. What can I do to help, Father?"

At last, Janus the Future smiled, and placed a hand on his son's shoulder, an action which had only occurred a couple of times before. As a rule, Janus did not touch people. One of his many quirks, Aeron supposed. "You are a good son, Aeron. I have something to show you."

Taking a key from his pocket, he stepped over to the ancient trunk and unlocked it. Lifting the latch and hood, he reached inside and produced a small box.

Aeron set down the trencher, now cold, wiped his greasy hands on his trousers, and accepted the small nondescript wooden box. Upon opening it, he discovered a green stone attached to a thin gold chain.

"A necklace?" It was similar to Gregorio's amulet in that it radiated some magic. But on the whole, the thing was exquisite. Not a spec out of place, perfectly polished, and likely worth a pretty penny. In the back of his mind, he thought that, should the whole plan go south, the necklace would be worth a small fortune. He shook his head. *No, the plan will work, and I will have what I always wanted.*

Janus shook his head. "A lifeline." When Aeron gave him a questioning look, he proceeded to explain. Loosening the strings at the top of his tunic, he pulled out a blue stone on a gold chain matching the one in Aeron's hand. "Should something happen to me, I need you to connect your amulet with this one. No matter what happens, or what risk, you must do it. The success of our mission depends upon it."

Frowning, Aeron studied the stone. He couldn't imagine what he'd ever need this for. They had taken all precautions to succeed. And yet, he still felt uneasy about everything to do with Medea. "How will I know that I must do this thing?"

"I trust you will know when the time comes."

Aeron nodded in understanding—the exact opposite of how he actually felt. "Do you think de Clifton and party will succeed in harming you, father? I shan't allow it. I swear it," he added to drive his loyalty home. Janus had been more of a father to him than the man he had grown up with had ever been. *This time, he will have no doubt about my loyalty to him.*

"Good lad. Keep this on you at all times, and do not let anyone take it from you. This will remain our little secret." He patted Aeron's shoulder again.

Pride swelled in his chest that his father trusted him in this, their secret. Aeron wished to ask more questions—*many more questions*—but knew a dismissal when he heard one. Perhaps tomorrow he would try again for more. "Yes, sir. I will not let you down."

CHAPTER 23

*T*alfryn watched Eliva stretch the bow string and release the arrow. It whistled through the air, missing tree trunks on its way to her set target. It disappeared from view, but then he heard it hit something solid. *The target.*

"So, what'm I aiming at?" Incredulous, Talfryn squinted into the middle distance but saw nothing but trees, a bit of grass, and ground cover. No arrow—so where was it? Bow in hand, he flicked at the green fletching of the arrow with his free hand.

They'd been given permission to practice archery in the forest outside the abbey walls yet still inside its bounds, but were warned to be cautious. Wings unfurled, Ulysses stood at attention in case something happened.

Eliva indicated the same place she'd just pointed at, as if that would help him see the invisible target any better. "That red apple next to the one I just hit."

"I don't see it."

"How do you not see it? It is very large and red. Quite unmistakable."

Talfryn's eyes turned to slits as he regarded the green girl. "Look, my eyesight's pretty darn good. But is this some sorta trick to make me look more foolish? 'Cause I gotta say, it's getting old."

From his shoulder, Miser confirmed that there was indeed an apple where Eliva pointed. He could leap to it with his eyes closed if need be.

"I bet you really could," Talfryn muttered, nocking his bow with all the confidence of a blind acrobat. "You two must have better than perfect eyesight."

"My mother thinks so," Eliva muttered in like tone. "She taught me everything she knows about bow craft."

"She sounds like a very nice dryad," Talfryn said. "Thimble spoke highly of her all the time." Thimble was Eliva's younger sister whom he'd met at Cataractonium. They'd become fast friends there. He still missed his friendship with little Thimble, although Eliva had done her best to let Talfryn know he wasn't allowed to spend time with her little sister. Eliva's protectiveness had pushed him away from spending time with either of them. Unfortunately, Nalini had other plans...

A light emerged in Eliva's eyes, and Talfryn thought he saw the hint of a smile. It was...nice, and suited her more than the scowl she always wore. "Thimble is her pride and joy."

"And what are you to her?"

Frowning, Eliva turned her gaze away and hastily plucked an arrow from the quiver on her back. "Let's return to the apple, shall we?"

"Oh, let's." Allowing her to avoid the question, Talfryn kept that piece of information locked away for another time. "Now, if only I could *see* my target."

Eliva rolled her eyes. "Why don't you ask your friends to move it?"

"All right, I'll...I beg your pardon?"

"Ask your woodland friends to move the apple."

Talfryn cocked his head. "The squirrels and deer? Why would they listen to me?"

Eliva huffed a breath. "Why does anyone listen to you?"

"Because"—he smirked—"I'm ruggedly handsome?"

The dryad gave him a blank stare, so blank it hurt Talfryn's chest. "No, that isn't it." Then she pivoted to look at the supposed apple he couldn't see and folded her arms over her chest in bored anticipation.

Well, that sounded like a challenge. He cast aside her rebuff and cleared his throat. Raising his voice, he spoke in what he hoped was a commanding voice. "Oi, squirrels in yonder trees. Bring the apple closer to me."

Nothing happened.

"Umm, please?"

Immediately, loads of chittering voices spoke up from above. Unfortunately, they were so jumbled, that Talfryn wasn't quite sure what they were saying. But Miser scrambled up and down his arm in excitement.

Leaves rustled in a cacophony of sound that swelled from directly above them, and moved straight ahead toward the supposed apple. Along the "tree path" they made, small branches and brown, yellow, and red leaves rained down on the forest floor. It was a wondrous sight and took his breath away.

Beside him, Eliva's eyes widened in astonishment as she followed the route of the rustling leaves and branches.

Moments later, Talfryn heard the clack of tiny claws scaling tree trunks before he saw them, even further than he'd imagined. Then they reversed direction along the tree path toward him. When they were directly above his head, their voices, leaves, and nails almost deafening, the apple dropped into his outstretched hand.

"Doubted me, didn't you? Just a little bit?" Talfryn said with his cockiest grin. To be honest, he hadn't believed it'd work, but she needn't know that.

Eliva raised her gaze to the trees, then down to the apple in his hand. "I will admit I had my doubts."

Talfryn chortled. Casting his gaze into the tree canopy, he grinned as the squirrels returned his look, their black eyes eager for more. And snacks. Loads of snacks. "Thanks, fellas. Now, can you deliver this apple thirty paces away in that direction?" He pointed to near where it had originally been placed, but in a spot he could see.

The chittering resumed, and he heard dozens of squeaky yeses in response. In their haste, they stumbled over themselves, rolling and tossing the apple along branches to their kin until they reached the designated spot and dumped the apple onto the ground.

Talfryn's smile couldn't have been wider as he strutted into place, nocked the arrow on his bow, and took aim.

"Will you just shoot the blasted apple, already?" Eliva jabbed her hands onto her hips.

Without looking at her, Talfryn could feel the heat of frustration and fury fuming off her green skin. He imagined her gray-blue eyes, so unlike the other dryads', darting daggers into his heart. *They're much prettier when they're green with her red hair.*

This didn't help his concentration one bit. Holding his breath and trying to ignore everything about her, Talfryn released the string and his breath at the same time. The arrow struck the tree trunk about six inches above the apple.

Clearly, that didn't work. A nervous laugh released from his mouth. "Uh, that was just a practice shot."

Some of the heat in the air seemed to lessen from Eliva's person. Her voice was less chill as she said, "Make sure your back is straight. Take even breaths, then hold it when you are ready."

Nocking another arrow to the bow, Talfryn cleared his thoughts. They were only for the apple. *Just the apple. There's nothing around but the apple.* This time when he released, the fruit shifted and then rocked back to its original spot. The arrow had grazed the top.

From his left shoulder, Miser *tsked* Talfryn's "poor shootsmanship," and said that anyone worth his weight in acorns could hit the huge, round target.

Frustration plinked at Talfryn's ego as he grumbled. "Then *you* shoot it," he said to his traitorous furry friend.

That got the little rodent to stop laughing.

As the rest of the squirrels in the treetops quieted down, one laugh remained. Cold, deep, and menacing, like it knew a secret about their futures that they didn't yet know.

Talfryn's chest constricted at the sound. *Not now. Go away, wolficorn!*

Instead of joining the laughter, Eliva handed him one of her arrows. "Try once more with this."

Feeling sheepish, and partly wondering if she could hear the evil laugh, Talfryn didn't even look at her as he reached for the arrow with turquoise-colored fletching. It was a hue he hadn't seen anyone in Derby or Nottingham use on their arrows or crossbow bolts.

He nocked the arrow with trembling fingers. The wolficorn's menacing growly laugh delighting in his failure. In his ruin. It crowded him until it became stifling, unable to take a full breath.

You're not real.

"Oh, but I am!"

Talfryn gasped. The wolficorn hadn't replied to him before. The large wolf's head emerged from behind a tree, the mottled gray fur and three bony protrusions on its face confirming its realness.

"Talfryn?" Eliva's voice broke through the wolficorn's deep timbre. It had an edge of something between boredom and irritation.

"Don't you see it?" he choked out. So much for sounding confident and brave.

"Of course I see the apple. Do you need to stand closer, or what?"

She doesn't see or hear it. It's not really there. He did, though, ignore what that meant about his own mind instead. "Nay, but— Oh, never mind." Drawing the string back, he ignored the monster and focused again on the apple. The wolficorn's voice didn't try cutting through his thoughts again, but its presence, whether real or not, still lingered.

When he released the bowstring, the arrow went quite wide. A high-pitched screech of anger and pain emanated from somewhere behind the apple. The next moment, a giant boar crashed out of the brush. Eyes red, it charged straight for them, the turquoise fletched arrow protruding from its side.

The wolficorn, however, was gone.

"Run!" Eliva shouted.

Talfryn didn't argue as, together, they sped away from the wounded animal.

Eliva leaped over a downed trunk. "You're not a very good shot."

"Not at apples!" Talfryn laughed as he avoided impaling himself on a dead, raised tree branch that aimed for his torso. "Bet you didn't know we were out boar hunting instead!"

Eliva just rolled her eyes and continued dodging trees in a graceful pattern, her brown and green skirts flowing behind her.

That night at the abbey, they feasted on roasted boar and spiced, skewered apples, much more than the cook's original idea for the evening meal had been.

While he ate the deliciously spiced meat, curtesy of the cook, Brynwen, and Gregorio in the kitchens, Talfryn glanced over at Eliva sitting by herself at the end of the bench near the other dryads. It was rare for her to speak very long with anyone other than Nalini.

She'd helped Talfryn take down the boar, and hadn't even threatened his life once during the ordeal. For a change, he didn't fear that she'd stab him in the dark. Well, maybe she still would someday, but not while Bryn and his friends were anywhere around. He took a bit of comfort in that.

Besides, whether she'd meant to or not, she'd gotten him to communicate with several creatures at one time. That was a pretty big deal, and such a skill could come in handy someday.

OUTSIDE THE ABBEY'S WALLS, Talfryn and Kett stood studying the giant elm tree, its egg-shaped leaves with serrated edges billowing in the light breeze. The latter held the drawing of the chariot he planned to build in his hands.

"Will this tree work?" Talfryn asked. He tugged his hatchet from the loop in his belt.

Miser complained that the tree was too nice to chop down.

Kett folded up the parchment, careful to make sure it didn't rip. "It'll have to do."

"How are we to get this done today?"

"We won't. But we should get pretty far, at least. We've still got four days until the full moon."

Talfryn hadn't chopped wood since August when he'd left the farm to become a squire. Luckily, his muscles remembered, but he knew they'd be mighty sore come morning. As they hacked at the elm, Talfryn's thoughts cheerfully roamed, glad not to have to be partnered with Eliva for the rest of the day. She was just as cold as the first day they'd met atop Cataractonium's hilly entrance. And yet, it felt odd not being around her.

Ulysses came by for a bit to inspect their work, then left them to their chopping, keeping within sight.

After the peryton left, Kett cleared his throat. "So, Talfryn, can you speak with Ulysses? I know you can with Miser."

Talfryn sawed for a few seconds in silence, trying to figure out how to answer. "Well, it's different with Ulysses. I can communicate with Miser easily, as well as horses and some birds. But Ulysses is special. He was once human, so I think there is some sort of a wall or barrier that blocks our communication. On the other hand, Gregorio can communicate with him just fine, but I don't know if it's because they've had thousands of years to practice or because they're related or what. My goats, however..." Talfryn chuckled. "They speak primarily with their stomachs, which are much louder than any other thought. It makes it nearly impossible to have a coherent conversation with them. When Padric turns into a goat, it's the same thing."

Kett paused in his chopping and wiped the sweat from his face with his sleeve. "That is interesting. I always thought it would be great fun to speak with animals. Do you know anyone else who does?"

"Bryn saw Circe communicate with Ulysses." Talfryn also stopped and wiped his sweaty brow and neck. "And I think several of the dryads and naiads can, but I haven't asked any."

"Because they're unapproachable?" Kett asked with a smirk.

Talfryn returned with a grin. "That, and they sing just about every time I walk by. It's unnerving, and beautiful, and discouraging all at the same time."

"I know what you mean," Kett said dreamily. "Gregorio said they sing to nature, that they're one with it."

That got Talfryn to thinking about Eliva. She didn't seem inclined to sing with the other dryads. In fact, he hadn't seen her sing at all. Not when he'd first witnessed the dryads singing in the stables of Cataractonium and not once since he'd been traveling with them. It was very *un-dryad-like*.

They chopped for another few minutes in silence to concentrate on felling the tree. It went quite a bit faster than Talfryn had anticipated. When at last it was ready, Talfryn took several steps back. "Go ahead, take the final swing. It's your project, after all."

With relish, Kett felled the tree with a proficient whack, his muscles tightening as his hatchet connected with the trunk. When it fell, they made quick work of chopping the wood into even sized logs, Kett's body almost a blur as he worked his craft.

Talfryn whistled at the pile of wood they'd made. "Well." Sweat covered his whole body, and he was ready to jump into the closest spring to cool down. Patting Kett's shoulder in appreciation, he said, "Ya know, I think you'll make journeyman carpenter before your seventeenth birthday."

Scarlet crept up Kett's dark features, but all he did was lug a pile of the wood into his arms. His eyes sparked in excitement. "No time to dilly-dally, Talfryn. We've got a chariot to build."

"Before you do that, Kett," Padric approached from behind. "I will require you to fix my boot."

"But, sir, I'm not a cobbler."

A spark alit in Padric's eye. "And that is why I require your skills. I wish to add a hidden compartment."

Kett grinned, likely contemplating such a thing. "Sounds like a challenge to me."

CHAPTER 24

The midday meal, consisting of fish and boiled vegetables, filled Padric's stomach after a morning of sparring with Nalini, Warin, Rawlins, and the other dryads in the haunted garden. He was just finishing the last sip of his ale when Brother Howell approached their group, his usual wide smile on his face. A short, rotund, out-of-breath brother in a rumpled white robe waddled behind him. His balding head gave off a dull glow from the light streaming in through the stained glass windows.

"Brother Howell." Padric greeted the monk with a smile. "It is good to see you."

Brynwen smiled. "We have not seen you in some days, Brother Howell. I hope all is well."

"Yes, quite well, Miss Brynwen. Forgive me for not visiting more often, but duties kept me away. However, this afternoon I am free and brought along Brother Fabian." He indicated the balding monk at his side, then turned to Gregorio. "I especially think you will be agreeable to what I have in mind for you all this afternoon. It is a treat." He rubbed his hands together. "Brother Fabian is the keeper of the keys, and will allow us a view of the relic room."

A few mutterings of displeasure emanated behind Padric. Padric, however, was intrigued. He loved history and was nearly as excited as Gregorio, whose fingers danced in anticipation.

"We would be most delighted," Gregorio said. He sent his tutor's gaze over all at the table, daring anyone to beg to stay behind.

"Perfect," Brother Howell said. "When you have finished dining, we shall go."

A few minutes later, he led the way through a long corridor to the right. The walls were bare except for the intermittent round wooden doors and sconces of small torches. The flames danced and created deep shadows as they walked past.

Near the end of the hall, Brother Howell opened the fourth door on the right. Sunlight spilled into the dreary hallway as he motioned for the guests to enter the room. Giddy with anticipation, Gregorio was the first to enter. Brynwen, holding Padric's hand, nodded to the monk and pulled him into the room.

"Oh, Padric, look!"

The moment he did, he was filled with awe. Coats of arms with labels of saints in beautiful calligraphic script were displayed on a short pedestal. Simple and ornate crosses and crucifixes hung on the stone wall. There were shelves lined with a smattering of chalices, some quite ancient, in gold, silver, bronze, wood, and clay. Tapestries depicting the Lord's Last Supper and other scenes from the Bible draped the open walls. Two small caskets filled with holy treasures occupied a table of their own on the far side of the room. Some items were beautifully crafted and others were plain, but each held as much religious significance as the item next to it.

There were so many things, Padric did not know what to look at first—but Brynwen did. Thus, she dragged him to the tapestry of Christ washing the Apostles' feet at the Last Supper.

"This is gorgeous." Hand hovering over the tapestry, Brynwen admired the artistry of the needlework. Flowers, grass, and vines filled the scene around Jesus and the twelve Apostles, giving it an air of reality.

The dryads looked at the chalices, whispering questions of why they kept these in the relic room when they could hold perfectly good wine or mead. Cornelia and Seia each raised one to get a better perspective of it. Brother Howell rushed over to ask them to please release the chalices as they were holy relics. Cornelia merely frowned at him but set it down. Seia, however, teased Brother Howell about how cute he was when he pouted and Howell had to pry it from her fingers as she flirted. His cheeks bloomed the deepest scarlet Padric had ever seen.

"Padric," Gregorio said on the other side of the room. "You should see this."

All of the men were gathered around the same thing. They parted as he approached. "What is so interesting about..."

He trailed off when his eyes fell upon a shimmering object hanging from two iron hooks drilled into the wall. It was a sword unlike any he had ever seen before. The blade was forged from a metal that seemed to drink in the very light around it. The hilt was one-and-a-half-hands long, perfect for wielding one- or two-handed. A soft hum emitted from the blade. Most magic hummed or buzzed to Padric, but this was like an angelic song, lovely and sweet, yet at the same time sending a note of warning to its foes. Not quite like magic, but certainly of power.

"The Sword of Saint George," Gregorio breathed. Soaking in its beauty, his eyes traced every detail of the blade. "The very blade he used to slay the dragon. I met him once."

"'Course you did." Rawlins folded his arms over his chest, trying to look relaxed, while he gazed on the sword with longing. "Looks like the sword in the tapestry."

"Amazing," Talfryn said, equally mesmerized.

Padric himself could not take his eyes off of it. It had little adornment, yet was beautiful in its simplicity. A single jewel rested in the cross guard, with an inscription lining the blade.

"It was given to him not long before he slew the dragon," Gregorio was saying, "but he had just received this sword from the king of France when I met him. Saint Demetrius blessed the sword. A most radiant piece of singular make."

The temptation too much, Padric rested his hand on top of the hilt. He could envision Saint George from the tapestry upstairs fighting the dragon and using the weapon's power to defeat it. *Loyalty. Purity. Faith.*

All of the things the saint depicted. A sudden discomfort clenched his stomach, and he realized all eyes were on him. "What? Why are you all looking at me?"

"N-it is nothing." Gregorio waved away whatever was on his mind. But his gaze slid back to the sword, then to him.

They ogled the long blade for a few minutes more, during which time the dryads came over to equally admire the sword. Then Brother Howell and Brother Fabian ushered them out of the room.

❧

OUTSIDE ON GUARD duty with Eliva that night, Talfryn stared up at the stars. He absently patted Miser, who rolled over and curled up in a sling hanging over his shoulder and across his chest. The abbey wall didn't impede their view of the moon.

The prophecy whirled around in his head, reminding him that the moon would be full in a mere few days. Its tug on him grew more pressing with each day, especially as a reminder at night. Janus would make his move that night.

Beside him, the dryad maiden in her human guise had barely spoken a word to him. Something seemed to be on her mind, but he didn't know how to ask without setting her off and getting a polearm down his throat for his troubles.

He still couldn't get the image of Medea blowing the purplish powder at the twin arrows Eliva and Luciliana had released her way out of his head, or how they'd hastily veered for him and Kett.

He couldn't figure out why, if Medea wanted him and Kett alive, she'd allow the arrows to hurt them.

Worse, he couldn't shake the dream with Faunus's warning, *"Talfryn, be ready."* He just knew it had to do with the aeternae and the prophecy. But did Faunus mean he should be prepared to find and kill it or to be prepared because it was hunting him? Gregorio and the dryads were just as clueless as him.

Sighing inwardly, Talfryn marched around and around the property, eventually falling two steps behind Eliva, his fingers absently tapping against the metal of his hatchet and the pommel of his sword.

Sometimes, he saw Eliva twitch and begin to turn as if to say something; but then she'd spin back around and pick up her pace. It was like some kind of cat and mouse game in which he hadn't gotten the full instructions to play.

A scuffle of tiny paws scurried away to his left. It was enough to send his heart racing and he nearly started hacking at the spot it came from.

But no, it was just a hare having a near-midnight snack. His heart hammered until the thing was out of sight.

At last, Talfryn could take the silence no more. "Eliva, can you tell me what you know about the wolfi—ah, the aeternae?"

The dryad's shoulders tensed, the darkness swallowing up her red hair and leaving only the outline of her lithe body illuminated by the bits of moonlight filtering through the forest canopy, accentuating all of her fine-toned features. Her shrug left him wanting. "Nalini can tell you more than me."

He sidled up to her. "But I'm asking you."

Eliva released a grunt. She bestowed a skeptical look upon him, but when she looked at the spot on his head where the arrow had grazed, she jerked her face forward again. For some reason, the gesture made Talfryn's stomach tighten.

"Eliva. D'you think I'm mad at you about the arrow? It wasn't your fault. Medea is a powerful witch; you couldn't know she'd be able to deflect your arrow like that."

Stopping in her tracks, Eliva waved her arms in frustration. "But I should have known. I have trained all my life to fight the witch, to know her schemes, and I failed. Any other dryad would expect her tricks. And you..." She took a few deep breaths as her gaze landed on the spot where the arrow had grazed his head, bouncing from foot to foot. "It shouldn't have happened."

Talfryn opened his mouth to ask how long she'd been training—how old she was—but caught himself in time. He'd learned from his grandmother when he was very young, that neither girls nor married women alike took too kindly to that question. Grandmother had chuckled at the incident when he'd made an older woman blush, and she was kind enough to explain that it wasn't polite to ask such a direct question. He never forgot.

The dryad beside him looked to be his age, but so did all the other nymphs. Still, there was something...different about Eliva that he couldn't place. Something that set her apart from the others, that made her always irritable. And also drew him to her, despite their first few horrible encounters.

"The aeternae," Eliva began, "is almost as old as time. It has stalked man and beast for countless millennia for the thrill of the hunt, for the taste of their blood. It has decimated whole villages. You met it. Didn't you find it formidable when you fought it?"

The saliva dried up in Talfryn's mouth. He was wrong. Talking about it only made it worse. His heart doubled in time and his nightmares crept through the cracks in the wall he'd been slowly building to block them.

"Talfryn Masson?"

Talfryn blinked, and he was back in the abbey's walls again, the moon trying to find purchase through the dying foliage, and only a sliver of Eliva's face catching its light.

"Yes." He fidgeted with the edge of his hatchet for whatever comfort it could provide. "It was." His reply was so quiet, he didn't think she'd heard it.

The silence was unbearable, and Talfryn took a step away to do... *something.* His greatest defense had always been humor, but somehow she'd managed to put a stopper in it.

"To be honest," Eliva said, finally, "I was surprised to learn that you had survived fighting with the aeternae."

Eyebrow raising, Talfryn couldn't help but note the challenge and grinned. "Is that concern in your voice?"

"What? *Nay.*" She folded her arms, and Talfryn could tell that she was scowling in spite of the darkness. "Merely an observation about someone much less trained than I am."

"Uh, huh."

"Diana might be impressed...if you'd killed it."

Diana was a goddess or someone, wasn't she? "Well, it's probably still got my hatchet in its back. Does that count?"

"Is that so?" she asked, interest sparking in her expression.

"Aye."

"That I would like to see. Er, that is, Diana would, by all accounts."

Mm, hmm. "Well, you can't; or she can't, because the hatchet's still in its back."

Eliva huffed. "Not the hatchet. The aeternae." This time, her eyes shone in the moon with a disturbing excitement. "If we can find it, we can kill it, and—"

"Nay, you wouldn't want to meet it," Talfryn retorted. "You don't know…" His breath caught, and he stumbled away. This time, he couldn't push away the memories of the monster, his cousin's lifeless body, and all the blood. His leg throbbed so much, he braced his weight against the wall before he could collapse. Leaning over, he gasped for breath as the images pressed in. *What's wrong with me?*

"Fight it, Talfryn," Faunus's voice said in his head. *"You cannot allow the* aeternae *to defeat you."*

"Well, it's doing a great job so far," Talfryn whispered.

"Its goal is to beat you down mentally before it comes for you physically."

"Just because I threw an old hatchet at it?"

A rustling in the grass put Talfryn on guard. He jerked the sword in his hand in the direction of the sound.

It was Eliva. Relieved, he dropped the sword tip to the grass.

"Talfryn Masson. We are relieved for the evening."

There's no danger. No danger. No wolficorn. Calm down.

Several minutes passed before Talfryn's heart slowed down so he could speak. "We…" He cleared his dry throat. "We are?"

"Yes." She paused to regard him. "Are you all right?"

He waved his free hand dismissively. "Never been better. Just felt something sharp in my boot's all. But you don't wear boots, so I guess you don't have that problem." He peered down at her bare feet which must have been freezing on the cool October night.

"Good." Her cold manner had returned, and she spun toward the abbey's side entrance without another word. Gone was the almost pleasant conversation they'd had. He sighed. It'd been nice while it had lasted.

As Talfryn carefully made his way into the abbey, Warin and Asinia passed them, the former nodding as he passed by. "Have a pleasant sleep," Warin's deep voice rumbled.

"Huh, no promises."

CHAPTER 25

The following day at late morning, having a free moment away from the kitchens and infirmary, Brynwen picked her way through the partially-cleared brambles and weeds of the "haunted" garden to where her friends were busy sparring. To date, no one had seen anything out of the ordinary to consider it haunted.

She found Padric, Rawlins, Nalini, and Seia facing off with their weapons. An invisible signal bade them to begin their sparring match of an all-out brawl, everyone on their own.

For some reason, every time Nalini sidled up to Padric, a wide smile on her face, Brynwen's stomach curdled. *Why does it seem like Nalini is always with him?* He had spent much more time with the dryad than he had with her in recent days. In fact, he appeared to be enjoying their match a little too much for her liking.

A cold realization dribbled over her, and her heart dropped to her feet. That was it, wasn't it? Padric would rather be with Nalini than her. She wanted to release the scream building up in her chest. But instead, she turned to leave. She'd scream in a different place where she wouldn't draw attention.

"Bryn?" Padric called. "Bryn, wait."

She didn't turn back as Padric jogged up and stopped in front of her, arms out, sword sheathed. "Bryn, where are you going?" he asked breathily.

"Padric. No need to stop your sparring match on my account."

She continued to walk on, tugging her dress away from sticky brambles as she pitched through the garden door and sped over the neatly manicured lawn, this time hoping he'd go away so she could stew in peace. In the distance, a handful of Cistercian monks worked in the vegetable garden.

"Bryn, please." Padric caught her arm and spun her around. Nearly losing her balance as she stepped on a small molehill, she collided into his chest.

"Oof! Padric, what are you doing?"

He clutched her arms so she wouldn't fall. "Forgive me, sometimes I forget my own strength. Why did you run off?" He looked down at her, his brows frowning in hurt.

A flush filled Brynwen's cheeks as his mossy green gaze pierced her soul. Desire for him to kiss her took over, but she shook her head to remove the notion from her mind. "F-forgive me, Padric. I know you must practice for our rematch with Aeron and Medea. I shouldn't have intruded."

"Nay, we have been practicing for hours and could use a break. Truly," he said when she gave him a skeptical side-eye. His hand hovered near her cheek and hooked a loose lock of auburn hair behind her ear, then caressed said cheek down to her chin.

Tingles of longing tickled her toes and stomach. Never mind her previous thoughts, she'd go anywhere with this man. To Pluto's underworld, if need be.

"Come with me. I have something to show you." He gave her a tentative smile that lit his entire face.

Unable to resist, she returned the smile and nodded. Taking her hand, he led her back through the haunted garden door.

"Where are we going?" Brynwen asked as she stepped through. The others were still there, but the fighting had stopped and they conversed amicably.

Polearm resting against her shoulder, Nalini examined Brynwen's and Padric's clasped hands, smirked, and placed her free hand on her hip. "Practice is over for the day, I see."

Brynwen's chest constricted at Nalini's free spirit.

"That is right," Padric said easily. "See you at Vespers?"

Trying not to look cross, Brynwen held her breath until they had passed the others, who had already begun heading for the door.

"Are we going to the back wall?"

"You'll see. I would tell you to close your eyes, but I am afraid you would trip on all of this overgrowth. I know I would." He pulled her close and gave her a peck on her lips.

Warmth spread through her torso. "Keep doing that and I'd walk backwards if you asked."

His laugh rang in her ears like a bell.

Shoulders back, Padric drew up to his full height and placed her hand on his heart, considering her words. "Promises, promises. But no need. We are here." Reaching out, he pushed aside the leafy branches of a short apple tree bursting with ripe fruit.

Behind what had seemed to be the back of the abbey wall stood a beautiful little clearing, where strong branches hung low enough that two could sit on them. A row of yellow chrysanthemum bushes lined the perimeter of the clearing. Through the center ran a stream, narrow enough to leap over without getting footwear wet.

Brynwen drew in a breath of surprise at the sight. "Padric, this is so charming! How is this here? There shouldn't be room for this. However did you find it?"

Padric pulled open his drawstring purse and fumbled a hand inside it. "Nalini and I stumbled upon this place earlier during our sparring session before Rawlins and Seia joined us. The moment I saw it, I wished to show it to you."

All the happiness which had bubbled up in Brynwen's chest burst like a bubble in the stream.

Padric's brows knit together when he saw her frown, and he froze. "What is wrong?"

"You and Nalini?" *Again?*

"Yes?" At first, his mossy green eyes swam in confusion, but then they cleared. "Is it Nalini that troubles you?"

Brynwen couldn't form words, her throat burned too much.

"Bryn, Nalini and I are associates. Allies. You know that we have trained with the dryads since they joined us. Being Circe's captain, Nalini outranks me in status and gets to decide on her partner."

"But why is it always Nalini?"

"Do you wish I would 'partner-up' with each of the dryads in turn instead?"

Brynwen wished to wipe the cocky grin off his face. "That's not what I meant." She could feel her entire body turning scarlet from their discourse. "But I have seen the way she looks at you. It's obvious that she has feelings for you—do you return them?"

Now Padric's eyes grew round as a set of soup bowls.

Chest constricting from her inquiry, it seemed interminable for his answer to reach her ears. Pressing his lips together into a thin line, Padric paused for a moment.

It was long enough to make her understand.

Tears formed in her eyes, blurring her vision. "I see." A tear trickled down her cheek, and she tasted salt on her lips. "I'll go now."

"Bryn—nay, hear me out." He grabbed for her hand. She struggled and glowered at him. Taken aback, he looked completely confused.

"You heard the lady." Warin Ingram came stalking in.

Where had he come from?

Not pausing, his meaty fist struck the startled Padric in the face. Padric spun in a circle and sprawled on the ground.

"Padric!" Brynwen screamed. She wheeled on the standing knight. "Sir Warin, why did you do that?"

The larger knight stood over Padric, who peered up at him in a daze. "He was bothering you. Come along, Miss Brynwen." Taking her hand in a gentleness she hadn't thought possible after the blow he'd just struck, he pulled her away from her swain. "We shall allow him to think about his sins."

"But..." For a few moments, she'd forgotten Padric's hesitation, and her chest tightened as though someone were tugging a sharp string around it. "Mayhap it is for the best."

Not peering back, Brynwen allowed Sir Warin to lead her away, part of her hoping Padric would come running after them, begging her for forgiveness.

"Really, Miss Brynwen, you can choose a better beau than him."

She startled at that.

Heedless, he tugged on her arm.

PADRIC'S HEAD SPUN, his cheek stung, and his back screamed something fierce from a jagged stick poking it. For a moment, he saw two pairs of people looking down at him, then they left. After a few seconds, his vision cleared, but he wished it had not. Ire built up in his chest as he beheld them leaving, Warin holding Brynwen's hand.

"Really, Miss Brynwen, you can choose a better beau than him." Warin's smile was big as he tried to coax Brynwen's other hand into his.

"You didn't have to strike him."

"I thought he was hurting you."

I thought we were friends...

The botched conversation replayed in his mind, every wrong word— or *lack of word*—a stabbing dagger into his side. *How did I get it so wrong?*

"Leave her be." Chest heaving, Padric leapt to his feet, prepared to fight with his fists against the bigger man. He had allowed the knight a little leeway in his attentions to Brynwen, believing it irksome but harmless; however, this was too much. They might both have shared the same several-great grand sire, but dash it all if he had to share his beloved with Warin.

Shoving up his sleeves, Warin grinned and planted his feet in the earth. "Ready for a re-rematch already, Padric? Who needs the tourney?"

For an instant, Padric thought the knight might have returned to his old ways of bullying. It mattered not now, though. As one, they made a slow circle.

"Is this really necessary?" Brynwen asked in her most annoyed tone. "Shouldn't you two be beyond brawling?"

"Not at all, my sweet," Warin said, voice like silk.

Heat rose up Padric's neck at Warin's using of his pet name for Brynwen. "Just last week, there were two brawls in the tavern, started by knights. Talfryn did not tell you?"

"Nay," she responded dryly. She rolled her eyes. "Well, while you two fight your silly brawl, I will be making the evening meal." Without another word, she turned to go.

As Padric tried to decide if he should strike first, he thought he heard something. His ears perked up as Warin made the first move, his thick arm soaring toward Padric's injured chin. Voices, and...wood chopping?

This time, Padric was prepared and dodged, the fist gliding across his curls.

Padric lowered his voice. "Stop, Warin. I hear—"

"No excuses." Warin's other fist rammed at him, narrowly missing Padric's chest as he leaped backward, transforming into his faun legs in midair. "And no fair using your abilities."

"Your ability is *strength*. You use it all the time." Strength almost as great as Hercules, and the haughty attitude to match. "I need every advantage I can get."

Warin smirked. "And?"

Frustrated that he would not listen, Padric looked for an opening in his opponent's stance. When Warin's hand swept past again, Padric sprang into the man and grabbed his elbow. Moving with Warin's momentum, they glided over the uneven ground. "I hear voices, and they are not our men."

When Warin failed to stop, Padric jabbed his friend in the neck with his palm—a technique Nalini had taught him only the day before.

Brynwen turned around. "And another thing..." Startled at Padric's action, she froze.

At last, Warin made an abrupt halt and clutched his throat. He struggled to speak. "I...yield."

Padric heaved a breath. "Forgive me, my friend, but you would not yield, and they might have heard us. It could already be too late." Padric released the knight and listened with his enhanced hearing.

Free, Warin staggered to the closest tree, rubbing at the sore red spot growing on his neck.

Somehow, no one seemed to have heard the ruckus they had made.

"What good will it do?" the voice on the other side of the brick said between the loud strikes of axes against thick bark.

Searing bile rose up Padric's esophagus as he listened to the familiar voice speak with himself. But no, he likely did not speak to himself, but to a silent partner—the Shadow Druid? Reaching for his sword, Padric pondered with all seriousness leaping over the wall and running the traitor through once more, this time ensuring he never gained his feet ever again.

He was so engrossed in his own thoughts, he did not hear Warin settle against the wall not three feet to his left. Padric berated himself again for not paying attention.

Recovered from her stupor, Brynwen took careful steps around twigs and leaves to join the two knights at the red wall, settling between the two. "Why are they chopping down trees?" Her whisper tickled Padric's cheek.

Has she forgiven me? Not the time, he berated himself with a low grumble. "I had the same question."

"She can't make me do it. It isn't right." Shuffling something that sounded like an armload of wood, Aeron Drefan's whine was harsh. "Surely my father wouldn't—" An impatient pause as he seemed to listen to the Druid. "Of course not. But how can I do that when he will not trust me? Wood-bearer—bah! I am worth twenty of her. Nay, thirty!" The wood slammed onto the ground. "Look, if we are to get everything into the portal on time, we should be in on making the plans, not carrying them out like eager pages."

"What is a portal?" Warin whispered.

A portal like the one that had pulled Brynwen into the underworld? Whatever it was, it must lead to Janus. But why were Aeron and the Druid here with their henchmen, of all places? Unless... It dawned on him, and he grimaced. Aeron, the Druid, and Medea had been here the whole time. He frowned and leaned in closer, hoping to glean more relevant information.

"When we rule Olym—"

Silence took over. Not a sound, no speaking or chopping of any kind could be heard.

"Oh bilge water," Warin said lightly. "We have a problem."

"I know," Padric replied. "We should leave before—"

He smelled the huntsman's sweat before hearing his boot crack the twig. Padric launched to his hoofs, sword drawn as he whirled, and parried the man's overhead strike.

Warin grunted as two more assailants joined the fray. Brynwen held her dagger, ready to defend herself. In seconds, they were all fighting in earnest. Padric tried his best to stay between their adversaries and Brynwen. Although her skill with the weapon had improved in the last few months, he had no wish to leave her vulnerable.

Where did they come from? he wondered.

Padric's adversary had a time keeping up with all the springing about on his faun legs. He elbowed the man in the temple, and the huntsman crumpled. He rushed over to help Brynwen with her adversary, although she was doing all right on her own. For whatever reason, the man seemed more interested in taking her alive. A frown crossed Padric's face, not wishing to know for what purpose that might be.

As Brynwen's strength waned, Padric stepped in. He was in the middle of sparring when a loud shout filled the air.

"Halt or he dies!"

Everyone stopped and looked in the same direction. Aeron and the Shadow Druid stood next to the stream. The former knight had Gregorio by the throat, a knife pointing at his chest.

"Gregorio!" Brynwen cried.

Fear laced Gregorio's whole being as Aeron held him near, the immortal tutor's thin frame seeming like a stick against Aeron's muscles.

"We found the *Signore* here attempting to run for help. But we asked him to stay for a reunion."

"How could I refuse such a generous offer?" Gregorio's attempt at levity heartened Padric somewhat.

Padric gripped his sword handle until his knuckles turned white. "A reunion indeed. Had we known, we would have brought dessert." Concern for his friend bade Padric try to surmise a plan of rescue while they bantered, but he found no quick solution. Glancing to his left, he spotted a door leading outside the abbey walls which had not been there before. Or had it?

He dared to take a step forward.

"Ah, ah." Aeron touched the sword to Gregorio's chest.

Padric's lips pursed as he tried to keep calm. "What do you want, Aeron?"

The former knight's mouth raised from ear to ear, quite eager to shed some blood. "Drop your weapons, and we shall parlay."

Brynwen dropped hers immediately, as though it were a hot poker. On the other hand, Warin and Padric hesitated to do so, unwilling to relinquish their blades. Yet Gregorio's fate depended on it—if Aeron spoke the truth.

"How can we trust you?" Warin glared at the villains. "You, a traitor. And you...whatever you are. Hearsay is, your entire family is dishonored and has disowned you after your betrayal this summer. Pathetic." He shook his head in disgust.

"Would you care to test my honesty?" Once again, Aeron jabbed the sword at Gregorio's chest. This time, a trickle of blood poured out, staining his tunic.

Brynwen drew in a quick breath.

With the greatest reluctance, Padric and Warin threw their weapons on the ground.

"Good choice," the Druid's utterance grated in Padric's head, and, he assumed, the others' heads as well. *"Huntsmen, stand aside."*

The huntsmen obliged and hauled away their fallen comrade whom Warin had bested. As soon as they fell in line beside the Druid and Aeron, the Druid's arms raised, his thin, translucent hands emerging from the long gray sleeves. In one hand he held a vial filled with clear liquid. In a swift motion, he unstoppered the cork and tossed it in Brynwen's direction.

Padric barely had time to analyze what it meant as it soared through the air. He dove to catch it, but was too late. It smashed on the ground by his outstretched hands. From the oozing contents came a white mist that hissed as it rose. There was no time to run, as it grabbed a hold of Padric like a sticky bur, on his clothes, hair, face, hands, and mouth.

"Run," he tried to say, but his throat was thick with the stuff. Panic gripped him as he gasped for air. All he could do was wheeze and cough. Around him, Brynwen and Warin fell to their knees, coughing and choking.

"Padric! Brynwen! What have you done to them?" Gregorio asked in helpless distress.

The Druid shrugged. *"Oh, dear, that must have been the poison vial. Oops."*

As Padric's body began to seize from the poison, his head became too heavy to hold up. He blinked as Aeron shoved Gregorio away and stalked toward him but could not move. The traitor's black boots stopped less than an inch from his arm. With his boot, he shoved Padric over onto his back, then thrust his dagger in Padric's face. "I could have my vengeance now. Eh, de Clifton?" Instead of stabbing Padric in the face, he lowered the blade to his abdomen and poked it until Padric felt it prick his skin. "Or I can watch you bleed out."

The Druid made an impatient gesture as Aeron continued to push and twist. The pain in Padric's abdomen and lungs burned as he lay helpless. Out of the corner of his eye, Brynwen and Warin also struggled to breathe. Then Brynwen stilled.

No!

Gregorio cried out and rushed toward Aeron, but two of the huntsmen pulled him back, struggling and screaming.

Lord, he prayed, *where are you? Help us!*

At last, Padric's pain and aching lungs gave out, and, with Aeron's twisted face the last thing he saw, he knew no more.

CHAPTER 26

Talfryn kept his attention pinned on the haunted garden wall, sword at the ready and bow hooked onto his back, Eliva beside him. They were just about to embark on another quick round of sparring and archery, with Ulysses's and Miser's help as distractions in combat—Eliva's brilliantly dangerous idea—and were on their way to the garden. Miser shifted and complained that Talfryn had disturbed his sleep. "Sorry, your highness," Talfryn mumbled. Miser berated him some more, curled up, and in moments his breathing normalized into slumber. Talfryn sighed. *What a life.*

To his right, wings hidden with an enchantment, Ulysses's eyes sparked in amusement, yet Talfryn knew the creature was as alert as Rawlins on any given day. If he looked close enough, he could see the taut muscles in the stag's chest and neck, near the diamond-shaped red mark Circe had given him long ago. That mark represented the transformation from a human into a peryton which Circe had to preform to save his life after a teenaged Telegonus—Gregorio—had accidentally cut him with a poisoned spear. The tale had been recorded in Homer's *The Odyssey,* only Circe's part in saving him in this fashion had never made it into the books for some reason. *Not enough drama?*

Talfryn was pondering asking Ulysses if the mark ever bothered him, when his stomach grumbled.

Eliva's eyes rolled, her fair cheeks releasing a huff. "How are you hungry again? We ate not that long ago." She marched on the other side of Ulysses, bow nocked and ready for any enemy to encounter.

Talfryn did his best impression of his grandfather. "'Hunger never ends for a growing lad,' my grandfather always says. And, if you must know, he really does *always* say that. I don't think a day's gone by when he hasn't." Grandfather was also rather grumbly about it—especially when he had *two* growing lads to feed on a daily basis.

"No wonder your sister makes so much food. It's enough to feed an army."

"Aye. And not a bit of it goes to waste."

"Aye." Eliva smirked, then continued to scan the walls for possible threats.

Talfryn grinned from ear to ear, imagining what sumptuous meal Bryn was cooking up with the kitchen staff next. He felt kind of bad for Grandfather and Sam that they didn't have her to cook for them. Last time he and his sister had left on their adventure, they'd had Brynwen's assistant Gerda help with the cooking—after all, Bryn had shown her a thing or two—and they were so pleased with Gerda's new skills, they planned to do the same this time.

A cold prickle itched at his neck, followed by the chilling laugh that sent Talfryn's heart rate into a sprint. *You are too late,* came its familiar eerie chant. Tired of suppression, the prophecy battered him, reminding him of his urgent task.

> *...Upon wing-ed carriage at brightest moon.*
> *In facing the monster thou must attend*
> *Lest Olympus meets an early end.*

Then the beast's laugh beat down on him again and again.

"*Talfryn.*"

Opening his eyes, Talfryn found both Eliva and Ulysses looking at him; the former with an annoyed scowl, the latter with concern.

"Umm, hi." The chill having left, all the heat rushed back and flushed into his face and neck. *Great!* His hand raised to rub his still prickly neck. "What, uh, happened?" He was afraid to know, and wished to shrink into a tiny mushroom like the ones by the trees in the forest.

Eliva huffed again. "You suddenly stopped and wouldn't respond to anything, not even to Miser. I've been calling your name forever."

"Really, forever?"

"You are incorrigible."

He shrugged his shoulders. "I know. It's a gift."

The girl clenched her teeth and suppressed a scream. Her discomfort lightened some of Talfryn's shaky mood.

"What is wrong with you?"

"I told you, I'm hungry. Let's hurry with our sparring match." He was trying to come up with another excuse when he heard a commotion coming from the garden and a sort of whimper.

Talfryn, Eliva, and Ulysses all looked at each other. Talfryn and Eliva drew their weapons, but Ulysses's ears perked. He shook his head and his black eyes bore directly into Talfryn's, trying to tell him something. Talfryn concentrated, and in a flash, a rough image of a scrawny young man in a crumpled red cloak appeared in his mind. *Progress!* Then Ulysses bounded in the direction of the noise and the image was gone.

"Ulysses, wait," Eliva hissed. She reached out for the peryton, but he was gone.

Talfryn was already following. "It's only Gregorio. Come on."

"But...Bah." With a grunt, she followed them, arrow nocked.

Opening up the garden door, they found him. Sprawled on the ground, Gregorio had a small, bleeding gash in his chest, a thin trail of blood running down his tunic. A huge purple bruise grew on his cheek alongside some smaller ones. Besides more signs of bruising, his arms had two sets of welts each, likely from being held down while someone else beat on him without mercy.

Talfryn winced as he beheld his friend, and he landed on the rough ground beside him.

Gregorio coughed. "I'm so sorry. I'm so sorry. I couldn't."

Couldn't what? Trepidation filled his lungs. The cold prickle turned into ice on his skin.

"Gregorio! Who did this to you?" Talfryn asked.

Having no hands, Ulysses rubbed his chin on Gregorio's head with affection.

"Pater." Tears spilled from Gregorio's eyes as he regarded his father. "It was awful."

Bow drawn, Eliva ran into the covered part of the garden to search for enemies.

As gently as possible, Talfryn raised Gregorio's shoulders so he could sit him up, keeping his hand on his friend's back. "Don't speak. We'll get you back inside the abbey and have Bryn stitch you up."

"Nay, nay, you don't understand..." His head slumped forward.

"Gregorio? Oh, that's not good. Eliva! He needs help, now."

Eliva returned without any enemy heads on her pike, so that was a good sign. But her teeth did snag her lower lip in worry. "I saw tracks and signs of a struggle. Did he say anything?"

"Nothing intelligible. He needs medical attention."

In short order, they made it across the abbey grounds with Gregorio's arms wrapped around Eliva's and Talfryn's shoulders, Ulysses at the rear, looking for danger, until they came to the east stable. Thankfully, no more danger arose. Gregorio hadn't said another word during their short journey.

They found Nalini, Rawlins, and Kett in the east stable where the chariot was being built. Their heads all turned as the group entered. Talfryn's stomach churned when he didn't see Padric, Brynwen, or Warin with them, and the cold prickle on his neck returned. "We need help."

Nalini and Rawlins were the first to react. "What happened?" they asked at the same time.

"We don't know," Talfryn said.

"We just found him like this in the garden. Alone," Eliva finished.

Gregorio's trembling in Talfryn's embrace increased, and they placed him with care onto a horse blanket which Nalini unfurled on the ground. Ulysses knelt on the ground beside him, rubbing his son's head with his own furry one.

Tears streaked down Gregorio's face as the immortal hugged himself, looking much more youthful than his seventeen-year-old appearance. Whatever happened had really rattled him. Talfryn kept glancing at the door of the stable, expecting his sister and the knights to appear at any moment.

Rawlins's full attention was on Gregorio, as though he already knew the answer.

Talfryn gulped.

"They've been...taken..." Gregorio shuddered.

Eliva asked, "Who has been taken?"

The air seemed to cool ten degrees with only the sounds of Gregorio trying to control his emotions. At last, the tutor reached out and clutched Talfryn's arms. For all his scrawniness, the strength in his hands was impressive. "P-Padric, Warin, and Bryn...wen." His head drooped, and when he brought it up again, new tears filled the corners of his eyes. "I could not stop them."

Stunned at the news, Talfryn set his jaw, the prickling becoming worse. "How? They didn't leave the abbey walls, did they?"

Gregorio shook his head violently. "In the haunted garden. I was near. Medea's huntsmen...grabbed me. Aeron and Shadow Druid...have our friends."

Worried, Rawlins paced around the stable. "But how did Aeron and his cronies get inside?"

Arms shaking, Gregorio gave a weary nod. 'Aeron and Sh-Shadow Druid came through...hidden door to outside. Said will exchange the three for Kett."

"Me?" Kett stared at Gregorio as though he had misheard. "Why would they want me? I only came along because I helped break Padric out of jail and wanted to help."

"So, they do not need Talfryn and the prophecy after all," Nalini said, saving Talfryn the trouble. Her eyes narrowed. "If it is not to do with the prophecy, then why?"

Everyone looked at Kett as though he knew the answer. His pallor changed from deep brown to ashen gray in a flash, and he shrugged in confusion.

Guilt puffed up in Talfryn's stomach as he realized Medea had really been trying to take *Kett* the other day. Oddly enough, he felt put out that he wasn't important to Medea at all. *And now Brynwen and my friends are in danger for my ignorance.*

"If only those rats'd died in the Labyrinth," Rawlins grumbled. "I never should've let them out of my sight." He glared at Nalini, who glared back in defiance.

"Little good will it do now." Eliva sighed. "Aeron and his friends could have killed them after taking them away."

Talfryn stared at the dryad in disbelief. "Don't say that," he begged under his breath. He didn't know if she'd heard him, but her sour expression didn't change.

Luciliana grabbed Kett's arm as she would a prized possession. "We cannot give them Kett. But what can we do?"

"We've got to rescue them." Talfryn leaped to his feet. "They'd do the same for any of us, wouldn't they?"

"Aye," came the unanimous answer.

Nalini nodded and gripped her polearm in both hands. "Then let us prepare."

"Gladly," Rawlins said. He cracked his knuckles in anticipation.

CHAPTER 27

*T*he tickle in the back of Brynwen's throat was irritating. She tried to ignore it, but it refused to be ignored. Without warning, she found herself gasping for air.

Tearing open her eyes, Brynwen coughed and coughed. Between coughs, she wheezed in a breath, which caused her to cough harder. Eyes watering, the choking receded as her breathing became more natural. In another minute, she was herself again, the tickling sensation gone but for an unpleasant memory. She tried to raise her hands to wipe her tearing, stinging eyes, but a sharp pain in both wrists bade her stop. They felt stuck. And she couldn't open her eyes without further irritation.

Birdsong filled the air, and smoke wafted from a nearby fire.

"What the...why can't I move?" Blinking rapidly did nothing to help her see any clearer. Nor could she wipe her eyes on her shoulder. *Bother!*

"Don't bother, Miss Brynwen." From her left, Warin sounded tired and resigned. "I'm afraid we're each tied to a tree."

"A tree?" Despite what he said, she jiggled her arms in experimentation. Sure enough, her hands and arms—what parts hadn't fallen asleep—chafed against rough tree bark. *Great.*

"The stinging will dissipate in a minute or so."

Thankfully, the stinging had already lessened, along with the shock. She looked to her left, and spotted a blurry version of Warin, likewise tied to a large tree, about five feet away. Several feet away, she spied men loitering or doing heavens knew what through her impaired view. She suspected Medea, Aeron, and the Druid were close by. The very thought of being near them gave her shivers. As she continued to blink, her vision finally cleared enough to recognize the villains. But Padric was...where?

After a couple more blinks, she could see better.

Stretching her neck to the right, she spied him, and gasped. "Padric? What have they done to you?" His head lolled to the side, eyes closed and arms tied to his tree like hers and Warin's. He looked a frightful sight. A trail of blood dripped from his abdomen and from a split lip, and his clothes were dirtied with Aeron's friends' filthy boot marks. Blood amassed on his forehead and three dried trails converged down to his chin. If not for his chest rising and falling, she'd have thought him dead. Her heart bled for him. If only she could reach him.

Warin cleared his throat. "From what I saw before I blacked out from that cursed substance, Aeron stabbed and kicked him. Then he encouraged his friends to rough him up a bit, too. Rotten business."

"He needs medical attention." She bit her lip and sought Medea to beg release so she could tend to Padric.

"We all need a bit of medical attention."

Scowling, Brynwen shook her bonds, which only cut into her wrists all the more. "Sir Warin, this is no time for jest. Medea might be moved to listen to reason."

"The witch who killed her own family for jealousy? Not a chance. Besides, wouldn't she have had someone patch him up already?"

"Mayhap they were in a hurry?" Brynwen asked wearily.

He gave on her a skeptical look. One, she was sure, his subordinates appreciated.

"Well, have you got any better ideas?"

"At the moment? Nay." The knight's broad shoulders deflated. "I've been trying to break these deplorable bonds, but they won't budge.

They used quality leather on these. Blast." He banged the back of his head on the tree and winced from the impact.

The thundering roar of trees crashing against one another sounded on the other end of the camp. Brynwen whipped her head around and spotted several men dealing with fresh-cut logs like the ones she had heard them chopping earlier. They brought the wood over to something covered by a tan tarpaulin. It was box-shaped, about waist-height. One of the men stumbled and bumped into it, knocking part of the canvas aside. Brynwen gaped. She had seen one like it before belonging to Helius—a chariot. But where Helius's was gold, this one was red.

Quickly, the man shoved the tarp back over the chariot, peeking around, hoping no one else had noticed.

"Why do they have a chariot?" she mused.

Warin must have had good hearing, as he answered, "To ride in?" After a short chuckle, he cleared his throat. "It looks quite a bit like the one Kett's building. Whatever this one is for, they've kept it meticulously hidden under that tarp. Didn't Gregorio say Medea had a chariot back when she was doing evil things..."

"You are right. I can't believe it survived after all this time, though. It could be important, and we must tell the others about it. But how do we escape?"

"We will think of something."

"Think of something for what?" a smooth, feminine voice asked. A shadow fell over Brynwen's skirt, and she looked up into a pair of fierce blue eyes. They reminded her of Circe's sapphire irises.

Behind her stood Aeron and the Druid, both as unpleasant as ever. She didn't like the way the false knight looked at her, as though he wanted to gut her like a fish.

I'll not give him or any of them the satisfaction.

Then, as her chest constricted enough to burst, she prayed for quick guidance of speech, otherwise she feared she *would* be gutted like a fish.

"Something pleasant to pass the time," Sir Warin said.

Brynwen picked up on his line of thought. She relaxed her face and imagined herself smoothing the wrinkles from her skirt to calm her nerves. "Oh yes. This is all most comfortable." She leaned fully back against the rough tree bark and smiled up at the witch, despite the moths flying around in her stomach. Moving proved a mistake, as her arms twisted and the leather cut deeper into her wrists, but she hid her wince.

"Could sit like this all day, myself," Warin said like an aristocrat. "A mug of ale would round out this most exquisite visit nicely." He gave Medea a lazy grin and crossed a leg over the other to prove his point.

Medea smiled like a queen—hadn't Gregorio said she'd been a queen once?—and curtsied. "Yes. Well, now that you are comfortable, it is time to be off to our next encounter."

Brynwen spared a quick glance at Padric. "Where will that be, m'lady? Might I tend to Padric's wounds first?"

"A lovely little village on the Welsh border, called Alesbury. We hope to find something quite…useful there. Your Padric has survived this long without treatment, I am almost confident that he will survive the next leg of our journey. Come along." She waved Aeron, Drogo, and two more burly huntsmen forward. Drogo regarded Brynwen with a bearded smile filled with brown teeth.

It was worth a try, Brynwen thought miserably.

"With pleasure, m'lady." Drogo pulled a long dagger from the sheath at his belt. Its glint promised pain for her and pleasure for him. He stepped toward her, but Aeron barked an order at him. "She's mine, Drogo. Get de Clifton."

The scathing glare Drogo gave Aeron sent Brynwen's toes curling. She didn't want to get between either of these horrible men. She'd almost rather be mauled by a boar.

As Drogo stomped off to cut Padric's bonds loose, Aeron knelt beside her, his scent of beechwood and ash mixing with the leather holding her to the tree. His scowl was enough verbiage between the two of them for a lifetime of words.

This time, however, he didn't threaten her or Padric. He simply cut her bonds and rose, flicking the knife between his forefinger and thumb as he did so. "Get up."

It took Brynwen a full thirty seconds to get her feet under her without getting entangled in her skirts, her legs screaming all the while.

"Let's go." Aeron grabbed her tired arm and pulled up. She tripped and bumped into his chest. As though disgusted, Aeron shoved her out to arm's length.

Meanwhile, Padric groaned as Drogo cut his bonds. Miraculously, his eyelashes twitched and fluttered. Hope swelled in Brynwen's heart at his rousing.

Before her wobbly legs could attempt going to him, though, Aeron's roughly spun her around and tied her hands behind her back with the remaining leather. "Don't even think of escaping."

Too scared to answer, Brynwen merely shook her head. She made eye contact with Warin, who tried to look at peace as two burly huntsmen almost his size bound his hands in a leather strap, but she could detect the worry in his face all the same.

CHAPTER 28

*O*utside the village of Alesbury, Padric hugged the tall pole, leaning all his weight against the post as Drogo bound them with the leather strap. The brown leather had a purplish sheen, meaning it had been treated with some sort of magic. Likewise, two other huntsmen tied Warin and Brynwen against posts on either side of him. A few people came out of the village of Alesbury to observe the curious visitors, especially the grand lady in the dark blue cloak and flowing raven hair. Padric heard her assuage the villagers that these were hardened criminals who were on their way to justice.

Smirking, Drogo tugged hard on the leather, causing the bleeding welts on Padric's wrists to open up again. "Oh, would ya look at that. Yer blood's getting everywhere. Tut, tut."

"Alas that it is not yours instead," Padric replied through gritted teeth.

Surprisingly, Drogo's grin widened even further as he gave the shimmering leather another good tug. Padric's abdomen bumped up against the pole, and searing pain rent through his entire body. A grimace escaped his lips as he tried not to scream.

"Oh, sorry, did I hurt you, your knightship?" He made a mocking bow, chortling as he did so.

On his other side, a huntsman with white hair and a long gray beard was finishing with Warin's magical trussing up but seemed to be paying more attention to the nearby forest than the prisoner. His fingers trembled as he hurried to tie the knot.

True to form, Warin protested. "Ouch. My arms are too burly for this tiny post."

"Ye'll make do, I reckon. Now, quiet." The huntsman's lip twitched and he glanced over his shoulder once more.

His disquiet sent worrisome shivers down Padric's spine. *Is he frightened of Medea?* Padric set his mouth in a line and shared a look with Warin. The knight's expression mirrored his own.

"Are you expecting someone?" Padric asked as though conversing about the weather.

"It's…" the older man said.

"Hush up, Caldo. They'll find out soon enough. Can't wait to see the look on yer faces when it comes."

"Jeffrey, why aren't you done with that knot yet? Here, let me do it." Drogo shoved over the young man with shoulder-length brown hair tying Brynwen's hands to her designated pole.

Jeffrey folded his arms across his chest. "Hey, I had it." Padric thought he looked familiar, but he could not place him.

Brynwen flinched at Drogo's not-so-gentle handling of the leather strap.

"Didn't I teach you how to tie a knot properly?" Drogo grumbled. "This is a mess."

"I was only making sure she weren't too hurt, Drogo."

"Well, we can't have her escaping now, can we?" In quick movements, he finished securing Brynwen to the pole and, after giving them all a final once-over, stalked with his fellows into the village.

Counting to five until their enemies were out of earshot, Padric gazed at Brynwen. She looked a bit harried but blessedly not the worse for wear, except for her wrists and forearms. "Brynwen, are you well?"

Brynwen rewarded him with a smile that lit up his heartstrings. "Besides my lovely new bracelets?" She raised them a fraction of an inch and blanched. In spite of this, she gave a slight shrug. "It could be worse." Her gaze slid over Padric, and he knew he must look as bad as he felt.

To his other side, he heard Warin grumbling and cursing.

"It will not work, Warin. These leather straps are enchanted, I assume with a strengthening spell that not even Hercules could break through."

Huffing a breath, Warin paused for a second and glared at Padric. "Challenge accepted." Then he resumed his grunting and cursing and pulling. His biceps and eyes bulged as he pulled at the leather. It creaked with the strain but never stretched so much as a millimeter. Padric just rolled his eyes and returned his gaze to Brynwen. She raised her shoulders.

A commotion picked up in the village, and Padric felt a sudden foreboding. All the hairs on his arms stood on end. As the birds in the forest took that moment to scatter, Padric's stomach clenched as with a vise. Harbingers. *Run!* He realized that the nagging in his chest was in reality the "goat" that had been lying dormant within him. It had left him alone for some time, but its instant fear made it attempt to burst forth from his chest.

RUN! its shriek pierced his brain.

"It is coming," he ground out through clenched teeth.

Warin continued to try weakening his tether. "What is coming?"

"Death." Padric fell to his knees as the goat tried to kick its way out of his stomach in painful bursts. His hands turned into hoofs.

"Padric!" Brynwen cried.

"Keep it together, man," Warin ground out.

Clenching his teeth, Padric willed the goat to calm down in spite of his own fear.

As soon as it had begun, the clenching pain stopped. The hoofs reverted to hands. Released from it, Padric leaned against the pole, sweat beads forming on his forehead and neck. Fear still emanated from his "inner goat," but it no longer tried to exit.

Because it was too late.

Out of the forest ambled a great, gray creature. Three sharpened bones protruded from its large head like a deranged unicorn. It gazed with great intensity at the village, baring gleaming yellowed teeth. More bones protruded from its back and sides. A rusting hatchet was sticking out of its back where Talfryn had slung it not four months before.

Screams filled the village as people began to run out the other side. However, Medea and her cronies, Aeron included, drew their weapons to keep the townsfolk in the streets.

"What...what are they doing?" Padric barely heard Brynwen's trembling whisper above his pounding heart.

"It appears that the townsfolk are to be sacrificed," Padric answered. "No survivors."

Warin cursed under his breath. "But for what purpose?"

As the aeternae loped past the poles where Padric, Brynwen, and Warin were bound, it glared at each of them in turn with hungry red orifices. *You are next,* it promised.

The "goat" inside Padric roiled again.

"Welcome to the feast, aeternae," Medea announced. She raised her arms in invitation.

With a deep, menacing growl, the beast lunged at the nearest villager, a man in his late fifties who stood in front of his wife to protect her. Blood spilled from his chest and neck and he fell. His weeping wife was the second victim.

In horror, Padric watched the monster rip through the villagers of Alesbury. Medea joined it with a disturbing laugh—a twisted version of her aunt Circe's—as she alternated between slashing with two daggers and blowing a strange purple powder into peoples' faces. They would beat at their faces as it burned their eyes and skin, before Aeron or a huntsman cut them down.

Aeron seemed to love this murder way too much. Sometimes, he stopped and looked at Padric, blood spattered all over him, and gave the most wicked grin. Then he would continue.

Blood covered everything.

An uncontrollable shudder swept through Padric's entire body. "We must escape. Now."

Brynwen cried and prayed for the people losing their lives one by one. It broke another piece of him to watch her like this.

Warin and Padric worked with furious abandon at their magicked bonds. While he fruitlessly sawed at the impossible bindings, he could hear Medea's insane musical laughter in his head mixed with the monster's growls.

When it was over, and there were no villagers left to slaughter, they still had not gotten even the slightest bit free. Shaken with exhaustion, Padric spied the blood-splattered Medea, Druid, Aeron, and the aeternae making their way toward them. He swallowed, warily eying the way they held their bloody blades in the air with deranged smiles on their faces.

CHAPTER 29

*I*n record time, Talfryn, Eliva, and the others gathered their weapons and set off. Talfryn checked that he had his sword, hatchet, dagger, and another knife in his boot for good measure. Still not quite himself, Gregorio was set on Ulysses's winged back as they gathered the rest of the dryads and rushed out of the abbey. It had taken a bit of time, but Gregorio had finally calmed down enough to relay the rest of the information Aeron and the Druid had given him.

The Druid had splashed their friends with a substance that choked the life out of them. Gregorio had despaired that they were dead, but the Druid told him they were only unconscious and would be freed in exchange for the carpenter when the sun set the next day. The location for the exchange was near the Welsh border.

Following Gregorio's maps, they surmised the fastest route passed through a small village called Alesbury, and they would arrive by early morning.

All the rest of the day, the strange, cold prickling resumed on Talfryn's neck. It constantly nagged at him.

They'd run for hours when Talfryn couldn't stand it any longer. His head ached with the cold prickling, the wolficorn's laughter, and dizzying bouts of prophecy invading his mind, and he announced that they needed a break. Without taking Eliva or anyone else with him, he took off into the forest to be alone for few minutes.

"Don't go far," Rawlins gritted out.

"Won't." Talfryn dashed off before anyone else could protest. After about thirty yards, he halted and listened to the sounds. Not hearing anything but Miser's annoyance at having missed all the lovely nuts they'd passed an hour ago, he cleared his mind as Faunus had taught him.

"Faunus? Are you there?"

After several seconds of silence, Talfryn began to despair. But then the familiar voice came through. At first, it sounded strained, as though from a great distance.

"I am here, Talfryn."

"Thank goodness! You had me worried there. Are you all right?"

"As well as can be expected. I fear it is more difficult to communicate in this place than usual. Are you well? Has something happened? Is it Medea?"

Talfryn's heart threatened to burst. He wanted to tell Faunus everything that'd happened, that he was about to break, but it sounded like his grandsire was struggling to keep their communication open.

Talfryn nodded, forgetting the faun couldn't see him. "I hope to be soon. I just wanted to hear your voice and let you know we're coming. Stay strong."

"You as well. And Talfryn?"

Yes?

"Be prepared."

The link ended, and Talfryn felt empty again. He sagged against the tree, knees shaking. *Be prepared.* Isn't that what he'd been doing this whole time? Being prepared and scared out of his wits? Slowly losing his wits to the beast that lurked after him day and night?

"Talfryn."

Talfryn nearly jumped out of his boots as Rawlins materialized in front of him.

"Why d'you always do that?" Talfryn hoped the knight hadn't seen him panicking.

"It's time to continue on. There's a nearby village where we can get supplies and ask questions about this area."

"Right." Talfryn pushed off the tree. "How's Gregorio?"

The knight grunted. "Alive."

Talfryn nodded, not anywhere near self-assured. As he followed Rawlins, he felt impelled to pray. Things were escalating fast, and they'd need all the help they could get. He sent up a quick prayer, thanking the Lord that Gregorio and his friends were still alive, and asking for help.

🐌

BY THE TIME they neared the village of Alesbury a couple of hours later, Talfryn thought he might pass out from the headache the prophecy had given him. And at every turn, he saw the wolficorn's red eyes. Or its slow, swishing tail. Or the hatchet sticking out of the mottled gray fur of its back. Once he'd blink, it'd vanish. No one else saw a thing.

Miser worried about Talfryn. Only one time about a month before, had Talfryn told him about his encounter with the beast. At the time, the creature had just started really filling his dreams with death and destruction, and he wanted someone to tell it to. Brynwen was the last person he wanted to bother with it, although he was pretty sure she'd guessed that something was amiss with him by now.

Oh, Bryn. Please be safe. We're coming for you.

He looked over at Kett. They would do everything they could to keep him safe from Medea as well.

About fifty yards from Alesbury, everyone felt the change. Miser had been in the middle of a monologue about the best place to stash nuts when everything went silent. The air grew thick with a stifling sense of foreboding. All the birds and woodland creatures were either quiet or had fled. And the smell of death was everywhere.

The wolficorn appeared at the entrance of the village and licked its chops in welcome. The bone horns stuck out of his mottled gray fur in a most menacing fashion. *You should flee, little humans. While you still can.*

"Good idea," Talfryn muttered.

"What's a good idea?" Kett asked.

207

"Don't you see..." Talfryn blinked, and the wolficorn was gone. "Um, I think going around the village would be a good idea, don't you?"

Kett nodded slowly. "If I have my say, then yes."

Eliva gripped her bow. "If the aeternae is here, I say we should kill it."

"If only it were that easy," Talfryn grumbled. Like every day since his nightmares had begun, he tried to imagine Faunus's home, yet the quiet place from his dreams was wrong. The animals were gone, the grass was dying, the trickling creek had dried up. Without Faunus, it was just another nice-ish place, although he could see bits of rot and darkness creeping in from the edges the longer the god was away.

"Quiet. We need supplies, and that's final." Rawlins glared at each of them. "Be on your guard for threats."

Everyone was quiet after that and extra vigilant.

When they reached the village, not a word passed between the group except the odd gasp. Talfryn shuddered at the scene. People of all ages lay dead in the streets. Adults, youths, children, and even newborns. Blood splatter littered the bodies, ground, houses, and businesses alike. As gruesome as it was, Talfryn couldn't avert his eyes. His nightmares would only grow worse after this. And all the while, the wolficorn's deep, evil laugh followed him. Mocking him.

"Aeternae," came the whispers from the dryads.

Rawlins wiped his finger on a dripping splatter of blood on the outer wall of the first building. "It wasn't here long ago. This blood is fresh."

Slash marks covered the bodies, the blood still dripping on many, and giant paw prints were on everything. They found evidence of several people who had put up a fight, but ultimately, they'd all failed. Talfryn wondered if anyone had survived and escaped or if the monster'd hunted them down, too.

"Stay together," Rawlins said. "The creature or our enemies could still be here."

A tear slid down Talfryn's cheek at all the senseless death. Seeing a small child still holding her rag doll completely undid him, and he crumpled to his knees beside her. She reminded him so much of his twin sister when they were younger, with her auburn hair and the rag doll their grandmother had sewn together. Numb, he arranged the child's hair and ruined, striped dress so she could be presentable to...he didn't know to whom, but somehow it almost made the process bearable. Trying to help, Miser set an acorn on her chest, and Talfryn placed it in her palm. "Thanks, buddy," he mustered.

As he laid the tiny maid's hands on her chest, which weren't even the length of his palm, a shadow slid over him.

It's back!

Startled, he reached for his hatchet. But only a hand reached out and touched his shoulder, green as a leaf, and squeezed. Peering up, he saw Eliva, devastation and determination in her expression. No tears, but... *is that compassion?*

Talfryn was just picking himself up when he heard it. It was low at first, like a waking baby's cry. It grew louder and louder into a wail.

A baby.

Eliva's eyes grew round. "Could it be? A survivor?" Face set, she darted in the direction of the wail.

Still numb, Talfryn didn't register her running until she'd already passed him, dirt from the street flying in her wake. "Eliva, wait!" He sprinted after her, several paces behind at this point. Miser clung onto his tunic for dear life. "It could be a trap." It took extra time for him to dodge and leap over bodies, but Eliva didn't seem to have that issue.

Kett called after them, but they didn't pause.

When the crying led her to turn into a two-story house, Talfryn was over a block behind. "Eliva, wait!"

Heart pounding after the nightmarish obstacle course and fear for Eliva, he nearly crashed into the doorframe to stop his momentum. The painted wooden front door was three-quarters closed, blocking his view of more than a chair by the farthest wall. The crying had stopped, although no one had come out.

"Eliva?" he whispered. "Are you all right?"

Silence.

Sword braced for anything, Talfryn slowly pushed open the door the rest of the way with his free hand. His chest threatened to explode as the stupid door creaked. *I'm dead.* Taking a slow step inside, the door opened in far enough that he could see the smoldering fireplace, all that remained were the dying embers and a bit of smoke that missed the chimney.

Humming brought his attention to his left. There, Eliva crouched, a worn orange blanket in her arms. She rocked the orange bundle and hummed a lullaby-like tune Talfryn had never heard before. Whatever the tune, the lilting of her pretty voice slowed the racing of his heart to its normal pace.

"Eliva?"

Her humming stopped, leaving the room eerily silent as she pivoted on the bare pads of her green feet. A baby was wrapped in the blanket. Talfryn surmised he was about seven or eight months old. Some brown frizzy hair adorned his head, and tear stains ran down his cheeks. He looked at Talfryn with a mix of curiosity and doubt. Talfryn feared he'd scream again and bring the whole building crashing down on top of them.

"It's all right, little one." Eliva wiped the tears from the child's face with the corner of his blanket. "We are here to help you."

Talfryn cleared his throat. "Uh, yeah, that's right. Helpers of others, we are. We, uh…"

"Talfryn, Eliva?" their friends shouted.

He poked his head out the door, waved, then ducked inside again. "We should probably go."

Nodding, Eliva rose slowly. "We must find supplies."

"Supplies?" Talfryn asked. She looked at him like he had drool dripping from his mouth.

"You know, for the *baby*?"

"Ooooh, yeah. *Baby* supplies. You shoulda said." Face aflame, he made quick work of the cupboard, shelves, and baskets lining the walls. Miser found things hidden under the cupboard and hard to reach places. Cornelia and Idaise arrived to help. In the end, they'd stuffed two baskets filled with blankets, some food, a tall jar of fresh milk, some pins, and on Eliva's insistence, a pile of small but clean, stained blankets which were supposedly for his bottom—*gross, gross, gross!* Those he packed at the very bottom of the basket. *Ewww.*

He narrowed his eyes at the baby, now cuddling in Idaise's arms.

"You'd better be worth all this," he declared with hands on his hips. To which, the baby gurgled and happily gave Talfryn the raspberry.

❦

WHEN THEY REGROUPED, Nalini's brows knit together as she leaned over a fallen family. "Not all of these marks are from a creature's claws. Some are from weapons. See here. And here." She pointed to marks which were different from the slashes. "Medea has a curved blade which she took off of raiders in the Mediterranean long ago. This cut must be from that."

"Some of these are huntsmen's weapons. Pikes and daggers." Luciliana pointed to a few of them.

"I noticed that too," Rawlins confirmed. "This one is the thickness of Aeron's blade. I'd know it anywhere."

Aeron. Of course, the traitorous knight was more than capable of killing on a whim. "But why kill everyone in the village? Were they looking for something specific?"

Eliva frowned and looked at Talfryn and Nalini. "Or someone." She'd gotten the baby back, his bottom resting on her hip, his head covered by a thin blanket and leaning against her shoulder so he wouldn't have to see all the death surrounding them. "What if Medea and the aeternae are working together?"

"I hadn't thought of that." Talfryn fidgeted with his hatchet. "They've been near each other this entire time, so that could definitely be the case. It could also be a warning that if we don't comply, they'll kill again." And he knew who'd be the targets.

Talfryn mulled all of this over as they continued their supply search. The sun was setting in earnest when they finished checking all the houses and businesses for survivors, but found none. Sadly, they didn't have time to bury the dead as they still needed to rescue their friends in a few hours.

As Talfryn filled his bag with supplies, such as rope and an extra tinder box, he slid his hand along his hatchet blade. "I feel bad about raiding their stores. Can we leave some money?'

"For who?" Kett asked. "There's no one left to care."

"Aye, you're right," Talfryn's heart crumpled. *But I'll care.*

"Talfryn, you should look at this." Nalini approached, carrying a short dark rope in her hand. But when she got closer, he realized with horror that it wasn't rope.

It was a bloody braid.

"B...Bryn?" His breath hitched. Snatching the braid from her, he studied every inch of it. The last eight inches of her long braid were shorn off with a sharp blade. It was the same auburn color, the same blue ribbon which had held it together the last time he'd seen her—but splattered with blood. His breaths grew ragged, not daring to imagine what had happened to her. "It's hers." He looked up in terror. "Is she—"

Nalini placed her hands on Talfryn's arms. "Nay, Brynwen is not here, nor are the others."

Talfryn's entire body shook.

"Where did you find it?"

"It was nailed to a door with this note."

Talfryn hadn't noticed the bit of paper before, his full attention on his sister's braid.

"What does it say?" Eliva frowned as she gazed at the shorn braid.

Eyebrows furrowed, Nalini continued. "You are not going to like it."

"What is it? Tell me," Talfryn begged.

"We can only choose one to save."

CHAPTER 30

The following morning, it was hard for Eliva not to notice how terrible Talfryn looked, with dark bags under his eyes, rumpled clothes and disheveled hair. After finding his sister's blood-spattered braid in the village, he closed in on himself. No more smiles or jokes. It was so unlike him, she didn't know what to do. He stared into the fire, barely eating anything. When at last Rawlins made him go to bed, he would only toss and turn, scream at nightmares, and wake up in cold sweats.

Now she walked beside Talfryn, each of them carrying the supplies from the child's home while Luciliana plucked the baby from Idaise's arms. Talfryn walked as one in a trance.

Eliva hadn't had a chance to hold the baby again since finding him in the abandoned home, as all the other dryads were busy coddling and cuddling him. She sighed, recalling the lullaby her mother had sung to her when she was little, and to her little sister Thimble after she was born.

"We should name him Beningus," Luciliana said. "He will be kind." Tickling the little lad's chin, his two-toothed mouth opened into a wide giggle.

"I think he should be called Zephyrus," Cornelia stated.

Luciliana said over her shoulder, "Nicolaus."

Nalini nodded. "Better yet, Nicomedas."

"Amphion. He should be Amphion," insisted Idaise.

Asinia shook her head dismissively. "Those names are all right, but I think he should have a strong name: Emidius. He will be a great demigod, mark my words."

Eliva scrunched her nose at all of those names. They would never do.

Talfryn must have snapped out of his trance to notice her expression, as he nudged her, and asked, "What d'you think he should be called?"

Alarmed at his touch, she shimmied away an extra foot from him. *Rule number one.* "Oh, I don't know…"

"You obviously don't like the other names. What would *you* name him?" His voice was soft. Thoughtful.

"I would choose Timotheus. After my…" She swallowed, having almost said too much. "Someone I once knew."

"Timotheus is a splendid name," Cornelia stated.

Luciliana nodded. "I like the way it sounds. Timotheus."

"Timothy or Timmy for short." Talfryn's approving grin made Eliva look away. How was she supposed to ignore him when he kept being so…so…annoyingly handsome and congenial? Steps one and two of becoming part of Diana's Huntresses had already slipped from her grasp. *Never speak to or touch a man outside of your family members.* Perhaps, though, she could still make it up to the goddess by killing the aeternae. That was her only option left, now. And she begrudgingly believed that with Talfryn's help, she could accomplish that task—as long as he didn't end up getting them all killed first.

WHEN THEY STOPPED for the afternoon meal, Talfryn found Gregorio by the cook fire, finishing up preparation for the first meal of the day. His left eye was swollen and black, and the rest of the bruises on his face looked even worse than the day before. "Good morning, Talfryn."

Handing Talfryn his meal of oatcakes and fresh fruit from the massacred village of Alesbury, the immortal tutor had a ready smile and sounded chipper, but Talfryn could tell he faked it for his sake.

"Good morning, Gregorio. Nice weather." Talfryn also pasted on a smile, which felt like it stretched out his whole face.

"That it is."

Talfryn nodded and pivoted to leave before they began talking about something awkward. Like his missing sister and best friend.

Seeking seclusion, he wandered away with Miser on his shoulder, but still within hearing distance of camp. Leaning against a giant ash tree, he shimmied down the bark to eat his oatcakes, the recipe of which Brynwen had taught Gregorio on their Labyrinth adventure in the summer. Thoughts of his sister made his throat parched, causing the oatcake to taste like wood shavings, which made his throat even more parched. Miser, however, was not so stingy in his appraisal of Gregorio's culinary masterpiece, and polished off whatever Talfryn didn't eat. Honestly, how the little rodent hadn't gained fifty pounds since leaving the marshes of Yorkshire, he'd never know.

Finishing up, he brushed the crumbs from his tunic and got to his feet in search of the nearby spring. He was just submerging his hands into the cool, clear water when he heard singing.

A different tune from yesterday, yet another one he'd never heard before. The melody brought on thoughts of sunshine and flowers and tall grass tickling his knees.

Without acknowledging it, he'd somehow gotten to his feet and they led him up the stream as though in a dream. As he walked, everything seemed brighter, more defined. The fall flowers were more pink and purple, the grass more green, the yellow and red foliage above more lavish, the water ever clear. A gorgeous maiden with red hair and alabaster skin sat near the stream, eyes closed, her face raised toward the sun shining through an opening in the forested canopy, welcoming its warming rays. *Is she a friend of Faunus's? Has he returned?*

The song stopped, and so did his feet. Everything around him seemed to wilt: the sun hid behind a great gray cloud, the colors of the flowers and grass resumed their muted autumn hues, and the water trickled as though hollow. With it, his content feeling vanished.

There, he found Eliva. In her natural green skin and dryad dress, she was sitting near the stream, holding baby Timotheus in one arm while feeding him a small piece of oatcake with the other. Watching their interaction made Talfryn's heart swell with warmth.

Talfryn blinked, feeling like he'd just woken up from a long nap. Hadn't that happened before?

Eliva stared at him as though he'd lost his mind. "What are you doing here?" she asked. Having lost her concentration on holding the oatcake, it bounced out of Timotheus's mouth and he gurgled.

"Umm. Dunno. I was just..." He licked his lips. "Taking a walk?" *Was I? I was, wasn't I?* Honestly, he couldn't remember *what* he'd been doing.

"Apparently, you have been eating too." She pointed at his tunic.

Sure enough, some crumbs from his meal stuck to his tunic. He and Miser brushed them off with ease, then he shrugged. "Sometimes I eat and walk. At the same time. I know, I know, it's a challenging feat, but I've learned to master it." And it came to him that he'd been eating Gregorio's oatcakes.

The green maiden set her mouth in a thin line and popped more oatcake into Timotheus's mouth. He chewed happily, wet crumbs accumulating on his little chin. "Do you wish to feed him?"

"Who?"

Without moving her head, Eliva's eyes rolled up to look at him in the most unnerving way. "Timotheus. The *baby*."

"Ooooh, feed the *baby*. Nah, I'd probably manage to break the food." *Probably break the baby, too.*

"Mayhap you would be better suited to changing him. He is beginning to reek." She leaned toward Timotheus's belly and scrunched her nose in displeasure. "Yes, he is definitely reeking something awful."

"Why does he need to change?" he asked innocently. "I think he's great just the way he is."

Eliva rolled her eyes. "*This* needs changing." She patted the baby's bottom, indicating the once-white cloth wrapped around it. That was exactly what Talfryn was afraid she was referring to...

"You are definitely selling me on the changing of the stinky baby job. Oh, wait, I think I hear Gregorio calling to me. I'd better go see what he wants." Talfryn turned to hurry away.

"Funny, I do not hear him, and I have excellent hearing."

"Oh, no?" Talfryn stuck a finger in his ear. "Could'a been a cricket calling me, then. Right, Miser?"

Miser's eyes rolled at the utter lie. Then the squirrel chided him and said he'd need a better lie next time. Like that he needed to go eat some more of Gregorio's delicious food.

"Well, since it was just a cricket, you can help change out Timotheus's most smelly swaddling cloth. After all, you did help find him and know exactly where everything is in the basket."

Timotheus finished eating the oatcake and squirmed in delight. From beside her, she lugged the huge basket which Talfryn had somehow missed seeing earlier. He took it from her.

"Oh, goody, the basket of baby items. So glad you didn't leave it behind."

"Go on, I must wipe off Timotheus's messy little face. Yes it is very, very messy," she said to the baby in the same silly voice he'd heard many mothers, sisters, and aunts use on infants.

Talfryn rummaged through the pile of blankets until he reached the bottom, where he'd strategically placed the stained cloths used for this purpose. He handed three to Eliva.

She shoved them back, dropping them into his hand. "*You* are changing him, Talfryn. Not me."

"But, but, we *both* found the baby. Remember?"

"I changed him earlier. It is now your turn."

Talfryn was about to argue more, but Eliva's stoic bearing would not budge. He grunted in exasperation. What was it with this dryad? All of the other ones were a lot less bossy. "Fine. How do I do this changing of the baby thing?"

A triumphant smile swept up Eliva's face before dropping back to a near scowl again. "First, you must remove the old cloth."

Talfryn reached for the baby's waist and untucked the corner. Then he drew down the cloth and his eyes began to water. Gagging, he slapped his hand over his nose and mouth. "That's disgusting. What did this little guy eat?"

A chortle escaped Eliva's lips. Then a full-on laugh. Her laughter made Talfryn feel like laughing. Until he gagged again. After a couple of seconds, she also gagged and raised a corner of her long brown and green skirt over her face.

They both spent a few heartbeats trying to recover.

Holding his breath, he removed the offending dirty cloth, wadded it up, and chucked it far away. A group of ducks squawked and yelled at him, calling him names like "short-feathered" and "lazy-flippered" that probably only a duck would find offensive.

Talfryn and Eliva both sucked in a glorious breath of fresh air.

"You know you have to clean that cloth too."

"It's not going anywhere." *Unfortunately!*

Quirking an eyebrow, she handed him a small cloth dipped in the fresh water and explained how to use it to wipe Timotheus's bottom.

"Do you fear for your sister?" Eliva asked.

Hand faltering, Talfryn's mouth became dry. "Yes. Aeron's got a vendetta against her and Padric. All of us, I guess. He's tried to kill us multiple times since May."

"But she is strong. Resilient. She would not be on this adventure if she were not."

"You are right. She's not one to be left behind."

"I believe she will be all right, as will the others."

"Thank you," Talfryn said, and meant it.

As he was scrubbing Timmy's bottom, he scrunched his nose and stared the gurgling baby down. "You are one stinky baby, Timmy, you know that? Yes, you are," he repeated Eliva's silly tone from earlier.

A snort came from his left. Glancing over, he saw Eliva covering her mouth again, this time trying not to laugh. He caught the smile as she released her hand, then cleared her throat to resume her serious expression.

Taking up a clean cloth, he wiped the baby's bottom dry. "She should do that more often, don't you agree, Timmy?"

"Do what more?" Eliva drew back.

He took the baby's hands to make them dance, continuing to talk to him as though Eliva weren't there. Timotheus beamed. "Smile. It suits you."

Eliva lowered her head, her red braids falling over her shoulder.

"Why don't you think she smiles very much?" he asked the baby when Eliva ducked her head even further, obviously feigning searching for something in the basket.

When the nymph finally looked up again, she'd pursed her lips. Huffing out a breath, she picked up the clean cloth and crumpled it up, unfolded it and smoothed it out on her leg, crumpled it up. Shrugged. "There is not much to smile about."

"Nay? Why not? I find there's lots to smile about." He placed the cloth like a diamond as she'd indicated and began folding it around the baby's bottom. Timotheus, thinking it a game, wiggled his legs all about while Talfryn tried to hold the cloth steady. *This is a lot of work!*

"Like what?"

"Well, like this little fella here." He tickled beneath his chin, and the boy giggled. Distracted, Talfryn hurried and folded up the cloth over his legs and tucked the corner in so it was snug. "A successful changing." He held up the little boy under the arm pits and looked at his handiwork. "A little lopsided, but it's not falling off, right?" He gave her a big grin.

The corner of Eliva's lip slid up just a tad.

Success! Maybe he could get past that stony exterior after all. Encouraged, he went on. "And, there's hunting. I think I saw you *almost* smile once. And during target practice."

Her lip twitched higher into a smirk.

"When I bested you."

Her bottom lip dropped open. "Nay, sir! I bested *you*, remember? You only got two arrows into the target, and I got at least three more than that." She folded her arms over her chest in challenge."

"I remember it differently. But you see, Timotheus, there's a bit of a smile growing right there." Without thinking, he raised his hand to poke the corner of Eliva's lips.

She drew away in alarm.

Stopping his hand in mid-air, he pulled it back. "Sorry. I, uh, where were we? Oh, your singing voice. It's so soothing. I—"

"I-I must go. Timotheus needs his nap by the fire." Eliva began clearing up the things.

Why'd I have to say that? I went too far. Flustered at his stupidity at saying the wrong thing, Talfryn tried to think of something to get her to change her mind. "But, doesn't Timotheus need a snack or something?" *Think, think!* "Eliva, I'm sorry. I won't do it again." *Whatever it was I've done.*

Timotheus, sensing disharmony, began to whimper. Huge tears formed in his eyes. *Oh, no.* Talfryn remembered the inhuman wail the little tyke had belted out in Alesbury, so he picked him up and bounced him on his leg. No luck. It just got worse. "Don't cry, Timmy. It's all right."

Having packed everything into the basket, Eliva hoisted it into one hand, took Timotheus from Talfryn, and settled him on her hip.

"At least let me help." Talfryn shot to his feet and reached for the basket. However, Eliva was swinging it around, and he missed, instead grabbing a hold of her wrist and the copper bangle surrounding it.

Fear sparked in her eyes. "Let go." She dropped the basket and yanked, but Talfryn was so taken aback by her reaction, he didn't know what to do. The bangle came off in his hand.

Her skin tone changed from green to fair and pink with freckles.

Surprised, Talfryn gaped first at her, then the bangle, then back to her. She wasn't wearing her amulet necklace that Nalini had made. "What the..."

Panic filled Eliva's expression, and her breathing deepened. "Please... give it back," she begged, holding out her hand.

Coming to his senses, Talfryn replaced it over her hand. The bangle slid into place, and she was green with gray-blue eyes again.

"Eliva? What just happened?"

But the maiden was already backing away in fear. "You can't tell anyone." Timotheus put on a full wail as Eliva spun around, skirts of browns and greens twirling around her ankles, and sped away.

"Eliva, wait!"

But she was already gone. All that was left was the spilled basket of baby supplies, her human-persona amulet lying uselessly on the ground, and a forested acre full of utter confusion.

§

AFTER WASHING his hands and righting the basket and its contents, Talfryn headed straight for camp, Miser chattering about how strange Eliva's behavior was and that female squirrels were just as confusing as human and dryad females. When he arrived at the camp, Talfryn was alarmed to find everyone running around and getting their weapons and gear together. But there was no sign of Eliva.

Gregorio waved him over. "Talfryn, over here." He held the baby in his arms.

If Timotheus was here, where was Eliva?

"Talfryn, there you are." Nalini was in the process of winding a long, thin blanket around Gregorio and Timotheus.

"What's going on? Where's Eliva?"

"Ulysses returned," she said. "He has found where Medea is holding our friends." She tied the ends off and tucked them into the underside of the blanket. The result was a seamless-looking garment holding Timotheus against Gregorio's thin form, giving him two free hands. It was ingenious. Nalini picked up her pike and other weapons.

"He has?" Talfryn asked in excitement as he checked his own weapons.

"We'll leave presently." The disembodied voice of Rawlins emerged next to Talfryn.

"You're way too excited about using your abilities, you know that," Talfryn said, trying to slow down his speeding heart. Most of his weapons were already on his person, but he stuck another dagger into his boot just in case.

"Did Ulysses say how they are?" He was eager to save his sister and friends.

The peryton loped forward and nodded at Talfryn, equally excited.

Talfryn scratched Padric's many-great grandfather behind the ears where he liked it best. "Where did you find them, Ulysses?"

Talfryn tried to concentrate on the winged stag's thoughts, but only a jumbled mass and a splitting headache came forth.

"Ulysses says they are east of Chirk Castle, only a few miles southeast of here." Gregorio adjusted the blanket. Timotheus seemed to enjoy it, especially when trying to stuff a wooden toy into his mouth.

"Where's Eliva?"

"Dunno." Rawlins fixed his arm guards. "She dropped the baby off with Nalini and sped off. Nalini's not happy."

Talfryn tapped his sword hilt. He didn't understand what the whole thing with her bangle and skin color change was about. Without thinking, his hand slid into his pocket to clutch her amulet necklace. *Why did she run away?*

Rawlins was restless to go, so Talfryn quickly secured his bedroll to his pack and hoisted it onto his back. They all rolled up their blankets every morning in case of the need for quick moving. Now he was glad he'd done it. He noticed Eliva's things hadn't been touched. Her green bag and blanket were neatly rolled up by a yew tree.

"Should I bring Eliva's things?"

"Leave them." Nalini's furrowed eyebrows left no room for question. "If she wants to follow, she will." With that, she moved east with the others.

Ulysses watched this exchange, his eyes sad.

The wolficorn's laugh penetrated Talfryn's thoughts. *"Soon, we shall meet again. Very soon."* His leg began to throb. *Go away.*

Talfryn cast one last glance at Eliva's belongings, shrugged his pack into a better position, and jogged up to his furry, winged friend. "Come on, Ulysses. I'm eager so see our friends back safe. How far is this castle?" Anything to distract himself from the persistent presence of the wolficorn breathing down his neck.

CHAPTER 31

By midday, Brynwen was tired of being tied up. Tired of replaying all the death Medea and her group had dealt to the poor, unsuspecting village of Alesbury in her mind. And tired of feeling naked without her braid. It felt like they had shaved her head, even though only about a third of her hair was in that shorn off braid. Aeron, of all people, had accomplished the task with delight, then nailed it to the dead herbalist's home. He knew that when Talfryn saw it, he would be devastated. She prayed he wouldn't worry for her too much.

Medea had been in a sour mood since leaving Alesbury. She apparently hadn't found whatever she'd had the village murdered and ransacked for.

Tired of contemplating her own worries, Brynwen cast her gaze on Padric. The wound on his abdomen bled again from the brisk walk, but he hadn't complained of the pain it caused him. If she didn't treat it in time, it would fester and become infected. Even though her remedies were very good, she wasn't God, so she prayed that she could help him in time, whenever she could retrieve her satchel filled with healing herbs and salves from the huntsmen.

Warin scoffed. "Don't you dare pass out, de Clifton, for I don't care to carry you to our next location again."

"Oh, come now, Warin, you don't care to take on a little bit of extra weight?"

"Only if it be the fair kind, then mayhap." His intense gaze swept to Brynwen, who felt heat climbing her cheeks. Drat the flatterer!

"Am I not fair enough for you?" Padric batted his eyes.

Warin pursed his lips. "I think those scruffy whiskers would scare off any maid."

"And what of your scraggly mane, man?"

"Lads!" Brynwen burst out, still keeping her voice low. "As much as I love your witty banter, is now really the time to decide who is more fair or scruffy?" *Why must they always act like they're five?*

"What else is there to do but while away the time, Miss Brynwen?" Warin asked sweetly.

"Exactly." Padric grinned. At the same time, his eyes scanned their surroundings. "It appears we are remaining here for a time. Look."

"What is it?" Brynwen asked, checking where Padric looked.

A nod from Warin. "They are setting up a perimeter. This must be where the exchange is to take place."

"Will they actually free us, do you think? And what will they do with Kett when he comes?" The poor lad didn't deserve the treatment he was likely to get with this band of murderers.

Padric clenched his jaw. "We can never know until it is done. But they have not outright killed us, so that is a tick in our favor. However, I would hate for Kett to be trapped with these killers. I pray our friends have a plan."

Thinking desperately for a mode of escape, Brynwen's gaze roved over the camp and rested on Aeron, who was again arguing with Medea, although she couldn't make out their words. The former knight glanced their way, then back again to argue some more. Thinking the matter resolved, the witch shoved him out of the way.

"He's not going to like that," Brynwen commented.

"Nay," both Padric and Warin agreed.

Seething, Aeron glared at the witch's retreating form as though he wished to strangle her—or worse.

Padric wrinkled his nose. "I wonder…"

"Padric?" Brynwen asked.

Warin, too, noted Padric's thoughtful expression. "What are you thinking?"

Padric tugged on the magic leather straps against his raw wrists. "A strategy of sorts."

ARMS TIED behind his back but this time blessedly not *to* a tree, but merely resting against a beech tree, Padric could find no solution to rid himself of the magic leather bonds. Because of them, he could not turn into a goat or faun to release himself. After Alesbury, Medea had strengthened each of their leather bonds so their "foolish attempts" to escape would do no good. For the second time in a week, he felt as Saint Paul, held in prison. But in this case, he could not write a letter to his protégé—having neither paper nor quill for one, and no free hands with which to write for the other. But, after spending so much time with Brother Howell and the monks in the abbey, he took a note from their daily lives. He bowed his head and prayed. For the poor souls who had lost their lives in Alesbury. For his friends. For Brynwen and Warin. That they could stop Janus and Medea from their wicked plans. The kidnapped gods. And, if worse came to worst, for the people who would suffer under Janus's grand scheme afterward.

When he was finished, he looked up to find Brynwen's head bowed, either dozing or praying; he was unsure which. His heart ached at seeing her uneven hair, the shorter parts from the shorn-off braid falling in uneven strands over her longer, untouched hair. After Aeron had sliced the braid off, her spirits had fallen. For a bit, she couldn't look at him, as though embarrassed at her appearance. Did she not know that she was still beautiful, both inside and out? She could have no hair atop her head and he would see her beauty no less. Oh, how he loathed Aeron even more, for frightening her with his knife as well as murdering all those innocent villagers.

Warin huffed, his face turning redder and redder. His biceps bulged, the leather creaking against his Herculean might, to no avail. Even he, descendent of Helius and Jupiter, could not break the enchanted leather.

"No one can break it," Padric muttered, disheartened.

Brynwen's head came up. "What did you say?"

"No one can break..." An idea came to him as an epiphany. "No one can break it," he repeated.

"No one can break what?"

Looking around, Padric saw all of Medea's henchmen doing their own things around camp. The guards were far enough away they could not hear him unless they had unnatural hearing.

He lowered his voice further. "What if we do not try to break the leather, but rather use it to our advantage?"

"How would that work?" Warin asked, finally allowing his arms to rest. He and Brynwen exchanged confused glances, until they turned their gazes back on Padric's determined face.

"I did it once before. I had no idea what I was doing then and am unsure if it will work again." This time, he had the amulet of obsidian ring in his possession hidden in the compartment Kett had crafted for him in the heel of his boot. It had protected him against Janus's plans the first time. Could it help again? Brynwen gave a slight nod of understanding, but Warin looked skeptical. "Just keep trying to break your bonds, Warin. Act like nothing has changed."

"They might break me first," he replied with disgust. "Here goes." Once again, his muscles bulged.

Padric bowed his head again as though in prayer, but this time, he pulled his memories of that first encounter with Circe to mind, when she had bound him, Rawlins, and other knights in a magical frozen state for several minutes. In addition, he pictured the amulet. He slowed his breathing and mind.

The light hum of the amulet of obsidian thrummed in his chest, like it was a living thing breathing in his boot. The noise it emitted was so faint, he had not noticed it much before now. If this worked, he would be in great debt to Gregorio's wisdom in bringing it along. *But how can I use it?*

"*Why not try asking me?*" a soft male voice said in his mind.

Taken aback, Padric held his breath. He peered all around but saw nothing.

Amulet?

"Yes, yes, it is I, known to you mortals as the 'amulet of obsidian.' A very mundane name."

Amused, Padric decided to play along. *Is there another name you go by?*

"Clarence. Or Charles. Nay, I am certain it is Clarence."

Clarence, then. Why have you not spoken before now?

"You never asked for my help before, silly mortal. The last time, I deduced that if I did not help you, we would both be destroyed, and that would have done neither of us any good."

Will you help me, Clarence? Please?

"I will consider it. What is it you need help with, young mortal?"

Padric was getting tired of being called "mortal." *Might you release Brynwen's bonds? They are impossible to break, so I had hoped there was a way to untie them with your powers.*

"The power of Medea flows nearby. Deplorable woman. Yes, I will help you, young mortal."

Padric.

"Mortal Padric."

Somehow, that seemed even worse than just "mortal." *Thank you.*

"Bryn," Padric whispered aloud. "Can you show me your hands?"

She dropped the slightest of nods. Without looking too conspicuous, Brynwen yawned and shifted in a way that made her appear to be finding a more comfortable position against her tree, baring her bound hands to him.

"Observe," Clarence said.

Warmth emanated in Padric's foot, extending through his wounded abdomen to bloom in his chest. It was a strange sensation, like going through an invisible magical veil.

Taking a deep breath, Padric observed the knot binding the leather around Brynwen's wrists. To either side of her hands, two transparent hands appeared, a right and a left, with long, thin fingers. The fingers wriggled, then plucked at the knot as though they were real fingers.

Brynwen gasped in surprise.

Sweat poured down Padric's face as though it were he expending the effort to use the magic while Clarence hummed a little tune. He continued to work it. To Padric's great surprise, a small bit of leather pulled out. It worked!

Clarence, why are you using my energy?

"Do you want this knot untied or not?"

Padric considered telling it not to, but begrudgingly let it pass. They needed to escape and this was the only option they had.

However successful Clarence was, the people were stirring in the camp. Medea was readying to go. *Time to hurry, Clarence.*

Not commenting, Clarence's transparent hands continued to work at the leather. Since the first bit had already released, the rest of the strap came apart more easily until it was free. Brynwen could pull it out the rest of the way from there.

Allowing the imaginary hands to dissipate into the ether, Clarence lessened the warmth in Padric's chest until it was gone. He released a long, grateful breath. It had taken much effort, and he was not looking forward to Clarence untying two more. With the camp getting ready to move, it was too risky to try speaking to Warin. The knight studied Padric with some interest, as though he knew he had a scheme brewing.

Steeling himself, Padric asked Clarence to try untying his own bonds. Clarence brought back the imaginary hands and had just begun to pluck at the knot, loosening it only a tad, when Padric heard boots approach.

His eyes shot open, some sweat stinging his eyes, and he frowned. "Well, Aeron, you do not seem as happy to be rid of us as I would have thought."

"Believe me, my ideas and Medea's ideas are very different."

"I bet." And yet, if not for the exchange, Padric knew Medea would have no qualms in joyfully ridding the world of all three of her captives in horrible ways.

Aeron gestured to the prisoners. "On your feet, then."

Brynwen gave Padric and Warin a worried glance.

Using the tree for support, the prisoners shimmied to their feet. The three huntsman guards each grabbed one of their arms to guide them to the next stage of their exchange.

Despite the guards, Padric felt hyper aware that at any moment, he could end up with a knife in his back, courtesy of Aeron Drefan.

THE CLOSER THEY drew to the meeting place, the more jittery Talfryn's nerves became. Worse, Eliva hadn't caught up to them. He worried something bad had happened to her. He envisioned Eliva sitting by the spring, singing, when the wolficorn pounced on her, tearing her to pieces.

Talfryn jolted into alertness. *It's just a day-mare. Nothing more.*

Except the wolficorn really *was* in the vicinity, and he wasn't just raving mad.

"I am coming for you, Talfryn. Fear not, it will be soon now," came the rough voice in his head.

Talfryn wasn't sure if that was his imagination or not. Did it matter? The beast would catch up to him sooner or later.

Again, Talfryn called out to Faunus, but the god of animals didn't respond. What had Janus done to him? And to the other gods?

As they traveled, Miser gave a suggestion to Talfryn about gaining further help from the squirrels. He couldn't see why they'd want to help them. But Miser just kept harping on about it, and reminded Talfryn that they'd helped him before, and besides, they were also friends of Faunus. They'd been quite upset when the huntsmen and lady in blue had dragged the faun off so fast. Having other worries weighing him down, Talfryn shrugged off Miser's idea.

He didn't see how it might help their predicament, that they could only choose one person to save, and would still lose Kett in the process.

When they were about a mile out, Ulysses flew reconnaissance. He returned and messaged through Gregorio and Nalini that they were in the agreed-upon place, but something was off about it. There weren't as many men in the camp as there were yesterday.

Nalini looked grim. "The aeternae was not with them, either. We must assume it is nearby."

Talfryn would definitely assume that.

Rawlins clenched his hands on his daggers until the leather creaked under the strain. "It's another trap. Be wary, and stick to the plan."

Everyone nodded at the gravity of the situation.

Except that Talfryn didn't want to acknowledge the gravity of the situation. "I've got an idea," he said. All eyes drew to him. "Actually, it's Miser's idea. It's either brilliant or harebrained, I don't know which."

"Spill it," Rawlins said.

Talfryn explained the harebrained plan, and for once, Rawlins didn't scowl, but looked almost impressed. *Almost* being the operative word. After a few minutes of argument and logistics, the final plan was agreed upon.

When they were a quarter mile from the meeting place, Talfryn's nerves threatened to give out. Miser tried to calm him and promised to find him some extra fresh acorns when this was over, but Talfryn wasn't really listening to his friend.

Despite his trepidation, he was to keep close to Kett. The carpenter's apprentice was flanked on his left by Talfryn and Cornelia. Eliva was supposed to flank his other side along with Luciliana, but after her disappearance, they had to use Idaise in her place. They were one person down, and that made Rawlins and all of the dryads very grumpy. They still didn't know why Medea wanted Kett, but they couldn't worry about that now. Yet, if she did get him, he'd also not be able to finish working on his current chariot project.

As though he needed another reminder of their predicament, the prophecy's warning practically shouted at Talfryn in red and gold bursts.

Things were going great.

FLANKED by at least six huntsmen, Padric marched along with Medea's group. Clarence the amulet tried to untie his enchanted leather tether but was thus far unsuccessful. As yet, though, no one had noticed that Brynwen held the leather around her wrists so they still appeared to be tied.

He was just wondering if he could cause a distraction so at least Brynwen could escape when he heard the chirp of a wren. Had he not heard it before? Sparing a quick glance at Warin, his friend's eyes slid to the left.

Padric followed Warin's gaze and spied Rawlins beyond the trees of the path, winking in and out with his power of invisibility. His friend pointed up to the sky or the tree tops. None of the huntsmen seemed aware of him at all.

Heart quickening, Padric dipped his head in understanding, then peered forward again as though nothing had happened. It had only taken a moment. Brynwen didn't seem to have gotten the message, however. He needed to warn her somehow.

Not ten or so steps later, the volley began.

Small, rust-red balls of fluff descended from the trees. Some dove directly from the overhead branches onto Medea's compatriots, some scampered down the trees, while others came from the ground. All chittering red squirrels. All pandemonium.

Startled, Brynwen gaped at the spectacle, unsure what to do. Her hands unclasped when a squirrel scampered up her dress with great enthusiasm. It was Miser!

The men to Padric's right shouted at their tiny attackers, trying to brush them off. In their haste to rid themselves of the rodents, a gaping hole in their defenses formed.

Padric rushed at Brynwen, using his shoulder to shove her out of the ring of enemies and into the awaiting arms of Nalini.

A hand clamped around Padric's arm and spun him around. Drogo.

"Not so fast." Drogo flicked an attack squirrel off his shoulder with his hand. He lunged for Padric when a dozen more squirrels bombarded his head.

"Argh! I hate squirrels!" Drogo screeched.

"That will not make them like you any better," Padric retorted.

Padric ducked from the huntsman's grasp. The open space Brynwen had gone through was now barricaded by a huntsman. He could no longer see her, but he prayed Nalini could keep her safe.

"This way," Warin bellowed, barging through two huntsmen toward where Rawlins fought.

Sending up a final prayer for his beloved, Padric followed Warin.

ॐ

AFTER DEPOSITING Timotheus into Nalini's arms, Eliva had run. Tears streaked down her cheeks as she bolted through the forest to escape.

"I hate being a dryad!" she cried to the skies. "I hate my life! And I hate this bangle!" Screaming, she tore off the offending jewelry and thrust it as far as it would go, losing it to the wood.

Low, thin branches cut her face and arms and legs in her haste to escape. "I just want to be free. To be a Huntress, away from the dryads who treat me differently because they know I don't belong. I don't want to be them. Is that so much to strive for?"

In her desperate plea, she hoped and prayed that the goddess would appear, to beg her to join the Hunt. To be *worthy*.

Eliva's feet slowed, and she stopped, placing her hand against a tree to catch her breath.

"But I am not worthy of Diana. There is a person who makes me"— face flaming, she swallowed the lump in her throat—"confused. And I don't know what to do about it." He was kind and handsome and smiled just for her, and...

Now she paced, hiccuping on her tears. "There is also a child who needs a mother. Parents." That would never happen as a Huntress. She'd never wanted a family beyond her mother, aunt, and little sister, along with Circe, who treated her like a niece or granddaughter. But did Timotheus make her want more? Did Talfryn?

Pounding her fist against the closest oak, Eliva sighed, resting her head against her arm. It scraped against the rough bark. Its branches surrounded her as though it would give her a hug.

"What do I do now?" she asked the tree. But it, like her other pleas, fell on deaf ears.

"Nalini is getting ever more annoyed with me. I always feared she would throw me out before I could make something of myself...and here I am. I have messed everything up." Talfryn and his friends came to her forethoughts. They had been kind to her, while she'd been—

Her ears perked, hearing a low growl, like a wolf.

The aeternae!

In a flash, she remembered the mission to save Brynwen, Sir Padric, and Sir Warin. Their lives were in grave peril, and here she was, sulking. Worse, she was supposed to help rescue them. The plan...

She grabbed her head in both hands. "Oh, no. I ruined the plan." She paced, uncertain what to do. Then, at last, "I have to go," she told the oak, who nodded with the cool breeze.

She dashed back the way she had come, hoping she could retrace her steps to find Talfryn, Nalini, and the others. It wasn't too long before she came upon her bangle, hanging from an overgrown bush. Hesitating, she picked it up and thought of chucking it again. Thinking better of it, she replaced it on her wrist and continued to Talfryn and the others. The growl grew in intensity, and she quickened the pace, chest constricting in hopes that she would make it in time.

CHAPTER 32

alfryn's sword slid with his attacker's as they fought in a circle. He stumbled back as their swords separated. Raising his arm to strike, dread spilled over him. All the hair on his neck and arms stood on end. The smell...ohh, he remembered the foul stench.

"Little fool...care to play?"

Talfryn gulped involuntarily. *It's behind me, isn't it?* His breath froze in his throat. His fingers lost all function, and his sword clattered to the ground.

"Here I am."

Taking the dropping of his sword as an invitation, his human adversary raised his weapon to strike. Before he could bring it down, though, his whole face elongated as he spotted something over Talfryn's shoulder. With care, the man stepped back.

Talfryn turned around, but it wasn't of his own volition.

The creature took slow, deliberate steps to meet him. As it approached, everyone stopped fighting and grew silent, still. They could tell who it had come for.

Excruciating seconds felt like hours as the wicked monster slunk up to Talfryn. He shivered when its shadow crossed him. His stomach churned at the stench it carried, that of carrion, sweat, and wet dog. What had Gregorio called it? Grave...*graveolency*, that was it.

"I have come to play."

No retort came to mind as the red eyes delved into his own, and Talfryn knew he'd lose his life this day.

The light footfall fell before he saw the blades descend onto the creature's back. Rawlins appeared, shoving two daggers into the aeternae's hide.

The monster growled and snapped at the disappearing Rawlins.

A war cry emanated from the dryads as they dashed in to shoot arrows and stab at it with their weapons. Despite its size, the aeternae was quite agile, ducking and outrunning their attempts.

"Your most cherished ones will miss you the most."

Fear for Brynwen's sadness at his demise bade him cast a glance in her direction.

As the dryads chased it, the monster constantly watched Talfryn, and, feigning an attack on them, rolled back on its paws and made straight for him instead.

Somehow, his hatchet was in his hand, but he didn't know how. His heart pounded in his ears. It seemed eons had passed before the creature was almost upon him, although it was a distance of only four yards.

"Talfryn," Padric screamed. "What are you doing? Kill it!"

Hearing his friend, Talfryn knew he should raise his weapon, but he kept seeing the rusted hatchet—his first botched attempt at its demise—embedded in its back. *What if I fail again? Can it even be killed? Will it go away if it kills me? It'll stop haunting me then, won't it? Will Bryn miss me? Eliva?*

"Little fool."

At the last second, the aeternae veered left. Talfryn didn't notice where it was headed until too late, as the wind whipped his hair and tunic, the beast sprinted, head down, horns pointed forward, at full speed.

Toward Brynwen.

From nowhere, Ulysses swooped down in front of her, white wings unfurled like an angel, his horns catching the light like a grand halo. He kicked his hind legs into the air in defense.

The aeternae plowed into him. Dark, red blood spurted in every direction as the aeternae's horns pierced through Ulysses's chest. The wolfish monster's momentum drove them both into Brynwen, knocking her to the side. She slammed into a thick tree.

"Nay!" Padric cried. He and Warin were running toward them, hands behind their backs. They were too late.

Ulysses and the aeternae fell to the ground in a heap. Wings akimbo, the peryton didn't move as the monster yanked its horns with unnecessary roughness from Ulysses's body. Blood flowed freely from his chest like a never-ending river to stain the ground. The once proud peryton's black eyes lay open, glazed over.

No one dared move, all eyes were glued to the next course of action that the monstrous wolf would take.

The aeternae glared straight at Talfryn and bared its bloodstained teeth. Blood dripped down from the horns on its head, onto the gray fur of its face and shoulders, plopping onto the ground.

"You killed Ulysses and my sister," Talfryn whispered through gritted teeth.

"My gift to you, little fool. Your next gift will come soon. Quite soon." Then it sauntered off to disappear into the trees. Bloody paw prints followed it out of sight.

Talfryn gasped in a breath.

Bryn.

Ulysses.

A flood of pain tore through him as his legs wobbled free of their hold. It took the greatest effort to move, as though he were wading through chest-deep water, walking through a nightmarish dream. The edge of his consciousness wondered what had happened to Aeron, Medea, and all the huntsmen. They must have snuck away the moment the aeternae arrived.

Padric crashed to his knees beside Brynwen and Ulysses, looking between the two as though not sure what to do. "Bryn. Brynwen? U... Ulysses..."

A loud sob burst from Gregorio. *"Pater?"* he cried in despair and rushed to his father's side, burying his head and hands in Ulysses's fur. Timotheus, still tied against his chest, cried with him.

Hands still tied behind his back, Warin knelt beside Brynwen. She moaned.

Praise be! Talfryn let out a shuddered breath.

Everyone gathered around as though also in a bad dream.

From behind, Eliva came running up, out of breath. "Talfryn? What happened?" She gasped as the others parted enough for her to see. "Oh, no." Her green skin grew ashen.

Padric's head flew up, body rigid. Tears streamed down his cheeks, and he gave Talfryn the most intense glare. *"Why?"* He rose unsteadily. "Why did you not stop it when you had the chance?"

A lump the size of a melon formed in Talfryn's throat. Stumbling backwards, he bumped into a dryad. "I'm...I'm so sorry. I..." Neither breaths nor words would come. *Why did this happen?*

Padric's whole face contorted in agony as he averted his gaze. "Just leave," he croaked.

"What?" Talfryn blanched. *Leave?* A thousand daggers pierced his heart. "P-Padric? You can't mean it."

But Padric would no longer look at him, his shoulders and curls shaking in despair.

Cheeks blotchy, Nalini said softly, "Mayhap you should go, Talfryn."

Talfryn flinched at his friend's anger and grief. He cast a desperate glance at his unconscious sister. At Ulysses's body, Gregorio's sobs. Rawlins met his gaze then looked away.

His chest burned, threatening to explode as he staggered away, moving as though drunk on emotions and pain. *How did this happen? Why?*

As his legs picked up speed to begin running, to just escape this nightmare, he thought he heard Eliva calling after him.

It was all my fault.

I killed them.

I killed them!

CHAPTER 33

"Oh, Ulysses." Padric stared at his friend, his many-great grandfather, who only a few minutes ago had been alive. Their adventures had only lasted a few short months, but he felt like he had always known him.

Padric wanted to wail along with the baby Gregorio held. He vaguely wondered where the child had come from but lost the train of thought as he relived Ulysses's death over and over. Of Brynwen being thrust against the tree. Of Talfryn, standing there, terrified and inactive. Why could he not kill it? It was right there, practically asking to be struck down.

Brynwen was hurt, Gregorio's utter despair making it all the worse. She had lain so still from the fall, he'd thought she had died. Lamenting not being able to hold her in his arms, Padric's bound hands clenched into fists until they ached, the tingling enchantment still holding strong.

"As for you," Nalini growled.

Padric's head popped up to see Nalini glowering at Eliva. The older dryad marched to her niece and took her arm. "Come with me, child."

Eliva flinched as she spun with Nalini's momentum. In a few steps, they had disappeared into the forest.

"Where is Kett?" Luciliana asked. She picked up one of his carving knives from the ground, holding it delicately.

The carpenter had disappeared.

"Medea." Padric and Rawlins spoke in unison. He must have been captured while the aeternae distracted them. In the end, Medea had gotten what she wanted after all—but what would she do to him?

Rawlins took charge, sending the dryads out to search for Kett and Medea but to also steer clear of the aeternae should it still be around.

Nalini returned after a few minutes without Eliva. Padric could only guess what had happened to her.

"Were you not a little harsh on the maid?" Warin asked.

Nalini folded her arms over her chest. "Nay. Indeed, I am very cross with her. She must learn not to be so soft." She raised her eyebrow and set her gaze on Padric, whose cheeks heated in response.

Warin frowned. "Eliva doesn't seem soft to me."

A snort came from Nalini's lips. "Nay. Please allow me to minister to Brynwen."

"Of course." Warin scooted back, but remained near.

Padric was too distraught to be jealous and let it go.

Removing some medicinals from her pack, the jars Nalini opened filled the air with scents of lavender and angelica, but they could no sooner soothe Padric's own mental ailments than bring Ulysses back from the dead. Raw pain grated into the wound in Padric's abdomen, and he made an involuntary wince. Useless as he was without the use of his hands, he could only watch Nalini work. "Will she recover?" His words felt thick in his mouth.

Nalini pressed her lips together. "I think so. It is likely a concussion and she should wake soon, albeit sore."

Padric nodded, not taking his eyes from her.

"Watch over her for a little while, won't you?" he asked Warin.

"I will ensure she is safe," the knight vowed. His hands were also still tied behind his back.

Nalini worked efficiently. "Then we will work on loosening those enchanted bonds of yours. Did you release Brynwen's?"

Padric's mouth dropped in surprise. "How did you know?"

She merely gave him a knowing look, then returned to her ministrations.

Making his way over to Gregorio, who hadn't moved but was now sitting up and petting his father's fur as though only trying to soothe him to sleep for the night. The only indications of his despair were his puckered face and the remnants of tears trailing down his cheeks.

Padric placed his head on the tutor's shoulder. He said nothing for no adequate words could be said. Warin rose to his feet. "We should go back to the abbey where our wounded can get aid."

Looking upon Ulysses's and Brynwen's faces, Padric vowed to find Medea and her despicable hench-wolf. They would pay the price for their crimes.

As for his squire, he did not know what to do.

Out of sight from the others, Eliva was finally able to tear her arm out of Nalini's iron grasp.

"Where were you?" Nalini demanded. "We needed you. Ulysses's death might have been prevented had you been at your post. We might have defeated the aeternae, the scourge of our people." Her voice shook with anguish. Tears formed in her eyes. Rare was the occasion when Eliva's aunt was overcome. She had always had the strongest constitution of the dryads who served Circe, and this display distressed Eliva terribly. That, and knowing that their beloved friend Ulysses was dead. Brynwen's death might be on his heels, too. Circe could not bring them back this time.

Tears slid down Eliva's cheeks as she reached for Nalini. Ulysses had been her friend, too. How could she explain? *"Matertera?* I am so sorry about Ulysses. If only—"

Nalini batted away her hand. "Where were you?" she repeated more forcefully.

Heat flamed in Eliva's face as she sought words to describe what had happened. About Talfryn, his soft eyes, his silly antics, his infuriatingly charming smile...

His look of utter wretchedness at being dismissed by Padric had likewise been a blow to Eliva. They had seemed such staunch friends. But for whatever reason, Talfryn had failed to kill the beast. Was it weakness or was it fright? Did he not deserve to be punished for failure?

"You had a responsibility to be here. All of your training was for this one purpose, and you deserted us. If only Diana knew."

"Nay, *matertera!* That isn't it."

"Are you telling me the truth?" Nalini's voice echoed through the still forest.

Eliva opened her mouth, but Nalini's hot glare stole her weary excuses.

Heart quickening, Eliva folded her hands over her chest, her head dropping to gaze at her green toes. "The truth, *matertera*, is that I am weak. Is that what you want to hear? That a young man distracted me, and I panicked? Because it is true..."

Nalini's gaze drew to Eliva's bangled wrist. Too slow to draw it behind her, the proof was already evident. Nalini grabbed it up for more study.

Shaking her head, Nalini released Eliva's hand. "And you ran instead of confronting him. Tell me, *neptis*, would you have confided in him with the truth?"

"I couldn't. You know I couldn't."

"It was foolish and petty, Eliva, and now one of our own is slain, another gravely wounded."

"Forgive me." Eliva's head hung low, and she held one elbow with the other in shame. "I know I shouldn't have left. It was foolish of me. I-I wasn't thinking."

"That is right, you were not."

Eliva raised her head, ready for her punishment. "What can I do to atone?" She didn't believe there was any possibility of atonement.

"Get out of my sight."

Eliva gasped. That couldn't be right. "But Nalini—"

"Enough! I have had enough of your wallowing. For years, I have watched over you, helped you where I could. Kept you safe. I have pampered your emotions because of my kinship with your mother. But

241

no longer. If you wish to be treated like an adult, then you must act like one. Take responsibility for your actions. Go." She waved her hand in the air as though swatting a fly. "I do not want to see you again until you have learned to be the adult you say you strive to be. If you want to impress Diana, you must act the part."

Eliva held out her arms in supplication. "But Nalini! Where will I go?"

"I care not." Nalini's face was hard. She'd not be swayed.

Tears streaming down her face, Eliva turned and sprinted away without looking back, a sob threatening to choke her.

Now she thought, perhaps, she knew how Talfryn felt, and she wished she were dead.

Dead.

No, that wasn't going to help anything. She had to fix this. Perhaps, if she could find and kill the aeternae, she could redeem herself that way.

And Talfryn...perhaps she could help Talfryn afterward.

She had only gone a short distance when she heard the low growl. *That must be it!* Picking up her pace, she listened for it some more, paying careful attention to the disappearance of bird song from the thinning forest. Only self-preservation kept her looking over her shoulder in case the thing attempted to pounce on her from behind.

Her foot stepped on something hard in the brush. Looking down, she discovered a thin cord. "It can't be." Reaching down, she picked it up. On the end was the amulet necklace Nalini had created to make her look human. The last time she had seen it was when she and Talfryn were changing Timotheus's dirty swaddling cloth.

She gasped. "Talfryn must have kept it." Grasping it, a strange emotion came over her. *Why would he keep it?* How confused he'd looked when he'd accidentally pulled her bangle off when her skin color changed. It twisted her stomach the way she'd cowered away from him in fear that he would find out the truth about her. Yet, he hadn't looked disgusted at all, only confused.

"He must have come this way." Eliva peered ahead to the edge of the forest and into the rocky hills, uncertain what to do. She had to defeat the aeternae. She had to prove to Diana and Nalini that she was worth their time.

Excited squeaky chittering emanated from the direction she had come, followed by the scampering of little paws in the brush. She would know that squeak anywhere. "Miser?"

The red squirrel bounded up to her, climbing her skirts with little issue, up onto her shoulder, down her arm, and into her palm, where he jumped up and down, excited about something.

"What is it, Miser? I cannot understand you."

Giving her an annoyed look, he chittered some more in great agitation.

"Miser, Miser, calm down. I think Talfryn came this way. Look, my amulet. He had it on him."

The squirrel touched the amulet and chittered some more.

She could guess what he was saying. "I can't, Miser. I must hunt the aeternae. It must be stopped." The squirrel's indecipherable higher-pitched squeaking made her wince. "I am sure he will be fine." However, the more she tried to tell herself that, the less she believed it. Talfryn had been devastated when Ulysses had died, and even more so when Padric had told him to leave. He had been haunted by something for a long time, and she hadn't ever given it more than a cursory thought until now. The few times she had mentioned the aeternae, he had blanched, his eyes distant and filled with terror. There was no way he could possibly be in any good state of mind right now. And if the beast hunted him now...

And he was all alone.

Her stomach clenched, realizing how thoughtless she had been. To him. To everyone.

Making up her mind, she cast her sights on the hills beyond the forest.

"You are right, Miser, he does need us." She set him on her shoulder. His tail tickled her cheek as he settled into a more comfortable position. "I think I know where he is going. Hold on," she said to both Miser and Talfryn. "Please don't do anything stupid before we find you!"

CHAPTER 34

The wolficorn breathed down Talfryn's neck as he ran. He knew his mind played tricks, that the beast was in the opposite direction, but that didn't mean it didn't follow him all the same. Leg muscles cramping, he refused to stop until he was far enough away.

Ulysses was dead.

Brynwen might be too.

Padric hates me. He has every right to.

Not caring where he went, his feet dragged with every step. When at last he tripped, he didn't get up. Body too tired to move anymore, he stayed for what seemed like hours. All the emotions exploded out of his chest. Pain. Tears. His morning meal. Everything came out, until in the end all that remained was an empty, depressed shell.

His best friend had abandoned him. But hadn't he abandoned him and everyone else, too, when he didn't lift a finger to stop the monster? He couldn't kill it over the summer, and he couldn't kill it today.

"That's right, little fool. Wallow in despair. Since they chased you off, why not finish the job? Show them you owe them no fealty."

"Go away," Talfryn whispered, too tired to raise his voice. "I want to be alone in my grief. I'm selfish and don't want to share it with you, wolficorn."

"Ah, so much pity! Look, there is a nice precipice from which to fling your-self. Never again will you have to feel aggrieved. Never again to feel alone."

"I'm doing great being aggrieved right here."

"But are you?" the aeternae asked, its foul breath just next to his ear. *"Really? Look at the precipice, Talfryn."*

Talfryn ignored him.

"LOOK."

The sharpness in its tone made him flinch. Forcing his head off the ground, bits of dirt and pebbles tumbled off his face. Now, he took the effort to take in his surroundings. Somehow, he'd managed to climb a small mountain, or what appeared to be one. Rocky terrain mixed with thin clumps of grass led up and up, kind of like the Yorkshire Dales, but much more craggy. *No, more of a big hill, just craggy,* he corrected. "I'm still in Wales," he realized. "Huh." Continuing his search, he found the precipice the beast had spoken of. It didn't look as inviting as the monster in his head had described it. "If you want to jump off of it, Wolfi, be my guest. It doesn't sound particularly pleasant to me."

"It will take away your pain."

"Sure."

"And your anxiety."

"Right."

"And, best of all, you will never have to remember again."

Images exploded into Talfryn's brain. Of Brynwen, lying crumpled on the ground beside the tree. Ulysses, bleeding out. His cousin Leowyn, lying in his own puddle of blood on the temple roof. All because he was too slow. All because he wasn't strong enough. All because...

"I'm a coward."

Another sob filled his chest. "I am. I admit it. Fool that I am, I thought that becoming a knight would make me strong and I could protect everyone I love. But I didn't. It's all worse. Everything. I was so wrong. I'm scared all the time."

"Now you understand. Good little fool."

Slowly, dislodging more dirt and rocks and scraping his hands and knees on the rough, gray ground, he made it to his feet.

"That is it," the wolficorn encouraged.

"Grandfather won't have to be more disappointed in me. Not like every time I leave home to go questing. Sam was always his favorite, anyway." Another couple of steps up. "Bryn'll get past any sadness I've caused. She's got Padric, now, and doesn't need me—if she's even alive."

"You are right, she doesn't need you."

"No one does."

Aching in body and spirit, Talfryn reached the top. It wasn't a cliff or anything, but just another side of a craggy hill, nice and steep, that'd break all his bones and probably his neck when he flung himself off. Beyond that were rolling hills, some regular hills, some craggy like this one. In the far distance, he spotted an actual mountain, so high the clouds covered the top.

Just one more step to end it all.

The wolficorn's throat rumbled. *"One final step. Go on, little fool. Be brave, and do it."*

Brave.

A final tear harbored on the edge of Talfryn's eye, as though afraid to fall.

"Faunus, I'm so sorry I failed you. I couldn't find you, although I looked and looked. Please forgive me. The others'll finish what I started."

Taking a final, shaky breath, Talfryn put out his foot and leaned forward, toward his destiny.

CHAPTER 35

*P*adric dug. He dug until his muscles hurt. He dug past when his muscles had really begun to strain. The bandage Nalini had placed on his abdominal wound was seeping with blood from the ordeal, but he did not care. After the beating he had endured and the wound in his abdomen, he should have been too weak. But somehow energy from the rage inside kept him going.

Raging at Medea, at Aeron, at the aeternae, at Talfryn.

At himself.

He dug some more.

"Padric?"

Not stopping, he continued, trying to finish Ulysses's grave so he could...he could...

A hand gripped his shoulder. He knew who it was.

All the strength left him as he dropped the shovel, watching it fall into the hole. His knees buckled. Gregorio caught his arm and they sat down, feet dangling into the hole.

"Why, Gregorio?" He tried to breathe normally, but his chest was too tight. "Why did it have to be him?"

"Would you rather another?"

Padric hesitated in thought, then shook his head.

The tutor squeezed Padric's shoulder. "Twice in my life, my father has died before my eyes. This time, however, he cannot return. Caron will take him down to the underworld, where Pluto will give him a hero's welcome."

Padric smiled at that, imagining a god in an expensive robe meeting Ulysses when he reached the other end of the River Styx. "Do you believe in God, Gregorio?" he found himself asking.

"The Christian God?" he asked. "Yes, in fact."

Padric did a double take. "You do? Really? Then at church, you really are praying to our Lord in heaven?"

A chuckle escaped the youthful immortal's lips. "Yes. Long ago, I became a Christian, much to *Mater's* chagrin. But she still loves me, regardless, and that is what matters. *Pater* understood. When I told him I had witnessed one of The Christ's miracles and could not turn back, he understood." He patted Padric's back and sighed.

"What is it?" Padric asked.

"I wish I could bury my father in a Christian grave with burial rites, but alas, he is of the old ways—nor is he fully human. Imagine trying to ask my mother if she would consider it."

A grin spread across Padric's mouth, imagining Circe's ire cast on her son. The fact that he was in the body of an animal would not go well, either. "I dare say I can. You would probably end up cursed as a hedgehog."

"That, I never wish to live again." He raised an eyebrow in jest.

Padric laughed, which felt good. Then his eye caught the edge of the grave, and all his mirth fled like a fish from a predator. Anger collected in his heart once more.

"Padric, you cannot blame yourself for this."

"But I should have been able to stop it. If I had been faster. Talfryn could have at least distracted it longer. He—"

"Stop it right there. Why are you doing this? Your hands were tied, quite literally. And what of Talfryn? Have you not thought about what he has been going through?"

"He should have killed it or fought it off." Padric waved his hand out over the grave. The growing darkness made the hole look bottomless.

"Padric, remember what I taught you and John in school? What was the first thing I taught you?"

Memories of tutoring lessons with his friend John Wilmot flooded back. "How to say 'good day' in Latin?"

Gregorio rolled his eyes. "All right, the second thing."

Pausing to think, the memory came up in another instant. "To stop and think, to analyze the situation. Much like my father's lessons on being a knight." His brows knit together in contemplation as he tried to set aside his anger.

"Precisely. What else?"

"Talfryn has been acting off. In between being his usual self, that is, but at times he falters. Panics."

"What else?"

"He did seem to know where the aeternae was, especially if it was near."

His friend nodded. "It seems he has been dealing with this in silence for a while now. Something that troubles him deeply, and I suspect it is to do with the aeternae. I do not think Talfryn has even spoken about it to his own sister."

Padric ran his dirty hands through his sweaty curls, huffing in frustration. "I am an idiot. I was so consumed in everything at home, and on our quest, that I did not see it. Mayhap I did not wish to." No one had a perfect life, not even his most jovial friend. "I failed him, didn't I, Gregorio?"

"We all have, I am afraid."

"But why would he hide it?" Padric wondered. "I have tried to ask him about it, but he makes excuses."

"Why indeed? Think on it."

"I shall. But first, I must finish this." He reached into the hole for the shovel, but Gregorio stilled his hand.

"It is getting dark and you need rest. And, I daresay, a bath and new dressing on that wound. Nalini has put a warding spell so nothing will disturb my father. We will finish the grave in the morning—together."

Padric nodded, feeling like he was twelve with his tutor. Rest sounded very good.

"How is Brynwen?"

The tutor smiled. "She awoke asking for you, but soon fell asleep again. Nalini says it is a good sign."

Relief flooded into Padric's chest. He picked up his step to the campsite, despite all of his muscle and stomach aches.

As he sat in his blanket that night to keep watch over Brynwen, his thoughts wandered.

I had hoped Talfryn would come back by now. I was too harsh on him. More than once, he had seen terror cross his friend's face, seemingly for no reason. But since he refused to speak of it, how could Padric know what was truly wrong? Well, now he knew, but he wondered what exactly had transpired between Talfryn and the aeternae. Padric's animal instincts could sense it the strange sort of communication between them earlier. *I should have tried harder to help him.* But Talfryn was gone, and Padric might never know where because of his own hotheadedness.

Padric scratched his face, the cuts now itchy, accidentally scraping his smarting bruises. His heart ached from his own callous actions toward his friend, the parting of Eliva, and his worry about Brynwen's recovery, all of which culminated into exhaustion. He sighed inwardly, trying, as always, to figure out the next steps.

The child Timotheus began to whimper and whine until one of the dryads shushed him and rocked him back to sleep. Poor child. He did not deserve to be orphaned at such a young age. On the morrow when they returned to the abbey, they would see about finding him a new home with the servants, beginning with the laundresses and milkmaids. The dryads would be sad to see him go, though. They had grown quite attached to him.

Peering down at his beloved, Padric brushed a strand of hair off her face and tucked it behind her ear. Brynwen mightn't have been so angry at her brother. At least, not for long. What would she do?

She would pray.

Another tear streamed down his face. He folded his hands together. *Dear Lord...*

CHAPTER 36

"*P*lease forgive me."

"For what?" a familiar voice asked.

One foot out over the steep, jagged side of the hill, Talfryn faltered. Waving his arms like a madman, he propelled himself backward, his heart hammering in his ribcage. For half a second, he thought he would still pitch over the edge. In a last effort, he righted himself to stand once again on both feet. Gaze landing on the far-down bottom, he couldn't believe what he'd been about to do.

"Talfryn?"

Eliva? Twisting around, he glanced down at the red-haired maiden in her human persona. The amulet was around her neck. Vaguely, he wondered if he'd dropped it somewhere, at it had been in his pocket earlier.

"What?" He tried to compose himself, certain she could hear his thundering heart from where she stood about ten feet away. *Why is she here?*

A fluffy red blur circled down her flowing skirts and darted up the hill to him. It scurried up his trousers and leapt into his hands. "Miser! You don't know how happy I am to see you." The squirrel was so agitated, he berated Talfryn for leaving him behind, and if he ever did it again he'd rescind his offer of giving him all the acorns he'd promised earlier.

"I know, I know, I'm sorry, buddy. I won't leave you behind again. Promise." He swallowed another growing lump in his throat.

"Talfryn?" Eliva waited. "Were you talking to someone?"

"I'm talking to Miser." He held out the red squirrel, who wrapped his tail around Talfryn's wrist.

Her brows narrowed which successfully made him squirm. "Just to myself," he muttered. *Maybe.*

Eliva studied him, her green eyes traveling from his face, down past his feet, then back up to his face again. "What is on the other side of that hill?"

"Nothing. So, how'd you find me?" he said quickly.

"I followed you. If there is nothing there, then why don't you leave it for now?"

Just seeing her made all his emotions burst up to the surface again. What could he say? *I really like looking at rocks? The grass is much greener on the other side?* In the end, he was worn out and didn't want to hurt her feelings again like he'd managed to do earlier. All he could think about was her green skin changing to fair when he'd removed her bangle. The other amulet was around her neck again—so why did she have two? "Look, Eliva, I'm not very good company right now. Please, leave me be."

With a determined shake of her head, she braced her bare feet into the angled ground and pounded her hands on her hips. "I will go nowhere until you come down."

"Eliva—"

"Please."

The next words died on Talfryn's tongue, and it was his turn to study her. She'd never said please to him before. Not once, to anyone. Demanded, yes, but never pleaded.

"All right."

The dryad didn't move until he was a couple of paces above her, then she led him down the steep hill. His tired legs tripped twice, and Miser's nails dug into his shoulder and neck as he stumbled. After that, she led him down slower to where the ground was smoother.

"Sit down here, and I will make a fire."

"You don't have to."

"Talfryn, please. I...I'll be right back." She darted away, presumably to get items for a fire.

Plopping himself and his pack—which he'd miraculously not lost from all his running—down on the hard ground, head in his hands, he'd never been so glad to rest his bones. Flashes of the wolficorn and all it'd done tore through his mind, and his heart raced again.

Miser pinched him.

"Hey, what was that for?"

The squirrel stared at him as if he should know why.

Well, maybe he did.

A few minutes later, Eliva came back, looking relieved that he'd done as she'd asked and hadn't decided to fling himself over the stupid hill after all. He wasn't so sure he felt particularly glad about it, though.

She assembled and lit the fire in silence, although he noticed her eyeing him frequently as though to make sure he wouldn't run off. Once it was built and had heated up a flat rock next to the flame to sufficient temperature, she cooked up a handful of palm-sized journey cakes from a little pouch tied to her waist. She worked in silence, which, for once, suited Talfryn just fine. No words would come, anyway.

Every time she moved, he caught a glance at the bangle sliding up and down her wrist. He didn't understand why she'd pretend to be green with one bangle while also pretending to be human with another amulet. It didn't make sense.

She handed him a pile of cakes on the plate from his pack, her cakes sitting on a "plate" made up of a big strip of bark. Her pack with her plate and gear were still back at their old camp.

When the meal was over, Talfryn realized he didn't want to be left alone with his thoughts any longer. Gulping down the last bites, he finished chewing and cleared his throat.

"Eliva." He gulped. "I appreciate you coming, but...why are you here?"

"To stop you from doing something stupid."

Talfryn didn't buy it. There was something she wasn't telling him. "But why did you follow me?"

Eliva chewed her last bite of journey cake and set down her makeshift plate by her feet. "I had nowhere else to go." Seeing he didn't accept that answer either, she blew out a breath, which puffed the hair on her head. "Nalini kicked me out because I was not there when I should have been. I wasn't there to back up my partner." Her gaze flicked to him, then back down. She picked up the plate again and poured water from a skin into it, swishing around the tiny bits her spoon didn't pick up. Then she dumped it into the grass behind her. "I followed you because I knew you shouldn't be alone. And, frankly, I didn't want to be, either." She gathered her legs together and hugged them to herself.

"You really shouldn't be near me. I'll likely get you killed, too, when the aeternae comes after me."

Her lips drew into a thin line. "That will not happen. I will not allow it—if you can stand to be around someone who is known for deserting her friends in need, that is." She gave him a quick imploring gaze before lowering it to her lap.

Talfryn sniffed. "I'm sure we can make do." He chose to accept it rather than asking more of the questions his tired brain wanted to ask. "Well, thank you," he simply said. After washing his dish, he bedded down on the brutally hard ground with only his cloak, although terrified he'd be up all night with terrors. "Eliva?" he asked tentatively.

"Yes?" She settled down, wrapped in the thin blanket from Talfryn's pack—which she had at first refused until he insisted she take it—arm curled under her head.

"Would you care to sing to Miser? He could use a song after everything he's endured today."

Cuddled on Talfryn's chest, he felt Miser's eyebrow quirk up, but the squirrel thankfully didn't argue.

Eliva's pause made Talfryn think she'd either fallen asleep or was deciding how to refuse him.

"Of course. I know a lullaby my mother used to sing to me." Then she began, her voice like an angel. After a few minutes, he slept in silence for the first time in ages.

CHAPTER 37

*T*alfryn awoke to a scream.

Bolting out of his blanket, he groped for his sword and hatchet. Upon finding them, he shot to his feet, spinning in a wobbly circle.

"What was that?" His head spun from getting up too fast.

Likewise, Eliva took up a defensive position with her bow drawn, polearm at her feet. She, however, looked nonplused about being startled awake.

Figures.

"It came from that way." Eliva jutted her chin out in the direction of the cry—up past the hill she'd found him on. "It is not human."

"Help me!"

Talfryn froze, listening. *"Help me!"* came again on the wind whistling through the grassy hills, followed by a screaming whinny— a horse. Its trembling sounded quite young. "You're right. It needs help."

Picking up his heels, he headed in the direction of the cry, gripping his weapons as he ran.

Eliva stayed on his heels. "Talfryn, what if it is a trap?"

He didn't have an answer, but it sounded so helpless. After the obvious trap by Medea and the wolficorn, though, they needed to be careful.

When he got to the top of the hill, the breeze blew his hair in his eyes as he bent down to peer over. Eliva squatted next to him. Seeing nothing, he looked for the best way down. Eliva didn't hesitate to bound over it, zigzagging a path around boulders, leaping off stones, and acting like a carefree creature of the wild.

Miser chittered in his ear as Talfryn watched in amazement.

"I'm going, I'm going. And no, I wasn't ogling after her. Also, she's not showing off. Just stop talking."

A little ways down, she stopped, turned, and looked up at him with raised brow. "Are you coming?"

Before Miser could further comment, after her he went, following her zigzagging path over the next couple of rocky hills, skinning his hands and knees only a couple of times. All right, a couple of times per hill. All the while, the foal's cries became more and more desperate.

Cresting the fourth and tallest rise, they darted around a few trees and gnarly roots.

"It's just up there," Eliva called.

Sprawled atop the last hill, Talfryn panted as he scanned the vast landscape for the foal. It whinnied again, this time sounding quite close.

"Next hill." Eliva didn't sound a bit breathless at all.

Talfryn rolled his eyes, not looking forward to the next stretch of hill. It looked more intimidating than the rest with more rocks and holes jutting everywhere.

When they reached the top of that hill, which he'd had to grab a hold of rocks to pull himself upward, the foal's whinny carried from their left. Peering over the edge, as one, he and Eliva spotted a *pegasos* filly not thirty yards away. She was flapping her sleek black wings in desperation, but something prevented her from rising. For a fleeting second, Talfryn sucked in a breath as the image of Ulysses's last action, his elegant white wings unfurled in selfless sacrifice, blared in his memory. He shook away the shame and recalled where he was. "She's caught on something," he said, already on the move.

Soon he saw what the problem was. A long, black iron manacle attached to a chain clung to the creature's left hind leg. The other end of the chain wasn't attached to anything, but had tangled itself terribly in a small tree projecting out of the steep side of the hill.

"How did she manage to get herself tangled up like that?" Eliva's face was drawn with concern.

"Panic?" he asked. "More importantly, why is she chained?" He frowned at the sharp drop. It was even more abrupt than the drop from the evening before. The pegasos was about seven feet down and flapping furiously, although it was clear she'd begun to tire. The tree trunk was too thin to carry her weight for more than a few seconds. "I don't suppose you've got a bit of rope on you?" Suspecting she wasn't hiding one on her person somewhere, he studied the rocks for any good hand and foot holds.

"How about this?" Eliva held out a thin rope looped tightly around itself.

"Where'd you get that?" He studied her skirts for extra large pockets.

"I borrowed it from the abbey. I thought it would come in handy someday."

"It looks old and worn to me."

"'Tis better than nothing." When he went to take the rope, she pulled it back. "I can go. I'm smaller and won't likely break the tree."

"I should go," Talfryn countered. "I can talk to her and coax her into calming down so I can untangle the chain and remove it. But you can hold the rope."

She bit her lip. "I don't know…"

"Let me try, eh?"

Finally, she handed him the rope. "Just be careful."

A smirk spread across his face. "Ah, so, you *do* care."

"Not one bit," Eliva retorted, folding her arms across her chest. Miser asked him not to die.

To which, Talfryn scrunched his lip. "Thanks for your vote of confidence."

Talfryn spied Eliva's blush before she ducked her head to peer at the terrified filly. It continued to try to release its leg from the manacle. It was uncertain whether she heard or smelled them, but the pegasos turned enough to see them. Talfryn saw the terror in her eyes, and she pushed even harder to escape.

"We've come to help," Talfryn called out to it. "Don't tire yourself too much. I'll be right there to untangle the chain."

"*Who are you?*" the pegasos asked.

"A friend. Name's Talfryn. And these are my friends Eliva and Miser. We heard you from a bit away and would like to free you from the tree. If you'll let us," he added.

Wings slowing down to flap less frantically, she seemed to be calming down. "*And then what?*"

"Then you can be on your way. We promise."

It was hard to see the black pegasos's expression too well, but Talfryn thought she looked skeptical.

Miser suggested offering her some acorns.

"What is your name?" Talfryn asked.

After a short hesitation, she said, "*Genia.*"

"That's a lovely name, Genia. You can trust us to help you. Don't tire yourself out. I'll be right there." He nodded to Eliva, who grabbed the end of the rope and looped it around a thick, sturdy rock sticking partially out of the ground while he tied the other end around his middle.

It wasn't until he began the turn to scale the hill that he really noticed how steep it was, and his bravery faltered a bit. Or maybe a lot. Heart fluttering, he saw the rare bit of concern spread across Eliva's face, heard the filly's wings flap, and his resolve hardened once again.

"I'm ready."

With a sharp nod, Eliva fed the rope while Talfryn found foothold after foothold. Miser's tail swished anxiously as he watched.

"I'm coming, Genia, just hold on," he said to the pegasos, who probably couldn't hear him above her own wings flapping.

Blood pounded in his ears with each step. When his chin was at the same height as the horizontal tree, which was no wider than his forearm, he reached for the chain. It gave the pegasos a lead of about three feet. Her leg, where the chain attached to a manacle, was raw and bled with the effort of escape.

"Miss Genia, could you please give up some slack?"

She complied, but he didn't expect the tree trunk to slump so low, and it dragged the winged horse down. Upon further inspection, some of the roots had been yanked up from the hill. That wasn't good. Even with her strength, if it fell, it would drag her down the hill. He needed to hurry.

Talfryn got to work chopping away with his hatchet near the base of the trunk. Even though it wasn't very thick, the bark was tough, and he couldn't get a great swing due to the angle. It was slow work, the trunk chipping away bit by bit as the sweat beaded up on his forehead, neck, and everywhere else. The rope chafed around his middle. Every time it creaked on the rock where Eliva held it, little bubbles of panic ascended his esophagus.

"How is it going?" Eliva asked after a bit.

"Getting closer." His arms, though strong from wielding a sword and bow and arrow from hours and hours of training, weren't used to this tedious labor anymore. At the same time, his thighs cramped from bracing against the rock at an angle.

When he was a quarter of the way through it, the pegasos flagged, one wing going limp. She swerved, and it was all Talfryn could do to swing away as her wing swept over his head.

Righting herself, she got her wing under control. *"Sorry. Are you almost done, by chance?"* she asked timidly.

"Just about." In another minute, he was down to one final swing that would sever the tree from the hill, when the whole thing snapped. The force of it jolted Genia's chain, and it ricocheted into his face.

"Talfryn!" Eliva cried.

The shock jerked his footing, and his shoulder struck a jutting rock on the hillside. Stars flew past his vision as pain shot through his shoulder and arm. Dropping the hatchet, he gripped the rope with his good hand, attempting to right himself, but kept feeling like he was sliding.

Eliva's voice was strained as she warned, "Talfryn...the rope is breaking...Hurry."

In spite of his efforts, he couldn't find his footing. The rope snapped.

He plummeted—sometimes head over heels, sometimes rolling, some-times sliding—down the rocky hill. As he went, he reached out for handholds, but found none.

Suddenly, a chained manacle fell from the sky. It was from Genia. It took several tries, but he finally got his hand around the chain above the manacle. She tugged, and he stopped with a jolt. Panting, he saw that he'd been less than a foot away from crashing into a boulder the size of his front door.

The pegasos landed a few feet away, still shy of him.

"Thanks," he said, head and stomach reeling. His heart tried to burst from his chest as he gulped in breaths.

Sickness came to his gut, and he retched. When finished, he wiped his mouth with his sleeve, self-conscious of the horse standing over him. It smelled wretched, and knew he must smell the same.

"Talfryn?" Eliva called. He could also hear Miser's worried squeaks from higher up.

He waved wearily at them. With slow movements, he checked to see if anything was broken. Nothing seemed to be, miraculously.

Genia's head lowered to look at him, then she nuzzled his forehead. *"Would you like a ride?"*

"I...if you wouldn't mind." He didn't think he could walk up that horrid hill anytime in the next week.

The filly was patient as he worked to get his sore legs over her back.

"Does Eliva look worried?" He patted Genia's head with gentle strokes, concentrating on staying upright.

"She is..."

But he didn't hear the rest of the answer as his head exploded in pain with visions of Faunus, Brynwen, Medea, Ulysses, Janus, and the wolfi-corn. Then everything went black.

Talfryn's dreams collided with visions of the future which collided with nightmares which collided with bizarre discussions between him,

Faunus, and the wolficorn. Having a polite conversation with tea. Yelling over one another over broken tea cups. Feeding his goats.

Somewhere in the middle, or near the end—he'd never remember exactly when—the prophecy presented itself, not just in words, but in images. Everything became clear. He even discussed it with Faunus in detail while the god spent some time locked away with the other gods.

When he awoke, hours later in the dark, he sucked in a shocked breath and wanted to scream at the pain that exuded from everywhere. Instead, he groaned.

Loudly, apparently, as Eliva rushed to his side. "Do not move, Talfryn. You will only hurt yourself more." Behind her, the fire only revealed her profile in the darkness.

"How can it hurt more, when everything hurts already? How bad is it?"

"Nothing is broken, but mayhap a bruised rib or two. Did you see that hill you fell down? You should have been smashed to bits on the rocks. It would seem your God made a less treacherous path for you."

"Didn't feel like it at the time, though." *But thanks, Lord, really.*

Next to him, a groggy Miser blinked several times and yawned. Then he proceeded to berate Talfryn for trying to get himself killed—again. *"It's like a thing with you, isn't it?"* he asked.

"I'm not trying to make it a thing." He coughed, which hurt every- thing even more.

"No coughing, either," Eliva warned.

Talfryn grinned, which was about the only thing that didn't hurt. "I'll try not to. Where is Genia? Is she all right?"

"She is fine. I put a salve on her leg, and she is sleeping off the harrowing day. She wouldn't leave your side for many hours, though."

"So, she likes me then."

"I didn't say that."

A chuckle erupted from Talfryn, who immediately quashed it as his rib screamed for him to stop.

"Don't laugh, either," they said in unison.

Eliva laughed, a lovely sound, making Talfryn's stomach flutter.

There was something he'd been dying to ask her. And a niggling of something he was supposed to tell her.

Eliva cleared her throat. "You should get some rest."

"Only if you sing to me again," Talfryn said before thinking. "Uh, only if you want to, though," he added quickly.

A pause. Then, "Of course, if it will make you be quiet."

As he settled down, soft notes emerged from her lips, words in an ancient tongue pronounced with finesse and grace.

Miser curled up against Talfryn's arm, and soon his soft snoring could be heard. Moments later, Talfryn drifted off to sleep, thinking of trickling streams and his goats, Hay and Stack, romping around the pasture with Miser, and a content smile on his own face.

CHAPTER 38

The Day of the Full Moon
October 28, AD 1356

*U*pon exiting the healing chamber two mornings later, every muscle and bruise in Padric's body was stiff. The wound in his abdomen still pained him, but spending time with the abbey healers and being confined to bed most of the previous day and all night had helped the bleeding to stop. The head healer himself saw to Padric's wounds and tutted him for getting into so much trouble.

Padric, released from the healing chamber despite the healer's displeasure, slowly headed for the refectory. His stomach growled, completely famished. Having skipped the evening meal because of his grief over the loss of Ulysses, he was also exhausted from the toll his body had taken by Aeron and his henchmen. Seeing anyone this morning was the last thing he wanted to do, but he knew that time was running out. After eating, he would spend a little time with Brynwen in the healing chamber before trying to figure out their next move. The moon would be full in a few hours.

Besides, there was an apology he needed to make, and he hoped the person in question had returned to the abbey and was at this moment sitting on a bench and stuffing his face with the cook's most delicious food served on silver platters.

His stomach growled as the heavenly aroma of eggs filled with spices and bread fresh from the oven guided his feet toward the refectory. A whiff of bacon set his salivary glands to working. Right as his foot scuffed across the threshold, a hand clamped onto his arm.

Padric drew his sword a fraction out of its sheath until he made eye contact with a short, round man in a white robe. Fear laced the brother's expression, and he drew back from Padric's most certain retaliation.

With the stay of his hand, Padric allowed the sword to slide back inside its sheath. "Brother Fabian?"

"S-Sir Pa-Padric, forgive me." The monk bowed twice and backed away, his fidgeting fingers causing tremors in his robe. "But I...ahem. May I have a w-word?"

Irritated that the little man could not wait until after he had filled his belly, Padric had half a mind to tell him to totter off. But something stayed his comment. That, and the realization that the goatish part of him nearly always tried to take over when he was hungry. Fear showed in Brother Fabian's shaking body.

Glancing inside the refectory, he spied his friends sitting solemnly at a table, but Talfryn and Eliva were absent. Padric sighed. They would have to wait. He returned his attention to the monk, who backed up in a panic.

Raising his bare hands, Padric smiled in contrite apology. "Forgive me, Brother Fabian, at times my stomach overbears my manners. Pray, what have you to say?"

Brother Fabian peered around them, lips trembling. "Not here. Meet me in the north cloister after the bells ending morning prayer."

"All right."

An hour later, content and with a full belly, Padric and Rawlins reached the north cloister as the morning prayer bells were ringing their last two chimes. Rawlins had insisted on tagging along, but Padric argued against it, as Brother Fabian was already uncomfortable being around one armed knight. Two would likely scare him off—or to death —especially if that knight were the ever stoic Rawlins. "You may stand nearby, however, should you wish."

On the last chime, Padric rounded the corner of the covered walkway, leaving Rawlins invisible near a dark recess on the other side. But nowhere did he see Brother Fabian.

After waiting another couple of minutes, Padric was becoming concerned that something had happened to the brother when an object popped in and out of sight at the end of the cloister. Curious, Padric watched until it happened again. When it did, he chuckled.

"It is but me, Brother Fabian. Sir Padric."

"Ah. Y-yes, so it is." The monk waddled out of the shadows, his white sleeves drawn together. "Thank you f-for meeting me."

"Of course. What did you wish to discuss?" Padric's curiosity was heightened by so much intrigue.

The monk peered around them again. "You are a f-friend of Brother Howell's so I know I can t-trust you. There are things I've s-seen which are most irregular. Some of my fellow brothers agree. Our whispers won't help, but I'm hoping you c-can." Agitated, his nerves caused his voice to stutter and hands to shake.

"As an outsider, I know not what I can do, but I will help where I can. What is the trouble?"

"For one, guests will arrive one day, then vanish the next."

"How do you mean?" Padric's interest piqued.

"For the past few weeks, a handful of the new guests we received went straight to their rooms without speaking to a soul. That part is not so strange," he hurried to say, seeing Padric's skeptical look. "However, the next morning, they were gone, and their beds appeared untouched. The stewards are most perplexed. When they brought it up to the abbot, he insisted that the visitors had left while we were at Prime—the sunrise service." His agitation lessened the more he spoke.

Padric rubbed his chin in thought. "The past few weeks, you say? Why did no one mention this before?"

The monk's cheeks reddened. "The abbot ordered us to not say anything to a soul. The guests' presence was to be kept secret."

Frowning, Padric regarded the monk. "If their arrival was so secret, why are you telling me now?" The abbot had seemed a bit peculiar, eccentric even, but he had expected nothing like this. Almost as bad as the Sheriff of Nottingham's behavior over Padric's murder charge. It was quite curious, but he very much doubted they were connected.

"Because"—Brother Fabian looked around nervously—"of the saint."

Padric quirked an eyebrow, waiting for a response.

"Your resemblance to Saint George's likeness in the tapestry when you were near his sword and the way Brother Herman trusts you. He mentioned some of the other odd things that were happening and...I had a"—his gaze raised heavenward—"premonition that you should know these goings-on."

Padric looked up, too, hoping for a heavenly sign. But alas, all he saw was the roof of the cloister. "I see. What did these guests look like?"

"That's the other thing. They've each worn long cloaks with h-hoods drawn low. Some men and some women, but nothing else we could note. What's more strange, is that their guides acted more or less normal, but those in their charge all walked sluggish and spoke not a word, almost as if they were half asleep, or..."

"Enchanted?" Padric offered.

The monk nodded. "Yes, mayhap. B-but of course, we could say nothing. There was one guest who tried to say something, but the guide shuffled her off straight away."

"This is most perplexing." Padric tried to connect it all. A creeping feeling overcame him. "I must confess that this is all very interesting, Brother Fabian, but what do you expect me to do about it?"

"That's not all."

"There is more? Tell me."

"A few days ago, I was on my way to morning prayer when I heard a commotion in the library where all the construction is taking place. I snuck up to it, and, for once, the doors were wide open. At the far end, the abbot had another door open, and some of the new monks were pushing something toward it. As they got closer, the abbot moved aside, and I was struck by a strange sight."

"What was it?"

"I only got a glimpse of it, mind, but, it looked like ancient Roman or Grecian ruins but—but *not* ruins. They looked new, still in use."

Padric leaned against the wall, pondering his words. "When are ruins not ruins?" He had a feeling he knew, but wanted to run it by the others. "The library door is always locked, you say? Who has the key?"

"The abbot has the only key. He...supposedly destroyed the others." He shut his eyes in grief.

"Destroyed? That seems rather desperate. And suspicious." Yes, it sounded like Abbot Caradoc was definitely into something nefarious. "I should very much like to inspect this library."

The monk's shoulders slumped in relief. "Brilliant! I've got a cunning plan for you to get the key." He grinned for the first time, and Padric noticed his gap tooth. "While we are at vespers, you could—"

Padric barely heard the shuffle of cloth before a monk darted out of the shadow-laden cloister. Quick as a stag, the hooded figure thrust a knife into Brother Fabian's abdomen. In the same stroke, he brandished a club at Padric's head.

CHAPTER 39

Genia huffed happily. *"You are heavy."*

Talfryn chuckled. A full-out laugh would land him on the ground again. "So I've been told. My grandfather states this fact all the time."

Eliva had scouted ahead while Talfryn rode atop the black pegasos. Miser sat amicably on her head. Whenever Genia had to take a step on her injured leg, she fluttered her wings enough so she wouldn't have to put much weight on it. Clever. After yesterday's ordeal, she was still too exhausted to fly any great distance. Every step hurt Talfryn's ribs, but he couldn't complain about the freely-given ride. *And she's too young to carry both me and Eliva*, he thought with stupid heat flushing his cheeks.

Eliva returned a few minutes later to report the way clear for the next few miles.

Talfryn disembarked without falling flat on his face, giving his backside a break. He patted Genia. "This little lady's told me her tale, and I think you'll want to hear it."

Eliva walked beside him. "Go on. I have been very curious about it."

"Genia here was most recently in the employ of one Medea, wicked witch of Olympus."

"Really?" Eliva asked, impressed. "And she escaped?"

Both Genia and Talfryn nodded in tandem. He went on. "Medea's not very good to her horses. Gets a new set every couple of years or so, she batters them so badly. I guess that's why she likes those dragony things better."

"*Dracones*," both Eliva and Genia corrected.

"*Dracones Rapuere Medea*, to be precise," Eliva added. "Winged dragons of Medea."

"All right, then, dracones. Now you sound just like Gregorio." His mood soured. "I don't want to know how many thousands of pairs she's gone through since she got that chariot. But anyway, she's been on the abbey's grounds for weeks. There's a separate abandoned stable on the abbey grounds less than a mile from the wall that's been be-spelled so no one can see it. Been that way for the last three"—Genia huffed—"the last four years, since they discovered the portal and began making their plots."

"No wonder we have not been able to see anything. Not even Ulysses..." She shuddered at what she was about to say.

A stone lodged itself in Talfryn's ribcage. "It's all right. Ulysses couldn't find it either. But Genia says that yesterday, the groom didn't lock her up very well, and she made her way out. She'd come down to land for a quick rest on that hill when the chain got stuck around the tree. She thought we were Medea's servants trying to take her back."

"That explains so much. Poor thing." Her eyes shaded in dislike. Then she turned to the winged horse and stroked her neck. "We won't let anything happen to you, Genia. We promise."

Genia whinnied and huffed in appreciation, rubbing her muzzle against Eliva's cheek. The maiden smiled and rubbed her muzzle in return.

Talfryn translated, "She says 'thank you kind lady.'"

Now it was Eliva's turn to blush.

They walked in silence for a time. Then Eliva moved a step closer to Talfryn. "Talfryn, there is something I...never mind." She bit her lip and drew away, speeding up.

"Eliva, wait." He jogged after her, biting back the ache in his ribs, and clutched her arm. Remembering how much she disliked being touched, he released her and stepped back. "What is it? Please, I know you've had something to say for a while. I won't get mad or sad or anything. I'll show no emotion at all, if that'll help." It was hard trying not to look desperate. She might be the only non-animal friend he had left.

The maiden halted and glared at him. But after a couple of seconds her lips fell into a sad frown. She nodded and clutched at the amulet around her neck. The same amulet that had fallen out of his pocket the day before. "I haven't told anyone about...about it. And you can't tell anyone."

"Not a soul. I can't vouch for Miser, however."

The red squirrel squeaked in indignation on Talfryn's shoulder.

"Very well." Removing the amulet, her creamy fair skin turned green and her fiery red hair became a more somber red. Then she unlatched the bangle from her wrist. When it fell away, her skin returned to the creamy white with freckles and radiant red hair from a few moments before.

Talfryn stood still. He didn't know what he'd expected to see, but he'd guessed as much. "So, it's not an illness. I'm relieved of that. Two amulets, huh?" He picked up both the wood and metal amulets in his hands for study. Heart thudding, he couldn't believe his eyes—she was actually a human after all.

"You are not mad?"

Talfryn dropped the amulets to the ground, took up both of her hands, and shrugged. "So you kept a secret. I have secrets, too. So do most people. Have you met Circe? *Big* secret keeper. I'll admit, I'm a little sad you didn't tell me earlier instead of running away. But you came back two nights ago and helped me, and for that I've already forgiven you a hundred times over."

Eliva shook her head and stared at their interlocked hands. Her cheeks became red as cherries as she dropped her eyes to stare at her non-green feet. "I don't think I'm deserving of it. And I don't know why, but I panicked. I thought you'd tell everyone, and then...I just couldn't take it, so I ran. I'm so sorry. It took me a while to catch up. Then everything went wrong with...I'm so sorry," she repeated, tears sliding down her freckled cheeks.

"Shh, shh, don't cry, now." Talfryn pulled her to him and held her tight, her head against his chest. He caressed her red hair, inhaling its scent of cherries and fresh leaves. He ignored his ribs as she sobbed into his chest, butterflies flinging themselves along the lining of his stomach with great abandon. This time, to his amazement she didn't pull away.

When at last she did step back, her tears had lessened. "That isn't all I must tell you. When I was about three years old, my family—all humans —were traveling near Yorkshire. We were attacked, and I was the sole survivor. My parents, older brother, and infant sister were all killed. I was left for dead."

"That's awful."

"But my mother—that is, my dryad mother, and her half-sister, Nalini, found me. Based on some evidence where they found us, they discovered a clue leading them to believe we were victims of murderers instead of a robbery gone wrong. They brought me home, and with Circe's help, made this amulet bangle to make my skin look green so I could hide with the rest of the dryads in case the murderers ever searched for me. They never told the others that I'm human, so I could fit in better. Some might have guessed, but they've not confronted me about it. And no one ever came searching for me."

"Is that why you don't sing with them?" he asked, his shoulder now completely wet.

Eliva's head shot up, her face all puffy and cute. "You-you noticed?"

Face paling, Talfryn rubbed the back of his neck. "Well, just the one time." *Me and my big mouth!*

A sigh escaped Eliva's lips. "I might as well tell you, then. Early on, Nalini and Circe realized I have some nymph blood in my veins, but it is from many generations ago and isn't as powerful as a full nymph's abilities. My voice isn't nearly as pretty or strong, and I knew I would stand out as...inadequate. Some of the others tried to ask why I refused to sing with them, but they gave up after a while. It's all made it very difficult to really *be* one of them." She shrugged as though resigned to it. "Mayhap someday..." She shook her head. "Never mind. We should keep moving. We've a ways to go before we reach the abbey."

Traversing the uneven ground, sorrow flooded Talfryn about his own failure to protect Ulysses and his sister. He hated not knowing if Brynwen would recover. He didn't care if Padric was still mad at him—and rightfully so—but he needed to go back, to finish the prophecy and be with his sister and friends. Padric could try to stand in the way if he wanted, but Talfryn wasn't giving up. Making it up to Ulysses and Bryn was all that mattered. He just prayed that by the time he returned, Padric would see it that way too.

"I am so sorry about your family and what you went through all those years," Talfryn said. "Will you tell the others now?"

"I am not sure."

"Well, then, what if Diana wishes to bring you on as a Huntress?"

Eliva's lips pressed together. "I am not so sure she will take me."

"Why not?"

She turned her head away, her voice gruff as she said, "It is of my own doing that she will not accept me."

"What does that mean?"

"Please, Talfryn, I cannot tell you—it is forbidden to speak of it."

"Ah. Gotcha."

Talfryn was a bit sad that Eliva wouldn't elaborate about what she meant, but he didn't push it. He was just grateful she'd confided in him at all. So instead, as they traversed the hills and forest, he told her about how the wolficorn—er, aeternae—had been terrorizing his dreams and daily life, and, haltingly, what had happened when the vile creature had made an appearance two days before in her absence.

But instead of recoiling from him, Eliva took his hand and squeezed it. "I am so sorry, I didn't know. I knew there was something going on with you, but..." She huffed a ragged breath. "We are a team, and I failed. I was so absorbed with my own problems and desires that I ignored yours. Nalini's anger at me was well-placed. I know Diana will never accept me, now, anyway."

Talfryn looked at her solemnly. "First off...you finally admit that we're a team?" Eliva play-punched his shoulder. He play-rubbed it. Distracted, he almost really tripped over a clump of grass. "And second, I'm sure Diana'd have you in a heartbeat if she really knew you." *What is she supposed to accept Eliva for, again?*

"You're just saying that to be nice."

Miser chittered and rolled his eyes, and Genia huffed in amusement. "Hush up, you two." Talfryn glared at them both. "I mean it." He would've said more had the prophecy not come forthwith into his mind. Images of the wolficorn. Of him and Eliva attacking it.

"Talfryn, what is it?"

Head pounding, Talfryn tried to concentrate on Eliva. "The wolfi—the aeternae—"

Eliva cupped his face, her fingers warm despite the coming night's chill. "Talfryn, you cannot let the beast haunt you forever. You must face it—your prophecy demands it. Mayhap that is what you needed to do all along—face the aeternae to conquer your fears: '*In facing the monster thou must attend.*'"

Talfryn sucked in a breath, then another. "I know. 'Spose I knew it all along, but just..."

"Did not want to admit it," she finished. "I understand that more than you know. But, Talfryn, you do not have to do this alone."

He slid his hand over hers. How could he say that he feared her death too? It took every ounce of effort to respond, his throat dryer than a drought. "Are you sure? He smells pretty bad."

Eliva smirked, and the butterflies returned to his stomach. "Then I will pinch my nose so as not to be distracted by his stench."

Talfryn grinned back.

Eliva's back straightened. She nocked an arrow and spun around.

Out of the trees ran Asinia and Idaise. They stopped in front of Talfryn and Eliva, not appearing even a tad winded. They looked at Talfryn in expectation, sending nervous glances at Eliva.

Idaise spoke first. "We have come to bring you back to the abbey, Talfryn."

"I can't go back."

The dryad nearly choked, her long brown hair flowing with her reaction. "But you must. As the Keeper of the Prophecy, you are needed."

Talfryn shook his head. "Nay, nay, that's not it. I will go back, but first I must take care of something."

"And that is?" Asinia asked in a rush.

"I'm going to hunt the aeternae."

Idaise smiled. "Then we are with you." Her green sister nodded, drawing her weapons.

Talfryn's gaze slid to Eliva. She nodded encouragingly. Rubbing his hands together to boost his nerves, he announced, "Then let's hunt us an aeternae. Also,"—he smirked—"how long have I had this amazing title?"

❧

THE CLUB SLAMMED into the stone wall, clipping Padric's ear on its way. Pain erupted in his head as he lunged at the escaping monk. The figure stumbled as Padric tugged on its sleeve, the fabric tearing at the shoulder seam. The club swung at his head and missed.

Stark memories of Aeron and his friends pummeling on him while incapacitated by the magical gas surfaced. *That shan't happen again.*

"Who are you?" Padric demanded, not expecting an answer. He slammed his fist into the man's stomach.

The man grunted in response, his foul breath filling Padric's nostrils as he slammed him into the stone wall. Gasps escaped Padric's lungs with the impact, his head cracking against the wall.

"Stop, you!" Rawlins hollered.

Sleeve still clutched in Padric's grasp, the assailant yanked, tearing it one last time to flee in the opposite direction.

Dazed and breathless, Padric fell to his bottom while Rawlins chased the man. A pair of hands clutched at his arm. Jerking his head up, he made a fist to strike.

"Easy, easy!" Gregorio said. "It is only me."

Padric's head and shoulders sagged in relief.

"Here, rest against the wall."

Leaning back, the growing lump on his head bumped the stone and he flinched.

"Sorry," Gregorio said. "What happened?"

"Brother Fabian." Padric indicated the wounded monk.

Gregorio moved to the other side of the felled man, and Padric grimaced at the small puddle of blood pooling under his rumpled white robe.

Padric shut his eyes. "Poor Brother Fabian."

A low groan caught his attention. Opening his eyes, he saw the monk quiver.

"Brother Fabian." He rolled to his knees beside the poor man. "We shall find help."

"S-S-S-Sir Pa-Pa-Pa—"

"I am here, Brother." He raised the monk's head to his lap and squeezed his hand.

The brother swallowed. A trickle of blood slid from his mouth. "I must g-give you s-some...thing." His chubby hand reached to his middle, patting his ample stomach, then his side. He slid his hand along his robe. After a few moments, Padric realized he was looking for a pocket.

"Here, allow me to help," Gregorio offered. Digging into the monk's robe, he found the pocket in question and retrieved a folded piece of parchment. "Is this what you wanted?"

"Y-y..." He gave the slightest nod. "You'll need this to-to open..."

Boots scraped against stone, and Padric jerked his head up, but it was only Rawlins, a scowl darkening his features. In his fury, he winked in and out of visibility. *Or is that just my vision going?*

"Probably not good news." Gregorio frowned.

By the time Padric looked down again at the monk's pale face, Brother Fabian had fainted. His stomach rose and fell, indicating life, thankfully.

While Gregorio left to find help, Padric stuffed the fabric of the monk's white robe into the bleeding wound. Rawlins stood guard in case the assassin returned.

Gregorio returned with helpers from the infirmary carrying a stretcher. On their heels were Brynwen and Brother Howell, rushing to their aid. Brynwen drew in a breath when she saw all the blood covering Padric, Gregorio, and Rawlins. Eyebrows drawing together, Brother Howell's skin paled at the blood and his friend's sorry state. He crossed himself, murmuring a prayer.

Allowing a healer to take charge of Brother Fabian's wound, Padric shook his head. "It is not our blood. We are fine."

Brynwen fell into Padric's waiting arms. When she looked up at him, she regarded him with skepticism.

"The assassin escaped," Rawlins grumbled, ignoring Brynwen's scrutiny. He kept his weapons drawn.

After verifying the two knights were not about to die, Brynwen followed the healers carrying the unconscious monk to the infirmary. "Please don't let yourselves get killed while I am away."

"We would not dream of it," Padric replied.

"We'll wait until you return, m'lady," Rawlins said with a deep, sloppy bow. "What's this?" Leaning over, he picked up a leather cord, dowsed in the monk's blood. Despite the blood, a purplish hue emanated from it.

Padric took it up to study. "This cord radiates Medea's magic." The blood in his veins ran cold. "It must have been on the would-be killer's wrist when I tugged on his sleeve."

A rumble emanated from his friend's throat. "Then the abbey's been infiltrated." Rawlins had sealed the haunted garden's secret outer door after the rescue, but it seemed it had done no good. Perhaps it never would have mattered anyway if the abbot had invited them into the abbey in the first place.

"No place is safe," Padric lamented, closing his eyes against an oncoming headache. "Not even in God's house."

Brother Howell made to leave with the others, but Padric put up a hand. "Brother, might you stay a moment? I know you wish to be with your brother, but this is urgent."

"Of course." Howell's face was still pale from the shock of seeing his friend in such a state. "How may I be of service?"

"Where might we speak in private? This is not the best of places after all."

"I daresay not. Follow me, I know another place where no one goes."

Howell led them to a recess under the church in the catacombs. It was so dark, their torches barely cast any light on the long-forgotten stone tombs of monks, monarchs, and saints. "Sometimes, when I need complete solitude, I come here."

"My kind of place," Rawlins said.

Padric grinned. "He does not jest."

Padric withdrew the folded parchment from his tunic. The edges were smeared with Brother Fabian's blood. He unfolded the parchment while the other two looked over his shoulder.

It was a charcoal drawing of an iron key. It had a rounded top and a large hole to fit through a key ring.

"He wanted me to get the key off the abbot," Padric explained.

"Sounds easy enough." Rawlins shifted.

"How do you intend to do that?" Brother Howell asked.

"If only Ombag were here," Rawlins muttered. The little *cobalus* thief Ombag, a sort of goblin, had helped them in their previous adventure in the Labyrinth.

"We have someone just as good." Padric clapped Rawlins on the shoulder. "Rawlins, a demonstration is in order."

The stoic knight eyed his friend. "Now?"

Padric nodded.

Rawlins rolled his eyes. "Fine."

Removing the dagger from its sheath, Padric placed it on the ground between them.

The next instant, Rawlins disappeared. Brother Howell gasped when the dagger disappeared from the ground.

After another couple of heartbeats, Rawlins reappeared holding a dagger in his hand.

"Perfect. I will take that back now, thank you." Padric grinned and held out his hand. Rawlins handed it back to Padric, who sheathed the blade. "There, you see?"

The initial shock over, Brother Howell smiled. "Mayhap we have a chance, after all."

CHAPTER 40

*T*alfryn was a wreck. After announcing that he would go hunt the wolficorn, he realized what a bad idea it was. His whole body threatened to tremor the closer they got to the monster of his nightmares. And the entire time, the beast was in his head, taunting him, awaiting his arrival.

"You and all your dryad friends will meet a most painful end. Especially your little red-headed swain."

"Get outta my head." Talfryn growled.

Eliva touched his arm in concern.

"It's close," he answered instead. Miser agreed, his red fur on edge, and he paced non-stop around Talfryn's shoulders.

"We will kill it," Eliva said with confidence. The tight grip on her polearm reinforced her words, her dagger and short sword also hung dangerously from her belt. The dryads glided through the forest in an equally deadly manner.

"Then we'll show Diana its pelt, and you'll be accepted as a Huntress." He managed to smile, but his insides hurt at the realization that he might never see her again after that.

Eliva bit her lip. "We will see what she thinks. Since I am not—"

"Eliva." He took her unencumbered hand in his. "She will. She'll love you." The tentative smile she gave brought some lightness to his chest.

Talfryn noticed Idaise and Asinia glancing back at them for the briefest moment, but he couldn't guess their thoughts. Idaise ran ahead several paces.

Miser asked him a question, drawing a snort from Talfryn in response.

"What did he say?" Eliva asked.

"He wants to know if you hunt acorns on Diana's Hunt, and if so, he's pondering joining too."

Eliva's full-on laugh enveloped him. The lovely sound made Talfryn even more hopelessly enamored. "That is a good question, Miser," she said. "I shall ask her should I ever speak with her."

Miser spun around, squeaking about being in love with her, that she was a squirrel—er, a non-squirrel after his own heart. Talfryn wasn't sure if he meant Eliva or Diana, and frankly, was afraid to ask.

Eliva raised a brow. "Now what did he say?"

"Just really excited about the acorns."

A cold feeling swept across Talfryn like a chill wind, but the calm evening had no wind. Not even the night creatures were making any noises. "We're getting closer," he said, breathless.

Eliva sped up to warn the others about the creature's imminent presence.

"Oh, little fool," came the wolficorn's rough voice. *"I can smell you and your little friends."* Talfryn shivered, legs frozen in place.

Again.

No, no, no, no.

*"Thank you for bringing them to me. They shall die such...*deliciously painful *deaths. And, my little fool, I will grant you the boon to watch first, before you follow them to the underworld!"*

"Get out of my head," Talfryn muttered. "Already been to an underworld, thanks." Sweat matted his wavy hair to his forehead. *I'm in charge of this mission. I need to act like it,* he told himself this despite the terror gripping his heart which begged him to flee in the opposite direction. Glancing up at Eliva, which was surprisingly hard to do at the moment, he gasped out a command. He grasped at some semblance of Padric or Warin's authority. Raising his voice, he announced, "Circle up. It's… here. Genia, get out of here."

Genia didn't hesitate. Her wings unfurled and she glided out of the trees.

Having heard his order, the leading nymphs spun around. Idaise was the farthest ahead. She took two steps before she whipped her head around, raising her polearm.

A giant gray blur darted into her, carrying her away. She cried out in defiance as the wolficorn sped off. Then all was eerily silent.

Shocked, Talfryn and Eliva made eye contact while Asinia cried out for her sister.

Poor Idaise.

In silence, the remaining three made a tense circle, their backs facing inward. Each breath was a struggle for Talfryn, trying to keep himself calm. Alert. He gripped both weapons in his hands. "Not panicking, not panicking," he mumbled under his breath. "Miser, could you please stop squeezing my shoulder? You should go into that tree and be our lookout."

If it can't sneak up on us, we might have a chance, he told himself.

"At dying faster?" the wolficorn crooned.

"I hate you."

"The feeling is mutual."

Miser'd bounded halfway to the tree before he shouted unpleasant things Talfryn's way.

The wolficorn only laughed. Raw. Ancient Loathsome. That was when Talfryn realized the laughter wasn't just in his head this time. Eliva and Asinia's heads popped up, stances ready, scowls marring their beautiful features. They'd also heard it and were searching for the beast.

Then it was there, its eyes glowing red in the dying daylight. The full moon was nigh.

His courage faltered and he almost dropped his weapons as he relived the deaths of Leowyn and Ulysses from the wolficorn's horror-inducing horns. He wished he'd practiced archery more. If he could shoot it, he might survive this night. But he only had his hatchet and broadsword. *You beat him before,* he reminded himself. He spared a glance at Eliva, her eyes bright and determined, then at Asinia on his other side. Next, his mind flitted to Brynwen and Padric and his other friends. Grandfather and Samuel. He'd not let them down if he could help it. *If we don't kill it now, it could attack Bryn and my friends later.*

"This is it."

"Talfryn?" Eliva asked, worry creasing her forehead.

Taking a deep breath, he answered. "Ready." Then he willed his legs to move, shouting as loud as possible while the ugly beast sprinted forward.

CHAPTER 41

"*E*xcuse me, Abbot Caradoc?" Gregorio asked as the monks filed out of the three o'clock service.

Padric and Rawlins watched from the shadows as the head monk looked down his nose at the youthful-looking immortal and his worn, rumpled clothes. Padric liked the abbot even less for it.

"Yes, my child?" the abbot asked, trying—and failing—to look attentive. Mostly he just looked annoyed.

"It is about Brother Fabian."

At the monk's name, Abbot Caradoc froze for a second, then his thin lips pinched together. "I am most grieved about Brother Fabian's attack. We are looking into the matter but have yet to find the culprit. I cannot fathom how it happened in our very walls." He shook his head sadly. "You were among those who found him, were you not?"

"Indeed, I was. A most awful business. I am glad he survived."

Gregorio continued, "I wonder if you might, perhaps, consider saying a couple Masses for Brother Fabian's recovery? I would be most happy to donate to the abbey."

The abbot's eyes lit up for such a brief moment before resuming his normal *I-am-holier-than-thou-because-I-have-a-title* look that Padric thought he had imagined it. "That is a most generous offer. But I could not possibly take your money."

Padric nodded at Rawlins to begin his task. In answer, Rawlins disappeared.

"But I insist. You see, I..." Gregorio trailed off as Rawlins's shadow hovered over the tile behind the unsuspecting abbot. "I...am discerning becoming a monk too. You know, leave the world behind, live a life of prayer and contemplation."

A young layman, late coming out of the church, startled when he saw the abbot. Padric thought he was the sacristan. He made the slightest bow before hurrying behind Abbot Caradoc. He slammed into thin air, stumbling back with a great "Oof!"

A ring of over a dozen keys crashed to the stone floor.

Padric winced. He hoped Rawlins would not materialize before everyone. Luckily, he stayed invisible.

Abbot Caradoc spun around in alarm. "David, for heaven's sake, what are you doing, man?"

Perplexed, David scratched his head and reached for the fallen keys. "F-forgive me, Abbot. I don't know what happened."

The abbot snatched the keys from David's outstretched hand. "See that it does not happen again." He re-attached them to his belt.

"Yes, sir. I mean, no, sir." Bowing twice, David gave Gregorio an incredulous look before scurrying away down the corridor.

"Where was I?" Gregorio asked, bringing the abbot's attention back to the conversation. "Oh yes, I wish to do more for the Church, starting with donating all of my worldly money and lands." The abbot would absolutely laugh himself off the belfry once he found out how much coin Gregorio Fiori, the tutor of maths, history, and languages, had to his name. Besides, the land his godly family owned was not only hidden where the money-grabbing abbot would never find it, but Circe and Helius would strike dead whoever tried to claim the land as their own.

Nevertheless, that seemed to do the trick, for Abbot Caradoc grinned. *Rather greedily*, Padric thought. "That is most delightful, *Signore* Fiori. Are you looking to join our order or one of the others, such as the

Franciscans? Our order and abbey, of course, is the most sought after. *In my humble opinion*, that is."

"Of course, I would like some time to decide."

"Splendid. Why, just the other day..."

Padric had no doubt Crucis Valle was the best adorned, with lush tapestries, silver platters, and unending wine—at least for the knights, nobles, and maidens of substance who visited.

"Have you decided, then?" Abbot Caradoc asked, arms folded in expectation.

Padric bit back a snort at the monk's enthusiasm.

Nodding, Gregorio bowed his head. "I believe white is best suited to me. Don't you think, Abbot Caradoc?"

The abbot grinned. "Precisely." His eyes shifted for a moment, then slid back to Gregorio. "Please forgive me, *Signore* Fiori, but there are matters I must attend to. I trust I will see you at the evening meal to discuss this further? Good." He brushed past Gregorio as a gnat might escape from a hungry frog.

The moment the abbot was out of sight, Rawlins reappeared and dangled a large ring filled with keys, the beginnings of a grin raising his lips.

AERON PACED AROUND THE LIBRARY. *So close.* Padric and his fool friends resided in the same building, and yet Medea forbade him and the huntsmen from destroying them all. It was bad enough that the huntsman had failed to kill the nosy monk earlier in the day. But Medea did not want them destroyed...yet. It would raise too many questions about how guests of the abbey had been murdered under their roof.

Instead, Aeron played babysitter to the carpenter's apprentice while he finished the final touches of Medea's chariot. Meanwhile, she got to visit Olympus for the final preparations before the full moon. Still, at this late juncture, she refused to relay her plan for the chariot, other than that it was needed for the ritual. Everything else was in place.

And the carpenter, Kett, kept throwing suspicious-looking glances in all directions.

"The carpenter is up to something," Aeron confided to the Shadow.

"He no doubt wishes to thwart our plans. Or hopes to be rescued. And yet, his friends are none-the wiser that we are here."

Aeron cracked his knuckles. "Mayhap I should go ensure he is following Medea's instructions to the letter. We wouldn't wish him to fail, would we?"

The Shadow glared in Kett's direction. *"Not at all, nay."*

With a wicked grin, Aeron strode up to the chariot Kett was fiddling with, his tools strewn about his work area: hammer, nails, saw, planer, and shave-grass. A couple of nails stuck out of his mouth. He seemed deep in concentration.

"Working diligently, I see," Aeron commented. Kett's work was exquisite, given the short timeframe he had been allotted to complete the task. Any non-demigod carpenter would have taken four times as long. "Are you nearly finished, lad?"

Instead of answering, Kett continued to hammer a nail into the bed of the contraption. As though he hadn't heard Aeron at all. This instigated fury in Aeron's chest.

"I said, are you nearly done?"

Silence.

Peering over his shoulder, Aeron called Stanley and Barnaby over. "Take him by the arms."

Kett's head popped up at that. The two huntsmen grabbed his arms, and the nails fell from Kett's mouth. "What...what're you doing?"

"I asked a question, and you failed to answer. That calls for immediate instruction." His lips drew up at the color draining from Kett's face.

Hauling him to his feet, Kett struggled against them.

"Now, Kett." He pulled his fist behind him and brought it forward to slam into Kett's stomach. "Tell me, or I shall strike you again."

Kett bent in half, the huntsmen's arms the only things keeping him on his feet. A cough escaped his lips as he gasped for breath. "Yes... nearly done."

"Nearly done…" Aeron leaned in for the answer.

Nostrils flaring, Kett spat in his face.

Aeron didn't flinch as the spittle covered his face. Very calmly, he stood to his full height and wiped it off with a white handkerchief from his pocket, a last birthday gift from his mother before she died. The only good person in his life until Janus came along. Without a word, he raised his hand and made a circular motion with his finger. The huntsmen gripped Kett's arms tighter.

"What are you doing?" Kett asked again, voice cracking.

"Continuing our lesson, dear Kett. What say you, fellows? What number of thrashings would teach Kett some manners?"

"Beggin' pardon, sir," Barnaby said, "but ya don't wanna kill 'im 'fore he's finished buildin' the chariot."

"Nay, I suppose not." Aeron sighed. Medea would have his hide if the chariot wasn't finished on time. "A short lesson, then." Making a fist, he dealt the first five blows to Kett's stomach and sides.

To his surprise and grudging approval, the lad didn't cry out or beg for mercy, despite his trembling body. *Brave. We'll see how long that lasts.*

Five blows later, the huntsmen dropped the drooping, panting carpenter onto the carpet.

Aeron bent down and helped Kett to his knees. In a few movements, he secured Kett's tunic which had gotten twisted around his torso. Kett only winced, but didn't make another sound.

"Now that that sordid business is over, let's finish the chariot, eh?"

Kett gave a submissive nod and shuffled slowly on his hands and knees the four paces to the chariot. Picking up his hammer and nails, he resumed his work.

Fifteen minutes later, at the chime of the tenth bell, he lowered his tools to the ground. Large beads of sweat covered his forehead. "Done."

"Very good, Kett." In three strides, Aeron was beside the chariot, inspecting every nail and wooden peg. Not a thing could be out of place, Medea had said. "Well done, lad."

"Can…can I go now?" he asked with big, hopeful eyes.

"You miss your friends, don't you?"

Kett said nothing, but it was clear in his expression.

"I am afraid your task with us isn't done yet. Drogo, I leave him to your capable hands."

"With pleasure. Lads," Drogo directed. A dark gleam sparked in his eye as he cracked his knuckles one at a time.

As they surrounded Kett, the carpenter searched each face, breathing raggedly with pain and fear. "What are you going to do?"

"Medea wants you as her guest of honor. We thought it best to tenderize you a bit first." He nodded at Drogo and his men. "And fear not. Your cries shan't be heard outside, as Medea so kindly enchanted the doors to keep all noises in."

What color had been left in Kett's face drained.

As one, the huntsmen approached and pounded on the lad with fists and boots. This time, Kett's screams echoed around the tomes and shelves surrounding them. Aeron grinned from ear to ear at the glorious sound.

CHAPTER 42

*B*rynwen wrung her hands in her skirts. She'd already nearly
ripped out the remainder of her hair via twisting too hard,
so now her poor skirts drew the short straw for her worrying hands, as
she willed the tall library door to open.

The healer had grudgingly released her from the infirmary only that
morning. Her head still ached, but the healer did not fear any damage
had been done. He did, however, tell her to take it easy—to which she
silently snorted in amusement.

"Please hurry." Brother Howell looked both ways down the deserted
corridor.

"I'm hurrying," Warin spat. He twisted the key into the lock of the
tall, ornate library door, and jiggled it. The scene of Saint Thomas
Aquinas at a scribe's desk, holding a quill, a thin yellow halo over his
head, peered up to heaven. Brynwen loved the detail of ink staining his
fingers.

Somehow, it reminded her of Talfryn. The stains on his fingers were
like the dirt and grime that always managed to attach themselves to her
brother's skin and clothing when he worked the land. Her chest
constricted all the more, wondering what had become of him after
Padric had sent him away, and if he would return.

Padric had confessed his part in telling Talfryn to leave after the aeternae's fateful attack, his remorse evident in his speech and bearing. She didn't remember much of the attack very well, but learning of Ulysses's death had upset her deeply.

With a grunt, Warin gave up on one key and attempted the next. And the next. Brynwen's stomach twisted with each failure. They would be discovered soon, she could feel it.

The sixth key, however, fit into the lock and turned with a loud *click*. "See?" Warin smirked with grand confidence. Quickly, Brynwen ushered everyone into the dark library after the knight.

In quick succession, Brynwen lit one candle while Cornelia lit another. Once the candles came to life, Padric made a direct route to the door at the other end of the room, not forty paces away, skirting piles of tomes, scribe desks, and other obstacles. "This is the door. It glows a pale blue." He touched it, feeling for what, she couldn't tell. Brynwen couldn't see the glow, and it didn't appear that anyone else could either.

When she reached Padric's side, she clutched his hand. *This is it, isn't it? We either save everyone or die trying.*

Warin went through the same ritual as before, trying and grunting with each key, but none of them fit the lock. "These wretched keys! All that work for naught." He wound up his arm to chuck them across the room.

"Let me see." Gregorio took the keys from a grumbly Warin and inspected them and the lock.

Brynwen sidled up next to him and did the same. "Is this door's lock different? It looks almost new."

"Yes," Gregorio agreed. "The door is old, but the lock and latch are new."

"How do we get in, then?" Rawlins shoved his way to Gregorio, glaring at the keys as though he could stare them into submission. Nalini and the dryads also pushed forward.

Before she knew it, Brynwen had been jostled to the back of the group. Fuming, she had a mind to shove her way back in. However, their bodies were like a wall, so she soon gave up and let her gaze wander around the candlelit room. They had been so entranced with the magical door, no one had noticed the rest of the room. Atop a great pile of discarded wood, tools, chairs, and ancient books that came up past her waist rested an upended oaken bookcase. It saddened her that someone had treated the books and furniture with such vehemence.

With a sigh, she was about to inspect another part of the room when she spotted a hammer on the floor, partly covered by the rubble. She reached down to pick it up, but it was stuck underneath the heavy ruined bookcase.

Nalini came up behind her. "What have you found, Brynwen?"

Brynwen sucked in a breath, not sure she wanted to speak to the dryad. But practicality, and manners, made her think better of it. "This looks like one of Kett's hammers."

"So it does." Nalini reached down to remove one end of the book case while Brynwen gripped the other. Together, they inched it up enough for Nalini to kick the hammer out into the open. After setting the bookcase down, the dryad picked up the hammer. The initial "K," carved with fancy curls, stood out near the head.

"It is his." Brynwen gasped. "Did he leave it here for us to find?"

"It is possible."

Brynwen and Nalini searched some more, but found nothing else. Having no luck with the door, the others moved to the center of the room.

"They have made a decision on something." Brynwen followed Nalini back to the others, disappointed there hadn't been more clues.

Padric held the useless key ring. "If we do not have the key, and it is not on Abbot Caradoc's person, then the only other logical place is his bedchamber."

Warin swiped the keys from Padric's hand. "And one of the keys will surely let us in."

"Please allow me." Brother Howell released a resigned breath, his expression solemn. He plucked the keys from Warin's grasp. "I know which key will open the abbot's bedchamber."

BROTHER HOWELL LED Padric and the others through the silent corridors of the abbey. Brynwen stayed by his side as they descended upon the abbot's room. They only met one timid brother, who, upon seeing the fully armed knights, turned and strode the other way.

"What if he's in there?" Brynwen asked.

Padric clenched his fists. "Then we shall bind him as Kett is most likely bound. It is plain he is in cahoots with Janus and Medea."

Brother Howell's lips pinched together, but he stopped in front of Abbot Caradoc's room without a word.

"What's wrong?" Warin asked.

"It is just that...it feels like such an invasion of privacy. And to tie him up? The abbot?"

"Remember, Brother, he is working with Janus," Padric pointed out.

Rawlins shrugged with disinterest. "Binding him's better'n he deserves."

The dryads nodded in agreement.

"You are right. Of course." Brother Howell sighed. "All right, let us get this over with." Taking a deep breath, he touched the key that would open the bedchamber door.

"Just let me do it." Rawlins grabbed up the key and stuffed it into the lock.

It unlocked with a soft *click*. He cracked open the heavy oaken door. When Brynwen's candlelight spilled into the room, Padric grimaced at the poor taste of the place. Large tapestries filled with scenes of the hunt, grapes above silver and gold chalices, and what looked to be Dionysius amid ewers of unending wine and unclothed maidens. A gold water pitcher sat atop a golden basin. The sheets of the four poster bed were pure satin, the curtains hanging from the posts a matching shade of crimson.

Gregorio wrinkled his nose in disgust. "He certainly has a taste for gaudiness."

"I could not agree with you more." Padric stooped beside a large, ornate chest, afraid of what horrible things the "holy man" kept inside.

To Padric's relief, it was only priestly vestments, rich in satins, lace, and linen. A few items of clothing had tiny holes. *And, apparently, moths.*

They took the place apart, searching for the key they needed, but they found not one key, even to the privy.

"If it's not on him, and it's not in this room, then where is it?" Warin asked.

Scanning the upturned room, Gregorio rubbed his thumb over his blue and silver amulet. "We must search again."

Padric and Brynwen looked at each other. They were running out of time.

"You heard him." Padric sighed inwardly. He had just opened the drawer in the delicately carved scribe's desk when at least two sets of footsteps padded down the hallway.

"Go on," the abbot's clear, annoyed voice said. "Open the door. I haven't got all night."

Rawlins motioned for everyone to go to the corner wall by the door.

A much older man's shaky voice answered. "Yes, Father Abbot. Mayhap you misplaced your keys in the—"

"Just open the door! Do you want to spend a fortnight in the stocks?"

"Ye-yes, sir—I mean, no, sir, not at all. Right away, sir."

Keys jangled, and Padric imagined the poor man's hand shaking as he noisily slid the key into the lock.

As the outsiders spoke, everyone scrambled over to the wall and Rawlins spared no time in grabbing a couple of arms instead of his weapons. With everyone squashed together, Rawlins sucked in a breath and made them all disappear right as the door creaked open. Brother Howell gasped in surprise, and someone slapped a hand over his mouth. Then the candles blew out.

"About time!" huffed the abbot.

"We could look in your room for the..." The man with white, wispy hair gaped at the ransacked room. Light from the candle he held in his gnarled hand spilled into the room.

The abbot gaped at his once resplendent room, all color draining from his face.

"Oh, my," said the servant. "Should I get the—"

"Nay, nay, nay. Get out, Bertram. Tell no one about this. I'll handle it."

"Very well. I—"

Abbot Caradoc took Bertram's candle and slammed the heavy door in his face. Breathing heavily, he leaned against the carved panels, staring at the room. Fright, the last thing Padric expected, pooled over his face. "Who would..." he muttered. "They better not have found it. They could not have found it." Wringing his hand in his robe, he moved into the room, straight away heading to his lavish bed. Stepping over the strewn silk sheets, he grazed a hand down the left post, down its ridges, then stopped about three-quarters of the way down. He slid his thumb along a ridge, then pressed in.

A little door popped open above his hand, about the length from the tip of his finger to the bottom of his palm. He sighed in relief as he stooped to look inside. "Ahhh, there you are. The master will be pleased. I should have our visitors drawn and quartered for their insolence." A chortle escaped his lips as he grinned. "Yes, that will be perfect. They have already failed, anyway."

"Who *are* you talking to?" Warin's disembodied voice asked.

Gasping, Abbot Caradoc clutched the key to his bosom and spun about, but saw no one. "Who is there?" he squeaked. He looked like a child who had been caught red-handed stealing a pastry from the kitchen before mealtime.

In an instant, Padric could see his body and all of his friends. Face set as stone, Rawlins's hands had released the others, and he strode forward, drawing his sword.

Padric matched his friend's stride, clapping him on the shoulder. Warin, not to be left behind, glowered at the abbot. All three loomed over the older man.

"Ah, thank you. This is exactly what we came for." Padric plucked the key from the abbot's frozen fingertips. "How thoughtful of you to find it for us, dear abbot. Rawlins, would you be so kind as to guide Abbot Caradoc to a seat? He looks a bit pale."

Taking the abbot by the arm, Rawlins's teeth gleamed as he smiled. "Gladly." Caradoc's eyes widened to saucers as Rawlins squeezed.

When he was settled, Warin began grilling him with Rawlins at his back, brandishing his own very sharp daggers. "How long have you worked for Janus? Where does the door to the library lead? What do you get out of all of this?"

The abbot stammered his replies. "I...he came to *me*. At the time, I was a struggling merchant with many connections, but the blasted plague killed off most of them. After the plague, times were hard, but I scraped together what I could, rebuilding my connections. About six years ago, I ran into a delightfully dark maiden, Madam Medea, who brought me to her employer. I had no inkling he was a god until he showed me his second face. Not wishing to decline the offer of a *god*— and it was a very good offer at that—I agreed. He set me up with forged credentials as an ambassador monk returned from Spain, and I quickly worked my way up to the appointment of the abbot of this fine establishment. It was so dreary when I arrived. But things changed quickly, so they did, thanks to my cunning." He beamed. "Don't you approve of the fine atmosphere and silver serving plates? That was all my idea."

All this time, Brother Howell stood seething, eyes rimmed in red. He took a trembling step forward, but Padric held up his arm. This was only going to get worse.

"And the library?" Padric asked.

"Ah, yes," Caradoc said slowly. "The library. Janus himself came and installed the special key and lock for it. We moved all of the scribes down to the basement near the crypt where they can work in peace. Oh, they complain about the oppressing darkness and draft, but—"

"Where does the library door lead?" Warin reiterated.

Caradoc shrunk in his chair. "To Olympus. This building is directly above a lay line which can reach Olympus with little difficulty. You see, Janus has a plan for the full moon." Sitting up to full height, he gave them a knowing smile, as though he were going to share a secret. "But, I am afraid, my friends, you are too late. My lord Janus will have already begun the ritual."

Padric studied the monk-impersonator and determined that he was, for the most part, telling the truth. "If the ritual has started, why are you not there?"

"I would have been had my keys not been stolen from me." He glared daggers at the dangling key ring in Gregorio's hand. The scholar glowered right back.

Standing beside the desk, Brother Howell exclaimed in great agitation, "How could you?" He took up a letter opener as long and finely designed as a priceless dagger. Quite a sharp blade, too. "I did not always agree with your ways, but you were our abbot, and I respected you as my elder and as a church father. But this...this *betrayal* of us all, of allowing *Janus* of all people, to turn your heart against us. It is vile. His way is most evil."

Warin dove in, clutched the fake abbot's pristine robe in both fists, and hauled him off the floor at least six inches. Arm muscles bulging with strength, Warin spoke through clenched teeth. "Listen to me very carefully, your abbotness. You will tell me the details of this ritual, and you will tell me now. Or else you and my friends Rawlins, the dryads, and your once-devoted monk here will become very closely acquainted."

Rawlins made a point of flipping his dagger in the air and catching it. The dryads brandished their weapons. Brother Howell seethed with the abbot's treachery.

"I might consider his words closely, were I you," Padric spoke calmly.

Eyes round with terror, the abbot nodded his head profusely. "Yes, yes. Um, well, I don't know much. Only that they needed all the gods on Mount Olympus and two flying chariots for various parts of the ritual. My lord Janus invited me as a means of good faith and immediate delivery of my previously agreed upon payment."

"Which is?"

"Immortality."

Everyone paused at that.

"Oh my stars," Gregorio mumbled, and wiped his face with his hands.

"What is it?" Warin asked.

"Janus." He spat the name out like a curse. "Janus can no more grant immortality than I can. Only Jupiter and Juno can grant that boon." His face dropped. "Unless..."

"Unless?" Padric prodded.

"Unless he takes Jupiter's power. Oh, no." If it weren't possible before, Gregorio's face became ever more pale. "That must be his plan. His original intention was to make him weak with sorrow when Apollo was to die by Helius's hand. And then the amulet of adamant was to drive Jupiter's power from him. Without them, there is only one other way, but it is difficult, and requires a particular ritual. *Mater* told me once."

Expression solemn, Nalini stepped forward. "It requires the sacrifice of a mortal whose blood must mix with the immortal's. Then the immortal is to drink the blood, which forfeits their power, making them mortal."

"And able to be killed," Gregorio finished.

Padric's chest constricted. "We must go. Now." He prayed they were not too late.

Eyes narrowed, Brother Howell charged forward and held the letter opener in surprisingly steady hands at the abbot's throat. "Have you ever stood a hairsbreadth from a lion, Father Abbot? I have, and I must profess that her bite was far more severe than yours."

Mouth agape, Padric could not believe the words coming out of Brother Howell's mouth. The young monk showed great spirit of character and conviction.

"Go," Brother Howell said. "I shall watch over our *dear abbot* until your return. Be safe."

"But first." Nalini looked at Caradoc severely and removed her amulet. In an instant, her skin turned green. "I need a hair from your head."

"And"—Padric grinned—"we will need the habit of the no-good abbot."

CHAPTER 43

"*W*hy could you not make me an amulet like yours?" Padric asked.

Nalini raised her brow in expectation as he held the stoppered pink liquid to his lips.

"Because you also need to sound like the abbot."

Point taken. Scrunching his nose, he steeled himself for a foul smell and taste...but what met him was in fact pleasant. Of peaches and apples and something on the tip of his tongue which failed to come to him. *Probably better that way.* He downed Nalini's concoction. And waited.

"Do not look so surprised that it tastes sweet, Padric," Nalini teased. "Even Brynwen here liked my tea."

Brynwen scowled at her. "You mean the one with the sleeping draught in it?"

"What will it feel like?" Padric asked to keep the maidens from bickering. A belch burst from his lips, tasting of peach and apple and...*ah, yes, honey!*

His stomach churned.

Nalini took the vial and stoppered it. "The discomfort will dissipate in a few moments, then your body will shift."

The churning continued, somewhat like when he transformed, but those he had mastered. This felt like having indulged in a plethora of poor food choices.

Brynwen cupped his face, her eyes shining with concern. "Are you sure, Nalini?" She glanced at the dryad, then closed her mouth. "Of course. How silly of me to forget."

Padric would never forget the way Nalini had pretended to be Brynwen. But, he reminded himself, she had done it on her master Helius's impulse, not her own.

An itch began on Padric's face and Brynwen's hand recoiled as though a snake had bitten it. Raising a hand to scratch his nose, Nalini swatted his hand away. "Do not scratch."

It was odd having everyone stare at him in amazement. His entire body itched with an intolerable insistence, but he could do nothing about it. Then, abruptly, the intolerable sensation stopped.

"Uncanny," Warin commented. He poked Padric's nose—quite hard.

"Ow!" Padric rubbed his nose and cringed. Touching his face, and his hair—which was *gone* except for a few wisps—he stood inside the body of a stranger. "I do not much care for this."

"You volunteered," Rawlins commented.

Nalini smirked. "Fear not, Padric, it is only temporary. Now that the transformation is complete, it will only last a short time. Half an hour at most."

"Then we must be quick."

They stopped before the door to Olympus.

Brynwen smirked up at Padric. "You smell sweet."

Unfortunately, Padric's nostrils were inundated with the abbot's choice of scent: rose water. *He must bathe his entire body in it. An awful business.* "If anyone else were to say such a thing, I should lock them in the stocks for a week."

"Enough yapping, flowery man," Rawlins growled. Yet Padric caught a glint in his friend's eye.

Recalling the task at hand, Padric's smile sobered. "On my mark. Three, two…one." Sword hidden under his robe, Padric swung open the door. It opened on silent hinges to a scene of pure beauty. White, marble columns lined a wide, curved walkway for a long distance.

Torches nestled in sconces on every other column to light the traveler's path. Low-hanging clouds made the sky look wispy. It was just as dark on Mount Olympus as it was in England, however, the air of Olympus was cooler, more crisp, like an early spring evening. There was not an enemy in sight.

After a few seconds where nothing happened, Padric felt somewhat relieved. However, he knew the hardest part was yet to come.

"I don't like it" Rawlins gritted his teeth.

"Nor do I." Padric clasped his hands together as the monks did.

"It's likely a trap."

"No doubt."

Warin snorted, his sword glinting off a torch from Olympus. "To you, Rawlins, everything is a trap."

"He is right, you know," Gregorio said.

Brynwen asked, "Gregorio, have you been here before?"

"Never. Since Helius retired from the sky, my family has had little cause to come here. And that happened long before I was born."

They had only gone about a half a mile when the dryad scouts, Luciliana and Cornelia, returned.

"Beyond those clouds is the city. We can make it in a few minutes' time," Luciliana said.

Down the winding path they trod, cautious as ever for enemies, but there were none. His gut squirmed at the bad taste in his mouth despite the land's beauty. *No wonder the ancients dreamed of living here.*

Rawlins scanned the area, but no enemies came to greet them. "I still don't like this."

Padric could not have agreed more.

Luciliana set the foot of her polearm on the ground. "There are two guards at the entrance just beyond the mist."

"They are waiting for me, then." Padric donned his hood and made to embrace Brynwen.

She held out her hand to halt him. He gaped at her in confusion. *I thought we were past this.*

"I'm sorry, but I must refuse to embrace you," she said. "You see, I am promised to another."

Heat pulsed up Padric's neck. His gaze shifted to Warin.

"Instead," she continued, pulling his face back to her. "I will give you a favor of my deepest affection."

Opening his hand, she placed a small, stoppered vial filled with powders in varying layers of color: green, red, pink, purple, yellow. It was just like the one she had gifted him—that he unfortunately had to destroy—in Cataractonium. Some of the worry slid from his shoulders. Clutching the vial to his chest, he bowed. "I thank you, m'lady." He smiled, and when he rose, met her matching smile.

Rawlins folded his arms and cleared his throat. "Now that's finished, get a move on, o' great abbot."

CHAPTER 44

"For Ulysses!" Talfryn shouted as he charged the wolficorn.

Eliva's arrow twanged as it left the bow. The monster dodged, but she already had another arrow nocked and released it immediately. This one struck its shoulder.

But it kept coming.

The aeternae only had eyes for Talfryn. *"The time has come, little fool,"* it taunted.

"Someone's got a high pain tolerance," he commented. At the last second, Talfryn drew out his hatchet. If he could get a well-placed hit to its throat, that might do the trick.

However, that *was* the trick. Those bony protrusions didn't help the situation, either. He hadn't forgotten the last time he'd fought the monster. Then, the aeternae'd fallen from Helius's chariot a hundred feet or more, Talfryn's hatchet protruding from its back. This time, however, there was nowhere steep to fall down.

The hatchet was still there, the metal rusted from the elements since midsummer.

Hacking down, Talfryn aimed for its neck. The hatchet glanced off a pointy bone. No damage.

Eliva disregarded her bow for her polearm. Asinia bore her polearm down on the creature.

They poked and jabbed in a sort of graceful, deadly dance. However, the aeternae didn't seem bothered by their polearms. He gnashed his teeth and thrashed the horns on his head. One left a huge gash on Asinia's thigh. She crumpled. Talfryn leaped back just in time to avoid a pointy bone in his stomach.

The monster stepped back and ran in a circle, then whipped its head around, as Talfryn's sword skidded along its rump, a sharp bone smacking Eliva in the side.

She went down with a short cry.

"Eliva!" He tried to rush to her, but the monster cut him off.

Between the wolficorn's laugh and Eliva lying on the ground holding her side, Talfryn's heart pumped wildly. He roared in rage. "I'm sick of your laughter, Wolfi. Why's everything so funny to you?"

"There is nothing for me except to laugh at my situation; and you amuse me, little fool."

"Stop calling me that."

"Oh, little fool, you are most entertaining."

"He is trying to rile you up," Faunus's voice cut in. It was soft, difficult for Talfryn to hear. *"Do not let him. Instead, imagine my peaceful meadow."*

Startled by Faunus's voice in his head, Talfryn wanted to grate out his frustrations at the elder faun. But no, there wasn't much use in it, not when the stakes were so high. Instead, as he took a deep breath, he pictured the meadow as it should be—no time for more. "If I'm so entertaining, how d'you feel about this?"

He darted forward, each hand clasping a weapon. Fangs bared, the creature charged. Then Talfryn pivoted and barreled past it on the left, slicing his sword along its side. Before anything else, he needed to get Eliva and Asinia out of its sights.

Rearing, the beast growled. Talfryn met it halfway. Swipe and slash, blade verses claw. The hatchet chopped at bone. The impact jarred against Talfryn's arm, and the wolficorn howled, jerking its head back, almost pulling Talfryn off his feet. His arm strained at the impact. *I really don't want to do that again!*

But he didn't release his grip, and he swung the sword at its hide. A red slash cut across the beast's side until it stopped at a bone protrusion. "Not so fast, huh, Wolfi?"

The wolficorn growled deep and swiped at Talfryn's stomach. "Ah, so, ya don't like nicknames. Age hasn't made you any prettier. Ugh"—he covered his nose at the stench it let off—"or smell any nicer."

Out of the corner of his eye, Talfryn spied Eliva taking ginger movements to get to her feet. He stepped over an excessively long root to keep the monster's attention on him.

"Fools lower on the food chain should never speak in such a way to their betters."

Talfryn chortled. "Is 'better' the right word, though?"

The beast clawed at him.

"Another question you should ask yourself—why're you working with a witch like Medea?"

Gray nose wrinkling in disgust, the wolficorn released a deep-throated growl.

Ah, that's something.

Now on her feet, Eliva took slow, limping steps toward the wolficorn, polearm raised in both hands for a death strike. She wore a determined face, but Talfryn could see how much pain she was in.

Images of the two of them leering over the wolficorn with their weapons came forth again. Followed by the three of them in Olympus. Janus. The gods. Padric.

Then the images were gone, and he was left gaping at the wolficorn. *What do they mean?*

They wolficorn's eyes turned to slits. *"It seems I am not the only one in your head. Let me guess: Faunus? The mangy old faun cannot save himself this time."*

"What d'you know about him?" Talfryn asked defensively.

Another paw swung at his stomach, but this time Talfryn didn't react in time. An explosion of light seared his body, releasing a gasp as the claws sliced through his leather jerkin and ripped into his side. He crashed to the ground, weapons sprawling.

More images crashed into him, intermingling with shocking agony and the monster making its way to him. Olympus—the gods—the wolfi-corn running around Olympus, the prophecy, and—Medea. Her tooth necklace.

No. We have to kill it. Don't we?

The beast's roar pulled him out of his head. The dryads' war cry on her lips, Eliva stabbed the wolficorn in the back. It spun to attack.

Talfryn reached out. "Eliva—don't."

She didn't hear him, fighting off the monster with her polearm.

Grabbing up his weapons, Talfryn scrambled to his feet. Clenched his jaw to ignore the three deep, oozing grooves in his jerkin.

Medea. The tooth necklace.

"Wolfi!" Talfryn shouted. He slammed his sword down on a bone sticking out of its back to draw the monster's attention away from Eliva.

With a yelp, the wolficorn rounded on him, backing up so both Talfryn and Eliva were in its vision.

"Children of man are the most vile of all species," it spat. Spittle hung from its ugly maw. "Allow me to finish you off once and for all, so I might—" He paused mid-sentence.

"Get your necklace back?" Talfryn asked. "Or, more precisely, your teeth?"

The wolficorn's hackles raised, but the creature stayed still.

"That got its attention," Eliva muttered. She kept her grip on the polearm.

"Are they yours?" Talfryn's thumb slid along his hatchet, twitching to use it to deal the monster a fatal blow.

The growl deepened so low, Talfryn wasn't sure if it were only in his head. He thought the monster mightn't answer, but then it did.

"They are from my mate and child."

Talfryn startled. "You have a family?" He couldn't keep the disgust out of his voice.

"What is he saying?" Eliva's keen gaze never left the creature.

Talfryn repeated it for her. He struggled to believe that any creature would want to mate with this vile monster and produce children, let alone the chance that there might be *more* of them roaming around the countryside. But it gave him an idea.

"How'd Medea get the teeth?"

Anger radiated off the wolficorn's fur and horns. *"When my son was still a pup, I was out hunting when Medea snuck into our lair and killed both him and his mother. She took a tooth from each of them. It is a grave dishonor to go to the afterlife without every tooth, every bone intact. I swore the most violent of vengeances. Yet, knowing how much the teeth meant to me, she bound me to her indenture until she discerned the right time to return them. That was over two thousand years ago."*

The story softened Eliva's hard expression. Just a tad, mind you. "That sounds unbearable. Medea is nothing if not ruthless in taking whatever she wants however she likes. For your family, I am sorry. But it does not excuse you for killing Ulysses and other innocent people."

Talfryn agreed. He couldn't imagine going through something like that. "I agree. But I've an idea, aeternae. Why don't we make a pact?"

"What?" Eliva asked, incredulous. "Talfryn, you can't be serious."

"I am listening," the wolficorn growled.

"I'm completely serious. Do you trust me, Eliva?" Gazing into her green eyes, he prayed she'd understand.

The number of emotions flashing across her face said it all. Indignation that he had to ask if she trusted him. Anger at having to give up her greatest conquest. And defeat that he was probably right. At last, she directed a look of disdain at the wolficorn, but then gave Talfryn a quick nod. "Of course I trust you, Talfryn. It is the aeternae that I do not trust." She attempted a smile but it quickly fell.

That made Talfryn's blood pump just a bit more. He turned back to his nemesis. "You help us defeat Medea and Janus, and we'll ensure you get your family's teeth back. And then we'll all go our separate ways. Right, Eliva? Asinia?"

Asinia drew her shoulders taut, chin up. "This beast has murdered my sister for sport. He must be punished."

Eliva squeezed her polearm until her knuckles turned white. "Despite our enmity with this beast, I believe Talfryn is in the right. Do not look at me so."

"Idaise is dead, and you would betray her with this alliance!" Tears threatened to fall from the corners of Asinia's eyes.

"And the rest of the world will be dead, too, if we do not make a temporary truce." Her next words were in Latin, so Talfryn couldn't understand what was said.

Asinia threw dagger eyes at the wolficorn. After another several heart-wrenching beats, her hands squeezed so tight at her sides, she finally gave a slight nod. She answered Eliva in Latin.

Talfryn drew his lips into a thin line. *Our only course.* "Aeternae?"

It nodded slowly. *"I accept these terms."*

"Good. We need to get back to the abbey now—it's already twilight. Luckily, the monks'll be at vespers, so we shouldn't run into anyone."

"There is one thing you should know, human. Medea expects your friends to enter Mount Olympus. The moment your alpha ascends the flying contraption, the trap will be laid."

"But the prophecy..." Talfryn began. No, it couldn't be. Kett'd been kidnapped before he could finish the chariot. To save the gods, Padric needed to ride it—didn't he? How would he do that now?

"Then we must really hurry," Eliva said.

"Is it over?" Genia trotted into view, Miser fidgeting on her head. In contrast to the squirrel's antics, the black pegasos seemed calm. She stopped beside Talfryn to nuzzle against his arm while Miser leapt onto his shoulder, all his fur sticking straight out like a hedgehog, eyeing the wolficorn warily.

He took Eliva's hand and squeezed. "I'm so sorry about Idaise," he said to the maidens. Talfryn's throat was thick as he thought about how the dryad's life had been snuffed out like an ember under foot.

She squeezed back, not releasing his hand, as though he were her lifeline. She glared at the beast. "She would want it this way, to die in battle."

Asinia nodded, her eyes betraying only the barest ounce of pain. "My sister will be welcomed with open arms into Elysium."

"Come on." Eliva finished tying a tourniquet around Asinia's thigh. "We've got friends to save." To Talfryn's surprise, the hint of a smile stretched her lips. A challenge.

Talfryn's stomach did another little flip, and he forgot what he was about to say. Instead, he helped Asinia to her feet.

Shaking her mane, Genia said, *"I know of a shortcut to the portal through the abandoned stable. Medea and her horrible underlings use it often."*

Talfryn translated for the dryads. "Will anyone be there?"

Eliva shrugged. "I doubt Medea would leave more than a few henchmen. They shouldn't be difficult for us to handle." She clutched her bow for effect. "Shall we go, then?" she urged, touching his arm.

Heat flew up his neck and face like a lit hearth. "Uh, uh, yeah. Let's um…this way." He plunged toward the abbey.

"Humans are most strange," the wolficorn muttered as it loped ahead.

Genia whinnied in nervous agreement.

PART III
OLYMPUS

"Any moment might be our last. Everything is more beautiful because we're doomed. You will never be lovelier
than you are now. We will never be here again."

— **Homer**, *The Iliad*

CHAPTER 45

*O*nce past the mist, Mount Olympus opened up into a large Roman city with structures and columns everywhere—similar to Circe's home at Cataractonium, but on a godly scale. Everything was huge, and breathtaking, and made of marble.

Up ahead, two guards with sharp pikes moved to greet the disguised Padric. Behind him, the invisible Rawlins stalked in silence. They were not huntsmen, but some other mercenaries Janus had picked up. Emulating Abbot Caradoc, Padric held his head high and spoke. It was strange hearing his own voice raised an octave higher. "There you are. I almost became lost in this blasted place." He huffed as though exhausted. "I was told there would be transportation for me, but I see nothing. Not even a winged horse or chariot. Incompetence!" He pierced them with his gaze to emphasize his great displeasure.

One of the guards looked bored while the other had a scowl that ran into a long scar from cheek to scalp.

"We weren't told about any transport. Come this way, sir. The ritual's about to start."

Padric sniffed. "Such insolence. Fine, fine, lead the way, young men." Extending a long sleeve, he waved them on.

It was hard not to gape at the magnificence that met him despite the late hour, with exotic flowers in pots painted with ancient pictures of gods and mythical creatures with inscriptions in ancient Latin, all appearing brand new. And yet, the place was deserted. The only people roaming the city were a few guards and huntsmen.

At last, the guards stopped at the edge of the city and motioned Padric down a short incline. It leveled out for fifteen yards before descending into a small valley with one white-stone staircase traversing the length of the steep hill. At the bottom, the stair path enlarged into a circle of white marble columns which extended toward the sky, much like a hippodrome. Secured by plant vines to each of the nearly twenty columns was a person in robes. *The gods.* Scanning the columns, he found Circe's blonde updo and blue dress, and three columns down stood youthful Helius in purple robes. Pasiphae was tied to a column on the other side. Midway between Pasiphae and Helius, Padric spied a faun whom he assumed was Faunus. He guessed at the identities of many others, such as Jupiter with his gilt laurel crown, impeccable beard, and muscled arms ripe for lobbing lightning bolts at the earth. Mars tried to break his green bonds with his bulging muscles alone, but to no avail.

Unmistakable to miss were Janus and Medea, standing on a dais on the same level where Padric stood, close to the steps leading into the valley. The former's future face was giddy with expectation of the ritual to come. Medea looked amused, her gaze flicking every few seconds to the chariot with two massive snake-dragon creatures attached, not ten feet away. *Dracones?* Behind them, the Shadow Druid clasped his hands together in anticipation.

Unfortunately, the chariot was on the other side of the dais from where Padric stood. How to get to it without bringing attention to himself?

Surrounding the columns were a couple dozen armed huntsmen and mercenaries. Padric scoured the group for Aeron but did not see him. *Drat, where is he? And where is Kett being held?*

Keeping up his facade, Padric made his way to Janus and Medea, studying the area for any advantage, while Rawlins was to veer to the left toward a red tent up the hill where Kett might be kept. The others would likely head there too. If they could rescue Kett before the ceremony started, all the better.

As he approached Janus, Padric's skin crawled. Here was the god bent on world domination or destruction, depending on the day. Now that Padric approached, the past-facing face showed worry, and mumbled unintelligibly to himself. Padric bowed to Janus and Medea. The god of time looked the same as before, with smooth black hair and goatee. His juniper green robes resembled the ones he had worn in Cataractonium.

Janus clapped his hands together. "Ah, Abbot Caradoc, you are just in time. I feared you might be late."

Heart quickening, Padric wondered if the god knew the truth. But if so, Janus did not let on. "Yes, it is a long, winding road. But quite beautiful, my lord. Quite beautiful indeed." He peered around as though to breathe in the tranquil air, despite the event about to take place at the full moon. "But please, do not hold anything up on my account. I am but your humble servant and wish only to—"

Janus waved a dismissive hand. "Yes, yes, thank you, Caradoc. Always so eloquent with the vocabulary. Must be an English thing." The last bit was muttered so low Padric would not have caught it except for his enhanced hearing.

On three ornate legs, a small, round table covered with a red cloth stood beside Medea, holding a small bronze brazier, three bowls filled with grainy substances, a bronze chalice, and a bronze pitcher of dark liquid.

Like Circe, she uses bronze for her magic.

Janus clapped a second time, bringing Padric out of his reverie.

The god raised his voice so all could hear. "The time has come. Behold, my friends. A new regime will begin once the full moon reaches its full potential. My son, bring the sacrifice."

Sacrifice.

The very word made Padric's blood turn cold. In a trice, Padric realized he had missed something vital.

At the top of the hill, the red tent flap opened. His stomach fell as he perceived who stepped out of it.

Kett, hands in chains, trudged behind two soldiers toward the dais where Janus and Medea presided. His face and arms were covered in purple bruises. It took much restraint for Padric to keep the hidden sword concealed under his white robe and not plow his way through the mercenaries to release the prisoner.

Yet, he stayed his ground in deference to the plan. Breathed in, released the breath. *Patience. Wait for the signal.*

❧

BRYNWEN LOOKED out from behind the thick column at the enclosed red tent at the top of a little valley. Poking their way into the cloudless sky, she spied the tops of a circular setting of columns. "What are those columns?"

Nalini gritted her teeth. "That is where the gods are being held."

"Oh," Brynwen said, feeling foolish. She counted eighteen columns. Were Circe, Helius, and Pasiphae down there?

Behind the tent, Rawlins, crouching low, winked in and out. Then Brynwen noticed the low flap in the back of the tent, tall enough to crawl through. She smiled, realizing Rawlins had carved the hole. *Clever.*

"That's the signal" Warin twirled his dagger.

"Cornelia and I will go," Nalini announced.

Warin wheeled on her. "Nay. We agreed—"

"I did no such thing. I allowed you to speak, but no consensus was made. You are too bulky." She poked his large bicep to make her point. "And your boots are too loud and squeaky. Stay here." Without another word, she and Cornelia scurried after Rawlins at an incomprehensible silent speed.

Stunned, Warin blinked, his face turning scarlet. "Well, good riddance, then." He grumbled under his breath.

Gregorio elbowed Brynwen's arm. "I think he's in love."

Biting her lip, Brynwen tried not to laugh at the knight's plight. It wasn't so long ago when she'd told him off too. Something she knew he wasn't used to. Luciliana and Seia covered their mouths with their hands, eyes crinkling in mirth.

Rawlins took hold of Nalini's and Cornelia's arms, and the three disappeared. The new tent flap moved. The grass swished under invisible boots and feet before the flap fell again.

"I hope Kett is all right," Brynwen said for perhaps the hundredth time. The blood by his tools still worried her. Something bad had happened to him. If they didn't rescue him now, it would be worse for him. In the meantime, her heart thundered in her chest, eager for their task to be over.

After a few heartrending minutes filled with desperate prayer, a loud drum sounded. Two guards strode from the valley, expressions with purpose and pikes looking quite sharp.

"Hurry, oh hurry," Brynwen urged her friends.

Warin grimaced, gaze never wavering from the two guards. "They won't make it."

"They've got to." Gregorio wrung his hands.

"I know they will make it." Luciliana's voice was firm until the last syllable, when Brynwen caught a slight hitch, as though she were trying to believe it too.

Nalini poked her head out of the little hole, grinning from ear to ear. Her nod was a welcome relief for Brynwen's nerves.

Crawling out, she helped Cornelia who emerged with care as though in great pain, one eye shut tightly. Her amulet swayed with her movements. Inching out, she was followed by Rawlins, his scowl as deep as ever.

The guards were almost at the front tent flap.

"Hurry," she willed them.

As Rawlins extricated his feet from the hole, the two guards flipped open the tent.

Getting the disguised Cornelia to her feet, Rawlins proceeded to make the three of them invisible. They reappeared right in front of Brynwen and the rest of the group.

Gregorio gripped Cornelia's arms and peered into her eyes. "Kett, is that you?"

Cornelia nodded with scrunched nose and muttered in Kett's voice, "I don't feel like myself, though. All dressed up in these frilly skirts."

Despite his obvious pain, Brynwen couldn't help but smile. "I'm glad you're all right, Kett."

"You let Cornelia go out there all by herself?" Warin asked, incredulous.

Nalini scoffed. "While I was untying Kett's legs, she grabbed the amulet and put it around her own neck. Before I could do anything, the mercenaries were at the tent. The brave fool," she muttered. Her eyes glistened with worry.

Unease gripped Brynwen's chest, knowing it was too late, as Cornelia had likely already made it down the valley to Janus and Medea by now. She couldn't bear to know what would happen to her. And if Padric had been discovered.

Brynwen heard the scraping of boots from behind. Reaching for her dagger, she was about to warn the others when a hand gripped her forearm.

"Drop it, vixen." Aeron's grinning face leaned into hers, his handsome features and ebony hair revolted her. She couldn't help but release a gasp as his grip became crushing.

A handful of other huntsmen surrounded them. Rawlins began to flicker out but a quick jab to his head with a dagger handle dropped him to his knees. With a groan, he clutched his head.

Warin let out a roar and tackled two smaller huntsmen. They grappled on the ground. Just as quickly, the fight was over. Warin made a choking sound. They dragged the struggling knight to his feet, and Brynwen groaned. A leather cord was wrapped around his neck, tight enough that he could only gasp for breath.

"Nalini. Pleasure seeing you again. Where's the farmer?" Aeron cast his gaze around the group. "He and I have a score to settle."

The dryad, held by two burly huntsmen, glared at him and spat in his face. "You disgusting human. How dare you speak to me. Talfryn is dead because of your pet wolf." One of the huntsmen slapped her twice, her dark hair flying in all directions as her head bounced back and forth. She only glared all the harder when he'd finished.

Aeron cast a glance at Brynwen, who didn't deny it. "Too bad. I wanted to see him squirm."

Luciliana struggled against her captors, but Gregorio didn't put up a fight. One of the huntsmen holding Kett's arms yanked off the amulet, and in an instant he was himself again.

"You knew we were here." Gregorio didn't look surprised, only devastatingly disappointed.

"Of course. I knew you pathetically predictable people couldn't stand by. We barely had to lift a finger to lure you here." He peered greedily at Brynwen and traced a finger along her jawline. "Now I can do with you as I will."

Brynwen recoiled from his offensive fingers, bile filling her belly. "Don't touch me." Without hesitation, she bit down on them. Hard.

Howling in pain, Aeron ripped his hand away. He shook his appendage, calling her several foul things in one long sentence. Rant over, he scooped up her face, pinching her chin. "You'll regret you did that, wench."

"I only regret that I didn't bite harder."

His other fist struck her face, so fast she didn't see it coming. Her head whipped to the side, hair flying in all directions. The next thing she knew, she was on the ground, panting, her cheek stinging from the force of the blow.

"You coward," Warin ground out.

The guard behind him pulled a string, and Warin's eyes bulged as it choked him.

A grin split Aeron's face. "Now that we're all reacquainted, it's time to reunite with your other friends. Shall we?"

Brynwen tried to inch away from him, but Aeron leaned down to clutch her arm and yank her to her feet. "Come," he whispered as a lover would, "your *handsome beau* is waiting for you." Then he laughed.

Arriving at the hidden stable, Talfryn opened the door with great caution. The hinges creaked so loudly, anyone inside with any sense of hearing would have heard it. Scrunching his nose, he could see why the monks didn't use it. It was in need of repair, with parts of the roof missing, beams leaning at wrong angles, and rotting hay piled in one corner. However, evidence in the stalls left no doubt of its recent occupancy: black feathers and fur, new and old horse shoes, buckets with fresh feed, and fresh, fragrant manure.

Oh, and the man leaping down on Talfryn from the loft.

Eliva and Asinia cried out, but the fellow fell so fast, he took Talfryn down with him. Crashing to the floor, all the air exited Talfryn's lungs as the man crushed him with his body weight. Another form leaped from the loft at Eliva, but she had the sense to move. He slammed onto the stone floor.

The man atop Talfryn raised to his knees, prepared to slam his club into Talfryn's head until he spotted Eliva. She pointed an arrow at his chest, pulling the string taut. "Care to surrender?"

He gaped at her.

For behind her, the wolficorn stalked, ogling the man.

"Drop it," Eliva ordered.

Gulping, the man dropped the club. Unhappily, it fell onto Talfryn's stomach. He let out an "oof" and rolled to his side.

"Talfryn, are you all right?"

A man just launched himself onto me from a height, then dropped his heavy club on my stomach. Do you really think *I'm all right?* "Mmm all...right," Talfryn murmured.

"Little fool, you are embarrassing yourself."

"Just...gimme a minute." It took loads of willpower not to whimper like a puppy, but Talfryn held it all in as he got to his knees. Genia nuzzled his head, which somehow helped a bit.

With a shrug of her shoulders, Eliva lowered her weapon and gazed around. Asinia leaned against a stall door that didn't appear to be rotting too much.

From behind her in the shadows, something moved, catching the light streaming from the ruined roof.

An arrow! "Eliva!" Reflexes surged as Talfryn unhooked his hatchet and underhanded it toward the shadowed figure. A strangled cry rang out, and the form fell to the floor, the hatchet protruding from his chest. The bearded huntsman with wild brown hair breathed his last.

"You killed my brother!" From out of nowhere, another figure emerged. He was wild with rage, facial features and build just like his dead huntsman brother.

Before anyone could move, a pair of knives struck him in the chest. Perplexed, he looked down at them, then keeled over, very dead like his brother.

Startled, Talfryn raised to his feet as he, Eliva, and Asinia looked around for the next assailant. A tall, hooded figure stood in the shadowed doorway, short knives in hand. Slender. Deadly. Familiar.

The hooded figure replaced the knives in her robe. "I heard you could use some help."

Talfryn let out a laugh. "Payla!" He rushed toward her and gave her a crushing hug. She still towered over him by half a head.

Payla laughed and squeezed him back. Too late, he remembered how strong she was.

"But how did you get here? Gregorio said you were busy."

Lowering her hood, Payla's dark hair flowed free, the bull horns standing out on either side of her head. "Gregorio reached out again a few days ago, and I begged the matron to allow me one more reprieve. It seems leaving twice within a year is not to Mithras's liking." She screwed up her lips.

"Ahem," Eliva said, hands on hips.

"Oh!" Talfryn spun around. "Eliva, forgive me. This is Payla. She helped us out with the Labyrinth. Payla, this is Eliva and Asinia."

"We have met." Asinia gave Payla a respectful nod.

Payla nodded in return. "You are one of my aunt's dryad guardians."

"You are Pasiphae's daughter?" Eliva gaped in awe. "Sister to the Minotaur?"

Lips betraying a slight twitch, Payla hid the sadness at her brother's passing. "That is right. And priestess of Mithras And *you* are pretending to be a dryad."

Eliva raised her brow. The temperature of the room got just a tad cooler.

Asinia gave Eliva a look as though she already knew or had guessed.

Talfryn clapped his hands together. "Anyway, we've got a bunch of gods to save before the full moon is up, so..."

The wolficorn stepped out of the shadows.

"There you are." Eliva pointed at it. "Were you even going to help?"

"I figured you had it managed. Besides, I wished to conserve my energy for our foray into Olympus."

Eliva folded her arms over her chest as though she could understand the beast.

Talfryn stepped between them, holding his hands up. "Easy now, easy. We have a truce, remember?"

Payla narrowed her eyes at the immortal monster. "Aeternae."

"Priestess."

"Since when do you side with mortals?"

"Only when our mutual objectives align."

"All right, great, now everyone's been introduced." Talfryn tried not to let his alarm show. "Can we go now? Genia, where's the special door?"

Wings furled against her sides, Genia pressed forward. *"This way."* Everyone followed her to the far stall, the wood so rotten it would probably fall to dust with the touch of a pinky finger.

"Here." She indicated the back wall with her black nose.

Talfryn looked at it, perplexed. "It just looks like a wall."

He could imagine Genia's eyebrow raise, if she'd had one. She stepped up to it, but instead of her nose bumping into the wall, it disappeared. The rest of her disappeared as she walked into the wall.

It was like the portal that *Dis Pater's* magician had made in the underground city of Rellea. The one he'd used to rescue Brynwen from being kidnapped by the Shadow Druid. That portal had been round and blinding. This one was...well, like a wall.

Payla helped Asinia step through it as though going through a regular door. Eliva looked at it tentatively.

Now Talfryn would finally have a taste of the portal. And yet, the hair on his neck raised just thinking about it. Would it hurt? *Could it kill me?*

"It won't hurt you. See?" Eliva took a step through, then held out her hand. "Trust me."

Talfryn nodded, accepted her hand, took a deep breath, and stepped through the wall-portal.

CHAPTER 46

The guards halted with Kett between them in front of Medea's table.

"Well met, Kett," Medea said with a sober expression. Then her mouth twitched, and she cackled a laugh, pretty with a large dose of insanity. "Ha! That rhymed!"

Janus only pressed his lips together into a thin line. "I hope your stay has been enjoyable thus far," he said dryly.

Briefly, Padric worried that Nalini had not made the switch. Inching closer, he was well aware of the mercenaries behind him. On the way down the short hill, he had counted twenty-two enemies, plus "Kett's" two guards. Plus Aeron and Drogo, who were elsewhere. Again, he took the briefest glance at the top of the hill for Rawlins's signal that the switch had been made but saw nothing.

On edge that their plan seemed to be failing, Padric surveyed the vicinity. To his left stood Janus and Medea on their dais speaking to "Kett." Beyond them, the hill sloped into the valley where the gods were tied by vines to the hippodrome's columns.

With so many enemies surrounding him, any attempt to save Kett or Warin or whoever donned one of Nalini's amulets and leaped onto the chariot would end in disaster. So he inched closer, pretending he had trouble hearing the proceedings, and waited for the signal.

Glancing up at the sky, the full moon, bright in its slow ascent through the atmosphere, would hit its zenith at any minute. *Hurry up.*

He could not help the sinking feeling that something was wrong. "Kett" was here, so where was Rawlins?

Medea pulled Kett closer. In a smooth move, she raised the amulet carved of wood from his chest and studied it. It glowed like the others Nalini had enchanted. "My, such a lovely necklace, Kett. Funny, I do not recall you wearing this before. What do you think, my dear Janus?" she singsonged.

Janus leaned forward to inspect the wooden piece. "It is quite a treasure, indeed. Pray, where did you get it?" He raised his gaze to Kett, who kept his lips sealed in defiance.

Heart pounding in his ears, Padric still had not received the signal. *Where is he?*

The smile Medea gave the carpenter was bittersweet. "Alas, my lovely, you shan't need it where you are going. But I will add it to my collection of trinkets acquired from my dead enemies," she cooed.

"Drat." Padric reached into his robe for his sword.

Medea tugged on the cord and it snapped. Cornelia materialized in front of her, unmoving, giving the witch her worst scowl.

Cornelia? What happened to Warin?

Cornelia cocked her head. "You will die first." She shot forward, hands clawing at Medea's throat.

Drawing his sword, Padric darted forward.

But not before Medea swiped a knife from the table and sliced upward in a diagonal line. The blade cut deeply into Cornelia abdomen and out the other side. Blood splattered all over the tablecloth, Medea's dress, and Janus's white robe. The god of time grimaced and looked away as though he would be sick.

Four steps away from Cornelia, a body slammed into Padric. Pain lanced up his arm as he and his assailant were flung into the air. They slammed off the edge of the hill and rolled down, down, down into the valley. The assailant struck at him, while he swung back, his sword long gone upon the blasted Olympian hill.

The slope evened out, and they came to a stop a handful of feet away from a column. Breathing hard, Padric stared at the great white cylinder dancing around in his vision. The mercenary, luckily, was in a similar bind. He closed his eyes against the dizziness.

"Thank you for the daring rescue, young hero," an unfamiliar sarcastic female voice said.

"Yes, I could taste the freedom." A man's voice. "For a brief moment."

"Mayhap, next time, lad, bring an army." The third voice sounded vaguely like Padric's father.

A melancholic male voice sighed. "Would it have made any difference?"

"You had better get up," came another female voice, this time wispy. "They are coming for you."

"Thanks," Padric croaked. Cracking an eye open, he saw a line of gods and goddesses tied to the columns staring down at him, some smiling, some leering, others indifferent.

Padric stifled a groan as he rolled onto his stomach, all of his muscles screaming. As he looked up, he spied Cornelia's body rolling down the hill like a child's rag doll. He might have been sick, if not for the number of mercenaries making their way down the hill chilling his insides.

"Your friend is waking up, dear," said the friendly female voice.

Launching to his feet, Padric kicked the head of his original attacker, who crumpled again. "Thanks, m'lady."

She giggled. "I wager a hundred gold coins he will perish from the second blow."

"The same for the third."

"That big looming one looks deadly—the first blow."

Deities argued behind Padric as he threw off the monk's rose-intoxicated robe, then braced himself for the onslaught to come. By the look of his hands, Nalini's potion had worn off.

The mercenaries touched the bottom and glared at Padric with equal amounts of ire. In no time, they encircled him but did not attack.

Instead, they sneered and waved their swords, cudgels, daggers, and meaty fists.

Janus's voice boomed from atop the valley. "Give up, young Padric. Lest you have not guessed, you are surrounded."

Padric did not take his gaze from the mercenaries, trying with all his might to come up with some way of escape.

"It was a valiant ruse," Janus continued, "but I am afraid you have been outwitted. See, I have your friends here, unharmed—for now."

Shocked, Padric's head jolted up to the dais. Next to Janus, he spied Gregorio and Rawlins and all of his friends. All except Talfryn, Eliva, and the two dryads who had gone after them, who for all he knew had been killed by the aeternae.

The god had his hand on Brynwen's shoulder. All the blood in Padric's body boiled as he beheld the god of time, whose future-seeing face smiled down at him as an adult to a naive child. *Mayhap I was naive to believe we could win against Janus so easily.*

The bitter taste of defeat crept into Padric's heart, he balled his fists at his sides.

"Most excellent choice, Padric. Now you can all join me in bringing in the new world. Now that the full moon is nigh, the time has come in earnest. Lads, you know what to do."

Greedy, laughing mercenaries loomed ever closer to Padric, until he could smell their weeks-old body odor and ale-filled breaths.

"Tal, if you're still alive, it is up to you now," Padric whispered under his breath.

"What's that ye say?" the ugliest mercenary with battle scars all over his face, a crooked nose, and fat lips asked. He was also the one with the meatiest hands.

"I said, if only I could break your nose, it would make my day. How many times has it been broken? Twelve? Thirteen?"

The last thing he saw before blacking out was the meatiest fist of them all careening for his face.

CHAPTER 47

*P*adric awoke with a start. His arms were above his head and tied to a horizontal pole.

Head spinning from the harrying trip down the valley and the punch to the face, he peered around the hippodrome. When his vision cleared, he found that his friends were secured likewise. The bindings were the same enchanted leather cords which had held him captive earlier in the week; something Medea seemed to have in plentiful supply. Their feet touched the ground. He straightened, his limbs protesting the movement.

At the center of the hippodrome, Aeron was directing some of the henchmen to set up the table on top of the dais identical to the way it had been at the top of the valley. A mercenary brought down the chariot led by the two small golden dragons. *Dracones Rapuere*, he remembered from his studies—"winged dragons." Behind it came a second chariot led by four black pegasi. They settled down behind the dais.

Padric stewed at his own stupidity. Of course there had been the greatest chance that Janus had expected them to try sneaking their way in. Their only hope was that the dryads had found Talfryn and Eliva, and that they had not been killed by the aeternae. Padric chuckled to himself. It would be like Talfryn to do the unexpected thing and die before accomplishing his own prophesied quest.

"Padric?" Brynwen's voice was breathy beside him. Her arms hung from the pole, like his, but she stood on her tiptoes.

Padric studied her—for perhaps the last time. His heart stopped just considering it. Attempting to keep his voice low, he said, "Bryn, I... please forgive me. I never had the chance to apologize for my behavior the day we were captured."

"Not counting this time, when were we captured?" Brynwen's eyebrow quirked up. Then winced. She frowned, likely remembering that fateful day. "That seems like so long ago. Much has happened since." Her mouth drew into a thin line, indicating that she had not forgotten his inaction in the garden, either.

"Will you take my hand," he blurted. Then groaned inwardly at his botched choice of words. The right moment had never seemed to come, and, to be honest, neither was this.

Her eyebrow raised. "Um, well, our hands are tied at the moment..."

The words jumbled out of his mouth. "Marry me."

Brynwen's mouth fell slack.

"If you would consider...if we escape," he finished in a rush, painfully aware of the dozens of eyes on them. His pulse quickened as he waited an eternity for her to recover enough to respond.

At last, her mouth closed, and she nodded. At first blankly, but then with more fervor, until she frowned. "Is"—she looked about and lowered her voice—"is now really the *best time* to ask this question?"

"Just say 'yes' and be done with it," Rawlins grumbled from her other side. Padric could practically hear his friend's eyes roll in his head.

Cheeks flushing, she bit her lip. "Yes—I will." Her eyes sparkled in the firelight, making her ever more radiant. "Deep down, I knew what you meant. I may have overreacted a bit."

Heart soaring, Padric had no doubt they would make a great pair. With all his heart, he wished he could hold her. Unable to help himself, his smile broadened, and he opened his mouth to say more.

Applause burst forth from the center of the hippodrome. One slow and methodical, the other excited and maniacal.

"Oh, bravo. Bravo." Medea clapped all the harder. "I do so adore a good love story. Mortals perform the best dramas. I do not recall that particular one from Homer, though."

"It was not." Janus looked perturbed beside her. "It is more in the style of—"

"Oh yes, how silly of me." Medea giggled. "It was Pliny the Elder's cousin, Pliny. How could I forget?"

"Yes, it is a conundrum." A vein bulged in Janus's temple, clearly trying to regain his composure. "Now, my dearest Medea, to proceed with our ritual, we must select a new sacrifice."

"Oh, goody." She wiggled, all excitement, and selected her knife. "Janus, bear with me, but our love birds have given me the perfect solution." When her gaze landed directly between Brynwen and Padric, his blood froze in his veins. "What a fitting way to end a dramatic love scene than with the sacrifice of one of the couple involved? Don't you agree, my lord Janus?" When Medea's gaze pierced into Brynwen's, Padric's heart sank to Tartarus.

To the side, Aeron sneered at him, soaking up every ounce of Padric's defeat.

"Nay!" *This is all my fault.* Padric struggled against his enchanted bonds. "Take me instead. Take me!"

Janus smiled from ear to ear. His eyes flitted to Helius and Circe, then to Padric and Brynwen. "Yes, my sweet. I agree wholeheartedly. Dramas are indeed the most beautiful form of art. But nay, young charioteer, I have a different plan for you." He snapped his fingers. "Take them."

٪

THE GUARDS GRUNTED and glared as they shoved Brynwen before the short dais. She'd dragged her feet all the way, but it only delayed the inevitable as Medea and Janus smiled down on her. The guards held her and Padric in place, pinning their hands behind their backs.

Why is this happening? It was the spider's web in the Labyrinth all over again. But this time, instead of a giant spider with a sticky web, it was an insane, immortal witch wielding a long, slender knife in her elegant hand and a vengeful two-faced god.

Brynwen's stomach flipped as she beheld the tip of the knife, glinting in the firelight. There was no question to its sharpness.

Hands clasped behind his back, Janus the Future looked at his peers tied to the columns, then his gaze rose to the stars. "The blood you share with us, young Brynwen Masson, will bring about the greatest reset the world has ever seen. The first was when Prometheus gave mortals fire. This, however, will be a much more dramatic change. You see, Jupiter, his siblings, and their children before you have become lax, unneeded by the people. Weak. That is why change is in order, where a new, strong ruler is required. Thus have I come. I see the future, and it is glorious." His eyes lowered, sparking in anticipation of what was about to happen. "The time has come. Let us begin. Medea." He motioned for the witch to proceed.

Medea regarded Brynwen with a hungry look that sent chills up her spine. "Come here, my dear. Your mortal blood is required." She brandished the knife with expertise. How many deaths had she dealt with that knife for her own ends?

The guard on Brynwen's right tugged on her arm to straighten it. Ice gripped her lungs as Medea drew the knife forward. "Why are you doing this?"

"What is in it for me? Why, a new world where Janus and I will rule over all as we see fit. A world of our making." She gazed at Janus with loving eyes and fluttering lashes. Then she kissed him, and he returned it with a deep passion. Many of the bound gods groaned. Brynwen's lips twisted in like thought about the unnecessary display.

"Janus, do you honestly believe Medea shares your love?" called a goddess. Brynwen twisted her head to see who spoke. The goddess's beauty outranked all others in this place, her long flowing golden hair reaching almost down to her ankles. Her robe might have been light blue in the firelight, but it was hard to tell. Even though her lips crinkled in disgust, it didn't mar her loveliness.

Medea unlocked her lips from Janus the Future and spun to face the speaker. "Oh, Venus. Are you volunteering to be our first test subject?"

The pallor of Venus's already alabaster skin paled to a ghostly white as two mercenaries chopped the vines binding her and led her to Medea.

"Janus," Padric said, "what does your past self think of all of this?" The young knight stood defiant, the guards straining to hold him at bay.

"He never listens to *me*," Janus the Past lamented. "He cares not a wit to reminisce about the great days that once were."

Janus the Future ignored him. "Proceed, Medea." He spoke through clenched teeth, all previous mirth gone.

The guard jerked Brynwen's arm until it was horizontal in front of Medea.

"Only a prick." Medea hovered the knife over Brynwen's flesh.

Brynwen bristled. "A prick? But you said my blood is required."

Medea quirked an eyebrow. "Would you prefer I spilled all of it?"

"Nay."

"Then hold steady or this will be very messy. We have no wish to see your sweeting become more irritable, do we?"

She was right. Squirming would only cause more damage than good. Allowing her arm to be manipulated by the guard, she braced herself for the cut. *A small cut, right?*

Raising the knife in an expert hand, Medea brought it down just below Brynwen's elbow and pressed firmly. Brynwen gasped at the stinging prick it made. Then it sliced all the way down her forearm, stopping just before the wrist, a fraction from the artery. In a trice, blood flowed from the cut. Brynwen hadn't even seen the Druid holding the bowl beneath her arm to catch the blood. And there was so much of it.

Padric's nostrils flared as he yanked against his restraints. "That was no prick."

"Oopsie," Medea singsonged. "I doubt it will kill you, young maiden." But Brynwen knew it hadn't been an accident. Less did she like the emphasis Medea placed on "it." The witch spun around to glide behind her table filled with bowls of colorful ingredients. Brynwen couldn't quite make out what they were in the torchlight. The flowing blood dwindled to a trickle. The silent Druid placed the bowl into the lit brazier and stepped back, translucent hands slipping inside the opposite sleeve of his hooded gray cloak. Once ready, Medea began her work with the intermingling of ingredients in the bowl while muttering a chant in Latin.

Brynwen felt lightheaded, and it was all she could do to keep her head up. No one bothered to wrap her arm or stop the bleeding. She'd run out before too long if it didn't clot quickly.

At last, slick with blood, she slid out of the guard's grip to clutch her wounded arm to her body. If she didn't stanch the blood flow soon, she might faint. Sadly, everything she needed to fix it up was in her confiscated satchel.

Scooping out a spoonful of the potion, Medea continued to chant and sprinkled some dark powder into it. The mixture bubbled and sparked, the emanating smoke amassed into the air around them.

Medea sniffed it. "Ah, perfection. Your blood is most exquisite, Brynwen. Aesculapius gave you the perfect blood." Then her hand whipped out and grabbed Venus's hair. The goddess cried out but couldn't move as the witch brought the spoon under her nose. "There you go, love, breathe it in. Does it not smell sweet?"

"Unhand her!" one of the gods cried. Brynwen heard him struggle against his bonds, but a guard blocked her view.

Medea regarded the speaker with slitted eyes. "Oh, very well, Vulcan. You never did know how to have a good time." She released Venus's hair. When Venus stood upright again, the witch splattered the spoon's contents all over her.

The smoking potion dripped down her hair and beautiful blue robe.

"Did it work?" Janus asked.

"Let us find out. Janus, would you do the honors?"

The god of time shrugged. "Why not?"

A giddy giggle emitted from Medea, and she bounced on her feet. From the table, Janus picked up the same knife Medea had used to slice Brynwen's arm. It still dripped with her blood as he offered it to Medea. "My love?"

"Oh, dear, it is dirty." Taking up some of Venus's light blue dress, she wiped the bloody knife off on it. "Thank you, my sweet."

Venus, for her part, breathed heavily but stood her ground. Not a whimper could be heard from her.

Medea bent to scoop up a lock of the goddess's golden hair. She admired it for a moment or two, then sliced the end off in one swipe.

"What do you need my hair for?" Venus demanded.

The witch sniffed the hair. "No reason other than that I have always admired your hair. It will be something to remember you by."

The goddess's eyes grew big. "To remember me by?" Her face blanched, and she swooned. A groan sounded from her throat. She doubled over, eyes bulging. Her body writhed and shot stick-straight. Scales grew on her skin, gold, just like—

Brynwen gasped.

Wings sprouted on Venus's back, and her whole body stretched, elongating into a giant serpent—a dragon!

When the dragon-which-once-was-Venus's growth ebbed, Medea petted its snout. "Yesss, my dear, you look lovely." Venus-dragon emanated a deep, happy rumble from her enormous throat.

Vulcan cried out in agony as he watched Venus, whom Brynwen thought he must love dearly, turn into a giant golden serpent. The gods made a deafening uproar.

The loudest was a god with bulging muscles, dark wavy hair down to his shoulders, and a deadly presence. "You both shall pay dearly for this!" Strange, he vaguely reminded Brynwen of Rawlins.

Trying to hold in her last meal, Brynwen couldn't believe how horrible things had become.

Medea threw the knife behind her onto the ground as Janus came to her side. "I say your experiment works. We knew of Venus's birth, and now her...death, of sorts. But most important, you can all be changed. Shortly, you will all share the fate of Venus and become mortal. Very hard to kill, but mortal nonetheless."

Oh no!

The gods protested, fear glinting in their eyes. The mercenaries laughed and brandished their glinting weapons in the torchlight.

Medea's hands came together. "At last, it is time for the true ritual to begin."

The moon was dangerously high in the sky.

Talfryn, Brynwen willed, *where are you?*

Janus the Future cleared his throat. "Your chariot awaits, my dear Brynwen." As he stepped to the side, he indicated the two empty red chariots depicting a different monster on the side of each. The one on the left, with four black pegasi at the lead. had a painting of a beast with a lion's head head and body, a goat's head out of its back, and the tail of a serpent; but she didn't know what it was supposed to be. The one on the right was led by the two giant, hissing, golden serpents of the same color as the Venus-serpent. Large for snakes, but smaller than dragons in the tales she had heard growing up. The painting on this chariot's side was the same kind of creature.

"Do you like them?" Medea asked, regarding the golden winged serpents. "Gregorio must have taught you about these fierce creatures."

Shifting to the other foot, Padric regarded the paintings. "A chimaera and the *Dracones Rupuere*. A matching chariot for each of you—how precious."

Brynwen recalled him and Gregorio speaking about the chimaera once, along with other monsters, but that was as much as she remembered.

This time, as the guards led her onto the chariot with the dracones, she didn't put up a fight. All of her strength had fizzled out with the blood in the brazier. Left untended, blood continued to leak from the long cut onto her blouse and skirts.

The guard on her left settled her onto a white cloth on the bottom of the chariot. Peeking over the edge, she spied Padric looking at her in devastation. It broke her heart to see him so.

"Where are you taking her?" Padric asked.

Medea grinned. "She and her blood may yet have a use for us. However, I am afraid young charioteer, that you have ridden your last ride."

CHAPTER 48

*P*adric seethed. They had planned this all along. Why was it that these gods enjoyed making life and death stakes into a game?

Clarence? Padric tried summoning the amulet. He berated himself for not asking a few minutes earlier. *Please, I have most urgent need of you. This is the last time, I promise.*

"Do you really promise, young mortal? Because I have much to do and little spare time."

Padric caught the sarcasm. *No time for games, Clarence.*

"All right, all right. Do you need release from your bondage?"

You know me too well.

"It is a gift. And, at times, a curse."

Today, please?

The amulet sighed as though very put out. *"Very well. Stand still."*

It was Padric's turn to sigh. Not much of a choice there.

In another moment, his chest warmed, and he could feel the leather strap being picked at.

The next time when Janus looked at Padric, he blinked, his lip twitching. The god took three long strides to him.

The guard on Padric's right jabbed a fist into his kidney. Air sucked from his lungs, he doubled over, then was shoved to his knees.

Janus grabbed Padric's chin and raised it forcefully. "Ah, yes, upon closer inspection, you do look much like Ulysses. Oh, *deer*, how callus of me," he said with false sincerity, "I forgot that he recently died." The coldness in his voice sent ice through Padric's veins. Then the god of time raised his gaze to someone behind Padric, whom he imagined was Circe. How did she take the news of Ulysses's death?

Shame and sorrow tore through his chest, and he wanted to scream. He ripped his chin from Janus's fingers. "You are heartless."

"I believe the word you are looking for is 'timeless.' Something you mortals will learn soon enough once I begin as your caretaker."

"I refuse to acknowledge you as our caretaker."

"A pity."

From the brazier, Medea scooped up the bowl into a white cloth and brought it with great ceremony to the dracones chariot. At its front, Padric spied a basket made of finely carved wood. He wondered if it was Kett's handiwork.

All the while, Venus-dragon sat still and regarded Medea's movements with interest.

Medea placed the bowl into the basket. Finished, she made her way to the table and picked up two bronze goblets and handed one to Janus who took it with a triumphant smile.

"To victory." He clinked his glass against hers. Together, they raised the glasses to their lips, Medea with a smirk on her face, as though she knew a secret.

As the Druid stepped into the chariot beside Brynwen, something *tinked* to the ground. He did not notice the corked green bottle rolling toward the wheel of the other chariot.

Drinks finished, Janus and Medea set the empty goblets onto the table. With ceremony, Janus took Medea's hand. She giggled as they walked with regal air to the dracones chariot. He handed her off to step into the wheeled contraption on her own. Once she was in position, he pivoted to the pegasi chariot.

"Begin!" Janus the Future declared. "I will be right beside you, my love." However, Janus the Past's face, cast in shadow, did not seem as enthusiastic as his other half.

The moment Janus touched the unmanned chariot with the pegasi, his hand rose to his abdomen. His lips twisted in discomfort.

Meanwhile, the Druid flicked the reins for the dracones to get going, unaware of Janus's plight. The beasts hissed and began to slither, their wings unfurling and batting with great thrusts, until they rose into the air. Padric's gaze followed the chariot holding Brynwen into the night sky with trepidation.

"Father?" Aeron stepped toward him with a frown. "What is wrong?"

A long groan sounded from Janus's lips, but he put up a hand at his son. "It is nothing. Finish what you started with the charioteer."

From above, Brynwen screamed.

Padric glanced upward, his lungs frozen in horror. A story off the ground, the Druid nudged Brynwen toward the edge of the chariot with his foot. She struggled, but was too weakened to stop him. Padric held his breath as he could only watch and fight against his captors.

"Hold on, Bryn. Please."

"For what?" Drawing his sword, Aeron marched toward him, eyes alight. "There will be nothing left of you for her to come back to— should she survive the fall."

Clarence?

The voice within the amulet of obsidian grumbled.

Still on his knees, Padric's guards' hands continued to clench his shoulders. Aeron bared down on him, sword aimed at his chest. Sweat poured down Padric's face and neck as he tugged against the magical leather.

"Clarence!"

"Try now!"

The leather fell away from his wrists. He brought his hands up and shoved against the guards. At the same time, he willed his body to shift into a faun. His powerful goat legs kicked off the ground as Aeron's blade sliced through the air where he had been but a moment before.

Aeron roared in frustration.

"Why won't you die?"

"You keep asking this question as though it has an answer." Padric jammed his elbow into the throat of the guard on his left. He wasted no time in sliding the man's sword from its sheath. "I need this, thanks."

Eyes wild, Aeron lunged. Padric parried with the borrowed blade, their metal crashing together. He wished he had his own sword as this one was not balanced as it ought to be.

"Medea?" Janus cried.

Aeron startled. Distracted by his father's fearful call, Padric punched him in the face. Aeron stumbled back a step.

Janus doubled over, his four eyes bulging. "What"—both voices panted—"have you done?" Then his body writhed and shot stick-straight. In grotesque fashion, his head split in two. The future face formed into a lion's head with full mane, the past face into that of a goat, its horns growing long and sharp.

Padric gawked at Janus's formation. If he saw the future, how had he not seen this coming?

"Medea, you snake!" Aeron shouted. He wiped away blood from a cut on his lip.

Before their eyes, Janus's whole body transformed into a large lion with enormous paws. But instead of a lion's tail, it grew long and scaly, ending in a serpent's head.

A chimaera!

Medea's ringing laughter spilled throughout the hippodrome as her partner's form continued to grow, his massive paws smashing the little table with potion ingredients. The brazier's fire sputtered out on the dais. Everyone in its way stumbled backward or ran. The tail struck one man in the chest and he went flying. Smoke puffed from Venus-dracones's nostrils, and her wings shook in agitation as she slithered away from it.

In opposition to them, Aeron broke away from Padric, stumbling toward his father. He moved with caution. "Father? It is me, Aeron. I can help you."

The monstrous lion and goat heads that once were Janus's two faces regarded its son. Recognition fluttered in their gazes for a heartbeat. Then they blinked, and their eyes were black—those of wild beasts. The chimaera raised its lion head and opened its mouth in a deafening roar. From the gaping maw spouted a flame that shot straight up more than fifty feet into the air. The roaring flame continued as the monster bounced its head from side to side. It sliced through a column with no effort. The top of the marble structure slid off the cut's incline and crashed to the ground, nearly smashing the gods directly beneath and to his left.

Startled, Venus-dracones squawked. She flapped her wings and took off into the night sky, disappearing into the white city.

Aeron beat a hasty retreat from the monster.

The pegasi leading the unmanned chariot on the ground skittered several paces away from the wild monster. They unfurled their wings to escape the hippodrome when Padric decided to hoof toward them. "If only I could speak to animals like Talfryn, this would be so much easier."

Brynwen's scream rent the entire hippodrome.

Staring up, Padric's heart pitched as she slid off the edge of Medea's chariot.

"Bryn!"

Her fall miraculously halted not four feet down. A white piece of cloth caught her, both ends connected to the chariot. The chariot's momentum swung her as though from a tree. Back and forth she rocked, clinging to the cloth, her wounded arm tucked to her chest.

"I am coming. Hold on." Padric galloped after the moving pegasi chariot. He was nearly there when Aeron appeared next to him. The former knight slashed at Padric's head. Ducking, he rolled, then bounded to his feet, sword swinging. He bashed at Aeron's blade, then sprinted to the chariot again.

A group of huntsmen and mercenaries had to get out of their way. It slowed the beasts down enough for Padric to catch up. He had one hoof on when a blade stung his arm. He crashed into the chariot, with Aeron crashing on top of him.

The chariot never slowed down despite the added weight.

Aeron punched Padric's cheek. "This is your fault, de Clifton!"

Padric shoved at Aeron's chest and face, his sword somewhere under him. "How is it my fault? *Your* father wanted to work with her." He jabbed the traitor in the chest, then scrambled to his feet. The chariot lurched as it ran over something large. A mercenary's body rolled out from underneath. "Now you know how it feels."

Aeron got to his feet. They clutched at tunics and struck at each other a few more times, trying to make purchase on the other.

"Aeron, if you want revenge"—he grunted as Aeron kneed his thigh —"take it out on Medea." He kicked him back. "She betrayed all of us." He ducked another blow.

Aeron stopped, and Padric took the opportunity to grab the reins. They were wound around a small wheel attached to the front of the chariot. The former knight's lips were pressed into a thin line.

The chimaera's fiery roar brought Padric's attention to their other problem.

"You might have a point there, de Clifton."

Padric hated when he called him that. Nor did he like his former friend calling him by his Christian name, either.

"But that doesn't make us friends."

"Hardly," Padric replied dryly. Flicking the reins, he directed the pegasi to the skies.

The chimaera's roar bellowed just behind them.

Talfryn exited the portal into a quiet, dark room still holding Eliva's hand. Nothing bad happened. The only thing that greeted him was the pleasant smell of old books and carved wood.

"See?" Eliva said, "we did not die."

It was then that Talfryn realized how sweaty his palm was. "Knew it all the time."

Eliva smirked.

Genia was nosing and sniffing at books and furniture pushed against the walls. Payla's daggers flashed in the rising moonlight from the windows. Asinia sat on the floor, examining her wound. The book smell turned into the stink of death and very dirty, sweaty fur. The wolficorn had arrived. Sadly, neither he nor his stench had gotten lost in the portal.

"Guess we found the library. It doesn't look so great." Talfryn's nose scrunched. Not with broken bookshelves and furniture and books strewn all over the place or shoved to the sides of the room.

"Where are we to go now, aeternae?" Payla asked.

"There is a door," the wolficorn replied.

Talfryn rolled his eyes. "That's helpful." He released Eliva's hand to explore the room. Several boot marks scuffed up the plush rug. "Lots of people've been here recently."

The wolficorn growled under its breath. *If this is the library, then it is here.*

While Payla and Eliva began feeling the walls for another invisible portal, Talfryn went straight for the double doors at the center of one of the walls. They opened into the hallway of the abbey. "Well, unless Olympus looks just like the abbey, this isn't it."

"How about these other doors?" Eliva asked. Talfryn followed her to the doors. The latch clicked and opened into the night just like outside the window. But here they saw column after column, with sconces and torches in between. The air smelled sweet on the crisp wind.

"Ummmm, this might be it," Talfryn said.

Before the others could join them, the door to the abbey hallway creaked open. Payla brandished her daggers to attack.

A monk sidled in, hood over his eyes.

He had just slid his hood off his head when Talfryn and Eliva both shouted, "Payla, stop!"

Payla's dagger stopped an inch from poor Brother Howell's face. Eyes wide in horror, Brother Howell stayed perfectly still.

"Are you sure?" Payla asked, her whole height and bull horns towering over the frightened brother. Behind her, the wolficorn sneered at the newcomer.

"Yes," Talfryn answered. "Brother Howell is a friend of ours."

Satisfied, Payla put her daggers away and sent a friendly smile his way. The monk, on the other hand, crumpled to the ground in relief. When Payla reached down to help him up, he cowered away.

"Sorry about that." Talfryn helped him up instead. "Payla gets a bit excited sometimes. Wolfi, down." He quirked an eyebrow at them both.

The priestess blushed. "Forgive me, Brother Howell, but I did not wish anything to happen to my friends."

"I understand," Brother Howell replied. Knees still shaking, he allowed Talfryn and Eliva to help him up and lead him to a chair that was still intact.

"What has happened since we left?" Eliva asked.

"There is much to tell you." Brother Howell explained what had happened after Ulysses was killed.

Although anguish still stabbed at his heart about his inactivity in saving Ulysses, Talfryn listened intently, taking in every word. "The abbot isn't really an abbot? *How abbot* that."

Miser's eyes rolled.

Without looking at him, Eliva elbowed his arm. "What has happened to him?"

Brother Howell's nose crinkled. "Brother Ambrose and a couple other brothers have him in custody. I explained everything about him to them but only said that he had a crooked employer. I had hoped you would come here so I could tell you a revelation I had while I was watching Abbot Caradoc. Do you remember the tapestry of Saint George in the welcome hall?"

Talfryn nodded, remembering the tapestry, as the knights and Brynwen had made a fuss over it. It was, he remembered, a very fine tapestry of a knight in silver armor so realistic he'd almost looked real, fighting a dragon whose scales seemed to pop out of the picture. A true masterpiece, if his own inexperience in art meant anything.

"Well, when you first came to the abbey, Padric stood directly underneath the tapestry, and I thought for the briefest moment that he *was* Saint George. Then in the relic room, I thought it my imagination, but I could have sworn that the sword sang to him. It occurred to me again while I was keeping guard on the abbot in his room with all his gaudy tapestries. That was when I made the two connections."

Arms folded over her chest, Eliva tapped her foot in impatience. "And where is this leading?"

Brother Howell smiled. "I think Sir Padric should use the sword to stop Janus and Medea. It once defeated a great monster, it must be able to stop a pagan god or two."

Payla tapped her chin with a dagger. "That is not a bad idea, Sir Howell. I wish to see this sword."

"Brother Howell," Talfryn corrected.

"Sir Brother Howell."

"Good enough," Talfryn muttered.

Brother Howell puffed out his chest. "I rather like the sound of that."

Eliva rolled her eyes. "Now that we've got that sorted, do we have time to get it?"

Payla moved to the hallway door and pulled her hood over her horns. "We'll have to make time."

"We will wait here," the wolficorn said, indicating the nervous looking Genia.

"I will stay as well," Asinia added.

"Don't eat either of them," Talfryn warned the wolficorn. "If they have even a scratch, the deal is off." *Great! I just threatened an undying, murderous beast.*

It took no time to descend the deserted hallways and staircases to get to the relic room following Brother Howell and his torch.

Senses heightened after the ordeals of the last couple of days, Talfryn felt constantly antsy. So, when he thought he heard a noise in the hall, the hairs on the back of his neck stood on end. "What was that?"

Brother Howell shrugged as he sifted through the key ring from Brother Fabian. "Probably rodents. The lower level is infested with them. We need to bring in some cats, but Brother Barnabas is highly allergic. Hives. A most unpleasant business." He found the right key and touched it to the lock."That's strange..." The door creaked open without him touching the latch.

Unease crept up Talfryn's neck. "Umm, I guess that wasn't supposed to happen?"

"Nay."

They all shared a wary look. Nothing happened behind the door, but Talfryn wasn't taking any chances. He motioned for the monk to step back as he drew his hatchet. Payla and Eliva stood to the other side of the door as Talfryn shoved it open, springing his arm back to his body immediately afterward.

Nothing happened. Inside was as dark as a moonless night.

Eliva studied the door without touching it. "Is this door ever unlocked?"

"Never," the monk replied, worry lines marring his young face.

"Whoever it was must have taken what they wanted and left already." Payla took the torch from a sconce on the hallway wall and stepped inside. Following behind her, Talfryn cast his gaze wherever the light touched. Everything seemed in more or less the same order it had been in before.

Until he saw the empty iron hooks on the left.

"Saint George's sword!" Brother Howell cried, running to the shattered case.

Sure enough, the sword was gone; all that remained was its display holder. Talfryn's heart sank. "Now what?"

"Now ye'll deal with us."

Spinning around, his heart froze. "Drogo."

Pounding his club into his meaty hand, the bearish man's body took up the entire doorway. He grinned, his gap-tooth making him look all the more brutish. Behind him stood at least three other men.

Miser chittered irritably, cursing all of the man's acorns to taste stale forever and other such un-niceties Talfryn wouldn't repeat in polite society.

"At your service." Drogo gave a mock bow. "My friends and I had a wager as ta what was locked up in this room." He whistled. "An' what a pretty sight 'tis, too!"

Eliva twisted her short sword's handle until her knuckles turned white. "If you have the weapon in your possession, then why are you here?"

"Unfinished business, let's say."

※

By the stricken look on Talfryn's face, Eliva knew there was a sour history between him and the large man. Miser definitely knew him as his chitters were very high-pitched. She remembered seeing this man in the forest the day her group had come upon the huntsmen attacking Talfryn's group. How could one forget him? His size alone could fill a small cottage.

If Medea already had the sword of St. George, then they could already be too late. It was of the utmost importance to warn Padric, but this huge man and his goons were in the way.

Eliva made an arc in the air with her short sword to get her muscles primed. "Unfinished business? Then by all means, let us finish it."

Drogo rolled his shoulders and cracked his knuckles. The men outside the room chuckled, the sound made all the more menacing by their voices echoing throughout the long, empty hallway.

Talfryn twirled his hatchet in his hand. "I'm pretty sure it was finished when Padric pointed that arrow in your face."

The daggers shooting from Drogo's eyes could have shredded Talfryn to pieces. He stomped on the ground like a bull, causing ceiling dust to rain down on top of him. "He's not here ta protect you this time, laddie, is he?"

Talfryn grinned, which only unnerved the giant. Drogo grunted and pounded forward. Talfryn rushed to meet him.

Both Eliva and Payla rounded him to get to the other huntsmen.

Somehow, the huntsmen got themselves entangled shoulder to shoulder in the doorframe.

"Geroff me!" one cried.

"Nuh, uh, you," cried the other.

Eliva could have sauntered over, for two of the daft huntsmen fought to be the first to enter the room. Tapping her bare foot on the stone floor, she and Payla waited while they poked each other's eyes with fingers and noses.

"Unbelievable." She rolled her eyes, anticipation waning.

"I could have brought snacks." Payla flipped a dagger and caught it. To the men, she said, "We will wait right here for you, gentlemen. Take your time." She waved, giving them an innocent smile. Her hood was still up.

Hiding her own laugh, Eliva decided she liked this horned immortal.

In a flash, they popped into the room. Eliva ducked the left man's swinging club as she pivoted around him, tapping his back with her sword. He plunged into the room and sprawled on the floor.

Meanwhile, Payla and her assailant danced around each other. When her hood slid off her head, he paled. "Do you like them?" she asked, nonplussed.

On the other side of the room, Talfryn sparred with Drogo. The bigger man's club beat down mercilessly on Talfryn's hatchet.

She brought her attention back to her man on the floor. He was just getting up when a warning went off in the back of Eliva's head. She looked up just in time to see Payla careening toward her.

Together, they crashed into a table filled with antique bowls and iconography. Sharp pain sliced up Eliva's side as she slid to the floor amid shards of the relics.

"I don't think he likes your horns too much," Eliva said. She glanced down at a long shard from a glazed bowl sticking out of her side. She hissed at its sting, then frowned as dark red blood seeped from the wound. There was no time to patch it up, and pulling it out could cause more damage. *I must be more careful.*

"Mayhap he is just jealous."

"Most likely."

As one, they rose as the two henchmen charged and battled them.

Being shorter, Eliva had the disadvantage of the man's long arm. But she was fast and dodged his lunges and swipes, then pivoted around him, cutting his arm. On her way up, she sliced through the back of his tunic. He cried out in rage.

Drogo's arm slammed Talfryn into the shelf holding ancient scrolls. His hatchet went flying, imbedding itself in the nearby table with the chalices, under which Brother Howell was cowering. All around Talfryn, priceless scrolls bounced off his head and shoulders.

Eliva seethed. It was time to end this and capture the despicable man responsible for framing Padric for murder.

Payla's hands opened to display a fan of small daggers in each one. The goon high-tailed it out of the room. She followed.

Eliva's huntsman looked after his friend, then back to Eliva. At last, Eliva saw an opening, and feinted left. As the huntsman appeared to take the bait, she spun, landing on his left side. As she brought her sword around, he grabbed her by the middle.

Raising her up, he slammed her onto the ground.

She screamed as the shard embedded itself further into her side.

&.

TALFRYN REELED as Eliva's scream filled the small room.

"Eliva!"

Somehow, her cry of pain made his shoulder throb all the more. His foot slipped on a scroll as Drogo's club came for his face, and it only struck some strands of hair as it whiffed by. Scurrying to his feet, he stepped toward the chalice table, but Drogo blocked his way.

"Not so fast." Drogo's menacing grin leered down at him.

"Nowhere to go fast, anyway." Talfryn shrugged.

Eliva was scooped up around her middle again, her red hair flying all over the place as she kicked and clawed at her attacker. Her short sword had fallen uselessly on the floor.

His heart lurched for her. *I need to help her!*

Where was Payla?

Giving him a stricken look, Brother Howell glanced from beneath the table at him and Drogo, then at Eliva and her attacker. Then his gaze traveled straight up to the hatchet. Nodding, he reached up with both hands to grab the weapon's handle and tugged.

Talfryn got buffed with another swipe of the club to his ear. Stars spun around as he stumbled away. Finally, he widened the gap and drew his broadsword.

"What's that going to do against my club?" Drogo sneered.

"'A sword in hand is better than one in the gut.'"

Drogo snorted. "Where'd ya hear that nonsense?"

"Old English proverb."

"Never heard o' it."

Talfryn shrugged at his made-up proverb and lunged, taking Drogo by surprise with an upward slice to his bicep. He leaped back just in time as the club came dangerously close to knocking out all of his teeth. "Uh, Brother Howell?"

"Getting there." The monk was slowly loosening it with up and down movements. Too slowly.

Talfryn and Drogo danced around some more, nicking each other, until Brother Howell finally pried the hatchet loose. The monk tossed it onto the ground near Talfryn's foot. Drogo heard it strike the stone and blocked Talfryn's path. When he attempted to feint, Drogo saw his bluff and rammed his shoulder into Talfryn's chest.

A sturdy wooden table against the wall broke Talfryn's fall—and, seemingly, his back. The painted wooden and stone statuettes on top wobbled precariously but then righted themselves. His hand brushed against one, its surface smoothed with expert crafting. As Drogo approached, Talfryn swiped one off the table. "Sorry, Saint..." He had no idea which male saint he chucked at Drogo's face. The man ducked, but the second flying saint got him on the nose with a loud *crack*.

Clutching his nose, Drogo stumbled back, howling in pain.

Eliva, for her part, plunged a dagger into her antagonist's belly. Shoving off of him with her foot, her blade released as he collapsed to the ground with a thud.

Face crimson from rage and pain, Drogo was about to lunge when Eliva, in one fluid motion, dove at the hatchet, scooped it up, and tossed it in front of Talfryn. Shoving off the table, he slid along the smooth stone, caught it by the handle near the ground, and sliced upward as Drogo's leg stepped into its trajectory.

Drogo's face quickly drained of all color as he realized the severity of his mistake. He collapsed to the floor, holding his leg which oozed much blood.

So much blood.

Like Leowyn's blood. And Ulysses's blood draining from his lifeless body after the aeternae murdered him. Talfryn's heart constricted, and he thought he might pass out.

"Quickly," Eliva said. "We must stop it from bleeding out."

It was then that he noticed the shard sticking out of her side. "You don't look in much better shape." A stream of blood soaked her green and brown skirts, making them an awful shade of brown.

She grabbed his arm. "If he dies, he cannot testify to his crime."

"If you die, I'll never forgive myself." He hadn't meant to say it aloud, but it was true.

Something shifted in her eyes. They stared at each other, faces not six inches apart. Talfryn's heart pounded so loud, he was sure the whole room could hear it. "Eliva..."

Payla marched into the room, twirling her daggers. They'd already been wiped clean. "Looks like everything's in order now."

The cutest crimson blush crept up Eliva's cheeks, emphasizing her freckles. She ducked Talfryn's gaze to tear a piece of her skirt to stanch the blood falling from Drogo's wound.

Surveying the room, Talfryn winced at the scene. Most of the relics had been smashed or worse. The tapestries weren't much better. Brother Howell, for his part, was still huddled under the table, face slack in shock.

"Sorry about the relics, Brother Howell. But at least they helped us defeat the bad guys?"

"Y-yes." Brother Howell emerged slowly from under the table.

Wheezing, Drogo looked up at Talfryn with hatred in his eyes. "You should've killed me."

"Mayhap, m'laddo, but that's not happening. We do need some rope, however...ah. This should do the trick." He picked up a long piece of rope coiled near where the Sword of Saint George had been.

Brother Howell looked horrified. "But that is the rope that bound Saint Sebastian to the tree."

Talfryn recalled that Saint Sebastian had survived his terrible ordeal by arrows. "And we're going to bind Drogo up too, so what's the difference?"

Brother Howell folded his arms across his chest. "I don't like this."

"I know. Hold his arms back while I tie him up, will you, Payla?"

A whole line of unsavory phrases came out of Drogo's mouth. "You'll all die horribly in the end, mark my words. By my own hands, I'll torture you until you beg me for mercy."

Gingerly, Brother Howell picked up one of the stone statuettes from the table as though to study it.

Drogo continued, "Until every ounce of blood is dripped from your bodies into the endless pits of Hell. Until—"

Brother Howell bashed the huntsman over the head with the statuette. Drogo's eyes rolled into the top of his head and he keeled over. Everyone stared at the monk in shock. Cheeks scarlet, Brother Howell stuffed his hands and the statuette behind his back as would a naughty child who'd been caught doing something he shouldn't. "What? His voice was getting very annoying and repetitive."

Talfryn outright cackled. He slapped his hand on the monk's shoulder. "Brother Howell, I knew you had it in you."

CHAPTER 49

"Hurry up, Payla. It's started." Talfryn tapped his fingers on the roof facade of the building overlooking what Asinia referred to as the hippodrome. When the witch had sliced Brynwen's arm, Eliva and Paula'd had to hold him back. The stupid wolficorn had just laughed at him and sat down on its haunches. Only Asinia stayed where she was since she couldn't move very fast, but her eyebrows furrowed, nonetheless. They'd left Genia on the outskirts of the city of white, but Talfryn would call her when needed.

"I am working as fast as I can." Spreading her fingers over all of the weapons they owned plus the ones Talfryn and Eliva had pilfered from the tent next door, Payla muttered the same chant for the fifth or sixth time.

They'd quickly patched up Eliva and Drogo (the latter still sitting bound in the ruined relic room), but Talfryn didn't like how pale Eliva's face was. She told him to stop fussing over her as though she were a wilting flower. "Dryads do not wilt," she'd said.

But Talfryn had frowned. "That's just it—you're not a dryad."

Nostrils flaring, Payla muttered the rest of the chant rapidly, her Latin so fast, she doubted Gregorio could've spoken it any quicker. "The incantation is finished." She pinched her lips, which seemed *so* convincing to Talfryn.

"We'll have to pray they work." Eliva scooped up her arrows, daggers, polearm, and short sword.

Talfryn picked up his weapons, while Payla grabbed the rest. When she freed the others below, she would hand them their weapons.

Assuming the plan didn't fail at the start.

"So what *is* the plan?" He beat his brain for an idea. "Unless you can shoot Medea from here, I've got nothing. Wolfi, d'you have any ideas?"

One front paw resting on top of the other in a relaxed pose most likely meant to drive Talfryn crazy, it looked him in the eye. *"Wreak havoc?"* it said dryly.

Talfryn snorted in surprise. "Wow, you made a joke. I don't even know what to say to that."

"What did the aeternae say?" Payla asked.

"'Wreak havoc.' I mean, Wolfi, if you wanna run around and take out Medea's pot o' smelly stuff, you could…"

"Talfryn." Eliva's voice raised a fraction in excitement. "That is it!"

Talfryn's head spun to look at Eliva expectantly. With urgency. This girl who did weird things to him, who might have the answer to their problems. "And that is…?"

She clutched her bow. "To wreak havoc. It's time to call Genia."

A FEW MINUTES LATER, Talfryn clung onto Eliva's waist—gingerly—as Genia soared off the roof of the columned building. His heart pounded, partly from having to leap off a steep roof, and partly from holding onto Eliva. Her earthy scent of strawberries and leaves intoxicated his senses in a way he didn't know could happen.

"I hate this part," he stated as his stomach plunged past his head, sure his face was turning green.

"You will be fine," Eliva yelled over her shoulder, her hands twisted in Genia's mane. Eliva's long, red hair whipped Talfryn's face no matter how he moved his head, the braids stinging his skin. *Next time, we each get our own flying horse!* Although, if that happened, he wouldn't get to hold her so close.

Below, Payla and the wolficorn darted toward the nearest group of enemies. In another moment, Genia flew past them toward the valley. Through Eliva's windblown hair, Talfryn could see one chariot with pegasi on the ground, and a second chariot rising from the ground via one set of giant, golden snakes with wings. Genia whinnied in excitement at seeing her friends—the pegasi, *not* the winged snake things.

"Not yet, Genia. Reunion later," Talfryn said.

She snorted in disappointment.

In the hippodrome below them, Janus writhed and then transformed into a huge lion with a goat head on its back and a snake tail!

"What the..." Talfryn stammered.

"A chimaera!" Eliva cried, pulling on Genia's mane.

The huge chimaera roared a great flame that destroyed a column. The blast was so strong, they could feel its heat from a distance.

Near the chimaera, he spied Padric and Aeron gliding on a chariot. The strange thing was that, for once, they weren't trying to kill each other but seemed to be working with one another. He couldn't help but wonder if it was a sign of the apocalypse.

Genia didn't care for the monsters, especially the fire-breathing chimaera, and began to panic. Meanwhile, Medea's cackling-but-strangely-pretty laugh could be heard all throughout Olympus.

Not only that, but Brynwen dangled from Medea's chariot!

"Should we go after Brynwen?" Eliva asked. "The chimaera's breath will kill them."

"My friends!" Genia urged.

Both Bryn and Padric were in trouble, but his sister looked in a precarious way. Padric could likely—*hopefully*—take care of himself.

"Go after Bryn. While we're there, we can distract our little Druid and witch friends who're up to no good. Drop me into the chariot, then you get Brynwen to take my place." Eliva nodded. "Got that, Genia?"

Genia snorted in agreement. Without hesitation, she veered toward the soaring winged-snake chariot.

Before flying off the roof, the wolficorn had told them as much about the potion Medea had concocted as it could, which wasn't a lot—but it was really bad for everyone, regardless.

"What are those snake-things called?" Talfryn asked.

"*Dracones*—dragons."

"Kinda scrawny dragons, aren't they?" He'd always imagined dragons being as large as a mansion. These were only about three yards long.

As they neared the chariot, Genia's wings beat with effortless agility, following the chariot's ascent into the sky.

Opening his mouth, Talfryn had to spit out the red hair that blew into it. "Eliva, be careful of his potions. They can have real nasty effects."

She twisted her neck around and smirked. "Do not fear for me."

His heart skipped again.

Talfryn readied himself as they drew even with Medea's chariot. Below, Brynwen held onto the cloth swinging from the chariot. Catching sight of him and Eliva, her eyes glistened in hope as she clutched the cloth for dear life.

Inside, he spotted a basket with a bubbling red substance—the potion. Medea chanted something while flicking her fingers over it as the Druid held the reins. They were so engrossed in their own doings that they didn't seem to notice the pegasos that practically blended into the night.

"Lovely evening for a flight!" Talfryn called as Genia's wing came within a couple of feet of the chariot.

Medea gave them no heed, but the Druid's hood turned to them with a double-take. Talfryn waved. The hooded figure recovered quickly and reached into his cloak. Before he could withdraw it, Eliva flung a small knife from her bandolier at him. The hilt knocked the bottle from his hand, and it flipped over the edge of the chariot. Talfryn hoped it hit a mercenary.

Shaking his hand, the Druid's hood whipped in their direction, and Talfryn could feel rather than see his cold eyes scowling at them.

Flicking the reins, the Druid swerved the dracones left, forcing Genia to veer left with it. She snorted in protest and tried to compensate. It was too late, however—the cloaked figure pressed the advantage by guiding them straight toward the column!

Genia swerved a hard left at the last moment, clipping her wing on a marbled column. With a whinny of pain, she spun out of control.

CHAPTER 50

*T*alfryn clutched at Eliva's waist for dear life.

Before crashing into the ground, Genia righted herself and shook her mane in frustration.

"You did great, Genia," Eliva coaxed. "Take one more pass at him."

With a determined huff, Genia was rising again with great speed. The Druid and Medea were ahead, the former weaving her arms in an intricate pattern that Talfryn didn't understand, but knew it couldn't be good.

"Medea's blocked, but can you shoot the Druid?" he asked Eliva.

"I can try." Eliva unhooked her bow and nocked an arrow to let it fly in what seemed like one fluid motion. They watched as the arrow struck the Druid's back and came out the other side, into the night sky, with barely an impediment to its speed. The Druid hunched forward.

"Amazing shot!" Talfryn said. "He didn't stand a chance."

The next moment, the Shadow Druid righted himself. A hole where the arrow had gone through the gray robe was the only indication that he'd been hit. As though nothing had hindered him, he continued with the flight. Medea remained unfazed.

Talfryn gaped. "How'd he do that?"

Eliva huffed in exasperation and spat over the side. "Shadow Druid."

As though that answered everything. "We will have to stop them on the chariot itself."

They were no more than five feet from the chariot when the Druid uncorked a potion. A cloudy substance spouted from it straight up toward the rising moon. About fifteen feet up, it gathered itself together to form into big, solid, and menacing bird. Its wings had the wingspan of two Talfryns and its claws were long and curved.

At last, Genia got them to within a couple of feet of the flying chariot.

"Genia and I will get Brynwen," Eliva said. Her hand grazed his.

Talfryn nodded. "Be careful." Bracing himself, he released the girl's waist and jumped onto the contraption. He grabbed the side and slipped, banging his knee on the wheel. The whole contraption dipped with Talfryn's added weight, making the Shadow Druid lose his balance and grab at the sides for support. *Maybe not my brightest idea.* The dragon things up front hissed in annoyance. They weren't happy one bit and let the Druid know it—if he even understood them.

Talfryn had just climbed over the edge when the Druid spotted him. *"You again!"*

"Yep, it's me," Talfryn replied, cringing inwardly at the Druid's grating voice inside his head.

Just then, a giant something from above swooped onto Eliva.

"Eliva!" Talfryn cried. He reached out to her, but the giant bird screeched and grabbed her arms with its enormous, sharp talons.

She screamed as it yanked her off of Genia's back, kicking and flailing. Her bow fell to the ground, arrows scattering out of her quiver as she struggled to free herself.

"Stymphalian bird," the Druid announced proudly. As though Talfryn should be impressed. Actually, he was. And also pretty terrified. Gregorio'd be disappointed he couldn't remember what the creature was.

With a brave whinny, Genia flew upward to help Eliva.

Ice cold hands clung to his neck. So cold, they burned.

"You mortals ruin everything," the grating voice shouted into his brain.

This time, it wasn't fear that froze Talfryn as he struggled for breaths and clawed helplessly at the Druid. Without warning, the prophecy shoved its way into Talfryn's vision—gold and red letters overpowering the chilling effect of the Druid's arctic touch.

"Get...off." Talfryn shoved him into the other side of the chariot.

The Druid's arm struck Medea's legs, but she took no notice. He grunted, his grip on Talfryn's throat lessening. Talfryn struggled to get the strange little man off of him.

Eliva screamed again.

No!

When he looked up, he couldn't find her. She was gone.

The Druid's fingers slid from Talfryn's neck. He came back to himself slowly. Too slowly. He watched as the Druid removed a vial from his gray cloak. Diving at him clumsily, Talfryn smacked his chin on the side of the chariot.

ELIVA STRUGGLED against the talons grappling her arms. They squeezed so tightly, she thought the bird would wrench them off. She was furious how the giant bird had snuck up on her, knocking her bow from her hand. Being unable to reach any of her weapons made her vulnerable.

She'd never liked Circe's Stymphalian birds. They were bad-tempered and foul-smelling. Whenever it was her turn to care for them, she did it out of duty, praying that someday she would be able to escape this life.

Raising her legs up, she tried to kick at it, but it was no use. Its legs were too long.

The magical Stymphalian bird lifted her higher. The wind brushed the hairs on her arm. The bird squawked in agony, a spear sticking out of its chest. It flapped its wings for all of three seconds, jarring Eliva until her head spun.

In a flash, she was falling. A scream tore from her lips. With a final glance up, she spied the bird puff into dust, sparkling in the torchlight. As she sped through the air, she wanted to say she welcomed death with finality. She had done her duty to save others. Instead, her chest tightened with the sensation of leaving things undone. Of leaving behind the chance of something more...with someone...

Would Diana be proud of her? Would her mother and Nalini?

The last things she saw were the hovering chariot, the Druid fighting with Talfryn, and smoke spilling rapidly out of it into the hippodrome.

She reached toward him. The boy who drove her crazy. The boy who tried so hard to impress her every day. Who put up with her moods. The boy who made her secretly laugh. "Talfryn..."

A SCREAM TEETERED on Brynwen's tongue, her heart threatening to stop as Padric and Aeron made a crash course straight for the chariot she dangled from. She couldn't believe it when she watched Padric in his element, curls almost straight and flailing in the wind, feet braced, with a wide grin on his face—in peril from the chimaera chasing after them, spouting great beams of fire. Padric was the true heir of Helius. He seemed to be enjoying this. Meanwhile, she was struggling to hold onto the sling, the remainder of her long hair biting at her cheeks as it struck them repeatedly.

Padric waved at her, motioning for her to jump onto the pegasi. He also looked up onto the chariot, presumably to Talfryn.

"You can do this," she whispered. Her injured arm throbbed. Could she make it in time? "I...might need some help, Lord," she prayed.

When Brynwen was sure it was too late for them to pull up, Padric called, "Jump!"

The pegasi dipped, as did the rest of the chariot. Brynwen's stomach plunged toward her toes as something warm engulfed her, and she slipped from the sling. Glancing up, she spotted Talfryn jumping. A purple cloud followed him on his descent. The breath was knocked out of her as she landed on the front pegasos backwards. Talfryn landed with no grace onto the back of the left-rear pegasos. Both pegasi whinnied in surprise and consternation.

"Talfryn!" she cried once her breath came back, but it was drowned out by the noises in the hippodrome.

Once they were "settled" on the pegasi, Padric banked right.

Just in time, too. Blinding flames licked the chariot, pegasi, and her hair. She closed her eyes against the brightness. From above came the crash of the chimaera's fiery belch ramming into Medea's chariot.

Aeron crowed in victory. "Take that, you traitorous b—!"

It took a few moments for her to comprehend that Padric and Aeron were on the same chariot and not killing each other. *Mayhap I lost more blood than I thought.*

Talfryn's scream startled her. He swatted at something in the air by his head, then brushed off his tunic and slapped his arms in frantic gestures. His wild look of helplessness took Brynwen aback. There was nothing there for him to fret about, yet he acted like a million insects crawled and flew all over his body and around his head.

The purple cloud...it was a potion! she realized. *It must be an illusion.* But she didn't know how to help her brother. Perhaps something in her satchel might help, but it was in the tent atop the hill. Right now, she feared he would wiggle himself off of the pegasos and injure himself in the fall.

"Hold on, Talfryn and Brynwen!" Padric shouted. Flicking the reins, he guided the pegasi toward the ground.

ALL THE AIR was crushed from Eliva's lungs in her abrupt landing. But, miraculously, not in a bone-shattering way, despite the great distance. Her wounded side screamed as she gasped for air.

"You all right?" Rawlins rasped.

Head spinning and stomach roiling, Eliva dared not open her eyes, but continued to try to breathe normally despite her racing heart. She could only grimace and nod.

After sitting on the ground for a few moments, she realized Rawlins had caught her in his arms. Her side ached something awful, but it wasn't enough to kill her. At least, not yet. All about her, a dozen of her blue-green fletched arrows lay strewn on the grass. She considered picking them up, but they would re-appear in her enchanted quiver within the next few minutes, regardless. When her head finally stopped whirling and her lungs were full of breath again, she raised her head. Rawlins leaned over, his eyebrows nearly connecting together in concern.

"Did you throw that spear at the Stymphalian Bird?" she asked.

"Not me. Warin." He cast a quick nod over his shoulder to where the other knight and dryads were fighting a monster.

"What of Talfryn?" She searched frantically about.

"He's still up there." Without moving his head, he looked up.

She followed his gaze to find the chariot still hovering in the same place, with Brynwen swinging on the sling, and Talfryn fighting off the Druid.

"Talfryn." So many emotions churned through her chest, she thought she would suffocate. The blasted boy certainly knew how to get himself into trouble. And yet, her fingers curled into fists, praying to the gods for his safety. She stopped partway through her prayer. Most of the gods she'd worshipped were no longer gods, but monsters. Could they hear her prayers at all anymore? They were all chained to the columns before her, making their prospects for answering prayers even less likely.

Talfryn's shout of pain reached her, and her resolve hardened. If anything befell him, the Druid would pay with his life.

The conviction in the thought startled her. Shaking her head, she tamped down what it could mean.

Shoving Rawlins's chest, Eliva scurried to her feet. "We must help them."

❦

PADRIC MIRACULOUSLY SETTLED the chariot down on the ground quite smoothly. Although that didn't mean that Brynwen's stomach stopped churning at once.

The second they landed, Eliva, Warin, Rawlins, and Kett descended on them and helped the twins down from the pegasi. Scanning the area, Brynwen spotted Payla and the other dryads still fighting Janus's henchmen alongside the handful of gods Payla had released. The remaining gods remained bound to their columns.

"What happened to Talfryn?" Eliva dropped to her knees, her eyes furrowed in worry at Talfryn's state. "Why is he swatting at himself and the air as though he were surrounded by invisible insects?"

Brynwen was bewildered at her concern. Eliva had always been so cold and distant to everyone. *When did she begin to care in the least about my brother?*

Padric looked down at Talfryn with regret, then grabbed Brynwen up in a hug, careful about her arm. "The Druid threw some potion onto him. Illusionary of some sort." He released her so she could help her flailing brother.

Warin bared his sword. "What is *he* doing here?" He aimed it and a fierce glare at Aeron.

"Hold, Warin." Padric lifted his hand. "We are currently aligned in stopping Medea." Behind him, Aeron nodded, although his eyes glittered disgust.

"Sir Padric," Eliva said, trying to prevent the screaming Talfryn from scratching his arm to shreds. "We tried to get Saint George's sword, but it was stolen. Medea or Janus must have it."

"It's not Janus," Brynwen muttered. She pressed her lips together, trying to figure out what could help Talfryn.

"Why would they want it?" Padric asked. Brynwen wondered the same thing. "Sword or no, she must be stopped." He knelt on a knee to peck Brynwen on the cheek then hopped back onto the chariot. Aeron hopped on behind him, unaware of Padric's frown. Clearly, the knight wasn't completely thrilled with the alliance either.

A deafening scream erupted from the Janus-chimaera. Puffs of smoke covered its face, and it flailed, fire spouting from its mouth in all directions. Glass shards littered the ground around it. The Druid had apparently found his mark.

With a flick of the reins, Padric led the pegasi airborne, Aeron clinging to the sides to avoid falling off.

"Wait, Sir Padric," Kett called after them. He held up a wooden contraption. "I have this—"

But Padric didn't hear him.

A band of tough-looking mercenaries approached. Brandishing his weapons, Warin turned to face them.

Kett's shoulders sagged. "He needs to know about the chariot."

"Which chariot?" Eliva asked.

"Medea's. I made a few adjustments, and using this device will help stop her. But now it's too late."

Eliva's gaze slid from Talfryn to them. "Genia could help."

"Who is Genia?" Brynwen didn't recall any of the goddesses having that name.

But Eliva had already raised her head to the sky and whistled. "Genia, I have need of you."

However, after a couple of minutes nothing happened.

"I am sorry, Kett." Exhausted, Brynwen dropped next to her writhing brother.

"Why won't you help get them off?" Talfryn demanded from no one in particular.

"What can we do for him?" Eliva asked, worriedly. "He won't stop it."

"Mayhap something in my satchel can help. It's in that building at the top of the valley."

Eliva nodded. Spotting Brynwen's bloody arm wrapped up in some of her skirt, she nodded more eagerly. "At once." With reluctance, she brushed the hair of out Talfryn's face then released him into Brynwen's care.

"Please hurry," Brynwen called to Eliva's retreating form. All around, she spied her friends fighting mercenaries and huntsmen. She caught a glimpse of Payla and her long horns fighting and slicing at the gods' vines. *And is that the aeternae chasing down huntsmen? Maybe I inhaled some of that illusion potion, too.*

CHAPTER 51

The smoke around the chimaera's head had already begun to clear by the time Padric was halfway to Medea's chariot. The chimaera silenced, and it swayed.

"He's going to fall," Aeron warned. His eyes glistened as he watched the beast. "Father."

"I see that," Padric countered. He tugged on the reins, trying to keep on the opposite side of the monster's fall. The pegasi hated the situation as much as Padric, and they began to panic. Finally, the chimaera collapsed, it's final fiery breath coming directly for them.

Tugging the reins for a hard right, they escaped the fire.

The loud crash of a column breaking apart from the blast, accompanied by a dozen screams, filled the air. Padric's chest constricted. He could not remember if a god was still tied to the crumbling column or not.

"Forget the gods," Aeron barked. "Medea's still performing the ritual."

Righting the chariot, Padric glanced up at Medea, his heart racing with a mixture of fear and anticipation as he watched her muttering the incantation, waving her hands around for effect. Now that the ritual was underway, the air crackled with tension. Each breath he took became heavier than the last.

With a renewed burst of determination, Padric guided the pegasi closer to Medea's chariot, his grip tightened on the reins. As he neared, he saw Medea draw a long sword from a scabbard, its edges shimmering with an otherworldly light.

Saint George's sword!

Medea's singsong cackle filled the hippodrome, making Padric's skin crawl. "Why did she take the saint's sword, Aeron?" When he had seen it earlier in the week, he had felt power radiating off the blade. Even if Saint George had not killed a dragon with it, he had certainly killed *something* requiring so much power.

"I don't know," Aeron replied, voice gruff.

"*Why?*" Padric persisted.

"Believe me, she has only ever told me what she wants me to know. My father is only slightly more forthcoming, but he never once mentioned the sword until today when he wanted us to steal it."

With reluctance, Padric believed him. Before the witch did anything else, he had to do something drastic. "Hold on to the sides."

In a daring move his father would have called nothing less than reckless, he steered the pegasi into a sharp dive, aiming straight for Medea's chariot. His sword rang with anticipation as it slipped from its sheath. Aeron followed suit.

"Oh, Aeron, foolish child," Medea said. "Never thought you would be the brunt of someone else's tricks, did you? And now you are a poor, lonely orphan." She laughed again.

"I always knew you were filth, Medea! No better than the slime on the bottom of my boot."

Padric had to admit that he could not have said it better.

"We will see who is filth." With a swift motion, Medea raised the gleaming weapon, readying for an attack. Beside her, the Druid uncorked a vial of green liquid. Padric prayed it was not the same acidic potion from their last encounter in the Labyrinth. The person who happened upon that particular potion had met with an unfortunate fate.

The tongues of the golden dracones attached to the chariot slithered at the pegasi, who quaked in fear. The wings of the front two seemed to petrify. "Pegasi, to attention!" Padric tugged on the reins. Unfortunately, they were not like his horse Firminus who knew all of his commands. They wobbled the chariot, falling a couple of feet, tipping to the left. Padric's heart nearly stopped as he released the reins to grab a hold of the side. Aeron slammed into Padric's back, releasing a loud grunt in his ear.

"I hate chariots," Aeron moaned.

Holding in his now aching ribs, Padric shoved the former knight off of him. "I am beginning"—he slid—"to hate them too." *Especially the tight spaces.*

Medea raised the sword of St. George into the air and hovered her free hand over the bubbling bowl in the basket. Her rantings in Latin became loud and clear as she bellowed to the universe.

> *Titanes antiqui*
> *Obtemperate Fatis!*
> *Tollite dona ab illis*
> *Gratia indignis.*
> *Dona illorum relinquite –*
> *Tuus minister exspectat te!*

> Titans of old
> Heed the Fates!
> Lift the gifts from those
> Undeserving of grace.
> Relinquish their gifts—
> Your servant awaits!

As she spoke, sparks like lightning pulsed up and down the sword, some siphoning into the arm holding it, through her body, and down her other arm to be released into the bowl. With each pulse, like a heartbeat, the concoction bubbled even more. Smoke poured from it.

The pegasi were in panic mode. Their wings could barely hover, legs kicking in fright. Padric reached for the retreating reins but they slipped out of his grasp and over the lip of the chariot.

"Blasted reins!" He banged his chest again on the side of the chariot. He was just thinking of climbing over the side when Medea screamed in shock.

Jolting his head up, he saw Medea's face pale, blue eyes widened in disbelief as her spell spiraled out of control. Her hair and robes blew around her face and body, caught in the vortex of a tempestuous windstorm. The very fabric of the world seemed to warp and bend under the weight of the power she wielded. Great rifts tore the night sky with deafening roars.

Face twisting in pain, she tried to relinquish her grip on the sword, but it refused to budge. Its power, Padric realized, was using her as a conduit.

Heart quickening, he recognized how dire their situation was. *Is this the end of the world?* "We must get out of here." Peeking over the chariot, he spied the cursed reins resting atop the center pole attaching the chariot to the pegasi. He lunged for them with his free hand, but the horses jolted again, and he dropped his sword. It was all he could do to stay inside.

"Hurry!" Aeron cried. He lunged for them, too. No luck.

Inconceivably, the energy in the air intensified. Padric's curls raised with the electricity. He made one last desperate attempt for the reins. This time, his finger hooked around them and hauled them up. He slapped the reins with all his might. The pegasi yielded and bolted.

They barely got five feet before Medea's chariot erupted into a blinding white light, illuminating every corner of Olympus. The light struck them with a raging force that seemed to shatter all of their bones.

CHAPTER 52

*T*alfryn kept in his screams as best he could, but the creepy crawly insects scuttled all over his body! Worse, Brynwen kept slapping his hands away each time he tried to scratch or flick the little devils away. He might've accidentally smacked her in the face once or twice, because they were beginning to creep all over her too.

"Why aren't you screaming?" he asked her, incredulous.

She just gave him a sympathetic look which only upset him all the more. "There's nothing there, Tal. Eliva will be right back with my satchel."

She's blind! "Are you gonna smack these little buggers with it, then?"

Beside him, Miser screeched and ran around in circles, his tail flailing at the tinier bugs skittering all over his little body.

Talfryn reached for an especially large beetle on his forearm. Brynwen slapped his hand again.

"Stop it, sis! Or I'll..." He blinked, and the bug on his forearm vanished. "I'll..." After a couple more blinks, the bugs *all* disappeared. *I'm free!*

He went in to pinch his arm to make sure he wasn't dreaming, but Brynwen slapped it again.

"Ow! Stop it, seriously, Bryn. I'm fine now. See, no bugs."

Her eyes rolled. "That's what I've been trying to tell you."

It was then Talfryn realized the chaos surrounding them. His friends fighting enemies. Deities tied to columns. A scream rent the air.

"Wait, did you mention Eliva?" His heart rate spiked, daring to believe she hadn't plummeted to her death. "So she's not…where is she?" He scanned all around but couldn't find her anywhere.

"She's getting my satchel. Tal, I'm so glad you're all right."

"Of course, I'm all right." His heart swelled at the news. "Hear that, Miser? She's all right! Eliva is all right!"

Miser, also bug-free, cheered and ran in circles by their knees.

Brynwen grabbed Talfryn's hand with her good one. The other, he noticed with horror, was covered in blood and wrapped in her bloody skirts.

"Are *you* all right, though?" he asked.

She pinched her lips together when lightning lit the sky. Glancing up, he saw two chariots. Medea's and the other with Padric and Aeron… *Aeron? What did I miss?*

It wasn't lightning but the sword in the witch's hand causing the lightning effect. *That can't be good.*

A voice entered his mind. *"Talfryn, my lad!"*

Turning to the columns, he made eye contact with Faunus, still secured by tight vines. Other gods also remained bound, including Helius in his purple robes. The air crackled with energy. There wasn't much time to release any of them before Medea unleashed chaos.

"Stay here, Bryn." Launching to his feet, he checked his weapons. Hatchet, sword, and dagger were on his person.

"I'm going with you." Brynwen stood beside him.

"Great. We're coming, Faunus!" In a mad dash to the god of dreams and animals, Talfryn thrust all his strength into hacking at the vines with the hatchet Payla had enchanted. Brynwen attacked it with a knife she'd found on the ground. Three strikes later, he'd chopped two vines, a thick one and thin one. Her knife barely made a dent, so he handed her his enchanted dagger. "Try this." With only one hand, Brynwen managed to sever a thin vine. There were still almost a dozen left. No wonder not even half of the gods had been freed. Only Circe, Diana,

Neptune, Apollo, Dionysus, Jupiter, Pluto, and Mars had been released. Payla had pointed them out when they were making their rescue plan.

Remaining resolute, they continued. As Talfryn raised his hatchet for a twelfth or thirteenth strike, the air thickened with whatever spell Medea was performing in her fancy chariot. He prayed Padric would stop her quickly, so they could all go home.

He'd just struck through another vine when Medea's scream broke his ears. And Olympus. Peeking up, he shielded his eyes from the brightness. A vortex surrounded her and the chariot. Its power increased, picking up inside the hippodrome. Talfryn felt his feet lift off the ground momentarily, his hair and clothes whipping about in all directions.

"Forget about me, Talfryn," Faunus commanded, still trying to free himself. His eyes reflected pure fear. "Get somewhere safe."

"Nay!"

From the sword of Saint George, streaks of lightning fingered out in all directions. They honed in on the tops of every column.

"Talfryn!" Brynwen braced against the column, but her feet rose off the ground. Grabbing her good wrist, he was about to grasp the vines when the wind increased. "Hold on, Bryn."

Tops of columns in the hippodrome cracked and splintered, chunks careening to the ground. *Are they supposed to do that?*

Then the whole vortex exploded in blinding white light. The force of the gale blew Talfryn and Brynwen several feet into the air before a huntsman happened to break their fall.

When the blinding light faded, Talfryn blinked until the world was lit with only an ethereal radiance. "Am I dead? Or dreaming?"

"If you are, then I am too." Brynwen lay curled up beside him. Opening her eyes, she scanned the night sky. "What happened to Padric?" she asked, frantically looking about.

Talfryn didn't see him either, but his heart stopped at what he spotted a moment later.

Out of Medea's chariot came something so sinister, the twins both gasped at the same time. All thoughts of Padric fled.

A nightmarish spectacle of spectral illusions danced around the columns of the hippodrome, twisting and warping to the uncanny music filling the air.

Talfryn's lungs froze as one of the specters floated toward him. It had an ugly, translucent, gaping maw and cloudy white, vacant eyes that looked straight through him.

Some of his senses returned, and he shifted to block his sister from the wraith. "S-stay away," he croaked.

At the last moment, the ghost must've thought better of it and flew over him. He sagged in relief.

Yet, the horrible visions weren't done with their menacing task. Screams and moans came from the gods still tied to the columns, their voices manifesting inside the hippodrome as the specters flew into their bodies. Writhing, the gods recoiled in their divine forms, shimmering and flickering like candle flames in a gust of wind.

Talfryn's skin crawled at the horrible visions, all of the fear he'd thought to have locked down came shrieking back.

"What has she done?" Brynwen wondered.

But Medea's work wasn't finished.

CHAPTER 53

alfryn and Brynwen could only stare as the horrors of Medea's plan unfolded. Faunus writhed and screamed. His horns grew and twisted around themselves. His legs doubled in size and turned golden. His body and face grew hair everywhere as he hunched over onto all fours. Great wings sprouted and unfurled from his back, severing the remaining vines which had bound him. Last, feathers and a beak took the place of his face.

It was like watching all the men at Cataractonium turn into animals; but instead of shrinking, Faunus grew to the size of a horse.

Screeching before them was a creature out of mythology Talfryn had seen once in a book Gregorio'd made him study. Since becoming a squire, he'd begun tutelage under Gregorio to catch up with the other squires. The name of the beast was on the tip of his tongue.

"A gryphon." Brynwen took a backward step away from it.

"I knew that." Talfryn gulped.

Every god or goddess who had been tied to a column had turned into a mythical creature. Some with fur, some with feathers and wings, but all big and nasty. Oh, and the hydra—*can't forget that one!*

The gryphon-that-once-was-Faunus looked at the twins like they were its next meal. As did the rest of the nearby monsters.

"Time to run?" Brynwen asked.

Talfryn searched for an escape. Seeing none, he replied, "Yes."

Cyclopses leaped from their former prisons, bellowing in primal rage. Harpies screeched as they flew overhead, piercing Talfryn's ears with their cries. The two dracones attached to Medea's chariot roared and expanded in size, their scales shimmering with an iridescent glow that shifted and changed through reflections from the fire. Their wings unfurled like a thunderclap, ten-times their original length, sending gusts of wind whipping throughout the valley. Worse, the wind carried their fiery breath to singe anyone close by on the ground. Talfryn's hair and eyebrows sizzled.

He had an eerie worry for Eliva. Where was she?

Holding Brynwen's good hand, Talfryn twisted and dodged outraged, hungry monsters. He avoided more than his fair share of swipes to the gut, expecting his luck to run out any second.

Except for the hydra, the monster-gods were dwarfed by the ever-growling dracones. The enormous gold dracones gave Medea's chariot such a sharp jolt that she fell backward, dropping the long sword. It glinted in the frenzied firelight as it plummeted, and Talfryn's heart lurched as he recognized it. "The sword!"

"What?" Brynwen peeked over his shoulder. "Where?"

He pointed beneath the chariot, where the dracones were now smashing it into the ground. Near their scaly bodies, several monsters paced, looking at the people in the hippodrome with greedy, murderous eyes. He groaned. *Just great.*

Payla and Nalini hadn't been able to release more than half of the gods. Near them, Circe gaped at the monsters—her family—in horror. He thought Helius had been on the side that hadn't been released.

Talfryn pulled Brynwen behind a column to decide on their next course of action when eager boots scraped against the ground.

"Talfryn! Brynwen!" Kett appeared next to them, breathless.

Gregorio threw his arms around Brynwen. "We looked everywhere for you."

"Kett! Gregorio! You're all right!" he said.

"Thank goodness." Brynwen sighed.

Talfryn frowned as he studied his friends. Bruises covered Kett's face and arms, and a cut on his forehead dripped blood into his swollen right eye. Talfryn knew he probably didn't look much better. At least Gregorio didn't appear to have any new bruises.

"The horned girl freed us all. But look"—Kett held up his wooden contraption. It looked somewhat similar to the one he'd made in Nottingham to release Padric from gaol—"I made this device which I think'll help disable Medea's chariot. It's—" He and everyone ducked as a harpy flew over their heads, her clawed fingers and toes an inch from grabbing his head. "It's to mess with Medea's chariot."

Talfryn swung his hatchet at the harpy. It missed, but the creature zipped off with an irritated screech.

"How?"

"Well, I may have tampered with it a bit during construction. But with this device, I can disable it so she can't get airborne again. Break it apart."

"How does it work?"

"It's too complicated to explain, and we've got limited time."

"Right." Talfryn nodded. "Let's go." In all the excitement, he'd almost forgotten about his sister. "Oh, no, Bryn!"

"Don't worry about me. Go get him. Gregorio and I will look for Eliva."

Talfryn squeezed her good hand. "Thanks. Love you." Following Kett, they found Warin and Rawlins taking turns battling with a huge echidna. The monster staggered as each knight struck the final blow.

"That did it, to the heart." A wide grin spread across Warin's face. Sweating, he kicked the ugly body off his foot. Blood had splattered all over his face and clothes.

"Nah," Rawlins argued. Dagger still in hand, he held up two fingers. "My two hits to the spinal cord finished it off."

"I disagree. I—"

Talfryn set a hand on each man's shoulder. "Fellas, fellas, you just killed a god—probably not good form. Also, we have to stop you-know-who." He indicated with his head upward to Medea's chariot, which was still spouting lightning left and right. The witch and the

Druid seemed at a loss. "But first, we have to get Saint George's Sword."

Warin's brows furrowed. "The sword? But it's inside the abbey."

No time to lose, Talfryn waved them to follow and talked while they went. "Not anymore. Long story, but it's here now, under that giant golden dracones."

Both Rawlins and Warin gave each other a look, then shrugged. Still armed, they followed Talfryn and Kett to the crowd of monsters.

ELIVA TORE through the storage tent filled with boxes and weapons and unique items that could only belong to the gods of Olympus. On any other day, she would have stopped to admire them, but not this day.

She gritted her teeth. "Where is it?" Talfryn was out there, scratching himself to death, his sister Brynwen not in much better shape. After another shuffling of fine cloaks and scarves, something heavy toppled to the floor.

Moving a silk blanket out of the way, she found it—Brynwen's satchel!

Lifting it up, Eliva's gaze was drawn to a bow that caught the moon's glow from the skylight of the tent. Before she knew it, she was standing before it, gazing at its beauty. Her fingers slid along the smooth mahogany wood covered in tiny carvings of animals near the grip. The grip itself was worn with use, but she could tell it had been cared for and oiled on a regular basis. A weapon worthy of a goddess of the Hunt.

A strong wind lifted the flaps of the tent, bringing a burst of blinding light inside. That, along with the angry shouts and monstrous roars from Olympus, drew her back to the present. Biting her lip, she made a split decision and swiped up the bow and the leather quiver filled with arrows in red fletching dipped in gold beside it. She flung the quiver over her shoulders beside her own quiver filled with blue-green fletching.

She tore out of the tent and had started down the valley hill steps, bewildered by where all of the monsters had come from, when a movement from the left caught her eye.

At the last second, she spied the winged, almost-human-looking gorgon fly at her, claws gleaming in the moonlight, screaming its high-pitched trill of death.

Without thought, she dove down the hill.

Down, down, down, she rolled, keeping a tight hold on her old and new treasures. Excruciating agony split her side with each hit to the ground. When she stopped more than halfway down the incline, she gasped as shooting pains tore through her hip and side. Blinking through the haze of pain, she spotted more monsters descending the dark hill. Also, a number of arrows stuck out of the ground where she had been. There was an archer nearby. Gulping, she got to a shaky crouch and continued downward, hunching as small as possible. Good thing it was night and they couldn't see her red hair as well.

At the bottom, a large group of hardened mercenaries and monsters sparred, so she gave them a wide birth.

From behind the second column on the right, a maiden beckoned to her. Her gaze shifted uneasily to the monsters and mercenaries before continuing to wave Eliva over to her again.

Her heart fluttered when she spotted Talfryn a long distance off, no longer affected by the potion, but speaking with his sister, tutor, and the carpenter. She would have rushed to them, but she couldn't take a straight path there without being noticed and set upon. Even with a full quiver of arrows, she'd never survive getting through all of that alone. The mercenaries were completely focused on Medea's monsters, but it was still a blood bath out there. With little choice, Eliva set her shoulders and darted to the maiden with long blonde hair and a commanding air.

Eliva's breath hitched—*Diana?* Never before had she seen her, but Nalini, her mother, and Circe had described her once. Nerves hastily took over as she stood in the goddess's presence. *Don't look stupid or inferior. And stop gaping!* Diana appeared as though she were on the Hunt in spite of being weaponless. How had she escaped being turned into a monster?

"I see someone here is prepared. Come, we will hunt down Medea and these reprobates from Pluto. And what is this?" She grabbed up the mahogany bow from Eliva's shocked hand and slid her fingers along the animal carvings. Eliva's chest constricted at it. The goddess eyed her with approval. "Thank you for bringing my bow to me."

"It is yours?" She winced at how inept she sounded.

"Of course it is mine. Come, we will hunt." She swiped the quiver filled with red and gold-tipped fletching from Eliva's shoulder.

"But—"

But Diana was already off, and Eliva had to scramble to keep up. Her hand pressed against the satchel filled with precious medicines, ignoring the biting pain in her side. Brynwen still needed help, and Talfryn might suffer some lasting effects from the illusion potion. And she could use one of Brynwen's miraculous salves, herself. "Please, wait, m'lady, but I must deliver this medicine to my—"

"After the Hunt. They will pay for turning my brother into a monster."

Eliva shut her mouth and complied. *This will be quick,* she tried to convince herself.

Drawing the nocked mahogany bowstring back to her ear, Diana sent a bolt into the group of mixed enemies. One fell, but it was hard to tell who it was in the dark. She prayed Diana didn't strike one of her friends. "Come on, lass. The more of them we kill, the less will follow us later."

It made sense, but Eliva didn't know what else to do. "My name is Eliva, m'lady." No response as the goddess aimed at another target. Disappointed, she shrugged off the hurt in her chest. Nocking her bow, she took a deep breath and targeted a manticore, but her arrow would never pierce its armored hide. Instead, she aimed for a soaring harpy bent on attacking Nalini's back. "Oh, no, you don't." Her arrow struck the creature's gliding wing, the next struck her back. The creature dropped with a strangled cry. Nalini spun around in confusion, then launched into battle with a gryphon.

"As long as there is no Nemian Lion," Eliva muttered.

"I saw no Nemian Lion," Diana answered, sending an arrow into the back of a huntsman in the shadows. "But that does not mean one shall not appear from the witch's cursed bowl." She spat "witch" with all the love of a scorpion to a praying mantis.

Eliva spied Circe and Mars fighting a group of huntsmen. "How is it that you were not turned into a monster like the others, my lady?"

Diana huffed. "I suspect it has to do with the columns. Everyone who was tied to a column was turned into a monster. Jupiter could answer better than I, but from what I gather, the columns are conductors of power."

Chewing on her lip, Eliva swallowed this information. She joined in a few more hits, this time at a group of mercenaries. When the villains and beasts caught on to where they were, they changed course and rushed to another column to hide behind. A score of dead bodies made for an additional barrier.

"Your aim is not bad for a mortal."

Eliva supposed that was a backhanded compliment, but a compliment nonetheless. Her lip curled upward. She was about to send another handful of arrows into some enemies when she spied Talfryn and their other friends taking up arms against some monsters beside the two huge dracones.

Why does Talfryn always run into trouble? She also found Luciliana and Seia alongside Nalini. But there was no sign of Padric or the second chariot. *He should be here.* Her stomach constricted. The prophecy needed the charioteer hero. Where was he? If he perished, they were all doomed.

"M'lady, my friends need help."

Diana didn't flinch as she took aim at another enemy. "They will be fine."

As much as Eliva wanted to believe that, she wanted to help them where she could. "They must stop Medea from releasing the creatures and fulfilling her promise to rid the world of the gods—your family. Would you see her win?"

Lowering her weapon, Diana's head moved slowly to peer down at Eliva, mouth set in a frown of disapproval. "Of course, I do not wish her to win. I suppose you do have a point, child. Come"—she tugged on the vines climbing up the column. Whichever god or goddess had been tied to it was long freed—"we will move to higher ground."

Eliva's mouth went dry. *Up there?*

Already, the goddess of the Hunt was climbing the vines like a squirrel. She was more than a third of the way up when Eliva placed a hand and foot each on the vines and tugged to test their sturdiness. Climbing the tall trees of the forest outside of Cataractonium had been a favorite pastime of hers growing up. Having never worn shoes since age three, the calluses on the bottoms of her feet helped give her the leverage she needed to climb fast. And yet, climbing a column had never been part of their training over the years. Now, she wondered why not. She would ask Nalini to add it to their combat training when they returned home. The last thing she needed was to fall flat on her face and embarrass herself in front of the one person in the whole world she wanted approval from. *After mother and Nalini, of course*, she reminded herself.

Hoisting herself up, she found it somewhat thrilling and at the same time unnerving, sliding her hands, knees, and feet against the smooth column while praying the thick vines would hold her bodyweight. They had kept Diana up just fine, but she was a goddess. Eliva had only gone up about six feet when a hand snatched her ankle and yanked downward.

"Got you!" came a deep voice.

CHAPTER 54

"**G**et. Off. Of. Me."

Coming to, Padric groaned. The moment he did, his entire body flared with pain, especially his head.

"I swear, de Clifton…"

"Just a moment." Padric's head swam as he lifted himself off of his nemesis. The young man's shoulder dug into his chest, and he knew Aeron would be less patient given another minute. Pieces of wood fell off his back. Dust sprinkled from his hair, making them both sneeze. Careful to avoid cutting his hands and knees on the jagged pieces of wood they lay on, he tried to remember what had happened.

When he saw the insignia of the chimaera on the broken piece of wood, everything came flashing back. The last thing he remembered was the blinding light. He thought their chariot had struck a column. If that were the case, it was a miracle they'd survived.

Giving him a death glare, Aeron shimmied out of the wreckage that once was a chariot. The pegasi were gone, either hurt or scared, and must have flown off. They had been through enough for one day.

The sounds of fighting, screaming, and monstrous roars came from behind Padric in the hippodrome. "I am going to stop Medea from this madness," he announced. "Do whatever you will." Turning around, he limped to the hippodrome, not twenty feet away. Inside, he spied monsters fighting with his friends. "Monsters?" He wiped his eyes, half wondering if he had hit his head too hard. "Did they come from Medea?" The power of St. George's Sword must have brought them there. Then he noticed that the vines at each column were loose, many of them torn to shreds. "Oh, no." Picking up the pace, he drew his borrowed sword.

"Aye." Aeron jogged up to him. "She wanted to release dead monsters to inhabit the bodies of the gods. With the gods gone from Olympus, they'd sic the monsters on the mortals of the world to beat them into submission. Janus didn't think they were necessary, and she got bothered by his refusal. I guess she never got over it. Didn't think she'd have the guts to go through with it, though."

The hippodrome was filled with nightmares. On the ground and in the air, monsters were everywhere. And in the remaining gliding chariot, at the end of two very large dracones, stood Medea and the Druid, looking less than pleased at the creatures fighting his friends on the ground. However, Padric did not see the sword on Medea's person.

Padric called over his shoulder, "If you ever had any regard for those who once called you friend, who would have died for you, you would help our—*my*—friends, and find the sword to defeat Medea."

Aeron grunted, and Padric wondered again if the former knight would try to stab him. It would do little good to remind him that they were even in that respect.

By the time they reached the monsters, harpies and gryphons had joined in the party to defeat his friends. Rawlins, Talfryn, and Warin had to periodically slash their swords upward as they fought two foes at once. Padric's heart lurched when he spotted Talfryn. When he had seen him arrive earlier, his feelings had jumbled up inside—happiness that his friend had returned, and grief at having turned his friend away in the first place. Talfryn would have had every right not to return. Were it not for the prophecy…he shook his head. First, they had villains to defeat.

As he approached his friends, he noticed two more gods whom he supposed were Jupiter and Mars based on their strength and the lightning bolt in the older god's hand. The aeternae slashed and bit at the creatures as well, much to Padric's shock. Talfryn even spoke to it. What bizarre events this evening held.

"About time you showed up!" Warin snapped. "Took a nap, did you?"

"You have no idea." His stomach pulled as he changed into a centaur, growing another couple of feet taller in the process.

His three friends were relieved to see him, even Talfryn, who nodded at him without any visible animosity. Shocked, Padric responded in kind. That was a good sign, was it not? Another surprise came when the others did not scowl and threaten Aeron again. But when Padric looked over his shoulder the reason for this was revealed. The former knight was gone.

"Did I miss anything?" Padric blocked an oncoming mace wielded by a cyclopes. Its single eye disturbed Padric as he parried the next strike as well. It reminded him too much of when he had discovered that the manticore he was fighting in Cataractonium was really Gregorio under an enchantment.

"Nah," Talfryn said. He twirled his glowing blue hatchet—it had never done that before.

Warin barreled into an injured gorgon. "Just a bunch of ghosts flying around, and us making new friends."

"I invited them to tea." Talfryn hacked at the god-turned-beast with his hatchet. "But, alas, they declined."

"Don't care much for tea," Rawlins grumbled.

Padric's eyes widened in mock shock. "What monsters! They are most certainly not English."

"Tal—" Padric deflected the monster. Guilt wrapped itself around his torso until he thought he might burst. He sidled up next to his friend. "Tal, I must tell you something. I..." A lump formed in his throat. "I should not have sent you away. I was wrong." He sliced at the arm of the chimaera.

Talfryn blocked a slash from the monster's sharp claws. "Honestly, you were right. I let you and Bryn and Ulysses down. I needed—" He leapt backward to avoid a claw to the gut. A pained expression changed his features for a moment.

"Tal…"

"—to face some things about myself."

Padric paused before saying anything else, wondering if it had anything to do with the murdering aeternae fighting alongside them. Instead, he and Talfryn took on the gorgon together, just like old times. Finally, he said, "Yet, you came back despite it all."

Talfryn gave a grim nod. The monster they fought tripped over its own tail and crashed to the ground.

"It seems we were both at fault."

"Seems that way." Talfryn frowned. "We're not killing these god-monsters, right?"

"Not if it can be helped." Stomach dropping, Padric pumped his four legs to launch at a chimaera as its gleaming claws neared Rawlins's back.

❧

STARTLED, Eliva cried out. Clutching at the vines, she kicked at her attacker with her free foot. Each kick jarred the wound in her side, but adrenaline kept her going. He cursed and pulled harder. "You little wench!" Diana had stopped to regard them as though calculating their value to hunt, her hand clutching the top of the column. The huntsman next to Eliva's attacker attempted to jab at the goddess with a spear.

Big mistake. With a grin, Diana plucked the spear out of his hand and twirled it around in deft fingers. "Thank you, kind mortal." Then she jabbed at *him* with its pointy end, followed by the man holding Eliva's ankle.

Eliva planted a good kick to her attacker's nose, and with a loud *crack* and another curse, the hand gripping her ankle released her. Seeing no more threats, she scrambled up after Diana.

"I'm not done with ya yet!" the broken-nosed man screeched.

"Looks like it to me," she called back.

Reaching the top was the most excruciating thing Eliva had ever done. Taking deep breaths, she forced her body to cooperate. *I will make it. I will make it,* she chanted to herself over and over until her hand slapped the top of the column in relief.

"Oh, thank the gods." She breathed deeply, resting her head against the cool marble. She felt feverish after the climb. *It is nothing. It has merely been a long day.*

A hand descended near her face. "You are welcome."

Diana's strength surpassed even Nalini's. She had once thrown a full-grown lion over her shoulder during a sparring match. Since that day, the lion had never let down its guard around the dryad.

"Thank you." Once her feet touched the cool surface, Eliva thought she might breathe easier, but she did not. In fact, she felt faint.

"Oh, do not try to impress me, child. Sit for a minute."

"There is not time."

"There will be less time if you plummet to your death from this height."

Point taken, Eliva grunted as she rested a knee on the marble. They had a wondrous view of the entire hippodrome. And lots of moving targets with which to hit with their bows.

After a minute, her breaths came slightly easier, but her side still roared. It would have to do, for Talfryn and the others hadn't made much progress against the monsters. *I should be down there with him.* Her thoughts drifted to the prospect of his soft lips against hers. Catching herself, she was mortified and hated the warmth blossoming in her cheeks. *Weak!* she accused herself. *Diana will never make me a huntress now!*

"If you are ready, we shall leap the columns and approach your friends where there are fewer monsters to contend with."

Eliva eyed the next column, which was more than ten feet away. She gulped. "I can't make that. There is no way."

"You can, child. Give yourself a running leap."

"'Give yourself a running leap,'" she muttered under her breath. "Of two whole steps. As though I am a goddess who can do miracles." Something she longed to be. To be free. To hunt all day and have no other responsibilities or worries. To rid the world of monsters like those below. Her resolve hardened. Then frayed, as she realized she couldn't do it.

"Suit yourself."

The goddess readied herself by kneeling on the stone next to Eliva, looked intently at the next column, and then...stood back up. "Well." She brushed off her arms and white robe as though they had gotten dirty. In the darkness, there was no dirt to see. "I suppose a great leap is not what is needed right now. We can shoot from here."

Eliva raised a brow but said nothing. How were they to get to Talfryn and the others? It seemed hopeless.

An idea struck like lightning. "Genia!" Rising to her feet slowly, she put a hand to her mouth to call out to the pegasos. Surely, she didn't only listen to Talfryn. "Genia, I need you!"

Nothing happened. Forlorn, she watched the scene below where her friends fought for their lives. Diana was already shooting with expert precision.

Resigned that something must have happened to Genia, she unhooked her bow and nocked an arrow. She was just aiming at a harpy when she thought she heard a small neigh. With a glance to her left, she spied the silhouette of a pegasos. Behind it, another.

Joy erupted in Eliva's heart. Genia and her friend hovered over either side of the column at a lower height to where Eliva didn't have to leap onto her back. She took a moment to rub the winged horse's long snout. "Genia, thank you for coming." The pegasos leaned into her touch, and she scratched under her chin.

Once they were both situated, Eliva directed the pegasi to fly to where Talfryn was last seen. Her breath hitched when she couldn't locate him. "Talfryn, where are you?"

※

THE MONSTER's powerful paw strained Padric's muscles. A volley of arrows descended on the monsters, the wind from their shafts like a sweet song of vengeance.

Two pegasi darted in and out, arrows slicing at targets. Eliva flew with another maiden in a white dress who wielded an impressive bow.

Waving his hatchet in the air, Talfryn cheered and waved at Eliva and the formidable blonde maiden as they drove arrow after arrow into the enemy.

Soon, the monsters had several arrows sticking out of them, yet they seemed never to tire.

Talfryn sidled up to Padric. "Padric, I know you're busy, but Medea dropped the sword under the dracones."

Shoving the echidna back, Padric took a quick glance at the spot Talfryn indicated, where the giant dracones's sleek, scaled body shielded the Sword of Saint George. Whenever the winged creature swayed as it jabbed its great tongue in the air, Padric saw a glint of the polished weapon.

"I'll take care of this...guy." Talfryn swiped his hatchet at the echidna. Another chimaera with a white goat head instead of gray, came up from behind Talfryn, but Warin launched at it.

Padric nodded in appreciation and sprinted over to the golden dracones, hoping it would not notice him. In an instant, his legs were human again.

"Sir Padric!" Kett called. Padric stopped and turned, impatient to get to the sword. "Sir Padric, I fixed your chariot."

"Fixed it, but how? It was smashed to bits." He knew the carpenter's skilled hands were quick with wood, but the reality of his gift still astonished him .

Kett scratched his neck. His fingers were bloody with cuts. "It wasn't easy, but it'll make do for one final ride. It just needs one thing."

Padric realized his mouth had gaped open. Slamming it shut, he said, "Kett, you are a wonder. What is it you need?"

"Wings."

"Alas, those we do not have in plentiful supply." Padric waited until the dracones shifted to breathe bright flames at a group of mercenaries, then he lunged for the saint's weapon. He tugged with all his strength, but it would not budge. The dracones slithered its weight onto the sword again, making Padric back up so he did not have the same squishing fate.

From above, Medea laughed. Oh, how Padric despised that laugh.

Glass shattered on the ground between him and Kett. "Look out!"

Padric shoved the carpenter out of the way. Purple smoke ascended from the broken bottle and dispersed into the air. It smelled rancid as it clung to the dracones's golden scales as some sort of goo. The monster screamed and twinged.

Another glass vial broke near Padric's foot. Then another near Kett's hand. "Get up!" He hauled Kett to his feet, and they ducked under the dracones's wing where the witch and Druid could not see them. "Eliva!" Padric called.

Somehow hearing her name over the ruckus, Eliva's gaze followed to where Padric pointed at Medea and the Druid, who continued to toss vials of liquid, making it impossible to get to the sword.

Eliva nodded, squeezed the pegasos's sides with her knees, and shot a number of arrows in quick succession at the witch and cloaked meddler. They ducked into the chariot at the first volley.

The glass stopped shattering around them; nevertheless, the humongous dracones was still very much resting on the sword.

"Help me pull the sword out, Kett. Once it is out, have Talfryn gather the pegasi or some helpful creature with wings."

"Yes, sir."

When the giant dracones leaned to the left, they dashed to the sword and heaved. On the third try, it came free, and they tumbled to the ground with the force of their pull.

"Eliva!" Padric raised the sword in triumph, laughter on his lips. Just like King Arthur pulling Excalibur from the stone. The pommel tingled in his palm, its power coursing through his veins. This sword, once used to destroy monsters, had now brought them back into the world. He only prayed he could return them to whence they came.

He peered around for Brynwen, but could not see her in the multitudes. Where had she gone?

FINGERS TO HIS LIPS, Talfryn whistled loudly as he and Padric followed Kett beyond the columns to the repaired chariot. When he stepped up to it, he couldn't believe his eyes. It looked not so much like a chariot but a child's attempt at a fort castle.

"It *is* in one piece as promised," Padric commented, although not with much assurance in his response.

Talfryn felt much the same. "Uhh, I applaud your carpentry abilities and all, Kett but, umm, are you sure this thing'll fly, let alone hold anyone in it?"

"Yes." Kett rubbed his hands together. "At least, it'll hold for a few minutes. It'll have to be enough; just don't jump up and down on it, all right?" He raised his eyebrows at Talfryn.

"Why are you looking at me like that?"

"The horses?" Padric reminded them.

As if in answer, neighing filled the air as four pegasi entered.

"Hi there." Talfryn beckoned them closer. "If you could please get back into line, laddies and lassies, I'd be forever grateful." He listened to their excited chatter as they resumed their places in front of the chariot while he, Kett, and Padric strapped them in. "Oh, yes, m'lady, Kett's a wonder with carpentry. I'm sure he'd be happy to update your stall in the stables once we're finished here. Yes, we'll include an extra bucket for apples." He nuzzled her muzzle.

She neighed in thanks and nodded at Kett, who grinned as he cinched the last strap.

"Let's go." Talfryn rounded the rickety chariot.

Eyes wide, Kett shook his head. "Oh, no, I'm not one for heights."

"Oh, yes you are. You'll be fine. Besides, if something falls apart, you're going to fix it."

"We need you," Padric finished.

Kett scowled, then sighed in defeat. "Why's it always me who has to fix things?"

As much of a rush as they were in, they stepped into the chariot's bed with the greatest care instead of jumping into it right away. It was a very tight fit. Padric flicked the reins. After the pegasi started cantering, Talfryn pretended he couldn't feel the repaired boards creaking under his feet. Miser, anticipating the heights they'd soon take, burrowed inside his tunic.

Returning to the hippodrome, Talfryn started. "What happened to the dracones? They're gone."

"Isn't that them over there?" Kett pointed to Medea's chariot, being led by smaller dracones no longer enormous and lounging on the ground, but swooping at their friends.

Eliva and the goddess kept shooting arrows at the witch, while at the same time trying to avoid a harpy and gorgon flailing their sharp talons at them.

"Look out!" Kett poked Padric's shoulder until he looked where Kett indicated. The Druid drove the dracones chariot in a downward path straight at them. "Don't stop!"

"They're bluffing," Talfryn said hopefully.

"Doesn't look like it," Kett replied.

"Drat." With a new burst of determination, Padric guided the flying pegasi in a semi-circle.

Kett's fingers gripped the sides. "Wha-what're you doing?"

"A diversion so we end up behind her." Padric swerved right, away from Medea.

Talfryn gripped the side of the chariot. His hand slid with the sharp turn, jabbing a splinter into his finger. Clenching his jaw, he tried not to howl as he jerked his hand away. He guessed Kett hadn't had time to polish it up before allowing them on. Worse, a couple of boards loosened below his feet.

"Oh, Kett?"

"I'll fix it, I'll fix it." The carpenter pulled out a hammer from his belt to somehow fix the cramped chariot mid-flight. "Don't move."

"Where could I go?"

They swerved behind Medea's chariot with ease.

Talfryn crowed. "Shall we hunt us a witch?"

Padric's eyes narrowed as he grinned. "We shall."

CLUTCHING the green stone amulet to his chest, Aeron ducked and weaved between the mercenaries and monsters Medea had created, along with some gods who had been freed before being turned. The place was a menagerie of beings. The creatures brought death to several of his father's and Medea's henchmen, people who had worked with them for months or years. Mainly for pay. Never for the cause. Not for the first time, he wondered if they'd ever known or cared one way or another about Janus's cause.

Aeron wanted to tell his father "I told you so" about the goddess, but would he ever completely listen? Of course not. And yet, Janus had knowledge that something like this would happen. The whole thing was surreal. Medea had stopped at nothing, and now his father had paid the price. If only he'd had early proof, he could have killed Medea before she turned traitor and the whole thing would be over, and he'd be living like a god in paradise by now.

And Padric would be a corpse right now as well.

So why wasn't he? *Why didn't I kill him when I had the chance?* A knife to the ribs would have done the trick with little fuss, then he could have saved his father. Aeron's stomach clenched at this whole sordid business.

Janus the Future had told Aeron he would know when to use the amulet. After he had turned, Aeron could never get close enough, so this had to be it, while Medea was distracted with Padric. If she killed him now, all the better.

But where had the chimaera gone? After the chariot crashed, he'd lost track of his father. But how hard was it to find a chimaera?

The familiar beam of fire launched into the sky, parting anyone standing nearby.

There!

Avoiding all of the mercenaries, huntsmen, and monsters swooping in and out of the hippodrome, he was ten paces away from the chimaera when another column of fire rent the air not twenty feet away. *Another chimaera?*

He grunted in frustration. "Medea! Curse you." He paused to consider. "Which one?" Aeron's own anger kept him going. At this rate, he wished Padric would defeat Medea. It would have been more pleasurable to defeat her himself, but his father took priority. And, if Padric defeated Medea before he found Janus, the whole plan to own the world would be foiled. *Yet,* he thought happily, *I can always kill Padric later.*

After another couple of minutes, Aeron began to despair. How could he tell one chimaera from the other?

He spotted a gilt laurel wreath atop the head of a gorgon. Even in the darkness, he would recognize the wreath of a god he had to see nearly every day recently. That god must be Helius.

Looking at another monster, he saw the crown of flowers from another goddess he'd noticed earlier, on the head of Hecate.

That's it!

Twisting the green gem between his forefinger and thumb, he scanned the hippodrome for which of the two monsters was his father.

At last, he spotted it. The gold chain was tight around the thick neck of the closest chimaera, one of the many "mythical" monsters Gregorio had had him learn shortly before their last adventure together. It was too dark and too far to tell the color of the gem around the chimaera's neck, but it was promising. Steeling himself, he joined the fray, striking at the gods in their current monstrous forms to get out of his way.

"Fear not, Father, I am coming for you. Then we shall rule, together."

CHAPTER 55

*W*hen Padric took up the reins of the rickety chariot—after taking a second to marvel that he had not broken through the contraption the instant he stepped foot upon it—he locked eyes on Medea. She looked somewhere between worried and furious. Good. That meant she would focus on him instead of causing more havoc to Olympus.

"She looks worried and furious." Talfryn echoed his own observations.

"That was helpful, thanks," Padric replied dryly. Clearly, they had spent way too much time together. "Kett, what is your plan to disable her chariot?"

"Of course." He pulled a small wooden box from his pocket about the size of his palm. On the top, Padric saw some gears that reminded him of tiny water wheels. "There's a piece connecting the draught pole and pole brace that I fiddled with while I was her guest. I can break them with this device without ever touching it."

Padric understood not a word of what Kett had said except draught pole and pole brace, but he nodded. "Good. Do it."

"I only need to get close enough to it to make it work."

"That can be arranged."

An arrow struck the side of their chariot. It was not from Eliva or the goddess alongside her—they were concentrating on the nearby harpy and gorgon—but an unknown archer.

Padric flicked the reins to encourage the pegasi to fly faster to catch up to the other chariot. Medea kept glancing back at them, her arms flinging into the air, fingers sparking, in the midst of conjuring up another spell.

"Where is the archer shooting from?" Padric asked.

"I don't think it's an arrow." Talfryn pointed to the left but he did not need to. The trumpet-roar of the manticore was a sound Padric would never forget. Having nearly died from its venom once before, he was not eager to encounter another one.

"Faster, pegasi, we must catch up to her," he begged.

The sleek beasts complied, and they began to catch up. *Where is Medea going?*

Just then, the hydra, over twenty feet tall with its three long necks and fierce snake heads, stepped in front of Medea's chariot. Its heads weaved in and out of each other, tongues flicking at the dracones and the people inside. The Druid swerved the chariot, the dracones hissing and breathing fire in protest at the quick turnaround.

Straight at Padric's chariot.

"Kett, be ready." Padric handed the reins to Talfryn.

"Sir." Kett focused all of his attention on his device, his brow furrowed as his fingers tapped against the strange little box, nervous energy radiating off his skin. The intricate gears whirred and clicked noisily in spite of its small size.

Medea glowered at Padric. "Return the sword to me, Padric!"

"I think not." Padric raised the saint's sword high above his head, its edge gleaming menacingly. He could feel the power of the sword seeping into him. It felt intoxicating, pulling him in even further. It was easy to understood the reason Medea wanted it.

Medea lunged at him, a pole materializing in her hand. Unable to avoid her advance, he received the pole in the chest. He knocked into Talfryn, then Kett, whose arm jerked mid-calculation.

"Oh, no." Righting himself, Kett shook the box and smacked it twice.

Talfryn looked over his shoulder. "Please tell me 'oh, no' means something great's about to happen."

Sparks flew from the box with a high-pitched whine. Kett's eyes widened in alarm as he frantically tried to stabilize the device. "It's malfunctioning. It's—"

Thinking quickly, Talfryn seized the box and chucked it at the Druid.

Mad shouts came from the dracones' chariot as Talfryn steered the pegasi away from it. For the second time that evening, a blinding light flashed in his face. The device exploded with a deafening roar, sending shrapnel flying in all directions. The force of the blast spun Medea's chariot out of control. Crashing to the ground, it screeched to a stop in a tangle of wood, scales, and wings.

"Hey, it worked!" Talfryn cheered.

The shockwave from the explosion jerked the pegasi's chariot. It groaned all around them. The right side came apart in Kett's hands. Padric grabbed the carpenter's tunic and righted him before he fell over the side. The draught pole rattled with such force, Padric thought it would shatter at any moment.

Heart pounding, he watched as the ground drew closer. "Land, Talfryn!" His right boot broke through the wood and scraped against its rough edge.

"What d'you think I'm trying to do?"

The winged horses' hoofs struck the ground, then the chariot wheels. The left back wheel immediately broke off, the front one cracked and buckled with the loudest snap. Flying out of the carriage, the three ducked and rolled away from the carnage which once was a chariot.

When they stopped, all the air fled from Padric's lungs. Two chariot crashes in one day—*I would much rather be jousting*, he thought with a wheeze. His friends groaned beside him.

Talfryn coughed and rolled onto his back. "You already did this once today? Think I'd quit first. Ughh."

"I second that," Kett proclaimed, rolling onto his back.

Eliva and the goddess who he suspected to be Diana landed nearby. Alighting from the pegasos, Eliva rushed over to Talfryn.

"Padric!" Brynwen cried.

He cracked his eye open to see Brynwen running toward him, her satchel on her arm. She looked revitalized now, praise the Lord. He sat up, his ribs and everything screaming at him to lie back down. This time, the chariot was little more than dust. Never again would it be resurrected into service. Falling to her knees, Brynwen embraced him in a severe hug, unforgiving to his ribs. There was no way to forego the wince it emitted. Even so, he held her, breathing in her scent, wishing they could be anywhere else. Gazing into her eyes, he cupped her cheek with a gentle touch, then very calmly extracted her hands from around his middle. "It is not yet over, I am afraid, Bryn." Holding her wrist, his fingers glided over a bracelet with more than a dozen charms. He did not recall seeing it before. "What is this?"

"But it *is* over, Padric. Look, her chariot is in pieces. She could not have survived."

Twisting around to look, he found she was correct. The two dracones lay in an unmoving heap of wings and long necks among the rubble. Medea and the Druid had to be somewhere underneath them.

"It's over?" Kett held his shoulder. Talfryn was already picking up his hatchet.

All of the tension dropped from Padric's shoulders. "It appears so." His eyes met Brynwen's again, her eyes dancing with happiness. Or was that mirth, or—

"Padric!"

He whipped his head around at hearing his name in Brynwen's voice. There she was, among the monsters, Warin, Rawlins, Gregorio, the remaining nymphs, Circe, and some mercenaries. The fighting had stopped. Brynwen's arm was bandaged, and she looked terrified.

Two Brynwens...

Mouth dropping in confusion, Padric's addled brain knew that was wrong, and recalled the sword. Where did it land?

"Looking for this?" The smiling Brynwen next to him held up the Sword of Saint George, one hand around the hilt with the blade resting in the palm of the other. Her skin tone darkened, hair kinking up into black ringlets around her face.

"Medea," he breathed, planning a method of escape. A little late, his instincts kicked in.

With a quick swipe, the witch pulled back on the hilt, then lunged the blade toward his heart.

CHAPTER 56

*a*eron skidded to a halt in front of the chimaera.

"Father," he called.

The monster cocked its head in curiosity. Then, apparently regarding him as a tasty morsel, bared its fangs. The amulet matching Aeron's hung from the gold chain dangling from the monster's neck.

"I don't think you're happy to see me in the way I had hoped, Father." Sweat pearled on Aeron's brow as he tried to figure out how to survive the next few minutes. *Please don't breathe fire on me.*

The beast roared, the wind from its mouth whipping back his black hair and tunic. Its breath he did not care to describe, but at least it wasn't fire. It put its head low to the ground, snake tail wiggling—ready to pounce.

Oh, no.

A few men were running through the monsters, not seeing the crouching chimaera. As one mercenary whom he thought to be named Jack rushed by, Aeron grabbed a handful of his tunic.

Jack gaped in surprise. "What the—"

The chimaera pounced as Aeron yanked the mercenary into its path. Jack screamed as its teeth and claws sank into his chest and shoulder.

Blood splattered everywhere, including all over Aeron. He wrinkled his nose in disgust.

The other men ran in fear before they were next.

While the chimaera dealt with Jack, Aeron waited until the monstrous face came up for air. A minute passed before the bloody lion face rose up from munching.

Aeron's nose scrunched as he reached for the amulet around Janus-chimaera's neck. Oozing grime and blood, it squeezed out of his fingers. Somehow, though, the monster hadn't noticed him—yet. It was too busy gorging on its meal. After another swallow, it dived back in for more. A gryphon with a huge beak sauntered up and squawked at the chimaera, wanting to share in its prize. The chimaera only grunted.

Not wishing to be the gryphon's meal, Aeron stood as still as possible until it got bored watching the chimaera and flew off.

When the chimaera came up for air again, Aeron took no chances and grabbed the amulet with green gem around Janus-chimaera's neck. This time, the slippery stone stayed in his fingers as he drew the two pieces together. Covered in blood, it was hard to find the right fit. He jammed them together, but nothing happened. With an angry hiss, he forced them together two more times, but they only came apart. Finally, he took the bloody piece and, with a scowl, wiped it off on his tunic, followed by his own piece. He wrapped the chain with his amulet around his wrist so it wouldn't fall to the ground.

This time, he noticed that the backs of the amulets might join together. Gingerly, he fit the two pieces back-to-back, and they clicked into place. A perfect fit. A soft glow emanated from them, casting his hands in light. The chimaera noticed the light and turned its enormous lion face to him in curiosity.

"Nice chimaera," Aeron said. The light brightened, and he could see every spot of blood on the beast, every speck stuck in his teeth. Aeron jerked back, confident the magic had worked. The chimaera's chain broke loose with no effort.

"It is working, Father," he said with a disbelieving laugh.

Both chains began to shrink and tighten around Aeron's hand until they pinched his skin. "What the—"

After another heartbeat, the pinching became excruciating. Crying out in shock, he fell to his knees. "Father! What is wrong with this thing?"

He yanked on the chain until it came away and chucked it at another monster. Blood spurted out from a puncture mark on his palm. It continued to tingle afterward, and he held it to his chest.

The chimaera made a low, drunken growling noise, then its face began to morph in a grotesque way, much worse than when Aeron had been stuck in the awful pens of Cataractonium when he doubled as a slave and spy.

At last, Janus's future face formed, the goat head diminished into his body, and last of all formed his nose. Aeron backed up as the lion's body began to tremble. Janus the Past's forlorn face became visible last. The head and faces of Janus were complete, but his body changed more slowly.

"Father, it is working." Aeron clenched his hand in his tunic to stanch the flowing blood.

"My son." Janus the Past's face smiled in that depressed joy he bestowed most days.

"Yes, about bloody time," said Janus the Future.

Janus the Past sighed. "My son, I wish you would have left us as we were. You should leave now, while you still can—"

"It is too late," came the future face, followed by a cackle.

"What do you mean? Father?" By now, Aeron's whole arm had begun to itch and his stomach twisted with pain. But he didn't remember getting hurt in a fight or from the crashed chariot. He itched his hand absently. Meanwhile, the two-faced god continued to become human, his arms taking shape, followed by the legs. "When will we finish with our task?" Aeron longed for his bed in Olympus, wherever it was to be. Then he could explore his new home on the morrow.

Great pain clenched in his stomach. It doubled him over, a scream belting from his mouth. He crumpled to his knees, stomach roiling. Every part of his body exploded in agony.

"Aeron!" The past's voice cried. "What is happening? Brother, what did you do? Let me see him."

"Nay," Janus the Future said, not turning his head in the slightest.

The pain ebbed for a heartbeat, only to gasp. His hands felt strange. Bringing them up, he gasped—they had grown large with fur and claws. "What is hap…penn…ing to me?" His voice deepened.

Gazing up at his two-faced father's hardened future face, Aeron blanched. At last, everything became clear. *I wish you would have left us as we were.* The future Janus had given him half of the amulet. He had foreseen this. Knew Medea would betray him and what the amulet would do when he put them together. Rage gripped his chest.

"You…tricked me." The words were hard to speak. His tongue puffed up, teeth filling his mouth. His hands increased in size, with golden hair growing like grass at an alarming rate along his arms and legs. A wail of despair left his lips, sounding like a huge roar to his own ears. Flames erupted from his mouth, startling him.

He managed to see the tears in Janus the Past's eyes while the Future's were hard as stone.

Getting to his feet, he stumbled between the stationary monsters, bumping into the creatures, until he fell to his knees within the open space at the center of the hippodrome.

PADRIC ROLLED TO HIS LEFT. Instead of piercing his heart, the blade sliced along his chest and right bicep. He rolled back, clamping his hand over Medea's on the sword hilt. The moment he touched it, a surge of energy radiated from the blade, forming an invisible barrier around him. Bolts of lightning flared outward, lighting up the entirety of Olympus. The energy the sword emanated filled the hippodrome with enough power to raise the hair on everyone's heads.

Clenching his teeth against the bleeding cuts, Padric squeezed Medea's hand. At last, she dropped the sword onto her lap. The lightning dissipated, and the night sky returned to stars and the full moon.

"Nay!" Medea hissed. "You foolish mortal. You will ruin everything I have worked for."

"Foolish mortal I may be." Scooping up the sword, Padric rolled to his feet and pointed the tip at her clavicle. "But your fight is over, Medea. On your feet, witch. You are surrounded." He knew to keep his distance, yet needed to be rid of her before she did anything more brazen. She was one of those people who always seemed to have a backup plan.

Talfryn and Kett were on their feet joining Eliva and Diana, their weapons trained on Medea.

Instead of rising, though, Medea touched two of the charms on her bracelet and muttered a quick, three-word spell.

Interficite eos omnes!

Kill them all.

THE MANTICORE and hydra shuffled forth, their roars intermingling together.

"Down!" Padric shouted.

Deadly spikes shot out of the manticore's scorpion tail, causing everyone to dive out of the way.

Medea's singsong laughter filled the air as she sprinted over to the manticore. It helped her rise onto its back with a deafening trumpet-roar.

"So the bracelet is how she controls them," Kett observed, climbing to his feet.

"Eww," Talfryn said, lips curling with disgust. "The manticore just called her its 'mistress.'"

"Medea always was the clever one. Devious, but clever," remarked Diana. She released three arrows at Medea but somehow they missed their mark, instead exploding with a purple flair within a yard of her.

"We must stop the creatures," Padric directed. "But do not kill them, if you can help it."

Another volley of spikes descended on them as Padric rushed at the manticore. This time, they went over his head toward his friends.

❦

IN ALL THE confusion with Medea in disguise, nearly stabbing Padric, and two monsters on the attack, Brynwen couldn't move.

Warin put a hand on her arm. "Brynwen, you should get back. Help the wounded if you must, but please leave."

"I can take care of myself." The last thing she wanted was to leave any of them at this juncture. She looked up at him with determination, but her heart pounded with the buzz of danger in the air.

"It isn't a request. It's—" He never finished what he wanted to say. Instead, he dove at her. The world turned black as he grabbed her to him. She heard several muffled *thunk, thunk, thunk, thunk* sounds, not realizing that she'd been screaming in the midst of it. The wind rushed from her lungs as Warin landed on top of her. Groaning, his body slumped against hers. Squished and unable to breathe, she couldn't push him off.

"Warin, what happened? You're squishing me," she tried to say, but it came out muffled, a bit panicked. Maybe quite a lot panicked.

A moment later, he shuddered, then raised his face, brows furrowed. "Are you all right?" he asked.

Still dazed, Brynwen couldn't speak. Rawlins and Nalini helped Warin up onto shaky legs.

Warin batted their hands away. "I'm fine, I'm fine. See to her."

"You are most certainly *not fine*," Nalini commented. Brynwen didn't like the worry on her face.

As Payla and Gregorio helped Brynwen up, she gasped when she spotted three manticore spikes sticking out of the ground around where she and Warin had been sprawled. "Warin, you saved me."

His eyes sparkled as he beheld her.

She blushed under his scrutiny. "Let me see to your wounds."

"No time. Monsters to defeat." Taking his sword from Gregorio, Warin cupped Brynwen's cheek and sighed. Releasing her, he clapped Rawlins on the shoulder and dashed after the hydra who was chasing the remaining mercenaries into the center. That was when she saw the four manticore spikes protruding from his back "Oh, Warin." Her chest constricted, her brain calculating how much care and time he would need to heal from such wounds and venom.

"Warin!" she cried after him, but he was too far away. "Rawlins, bring him back here so I can tend to his wounds." Stomach twisting, she prayed this manticore's barbs weren't as deadly as the last one they had encountered at Circe's home.

The knight's usually stoic face crumpled in defeat. He knew as well as she that it was too late for their friend. "I'll try," he choked out before he and the dryads bolted after Warin. The hydra was already coming this way.

Brynwen and Gregorio were left to tend to the wounded. And there were many, many wounded.

WHILE TALFRYN and Padric chased after the witch atop the manipulated manticore, Eliva and Diana shot arrows at her. Hearing Brynwen's scream, Talfryn spun on his heel. Frantic, he looked for her among the crowd, barely noticing that the spikes had stopped, and that Eliva and Diana continued their onslaught on Medea.

He couldn't find Brynwen, only Warin on the ground with spikes protruding from his back. "Warin, nay..."

Beside him, Padric grunted and sprawled to the ground on his stomach. Fearing more spikes, Talfryn fell to his knees beside his friend. What he saw alarmed him—an arrow protruding from Padric's hip. In the firelight he was sure it was red and golden-tipped.

"Padric!" Eliva called out. She skidded to her knees beside them. "Forgive me, my arrow ricocheted off the beast's armor."

Talfryn shook his head. "It's not yours." He pointed at the red and gold fletching. The arrow in Eliva's hand was blue-green. The goddess continued to shoot, either unaware or uncaring about the accident.

"Padric, are you all right?" Talfryn asked.

Nodding absently, Padric peered up to where Brynwen now stood safe. "I am fine. It only struck my sword sheath."

"You are one lucky knight," Eliva said.

A deep howl filled the hippodrome, sounding over Medea's laugh. Every nerve in Talfryn's body froze. *No, no,* he reminded himself, *it has no control over me anymore.* Eliva placed a hand on his shoulder for support.

"Talfryn, breathe."

He couldn't look at her for fear of breaking down. Taking a deep breath, he attempted to control his breathing as he thought of the next steps to defeat Medea.

From out of nowhere, a giant blur of gray tackled the witch.

They crashed to the ground in a heap of fur and cloth. Medea's screams of fear, outrage, and pain filled the hippodrome as the aeternae growled and snapped at her. "I am your master!" she shrieked. "Obey me, aeternae!"

But the creature did not stop.

On the other hand, Talfryn noted, the hydra and manticore *had* stopped.

"Stay here." Picking up his hatchet, Talfryn sprinted to the wolficorn and Medea. Mustering every ounce of courage he possessed, he ground out, "Stand down, aeternae."

Shockingly, the wolficorn stopped, blood dripping from its lips and bone protrusions to glower at Talfryn with its chilling red eyes. Blood covered Medea's once blue robe as she breathed heavily from several gaping wounds on her person.

"I will have my payment," the beast said. *"Your foes have the bravery of coddled cubs, and I have the manipulator in my claws."*

"And yet, we have questions for her," Talfryn countered. "Of course, she *could* bleed out from her wounds." He eyed the witch, not wishing to risk Medea or anyone touching the charms on her bracelet again. "Stand down, and I will return what is yours. As for you, Medea, if you so much as twitch a finger, I *will* allow Wolfi to gnaw on you some more. You don't need *all* your fingers and toes, do you?" He grinned wickedly.

Getting to her elbows, Medea's glare could have driven an arrow through his head with one stroke. "You would not dare. You are too soft."

"Well, let's see now." Talfryn tapped his chin and peered around.

"Which of these monsters likes to play with naughty witches the most? This one looks nice." Bending over, he moved his finger dangerously close to a charm on Medea's bracelet.

"All right, all right, I concede." Then she spat in the direction of his feet.

"That isn't very nice."

Hatchet gripped until the wood creaked, Talfryn reached with care. He slid the bracelet off the witch's blood-stained wrist. Feeling the wolficorn's rotten breath on his neck—not at all imagined, this time!— he choked down his growing terror as he removed the bigger chain from around her neck: two wolf teeth, one molar from a large adult wolf, and a cub's molar. "No more leverage for you, evil lady," Talfryn stated.

Standing up, he extended the tooth necklace to the aeternae. "But first," he said, holding it back, "you're not to kill any more mortals."

It regarded Talfryn with a snarl. However, it nodded, then took up the chain between its teeth. *"I swear it. Yet, this does not make us friends."*

The very thought made Talfryn throw up a little bit in his mouth. "Oh, I dunno. Mayhap you owe me one. It certainly doesn't make us even." Thanks to him, his friend Ulysses was dead. He missed him more and more with each passing day.

The beast growled one last time, then the creature of Talfryn's nightmares departed up the steps to the abbey's portal. *And hopefully forever out of my life.*

CHAPTER 57

*I*t was over.

Relief flooded through Padric's chest. He hugged Brynwen—the real Brynwen—tightly as she crushed into his chest. He winced at the cut along his chest and arm, but could not care less as long as she was with him.

Much to his relief, the manticore had stopped attacking when Talfryn took the bracelet from Medea, but the hydra would have none of it. His friends and some mercenaries continued to fight it. Despite everything, Medea smirked at their uncertainty on how to stop the huge monster.

"How does this bracelet work?" Padric demanded.

Talfryn handed it to him. It was an exquisite glowing bronze bangle with charms dangling at perfect intervals. Each charm was the detailed shape and likeness of every monster within the Hippodrome.

"Where is Circe?" Padric asked. "She might be able to stop the hydra with it."

"And turn most of the gods back to themselves," Talfryn said.

"I will get her," Eliva offered. She took half a step before sagging against Talfryn.

"Eliva?" Talfryn caught her as her knees buckled. Her face looked pale even in the firelight. For the first time, Padric noticed how much blood coated her clothing.

The goddess Diana held up her arm to bar Eliva. "Nay, I will go."

"I will live." Eliva scowled, pushing Talfryn's arm away. To demonstrate how well she was, she stood tall, shoulders back. Yet, she looked ragged, hair limp, fair skin ghostly pale.

Everyone looked at her skeptically.

"I am here," Circe said, pushing through the dryads. "I was dealing with my monstrous father." She sighed.

A despondent roar that sounded oddly human and yet not filled the hippodrome. Padric's smile faded.

"What was that?" Brynwen peered around, searching for the sound.

From around a gryphon stumbled a grunting, whimpering figure. At first, Padric thought it to be a beast, but as it came into the light, he realized it was partly human.

"Aeron?" He gaped as the young man fell to the ground. His face was still visible, but golden hair covered his body as it continued to grow. His arms and legs were extended, and where once had been hands were now paws with long claws. A large, dark hump grew out of his back. He wallowed in agony and despair.

A second figure emerged behind him. Another part-god-part-beast. His monstrous appearance was the opposite of Aeron's, however. The more Aeron became a beast, the more Janus became himself.

"Well, well, champions. Thank you for taking care of my nuisance for me." He peered at Medea.

Padric's blood chilled at hearing Janus's voice. Even the stationary monsters' heads paused to see what was happening. Talfryn and Eliva startled when they saw him, but along with Diana, they kept their weapons trained on Medea. The witch, for her part, seemed just as surprised as everyone else. As for the gods who had escaped Medea's spell, they were mainly dealing with their kin in monster form. Otherwise, he had no doubt they would be here to exact their revenge on Janus as well.

From behind Talfryn and Medea, the Druid, along with a handful of armed mercenaries approached, pointing their gleaming weapons at

Medea's captors. More mercenaries surrounded the dryads, but after a short altercation, they begrudgingly dropped their weapons.

Padric grimaced.

Now human in all but his legs, Janus bared his white teeth in a smug smile at Padric. "Well done, Druid. What a thoughtful gift to bestow upon your god. How are you, Medea, my dear?"

She answered by spitting at him.

Padric pulled Brynwen behind him, and muttered, "I wish Talfryn had not dismissed the aeternae so soon."

"Me too," she replied.

Aeron's gaze met his. The former knight looked so wretched as the last vestiges of humanity left him to embrace becoming a chimaera. Having been twice duped in less than an hour, Padric almost felt sorry for him. *Almost.*

It occurred to Padric that he no longer had Saint George's sword. He groaned inwardly as he spotted it lying several feet away in Janus's direction amid a half dozen or so arrows. It must have fallen when Diana's arrow struck him. The borrowed sword was in his hand, but the glowing saint's sword called to him, begging him to finish this.

Padric steeled himself. "It would seem you two have had a lovers' tiff, Janus. A shame." His gaze fell on Medea, who scowled. "What will you do now that your plan is thwarted?"

"Yes, well, it seems the help is not always trustworthy." Janus advanced on Padric and Brynwen, bypassing Medea without another glance in her direction. "Be that as it may, it does not mean that my mission has been anything but successful." He grinned from ear to ear. "I knew Medea would betray me, as she has on numerous occasions in her colorful past."

Medea hissed at him.

"And what about your son?" Padric indicated the chimaera behind the god. "What did you do to Aeron?"

"I did nothing to him. He merely followed my directions. The side effects may have slipped my mind, however."

"He is your own son!" Brynwen gasped. She and Padric shared no love for Aeron, but this seemed quite extreme for a parent to do to his own child. Even for a god.

Padric calculated how he could get to Saint George's sword before Janus. If only Rawlins and Warin were not busy with the hydra, they could get it easily. There would be no immediate help from Talfryn and the others, either, thanks to the Druid. "I presume your foreknowledge helped you with Medea's betrayal. But what is your ultimate motive?"

Janus clapped his hands together. "Aha, at last we have come to it. The truth is, my young knight, that it was not only the gods whom I required to bow to my will. Turning them into monsters was a nice touch by Medea, if I do say so myself. Nay, it is you, charioteer."

Too shocked to say anything, Padric could only watch the god's triumphal mirth. "Why?" he finally asked, voice thick.

Picking up the saint's sword, Janus twirled it in his hand with an expertise Padric never would have fathomed the god to possess. The blade shimmered under the firelight of the hippodrome, Janus the Future's face appearing bored as his fingers demonstrated their dexterity. "Because, my dear Padric," he began, his voice smooth like honey, yet with a hint of a snake lurking just beneath the surface of a stream, "you possess a power unlike any other mortal I have encountered. A power that even the gods would fear, should they know it existed. Although I believe Circe has guessed it."

Padric's mouth set in a line, his mind racing to make sense of Janus's words. "What power do you speak of?"

Janus's soft chuckle sent shivers down Padric's spine. His eyes gleamed with an otherworldly light. "The power of choice, my dear boy. The power to defy fate and forge your own path. The gods may think they have sway over mortals, but they are wrong. It is free will that truly rules us all."

"And you have concern for me because I possess this trait?"

"It is because power is never given, young Padric. It is taken." The sword twirled and gleamed again. "And you, being the exception, are an abomination. When mortals begin to realize they embody this trait, the gods fall. Again. But once you and your sniveling friends are gone, that will all change. I will come to be the most powerful being of this age.

With these monsters at my helm, the people of this earth will learn to fear me."

"And to worship you."

"That is the idea. Now, hand over the bracelet if you would."

As Janus spoke, heat seeped through Padric's chest. "Never." He glanced at the beast that once was Aeron; a traitor who had formerly been his friend, who himself had been betrayed—twice. "And throughout all of your cunning planning and manipulation, this was Aeron's fate all along?"

Janus lunged. "Predictable, as always." Padric barely managed to push Brynwen to the side and raise his sword to deflect the blow. Sparks flew as the clash of metal rang throughout the hippodrome, over the roars of the hydra's three heads. Padric's boots rolled on the arrows strewn along the ground.

Janus's fighting style was bold and powerful. Each lunge with the saint's superior sword drove Padric back another step toward the monsters until they were in their midst. The hydra roared to their right.

"I groomed Aeron to be much stronger than his bore of a family ever bothered to. I offered him more than the pittance of an inheritance his family would give him."

"For your own means. We were his family." Again, Padric remembered when they had played as children in true friendship. But things had changed after Aeron's mother died.

Stars filled his vision. Next thing he knew, he was sprawled on his back. Face stinging from the god of time's fist, he rolled as Janus chopped down at him. It clanged on the ground where he had been.

"You are a slug in the eyes of the gods." Janus chopped again. Dirt rained on Padric's face and neck as he rolled, this time bumping into the leg of a motionless cyclopes. *Dead end.*

"Aren't we all?" Padric replied.

Raising his sword for a block, Padric took a breathy second to kick the god's leg out from under him. Janus landed with an undignified squeal. The saint's sword went skittering away.

Reaching for the weapon, Padric rolled to his feet, tipping the sword point at Janus's throat. The white weapon tingled on his fingertips, the faint glow returning and flooding him with confidence. "Surrender, Janus. It is over. The gods of Olympus have no comparison to the God of Heaven. He is almighty and might take pity on your pettiness."

The god of time's jaw set, eyes roving the glowing weapon with jealousy and contempt. "Surrender to you, a lowly, abhorrent mortal? Never." He flung a handful of arrows at Padric's face. "Lies! Your God is nothing. Nothing!"

Though light, the arrows surprised Padric, a couple shafts hitting him in the face and chest. As they fell to the ground, Janus was quickly on his feet. Padric saw the glint a half-second before the god's hand moved in a downward arc.

CHAPTER 58

When the Druid and his mercenaries approached with weapons drawn, Eliva knew they were outnumbered. She sucked in a breath. Never in a thousand years would she admit it, but she had been looking forward to a bed, bath, and soothing balm for her side. But these enemies were insufferable.

"Care to surrender?" Talfryn asked. He got a club to the gut for that. Doubled over, he dropped his weapons, wheezing for air.

"Shadow, thank Olympus you are here." Medea's voice was weak with the loss of blood. "Take me away from this place. I weary of it." She held up a shaking, bloody hand.

The Druid's hooded face regarded her, and the temperature dropped. *"I think not. My lord Janus has no more use for you."* He reached out a hand to her throat.

"You would defy me, too?" she wailed. The Druid's fingers clasped her throat and squeezed. Air cut off, she made a horrid choking sound. It made Eliva's throat hurt.

Desperate for a way out, Eliva made eye contact with Talfryn. He shook his head faintly, but she had no other good options. She reached for the closest mercenary's spear. Too slow, she was unable to avoid the punch to her face.

She spun and crumpled to the ground. Stars flashed before her. It hurt much more than she'd expected.

"Eliva!" Talfryn wheezed.

Her heart melted at the fear for her in his voice. She heard scuffling and his grunt.

Talfryn!

"Take the bracelet from his pocket and their weapons," the Druid commanded.

Nalini, Circe, Diana, and the dryads shouted in outrage.

Eliva cracked open an eye to watch Talfryn struggle as a mercenary removed the bangle with dangling charms from his pocket.

Heart quickening, Eliva shut her eyes and waited for the mercenary to leer over her. The instant his shadow darkened over her, she grinned. Flinging her palm into his throat with one hand, she grabbed his spear with the other. Surprised, he fell to his knees as she rose to her feet, swinging the spear shaft into the face of a lunging huntsman. He went down in a tangle of limbs.

She caught Diana's approving nod, then the goddess plucked a dagger from the ground and drove it into the nearest mercenary.

Emboldened, Nalini, Luciliana, and Seia joined the fray with their war cry.

Diana swung a club at the Druid's head, but his hand touched a shadow and he disappeared.

"Where did he go?" Eliva spun, which was a mistake. Dizziness overtook her. When her vision cleared, a spear was hurtling toward her.

Talfryn pulled her out of its path. As he did so, she spied a huntsman swinging a hatchet at his back. He did not stand a chance against her spear.

"Thanks, I didn't see him," Talfryn said.

She stood panting, Talfryn clutching her to him as he checked for the next threat. She gazed up into his handsome, grime-slicked face. Her heart thudded within in her chest of its own stupid volition. She had a great urge to kiss him. That if she didn't do it right now, she never would.

"Talfryn…"

His eyes widened as another onslaught of mercenaries and huntsmen emerged, weapons blazing.

❧

BLINDING pain seared Padric's shoulder, lancing through his chest down to his toes. Staggering backward, he whipped a lazy slash at Janus. The god stepped aside with ease to avoid it.

Padric's knees buckled beneath him. As he fell, he saw the red and gold-fletched arrow protruding from his shoulder. He could not catch his breath, it hurt so awfully.

Vaguely, he saw Brynwen shouting his name, and his friends fighting with the Druid and his minions.

A moment later, the Druid appeared by Janus's side. He handed the two-faced god the monster-charm bracelet and a sword.

"Thank you, Shadow. You are indeed my most loyal follower." Slipping the bracelet onto his wrist, he touched every charm.

"Jewelry does no help in making your likeness more fair, Janus." Padric wheezed an aching breath. He tamped down the fear that the arrow had pierced his lung.

"Oh, I do not know, I think it is charming."

Padric rolled his eyes, just about the only thing that didn't hurt.

Rumbling filled the hippodrome. All of the monsters began to move, including Aeron-chimaera. Roaring filled the air as they shuffled forward, surrounding Padric, his friends, the minions, and the remaining gods within their formidable circle. The gorgons, harpies, and gryphon swooped in and out, their claws gleaming in the firelight.

"Do you like my monster menagerie, Padric?"

Rawlins, Payla, Warin—who miraculously had not yet succumbed to manticore venom—and two male gods rushed into the circle, chased by the gigantic hydra. The creature's three long necks towered over the columns of the hippodrome, its huge feet shaking the ground with each step. It was easily three times larger than any other monster in Olympus.

His friends, Circe, and Diana backed up warily toward the center, keeping their sights on the monsters. The Druid disappeared into a shadow again.

Gripping the hilt of the saint's sword, Padric drew himself to his feet. "I cannot say that I do," he managed to say. Padric stalked toward the two-faced god, the Sword of Saint George infusing its strength into him. "But I think it is time that they take a nap."

"You must catch me first." Janus smirked, his body becoming transparent and filled with dazzling white stars like a constellation, until he disappeared. The same thing had happened the first time Padric had met him. "If you can," he said, reappearing behind Padric, bearing down his sword toward Padric's head.

BRYNWEN STARTLED when a cold hand gripped her good arm.

No!

Ice cold dread from the Shadow Druid's translucent hand seeped into her skin. Fear gripped her chest as she struggled to get free of his grasp. *Not again!*

"Let go of me!"

Gregorio came up and attempted to detach the cloaked figure, but he was incapacitated when the Druid clenched his arm. Releasing his grip on the tutor, he punched him in the chest. Gregorio went flying several feet to crash at the feet of one of the monsters.

"Gregorio!"

Thankfully, Luciliana dragged the bedraggled tutor out of harm's way before the Cyclopes stomped on him.

The Druid pulled Brynwen away from Talfryn and the others.

Finished fighting the Druid's minions, Talfryn's head had whipped around when she'd cried out.

"Bryn!" Hatchet in hand, he rushed toward her, Eliva trailing behind. "Let her go, Druid."

Brynwen couldn't see the cloaked figure's eyes now, but she remembered his weathered, tattooed, scarred face. His frightening beady eyes.

"This one almost ruined all of my carefully-laid plans. It shall not happen again."

Meanwhile, the hydra's monstrously long tongue knocked Rawlins to the ground. He found his footing again and swung at it with a sword and dagger. Warin, manticore barbs still protruding from his back, jabbed at the face with his sword, shouting taunts in its direction while the two muscled gods took on the other two heads.

Talfryn swung his hatchet at the Druid. He ducked, releasing Brynwen's arm, as he pulled two vials out of his cloak.

"You are no match for me," the Druid taunted. He tossed the vials at Talfryn and Eliva.

They both dove out of the way as the vials broke harmlessly on the ground. One splashed ooze, the other filled the air with a vile-smelling smoke.

Eliva rolled to her feet, twisting the spear in her hand as she rose, skirts flying in all directions around her like fluid flower petals in the wind. She lunged for the Druid. Somehow, a dagger appeared in his hand. He slashed at her even though she had the longer weapon. He ducked and weaved as she and Talfryn took turns slashing at him in a beautiful but deadly dance. Brynwen was mesmerized by their movements, how well Talfryn and Eliva fought together, as though they were meant to be. The way they stole glances at each other made her gasp.

She shook her head in disbelief. *When did that happen?* Talfryn hadn't said a thing, had he?

Miser descended from Talfryn's shoulder to the ground. In a flash, he disappeared under the Druid's robe. A head-splitting scream erupted from the Druid. He shook his leg while desperately trying to fight off his attackers. He reached into his robe for another vial.

Eliva's lightning-fast reflexes grabbed his arm and pulled it forth. He gripped a vial with sparkling dark liquid.

"You shall all die foul deaths," he rasped. *"You shall—"*

Releasing his hand, Eliva stabbed him in the heart while Talfryn's hatchet chopped his head clear off. The head, still in the hood, soared twenty feet to land at Janus's feet. The god stared at the hideous face in disbelief.

"...not speak badly about my friends," Talfryn finished. "I'm sure he was going to say something along those lines."

Eliva chuckled and nudged him. Then she gasped, clutching her side. Her eyes rolled heavenward.

"Eliva!" Talfryn caught her and lowered her limp form to the ground. "Bryn, please help her," he begged. He looked lost, eyes glistening. "I can't lose her."

"I'm here, Tal." Brynwen took a hurried step toward them when the hydra's deafening hissing roar paused all fighting.

"Brynwen, look out!" Warin shouted from behind her.

She spun on her heel. The hydra's giant head came straight for her, its mouth big enough to swallow her hole. It's enormous forked tongue lashed out at her.

Warin burst into view, slicing the hydra's middle head from mouth to eye. Again it roared, forked tongue flailing, and dove at him. He was too slow, and it snapped him up in its huge mouth. Payla flung her daggers at its head, but it was too quick.

Brynwen's heart stopped as she watched helplessly.

The knight stabbed at the creature's head three times. He bellowed a cry as it dug its venomous teeth into his body. Having had enough of the toy, the hydra flung him to the ground. He bounced twice before stopping in a heap of limbs.

"Warin!" Brynwen screamed.

He lay so still, she thought him dead, but he rallied once more to his knees, then keeled over.

Payla dragged him out of harm's way while the beast roared at the night sky.

Not caring that she was too close to the monster, Brynwen ran after them and knelt by Warin's side. Eyes closed, his breathing was erratic and wheezing, similar to when Padric had been infected with the deadly manticore venom.

Payla placed a hand on her shoulder. "I am so sorry, Brynwen. I could not get to him in time." Payla's face screwed up in remorse.

"There was nought you could do." The knight stirred, and Payla sprang back into the action alongside Rawlins.

"Warin?" Hope swelled in Brynwen's chest. She moved a stray brown lock of hair from his sweaty forehead.

His eyes fluttered open, and he smiled up at her. "Brynwen, my sweet. Alas, that I am at death's door and cannot woo you as I would wish."

Tears flowed freely down Brynwen's face. She picked up Warin's hand. It had grown cold in the time since the barbs had struck him. "Don't speak like that. I have a remedy, I know it." Digging through her satchel, she found the Miracle Mix and angelica ointment. Frantic, she dumped them into a little bowl, praying over it, swirling it.

Warin pulled her hand away. "Brynwen, you have already done everything for me."

"But Warin—"

He placed a grimy finger on her lips. "You were the first lass who challenged me."

"Warin..."

"Let me speak." He coughed and wheezed for a few extended heart-beats. "I know your heart lies with de Clifton. He is a good man, and I respect him. He loves you as much as you do him, with all your hearts. Mayhap if we had met at another time"—he wheezed again—"I only wish to say that I am honored to have known you." Raising a hand, he caressed her cheek.

"Oh, Warin. I-I..." She choked on her tears. "And I am honored to have known you and called you my friend. Your noble heart has saved me and my friends on numerous occasions. I am forever in your debt."

"That means the world to me. I—" He gasped, then clenched his eyes shut as he spasmed, the venom overtaking his body. His head and hand fell limp with his final breath.

A sob wrenched from deep within her chest, her heart breaking at the loss of her friend. She barely noticed when Gregorio knelt beside her, but she fell into his arms and cried on his shoulder until the tears dried up.

Gregorio wrangled a handkerchief from his pocket and held it up to her. "I am so sorry, Brynwen. Warin was a good man."

She sniffed, swallowing a huge lump in her throat. "Oh, Gregorio, why did this have to happen? Why?" She frowned, staring at the fresh stain on his tunic and remembered. "You are hurt."

"I can wait. Eliva needs you more right now."

The clash between Rawlins and Payla against the hydra brought her to her senses. *Please don't let them fall, too. I can't take another loss.*

"Yes, she needs aid." With resolve, she nodded and stood up to finish ministering to Eliva, Gregorio, and her other friends.

PADRIC GRITTED his teeth as he blocked the strike. Putting his legs into it, he grabbed a handful of the god of time's tunic with his injured hand and shoved with the sword. Their weapons rang in disharmony as his slid along Janus's. Not once did Padric take his eyes off Janus the Future's intense blue gaze. Along with his ebony hair and Roman nose, Padric could not fathom how he never saw the resemblance to Aeron before their Labyrinth adventure.

When their weapons parted, Padric still held the fabric, causing Janus to stumble. He bit back the pain but had to release too soon.

"Oh, forgive me, are you ailing?" Janus pouted. "Poor little champion. When I am finished with you, you will be begging for me to end your suffering."

"Is that a promise?" Padric circled the god. He knew Janus had more tricks up his toga.

"I only make promises I can keep."

"Is that how Aeron saw it?" Padric did not understand why it bothered him so, but it pleased him to see Janus's forehead crease in irritation.

"He was weak." He bashed down on Padric's glowing sword. "He had no discipline." He bashed down again.

Saint George's sword hummed, its radiance encouraging Padric not to give up. "What of your other half? What promises did you make to him?"

Janus slammed his sword down a third time. But this time, as their swords made contact, Janus's future face froze.

"He has a point," Janus the Past's voice came from the other side of the god's head with an audible sigh. He sounded even more forlorn than usual. "What did you promise me again? Peace? And Helius—revenge? I am sorry, dear brother, but we cannot have it all, and I believe none of what we want aligns with what *you* want."

"When we rule Olympus and all beneath our feet, then you shall taste the sweetness of all we have suffered through, *dear brother.*"

"I have come to terms with my suffering, brother. Bringing it on others does little good for the world. Have you learned nothing from the past?"

Janus's jaw clenched. "Silence."

It was eerie, watching the god have a conversation with himself. Padric thought about killing the two-faced god while he—they?—were busy, but decided to wait, with wariness.

"I have been silent long enough," the Past said.

The Future's eyes widened in surprise. "I am in charge. Live in the past if you must, but I *will* ensure our future."

"Yes, you are always in charge." Now the Past's voice became agitated. "Part of the past is to see what mistakes you or others have made. And I have witnessed them all."

"What are you saying?"

The Past paused. Then, "When will you learn that you cannot control everyone? You controlled our son, and look what has become of him. He trusted us. I trusted you. Now, look what we have done. I cannot stand by any longer and allow it to happen again. Young charioteer, I stand with you. Forgive me for sitting in the dark and allowing this to come to pass. I—"

"Foolish." Future Janus scoffed at his past-self. "Of all the stupid ideas, this is your worst yet. You think to stop *me*? You are merely a face. It is I who hold all the power. Now, if you are finished, I will destroy this abomination and his unworthy comrades so we can continue."

Without waiting for a reply, Janus bounded at Padric. He struck so hard and fast, Padric could barely keep up. Unable to use his left arm much, his right took the brunt of the attacks. Too fast to find the god's weakest point. Breaths became harder and harder to obtain. His vision blurred, but he managed to blink it away most of the time.

They came to a standstill when their swords locked, neither giving way. Padric panted. *He must have a weakness somewhere.*

"Young charioteer," the Past said quickly. "His weakness is..."

"Stop it!" the Future ground out.

Padric found it and grinned. How had he missed it before? "In the wrist. Thank you, Sir Past."

"What? What are you talking about?" The Future growled. "I have no weaknesses."

Padric prayed for one last burst of energy. *Thy will be done.* After the quick prayer, he had an urge to close his eyes. Through his lids, the sword glowed pure white. It blinded Janus, who cried out and brought his free hand up to cover his face.

Wasting no time, Padric opened his eyes as the blade's radiance faded and struck Janus's sword wrist.

"Ach!" he shouted as the blade flew from his grasp. It skittered along the ground a few yards away. "Why, you little—"

"Nay!" the Past cried. I am not just a *face*, brother. I have some strength of my own which you have never cared to ask after."

Brows wrinkling, Janus the Future set his lips in a thin line. "What do you mean?"

His body went rigid, eyes wide as saucers, mouth agape. Sweat poured down his face. He fell to his knees, head up, defiant, yet fear glistened in his eyes.

"Finish it, young charioteer." The Past said. "We can no longer stay in this world as we are. We have not learned, after all this time, that the mortals must choose. This God of yours is stronger than us."

"No one is as strong as us."

"Kill us, now."

Padric shook his head, then remembered Janus the Past could not see him. "I will not kill you. The gods can have you—once they are themselves, that is."

"You cannot hold me, brother. I—ahhh!"

Janus crumpled to the ground and dissolved into stars.

"Is it finished at last?" Padric had seen the god materialize from stars before, but this looked final. He looked at Rawlins, Brynwen, Talfryn, and his other friends. Brynwen made her way to him slowly but stopped short. Her eyes went wide.

The sound of a sword slid across the ground.

In the next instant, the god was behind Brynwen, a man's silhouette of stars formed into the physical form of Janus, holding her by the waist, the other with his sword at her throat. His laugh was most wicked.

CHAPTER 59

"Janus!" Padric took two long strides before Janus jerked the sword closer to Brynwen's throat. He looked just like Aeron when he had held Simon, the young son of a tracker, captive in the Labyrinth. She stood still, wounded arm clenched at her side, but dared not whimper. Padric's heart ached to tear the god apart. "You are a coward! Hiding behind your sword and lies. I came here to fight a deity, not a frightened *man* who would use a maiden as his shield."

Rawlins and the others grumbled their thoughts on the matter.

"He is right, Janus," Circe said.

Diana shoved her blonde braid behind her back. "I could not have said it better myself, mortal. I like him," she told Luciliana next to her.

"That's my sister!" Talfryn's shout filled the hippodrome. He threw his hatchet into Janus's back.

Janus lurched forward, releasing Brynwen to regain his balance. She skidded onto her knees.

Enraged, Janus spun around, slashing his sword at anything and anyone who tried to get near. His sword came dangerously close to striking Brynwen.

"Janus!" Padric grabbed the god's attention so Brynwen could scramble away.

Janus spun at Padric, his face ugly with desperate hatred. "This is your fault!" He dissolved into stars again.

Where did he go now?

"Two can play at that game." Padric pulled on his own resources and transformed into a faun. He calmed his breathing. His father's lessons, knight training, those he had picked up from Circe, and Nalini, they had all taught him something important. Perhaps Janus had thousands of years of training for combat, but he seemed to have missed a vital ingredient to his regimen somewhere along the way. Even with only a minute fraction of Janus's training, Padric had learned many invaluable things, while the immortal's future self had learned nothing.

Using his "abominable" faun senses, he heard the slight rustle of fabric. With speed gifted by the Lord and the blessed sword, he pivoted out of range of a possible strike. He thrust forward, the long blade glistening, humming as it sought its target. It met with resistance.

Janus reappeared. On his tip-toes, he had halted mid-swing, Padric's gleaming sword pierced through his abdomen. He staggered forward, half-heartedly swinging the sword. The blow, Padric realized, was almost the same as the one he had given to Aeron. Like son, like father.

Heels meeting the ground, Janus worked his jaw. The shock at being struck lasted but a moment, however.

"The abomination has dared to strike me. My monsters will defend me." He fiddled with the charms on his wrist, but his fingers shook too much.

"Nay, Janus." Padric approached to less than an arm span away. "This abomination knows *you* are the monster."

The sword falling from his limp fingers, Janus gaped at the sword of Saint George protruding from his stomach. Golden ichor welled up to ooze out of it. Gripping his abdomen, he fell to his knees, swaying.

"What have you done?" the two-faced god cried. Golden ichor spilled over his fingers and the bangle holding the monster charms.

Exhausted, his shoulder screaming, Padric regarded the immortal who had caused so much trouble and pulled the sword out, lest Janus get his third wind. Rawlins came up beside him, his features hardened, as he grabbed Padric's good arm to steady him.

Curious, Padric brought the Sword of Saint George closer to his face for further study. It still glowed a brilliant white, its power coursing through his veins. Otherwise, he would have fallen over long ago. "This is a monster slayer. I believe that includes you, Janus."

"Do not just stand there," Janus pleaded. "Help me."

"As you would help anyone of us here? Especially an *abomination?*"

Rawlins's eyes sparked. "Shall I finish him off for you?"

"I cannot say I am not tempted."

Janus's face paled even further.

The others approached, Circe in the lead with a sour expression on her face. "Janus, Janus. How low we have come."

Nalini came up behind her. She removed the ichor-covered bracelet from Janus's wrist and handed it to Circe.

"This bangle is of an intriguing design." The goddess touched a charm, saying a short chant that Padric's brain was not capable of translating in his current state. The monster closest to Janus's left moved ominously close to the two-faced god. Its claws struck him in the shoulder. Circe bit her lip. "Oh, heavens, *that* was not supposed to happen," she said in a deadpan.

Gregorio cocked an eyebrow at her.

She rolled her eyes heavenward. "Oh, very well." With a touch and similar chant, the monster moved back a step, its paw bumping into Janus again. "Do not look at me so, it takes getting used to."

Gregorio sent a look to Padric of *this is who I grew up with.*

"How do we turn my family back?" Diana asked.

"I am still working on that." Circe raised the bracelet up to the firelight. The moon was well past its zenith by now, providing little help.

"Janus?" Gregorio asked.

"Do not look...at me," Janus wheezed. "That was all Medea's doing."

"Thanks to the Shadow Druid, she is incapable of speech at the moment...or perhaps ever again." Diana's lips curled up in a grim smile.

Circe lowered the bracelet in frustration. "It could take weeks or even years to decipher this."

Still holding Saint George's sword, Padric watched its glow radiating onto the bracelet. Circe's brow raised as she saw what it did. "Yes, I see. The monster slayer must destroy it."

"Are you sure?" Padric trembled. All of his strength seemed to be seeping out along with the blood from his shoulder. His whole arm and half his tunic were soaked in dark blood.

"Yes," Gregorio agreed. "Saint George would have done the same thing."

"Hold up the sword," Circe directed.

Janus gave a strangled cry. "You cannot! You would ruin everything I have worked for. Strived for."

"I warned you," the voice of Janus the Past said. "I warned you that we would come to ruin in the end. But you are never satisfied. Always looking to the future, never to the present, or the past."

Talfryn shook his head. "Guess he didn't learn from the past."

"Alas, you are speaking on deaf ears, my friend," said Circe. "Now, Padric, hold out your sword. Perfect, hold it still." As she slipped the bracelet around the blade, the charms tinkled against the metal, making a musical sound. Closing her eyes, she chanted in ancient Latin.

> *Vinculum frange*
> *In candida igne,*
> *Venerunt unde*
> *Illos omnes redde.*

> Break the binding
> In bright white flame,
> Return all those
> From whence they came.

The moment Circe's chant finished, the sword grew brighter. Energy flowed from Padric into the weapon. The little pieces of metal around the bangle began to pop and fizzle. Gray smoke emanated from them. A high pitched scream filled the air, and a spirit ascended from somewhere ahead of them. It arced overhead, screeching all the way on its trajectory to the sword, which sucked it up with a fizzle of energy. One by one, the charms smoked and dropped, and with each one, Padric felt a great weight overcome him. He was grateful for Rawlins's arm. Sweat returned to his brow as the magic worked. As the last charm bounced on the ground, they all broke apart into ash. The wind carried them away, each speck.

With the wind, the last of Padric's strength waned. Black spots and bursting stars swam across his vision. Legs buckling, he would have crumpled to his knees had Rawlins and Payla not kept him upright. The sword fell from his tired fingers.

"It is done," Circe proclaimed.

When Padric looked up, the gods were themselves again. Each bore a frightening countenance, made ten times more so in the flickering firelight. Only three or four were missing, but there were whispers that those fallen should be hale again within a fortnight—however that worked for immortals. As one, the remaining standing gods collected around Janus. When it was clear they would surround him, Rawlins helped drag Padric away.

"Time for the gods' justice," Gregorio whispered.

"At long last," Padric replied, thankful it was not he who was being scrutinized under the wrath of the Olympic beings. His eyelids drooped. "Now I can sleep for a week." *As well as hold my betrothed in my arms for the next foreseeable future.* He smiled, imagining it. He might have fallen asleep for an instant.

It was then that something bade him open his eyes. Up on the hill, he spied the form slinking up to the city, the firelight catching his raven hair, and a final wary look their way before disappearing into the darkness.

"Should I go after him?" Luciliana asked. Her polearm was poised for a final combat.

A voice filled with authority spoke behind Padric. "Allow me— Mercury!"

Padric startled. Turning, he found Circe with Helius and Faunus to one side and a formidable god with long, white-blond hair and trimmed beard on the other. Lightning bolts flashed in his eyes as he appraised Padric up and down. *Jupiter.*

Within the next moment, a youthful-looking god sprinted up to Jupiter. "Yes, my lord?"

"Gather up that rapscallion offspring of Janus and the rest of his underlings. They will see justice served like their masters."

Mercury raised his fist to his heart. "Right away, my lord." The wind he created as he passed them was the only indication he had been there.

"M'lord." Padric dipped his head to the Olympic god. Any further and he would have pitched forward.

The others gathered around them. Talfryn carried an unconscious Eliva in his arms. He wondered where Warin and the dryad Cornelia were until he spotted them lying on the ground a ways away, arms crossed over their chests. His chest tightened at the loss of his friends.

"Young charioteer."

The strong voice brought Padric's attention back to the god of lightning.

"We have you and your friends to thank for bringing us back to ourselves and defeating our great enemy, Janus. I assure you, your dedication and sacrifice are not in vain."

"What will become of Janus and Medea?"

Lightning sizzled in Jupiter's eyes. "They will be punished for a long time—for the rest of eternity if I have any say."

"How punished are we talking?" Rawlins asked, intrigued.

"Think of the fate of Prometheus, but on a grander scale." He grinned mischievously.

Padric winced, remembering reading about how the Titan Prometheus had been chained to a mountain and an eagle devoured his liver every day for his crime of teaching mortals how to use fire. Padric could not imagine what could possibly be a worse fate than that.

Jupiter continued, "In light of your service and sacrifice,"—his gaze flicked to Warin's and Cornelia's bodies for an instant—"what can we do to repay you for all that you have done for us?"

Padric found himself gaping, not sure what to do or say. His head swam with loss of blood and the never ending night. Yet, when he began to speak, the right words came to him.

"We ask, m'lord, for nothing in return. We are…" he looked to Gregorio, who urged him on. "We are only happy to have saved you and your estimable family from a fate worse than death."

Jupiter blinked in surprise at Padric's statement. Padric hid his smirk, wondering if the Olympian had expected him to ask for immortality or riches. "The honor is all ours, young charioteer. You no doubt know that your world would have been affected as well, so it was no little matter for both our benefits. Since you ask for nothing in return, I will grant you a quick exit from Olympus to the last place you haled from."

"You honor us." Padric dipped his head again. This time, however, when he breathed in, no air came. His lungs burned as he attempted to catch even an ounce of air.

Lips drawn in a worried line, the Roman god of gods snapped his fingers. Padric blinked, and he and his party were in the library of the Valle Crucis Abbey. Everything looked exactly as they had left it. Brother Howell stood gaping at them. Warin's and Cornelia's bodies lay in repose at the center of the room as though they only slept.

The doors to Olympus abruptly shut, and white sparks spat out of the lock. The glow which had surrounded the door faded. It was now just a regular door.

Brynwen came up to Padric, but still, he could only catch snippets of air. The last thing he saw was her lovely face looking down at him before the world went black.

CHAPTER 60

Two days later

"I don't see why I cannot polish my polearm while I sit in this horrible bed," Eliva whined. Her side hurt and she was bored out of her mind. At least Asinia, her leg bandaged and propped up on her bed, crafted with twine. Eliva had never been good at crafting with twine. She would rather use it as a snare for a hare.

Nalini pinched her lips together. "Shockingly, they do not allow such weapons in the room of healing. There are also enemies here who could take advantage of such a weapon." She side-eyed to Eliva's left where Drogo, chained, leg bandaged, and looking ready to kill, convalesced in the far corner. A few monks and injured mercenaries who had surrendered in Olympus occupied other cots. Brother Fabian, who had given Padric the knowledge of the key to Olympus, was propped up on a pile of pillows, praying fervently over a string of beads.

A courier had been dispatched the day before to tell the Sheriff of Nottingham the good news that the murderer of Daniel Lambert had been caught. Now they just awaited his response.

Eliva held in her huff of annoyance, as it only caused her more pain. If not for Brynwen's treatment with her Miracle Mix, she would be in much more pain. The healer had been nothing but kind during Eliva's recovery. When she'd tended to her yesterday, in good humor, Talfryn's twin had told Eliva how he had managed to ruin *yet another* perfectly good tunic.

"You must thank the gods that your wound was not more severe, Eliva."

Unfortunately, not everyone from their party had come back alive. Circe and Pasiphae had put a spell on Warin's body to preserve it until they could transport him to Nottingham for a warrior's burial. Cornelia and Idaise would be laid to rest in nature among the trees of the forest.

Eliva brushed her hand along the bandage on her side. "I know," she had told Brynwen. "I am thankful." Yet her faith in the gods of Olympus had fallen greatly since they had fallen into Janus's and Medea's trap and couldn't lift a finger to stop it. She wondered if Talfryn's God was so easily swayed and overthrown. The monks of this abbey sure didn't believe so. Their God didn't seem weak at all. They praised their deity with love, not fear. What did that say about everything she'd ever known? Instead of answering, she found herself looking at the doorway in earnest for Diana, hoping that the goddess would prove her wrong. Yet the doorway remained empty.

"I am sure she will come," Nalini stated. "She's likely engaged with helping to rebuild Olympus and figuring out what to do with Janus, Medea, and their other prisoners."

"I suppose." Eliva looked down at her hands, so pale without her amulets and nothing like Diana's beloved dryads. What reason would the goddess have to visit a lowly human? Nonetheless, it was grand to remember them having taken down their enemies side-by-side.

"And yet," Nalini went on, "what if a certain young squire showed his face instead? What will you do then?"

Eliva glared at her aunt, even as her heart betrayed her by thumping against her rib cage. Horrible, traitorous heart! Her gaze fell to where Brynwen now sat beside Sir Padric's bed, their hands entwined as they conversed in gentle, happy tones. Several layers of white bandages were wrapped around his shoulder, chest, and arm, yet Brynwen's eyes held him in such admiration. What would it be like to have Talfryn look on her like that? No, she couldn't think this way. She wanted to be part of Diana's hunt. It's what she had worked her entire life for!

Instead of being taken aback, however, Nalini cracked a smile. "That is what I thought. You know…" She paused as a shadow fell across the doorway, and all heads turned to see who had entered the room.

Tall, the goddess Diana appeared exactly as she had in Olympus but in a clean dress with a cloak overtop. Her blonde hair was wrapped around her head in one long braid. She looked every bit as regal and dangerous as she had been in Olympus. Diana's gaze pierced each of the residents of the healing chamber until they came to rest on Eliva.

Eliva squirmed, part in excitement, part in fear.

The goddess stalked down the aisle, her steps light, sandals making not a sound on the hard stone until she stopped at the foot of Eliva's bed.

"Eliva. You are awake. Good." No doubt, it was the same goddess, as brusque as ever.

Eliva and Nalini dipped their heads in reverence. When Eliva peered up again, her voice faltered. "My lady. I…" She managed to swallow. "I trust you had a good trip…here?"

"I did."

Nalini stood. "Forgive me, my lady. I will check on Asinia. Pray excuse me." She bowed and turned to the next bed over where Asinia rested.

The seat left vacant, Diana took it with elegance and peered down her nose at Eliva, giving her the hint of a smile. "I wish to speak with you about your future."

"Oh?" Eliva's heart thrashed around in her chest so loudly, there was no way Diana didn't hear it. It was difficult to keep her voice from trembling as she answered. "What would that be, my lady?"

"What are your plans for the future?"

"I do not have any," she said quickly.

Diana quirked an eyebrow at her, perhaps in amusement. "Very good. I have a proposition for you." She leaned in a little closer, which put more strain on Eliva's nerves. "You have shown great skill and resilience in Olympus, much of which I witnessed, and for this I wish to reward you. I have considered creating an opening for you amongst my huntresses."

Eliva's breath caught. No words would come, so she merely nodded —not too eagerly, she hoped.

"But before I can do this, you must answer some questions. Only the truth will I accept."

Startled, Eliva knew what she would ask and inwardly cringed.

"Have you followed my four main principles to the letter?" She paused for effect. "Never speak to a man outside of your family?"

Talfryn. Conflicting emotions ate at her. Everything in her wished to shrink to an inch tall, but she knew Diana wouldn't accept her if she crumbled before her now.

She couldn't lie, and Diana already knew the truth of this question and the following one, having been in the arena at the same time as they occurred. "Nay. I, I have spoken to Talfryn and some of the knights on numerous occasions since midsummer. And we...that is Talfryn and I... touched, too." Their intertwining hands. The time he had embraced her when she'd been upset, his arms and chest warm against hers, his scent of leather and oak mingling with the Welsh air—

"So, the second question is answered." Diana's expression was severe, yet, she swatted at the air as though it were old business. "These things I knew already, and not everyone decides at their birth that they strive for the Hunt. But in future, you will accommodate these first two conditions once you join our ranks, yes?"

She nodded. "Yes, my lady."

"Good. The third question: will you remain a chaste virgin all your days?"

"I will, my lady."

"Last question. Will you devote the rest of your life to the Hunt? Barring the possibility that you rescind your position as a huntress before the probationary period is over, of course."

Eliva's eyes brightened, her heart leaping in her chest. "With all my heart. There is nothing I desire more, my lady." She meant it, yet guilt tightened her chest. *Why do I feel guilty? This is what I want!*

Diana's lip raised the slightest bit. "Then, Eliva of Cataractonium, I hereby invite you on a probationary basis to become a huntress. As you are on the mend, it would not be for some little time until you are fully healed."

Elation bubbled up in Eliva's chest. It was all she could do not to squirm in excitement but to keep a straight face. "I understand, my lady."

"Good." She rose and nodded. "I will see you in a few weeks, then. We will keep in touch by messenger." Her eyes flicked to the door and her lips tightened. "It appears you have a visitor. You will take care of him, I expect."

Turning her head to the doorway, Eliva spotted Talfryn, bouquet of wildflowers in his hands, his gaze meeting hers, eyes shining, and smile ever-growing. Then his attention roved up toward Diana, and he tensed. The blood drained from Eliva's face as she beheld him, even as the butterflies flew around in her stomach. She was eager to tell him about Diana's visit, but all of these conflicting emotions ate at her.

Diana stood and took her leave. She nodded at Talfryn. "Talfryn Masson, well met." Her gaze landed on the flowers in his hand with intense scrutiny.

"M'lady," he said with a deep bow.

"You fought well. I hear you are a knight-in-training."

"That I am."

"Keep it up."

"Thank you, m'lady," Talfryn said in awe as the goddess continued out of the infirmary. When he turned back to Eliva, he still looked somewhat stunned.

Eliva admired him as he recovered from his encounter with the goddess of the hunt. He looked quite well after being patched up. Recently shaven, although with stubble already dotting his chin, his hair combed back, and a new maroon tunic made him a dashing figure. Not that he'd ever looked *un*-dashing.

Stepping up to Eliva, his words came out in a rush. "Eliva, you are looking welly good. I mean, very good...that is, you look well. And beautiful. And, um, did I mention you look good?" He ran a shaky hand over his neck while she grinned up at him. His very presence jarred her memories. After succumbing to the pain and blood loss from her side wound, only bits and pieces of what happened next had come to her. She recalled Talfryn carrying her to the infirmary, his face set in fear and devastation. Of her trying to tell him that she was all right, but her mouth wouldn't work. Then there were flashes of waking with her hand in his, he sitting beside her on one side of her bed, Nalini on the other. When she awoke later, he was gone. The warmth seemed to have left the room at his absence. Nalini explained that he'd been exhausted and she'd encouraged him to get some sleep in his chamber.

"Talfryn! I am glad you are here. I have some great news to share with you."

"Oh?"

"But first, what are those for?" she asked, nodding to the flowers

"Oh, these?" He shoved the bouquet in her face a tad more forcefully than he'd intended. "For-for you. To help aid in your recovery."

Beaming, she accepted them and took a long whiff. "Aster! You remembered. They are lovely and smell wonderful. Thank you, Talfryn." She admired them another few seconds, wondering how long it had taken him to pick them. "How is Miser?"

"He's fine, just hungry, like usual. Sorry I couldn't visit until now. Rawlins dragged me all over the abbey checking for rogue villains. We looked in every single room. Do you know how many bedchambers there are in this place?" he asked with incredulity."

She chuckled, then winced, reaching for her bandaged side. With an inward groan, she berated herself for doing such a foolish thing.

"Are you all right?" He reached for her, but drew his hand back.

"Yes, I am just not used to having to sit in bed all day."

"I hear ya. So, what's the good news?" he asked.

Her smile returned. "Diana offered me the chance to be one of her hunters! On a probationary trial at first, of course."

"Of course."

"Then, if all goes well, I will be initiated into the Hunt."

Talfryn dropped onto the bed by her legs, giving her the biggest smile yet. "That's wonderful, Eliva. I am so proud of you. See, I knew she would love you." He picked up her hands. His were warm and calloused. "You will be the best hunter Diana's ever had. She'll never wish to be rid of you." Seeing a lock of red hair out of place on her forehead, he looped it around her ear, and his hand strayed against her cheek, his touch like lightning. She couldn't pull her eyes away from his gaze, and his cheeks, his lush lips... Just once, she wished she could kiss him.

A loud bang occurred as Drogo dragged his chain along his bedpost.

The action startled her out of doing something she'd regret. Recovering, she squeezed Talfryn's hand. "I won't leave until I am fully healed, however."

"That's great." Something seemed to die in him as his hazel eyes lost their luster.

Suddenly, she found herself clutching his hand. "We could still train together once more before I go. Archery shouldn't be too straining, right?" Just a little more time together until she became a huntress couldn't hurt, could it?

"I wouldn't think so," he said absently, dropping his gaze. "I think...I will leave you to rest now."

Eliva flinched at his hurt tone, but he didn't see it, or at least, didn't acknowledge it. It was probably for the best. " I will see you later?"

Looking at the wall behind him, he mumbled, "Of course. See you later...Eliva."

As Talfryn exited the infirmary, Eliva's heart crushed to powder. *Being a huntress is all I ever wanted to be. Then why do I feel so guilty about it?*

CHAPTER 61

*N*early two weeks later, they made it to Nottingham. A handful of knights on horseback saw their approach from a distance, sending one off into the city, urging his horse into a gallop.

Padric grinned grimly. "Our arrival has been noticed."

The forest looked the same as it had before their nighttime exodus a few weeks before, only colder, the air more crisp. Padric breathed in the scent of the trees, some holding onto the last dregs of leaves before the first frost came to finish them off. Brynwen's scent of honey and lavender intermingled with the trees, calming his speeding heart. He'd never forget it as long as he lived. If this went wrong, if the Sheriff really was not forgiving, they would all end up in gaol. He did not care to think about what might happen after that.

"We have made it." Gregorio shifted his drab red cloak about his shoulders, looking as nervous as Padric felt. In three heartbeats, his face aged and dark curls donned gray streaks. One would never guess at his disguise.

All of the real dryads had already donned their amulets to hide their green skin. Eliva seemed happy enough not to have to wear any amulets to hide her identity anymore. Talfryn likewise seemed happy that she hadn't donned them, either. It was a surprise to Padric when the truth came out that she was human all the time.

"How d'you do that so quick?" Talfryn asked of Gregorio.

"Practice. Much practice," he said, bringing back his Italian accent for full effect.

Payla snorted. "You should have seen him practicing when we were young. It was adorably hilarious." She reached over with her long arm and pinched her cousin's cheek. Padric laughed at Gregorio's mortifying grimace.

"Do you think the Sheriff of Nottingham will really keep his word?" Brynwen asked. She squeezed Padric's hand. He curled his fingers around her smaller one. She looked at Eliva. Ever since Eliva's convalescence in the infirmary, she and Brynwen had exchanged stories and war wounds with one another—mostly at Padric's and Talfryn's expense. To his relief, they'd become fast friends. Brynwen and Talfryn had even managed to drag a few smiles and laughs from the red-haired maiden. Eliva brought forth her bow. "I don't suppose these men could be persuaded to release us?"

"Hardly," Talfryn replied. "But you may want to put that away before the knights see it and begin drawing their weapons."

Grumbling, Eliva hooked the bow onto her back.

"I pray they don't bind us again." Brynwen rubbed her wrists, even though they had healed. Padric still felt his wrists chafing at times, too, since their time with Medea.

Talfryn shrugged. "Padric says he's a good man and is as good as his word."

The wind caught up Padric's dark-blond curls, flipping them in the breeze as he slapped a hand on Talfryn's shoulder. "You took the words right out of my mouth. In the letter, the sheriff said he would release the captain and the knights once we returned. I trust him. But Rawlins, mayhap you should put your daggers away. You too, Nalini."

The knight grunted. "These aren't for those knights."

He turned toward their prisoner, Drogo, sitting atop a gelding they had purchased from the Valle Crucis Abbey. His arms were tied to the saddle. Drogo's face and neck were red with anger at being caught and trussed up like a prized hen.

A smirk slid up Rawlins's lips. "It pays to be wary."

"I concur." Nalini's eyes narrowed as she looked upon the sheriff's men.

"Rawlins. Nalini." Padric gave them the eye.

With a deep grumble, Rawlins sheathed his blades, but his gaze never left the approaching Nottingham knights. "We'll know in a minute, I s'pose."

The knights approached, all strained politeness, calmly taking their weapons and immediately led them to the gaol. Sheriff Herbert Herrington was inside, waiting for them behind his desk. The knight who had warned him of their coming plus an extra five armed knights stood on the other side of his desk.

Next to the door to the cells stood Captain Garrick de Clifton flanked by the Nottingham knights. His lips raised at seeing his son and friends in one piece. He gave the sheriff an *I told you they were quite innocent and would return with the real culprit* look.

Sir Herbert merely huffed out a breath, but Padric thought he secretly looked relieved. "Sir Padric. Gentlemen. Ladies." He gave a slight bow at the shoulders, his gaze never leaving Padric or Rawlins. "I trust you had a fruitful trip?"

Padric returned the sheriff's gaze as though it were a casual visit, and returned the small bow. "It was a most enlightening trip, thank you, Sir Herbert. Captain. How do you fare, sir?"

"I am well. Sir Herbert has been a most gracious host." Garrick's smile widened.

Sheriff Herrington returned the smile, but it soon fell. "Your letter mentioned you would bring back Sir Warin Ingram's body. Is this so?"

Padric's chest constricted, the loss still fresh. "Yes, sir. The brothers at the abbey prepared his body for travel." Sadly, they could not have brought Ulysses's body back. Circe and Helius were truly heartbroken that he had died.

"I thank you," Sir Herbert said. "I was most saddened to hear of his passing. He was a fine knight. All of Nottingham feels his loss."

Padric took a breath. "He fought bravely for our freedom against Drogo and his minions until the end. He saved Brynwen from the same fate he shared. Sir Warin was a true hero." Padric had not seen all of how Warin had fallen, but he knew it was to save Brynwen from the hydra and in the service of saving Olympus and the world from Janus and Medea's tyranny. He would be forever grateful to him and prayed he had at last found peace in heaven.

"My men and I are most proud of his brave actions. May he rest in peace."

There was a brief pause.

Finally, the sheriff gave Padric the side-eye. "I trust you have the real culprit responsible for Lord Daniel's murder?"

"Yes, sir. He is here." Padric stood aside. "Drogo Blane, a huntsman from the north. Alas that the rest of his men escaped capture or were taken by the local Welsh constabulary, but this is the culprit who stole my dagger earlier this year and killed Lord Daniel with it." He did not dare mention anything about Drogo's immortal masters.

Talfryn and Rawlins shuffled the limping Drogo forth. The prisoner's glare shot daggers at Talfryn and Padric and anyone who dared to look at him. "I did no such thing. These men accosted me while I was minding my own business."

Herbert and Garrick shared a knowing look.

"Of course, Master Drogo," Herbert said, holding his arm out toward the cells. "If you will step this way, please, we will hear all of your complaints."

Three Nottingham knights stepped forward to take him away.

"Don't worry, Drogo," Talfryn said, "I have it on good authority that the food in the Nottingham cells is excellent."

The bearish huntsman shot Talfryn a dirty look. Behind his back, his hands bunched into fists.

"None of that, now," one of the armed knights said, turning Drogo toward the cells. "We have a nice room with your name on it."

Once Drogo had been carted off, Padric turned to the sheriff. "Sir Herbert, what of the release of the captain and our fellow knights?"

The sheriff grunted and looked at his friend, Captain Garrick. "I suppose staying in the cells for a couple of weeks was long enough."

"It was nearly a month, Herbert."

"Come on, the food was not that bad, surely."

"Not so bad, no," Garrick conceded.

Padric's heart warmed at the friendship between his father and the sheriff. "Thank you, m'lord."

"Regardless, Garrick, you and your knights are free to go. As are Sir Herman and our other Nottingham knights. As for you, Sir Padric, as much as I disliked your friends breaking you out of gaol, I applaud them for their belief in you."

"I do have the best of friends." Padric looked at his father and friends, truly appreciative of their kinship and loyalty. He did not feel he deserved them, but he would go through the same trials for them.

Always.

CHAPTER 62

*T*alfryn stood on the road at the northern edge of the Derbyshire border, wishing there were something he could say or do to make Eliva stay. Nalini, Luciliana, Seia, and Asinia—the only dryads left—spoke with Padric, Brynwen, Rawlins, Gregorio, Payla, Kett, and Miser a few yards away. Captain Garrick, his wife, Tabitha, and daughter Chelsea were also in attendance, the younger girl questioning the green warrior maidens on their lifestyle and adventures.

"Can I visit you from time to time?" Talfryn asked Eliva, hopeful.

Eliva's face fell. "Diana forbids men to enter our camp."

Oh. "What about if I stayed on the outskirts?"

She shook her head.

"What if I snuck in?"

She snorted. The action accentuated the freckles on her nose. "You have seen how well she shoots. Imagine a dozen maidens with similar skill pointing arrows at your heart. Perhaps using you for target practice."

Talfryn laughed. "Oh, you are hilarious, Eliva, you know that?" He shoved her playfully. But she didn't smile. "Uh, Eliva? Please tell me she wouldn't use me as target practice." He didn't want to be a pincushion.

"All right, I shall not tell you," she said in all seriousness, hands behind her back.

Talfryn gulped. *Well, there goes that plan...*

Eliva burst out laughing. She poked him in the chest with her index finger. "I got you, Talfryn Masson. Oh, you should see your face. It is as white as a calla lily."

Her bubbling laughter was contagious. Before he could think, he'd grabbed her hand and drew her to him in an embrace, his hand on her back, their faces mere inches apart. His heart almost seized as he got lost in those green eyes. Those lush red lips. The whole world stopped as he breathed her in, fresh leaves and cherries.

He leaned in.

But instead of closing the gap, she leaned back with a whimper. She shoved against his chest with both hands.

"Please, Talfryn." Her eyes glistened as she pleaded.

"But...Eliva..." He raised a hand to caress her cheek, but her look of horror stilled him. His chest felt full of boulders, leaving him cold. Dropping his hand, he released her. "Forgive me, I forgot myself for a minute. I know you must go, it's just..." *Hard.* He couldn't look at her. Because if he did, he'd scoop her up and take her back into Derbyshire, never letting her out of his sight ever again.

But that's not what she wanted.

I'm not what she wants.

He would let her follow her dream.

Instead, he took a deep breath. Forced himself to look at her like he was calm and collected and not madly in love with this infuriatingly beautiful, intelligent, brave non-dryad. Like she wasn't breaking his heart.

"I wish you all the best, Eliva. I meant it when I said Diana will be lucky to have you."

He was turning to go when there was a tug on his arm. Spinning back, Eliva's warm hand cupped his arm. In her other hand she held her bangle—the enchanted one which had turned her skin green for so many years.

"To remember me by." She picked up his hand. Placing the bangle in it, she closed his fingers over it, the metal warm from being in her invisible pocket.

Talfryn thought he saw her eyes glistening as she spun on her bare heel toward Nalini and the others. She bid a final farewell to her new friends, then, with a final heart-stopping look at Talfryn, she and the dryads faded into the pre-winter's forest.

Talfryn sucked in a breath. Smiled. He realized for the first time in a couple of weeks that the wolficorn—aeternae—hadn't bothered his daydreams or nightmares. Eliva had helped him with that. Helped him conquer his fears.

He joined his friends. Padric patted him on the back, and Brynwen hugged him.

"Are you all right?" she asked in a whisper.

Not one bit. "She's following her dream."

She squeezed him, letting him know she was there for him. Padric patted him twice on the shoulder.

Rawlins, however, punched him in the other arm, letting him know that he'd failed to keep the girl. It smarted.

Gregorio, with his youthful face and dark curls, picked up an oak leaf and twirled it in his thin fingers. "Allow me to tell you all the thrilling tale of how this oak tree received its name."

Rawlins rolled his eyes.

Padric put his arm around Brynwen, ready for the tale.

Talfryn cracked a smile. His heart ached, but he'd be all right. Someday. Under his breath, he whispered, "I wouldn't have it any other way."

EPILOGUE

"There is nothing more admirable than when two people
who see eye to eye keep house as man and wife,
confounding their enemies and delighting their
friends."

— **Homer, *The Odyssey***

A perfect July morning, AD 1357
The following summer

Talfryn chuckled, watching Padric pace near the altar of Saint
Mary's church in Chaddesden. All of their friends and family
members were there, including the Sheriff of Nottingham, who still felt
awful about blaming Padric for murder last year. Circe, Helius, Faunus,
Payla, and Nalini had come. Brother Howell and his cousin Herman
were also in attendance. Talfryn's brother, Samuel, looked just as
nervous as Padric.

Talfryn placed a steadying hand on his friend's shoulder. "A little nervous, are we?"

Miser, ever on Talfryn's shoulder, squeaked some encouragement to Padric.

"Never," Padric said, although the word was shaky. "Where is she?" He tried to pull his arm away to pace again, but Rawlins blocked his path.

"Right on time, mate." He indicated the back of the church. "See?"

There, beneath a long white veil, in a beautiful frock made of light blue with lace trimming the bodice all the way down to her lace slippers, Brynwen clutched her grandfather Eduard's arm. She beamed, her whole countenance resplendent in the stained glass of the church.

Padric's breath hitched as he beheld her, and Talfryn chuckled.

Once they got to the altar, the second Eduard handed her off to Padric and their hands touched, they didn't release hands again. Not when Father Clement began the ceremony, not when they exchanged vows and rings, not when the priest blessed them, and not when they shared their first kiss as husband and wife. It wasn't until sometime after they left the church, and only then because Brynwen's cousins and friends dragged her away for a few minutes to "freshen up."

The wedding feast followed soon after, and Talfryn and Miser stuffed themselves with all of the food. The townswomen had outdone themselves, with trenchers of roast mutton, meat pasties, well-seasoned vegetables, sweets, and a cake as tall as Talfryn. He and his friends joked around and talked about knightly topics, per usual.

It wasn't until the musicians picked up their instruments for the dancing part of the celebration to begin, and the newly married couple performed their first dance, with Brynwen and Padric peering at each other with adoring eyes, that Talfryn began to not feel well. His stomach ached, and he thought of leaving after their dance ended.

The revelers picked up their feet and dresses and danced around the couple in the most jovial way, at the end making a "covered archway" with their hands over head clasping the person's on the other side. The newlyweds marched through, laughing all the way, their joy contagious.

The moment Padric and Brynwen were through, Talfryn began to make his excuses to his friends.

"You've got to stay," Rawlins admonished.

"Right," Serill said. "There are too many pretty maidens needing partners. As knights, we would be shirking our duty should we abandon them in their time of need." He raised his eyebrows knowingly.

Byron nodded, raising a goblet of wine. "Leave now, and you know you'll never live it down with the lads. Also, this wine's pretty good." He tipped his cup to his mouth for a big gulp.

"And us," Serill said. "Look, your cup is empty, too. It needs refilling."

Rawlins gave him his normal glare. "If I have to dance, then so do you."

As part of training to be a knight, Talfryn had been forced to take dance lessons, something he'd never dreamed he'd have to do growing up. But once he got over the initial stepping on his poor partner's feet, he actually began to look forward to the lessons. What was the most entertaining was watching Rawlins trying to impress his partners. He was a marvel at fighting but almost helpless at dancing. And yet, secretly, he enjoyed it too.

Brynwen danced next with their grandfather and Padric danced with his mother, resplendent in a fine yellow frock.

Afterward, couples were invited to the dance floor. The minstrels began to play a lively tune.

Talfryn was pushing himself up from the bench when his friends all looked at him with expectation.

He released a huff. "Fine, fine, fine. One dance."

Cheering, the friends raised their goblets and downed a drink, then they each found a girl to dance with. Talfryn's chest constricted as he looked at all of the available girls, and he really wanted to flee. The last time he'd tried to woo a girl, it had ended terribly. What if he messed up again? Any woman he saw with red hair gave him a complex. Maybe it'd be easier to just be a bachelor forever. It seemed to work for Sir Kensington, in his mid-fifties and never married.

A hand grabbed him from behind. Turning, he found his sister smiling up at him. "Tal, why aren't you dancing?" She was giddy and lovely, and he was so incredibly happy for her and Padric. His best friend was his new brother.

He scooped her up in a heartfelt hug. "Congratulations again, little sister."

"You mean older sister."

"I meant what I said. 'Sides, the midwife was always more partial to you anyhow."

"True. Will you dance with me, 'little' brother?" She beamed.

Giving a fake groan, he couldn't argue with her on her wedding day. "With the loveliest woman at the feast? It would be my greatest pleasure." He gave her a deep bow.

Laughing, Brynwen responded with a pretty curtsy.

They danced, chatted, and laughed through the song. When it was over, he gave her an even grander hug. "I'm so happy for you and Padric," Talfryn repeated. "It's been a wonderful day. But I'm tired, and I think I'm going to leave now. I'm not feeling myself."

"Are you sure, Tal? There's still some food left." She indicated the table still overflowing with tasty morsels. Miser was helping himself to a bowl piled high with acorns.

His stomach growled in repugnance. "Ugh. I think I'll pass."

"I could make you some chamomile tea."

"Ha, that's your solution to everything, isn't it?"

His sister had the biggest heart, even considering to work on her own wedding day.

She raised an eyebrow at him.

"Seriously, Bryn, you'll do no such thing. I'll manage. You enjoy yourself."

Someone tapped him on the shoulder. "May I have the next dance?" a familiar voice asked. Turning, he found himself staring into a pair of green eyes. Brown freckles dotted her fair nose, and fiery red-orange hair had been braided and half piled atop her head, the rest spilling down her back, begging for his fingers to comb through them. Lucious red lips smiled up at him.

Talfryn's breath hitched. "E-Eliva?" he breathed.

"The next dance is a slow one." Brynwen grinned at him and winked at Eliva conspiratorially.

Taking his hand, Eliva returned the smile, then hauled Talfryn away from his sister to get situated on the dance floor. His heart threatened to burst as he took in her dress, a gorgeous green that enhanced her eye color. A sash of fresh flowers adorned her outfit, making her look ever more like a nymph sans green skin.

Mind swirling and heart hammering, he couldn't remember the steps of the dance. "Am I dreaming?" he finally asked. "Is it really you?" The music slowed, and he cupped her face. She felt real. He really, really wanted her to be real!

"It is."

"Did Diana release you to come to the wedding?"

"I wouldn't miss it for all the world." She glided with him, then winced.

"Sorry," he said, heat rising to his already flushed cheeks. He hadn't recalled stepping on her foot.

He spun her, his feet finally remembering the steps where his brain hadn't. He noticed Rawlins with a raised lip that resembled something akin to a smile as he danced with a brunette. Byron and Serill grinned as they spun their partners.

Talfryn pulled Eliva closer, still not daring to believe this wasn't a dream. "How long do you have? Wait, are you wearing *shoes*?"

Eliva's eyes rolled. "Yes!" she hissed. "They told me I had to wear these vile slippers to this celebration. I want to tear them up and feed them to the lions."

"Unfortunately, Derbyshire is fresh out of lions. You'll have to feed them to the badgers instead."

"What?"

"Who told you to wear them?"

She glared at Circe, Nalini, and Helius, disguised as visiting nobles. Nalini's green skin was hidden by the amulet necklace she wore. They grinned and waved.

Talfryn burst out laughing.

Eliva pouted and punched him in the chest. "It is *not funny*. They squeeze my toes. I think they are falling asleep as we speak."

"Then why not kick them off?"

"I can't. I…oh, I had not considered that." She bit her lip, then looked down at her feet. It took only a second to fling the silver slippers off her feet to launch into the crowd.

She sighed with relief. "That is so much better."

They continued to dance. When it ended, he kept hold of her hand, rubbing her palm between his fingers. She really, really felt real. He couldn't let her go. Not yet. "Another dance?"

"I could use something to drink."

"All right."

A few minutes later, goblets in hand, he led her to an open table. Once settled, he took a long drink for his parched throat while she took small sips. He still couldn't believe that she'd come.

After swallowing practically the entire goblet, he wiped his mouth with his sleeve. "Tell me about Diana and the huntresses."

Her smile met her glistening green eyes. "It has been wonderful. I have learned so much from my lady and the other huntresses. Although strict, they are patient and easy to speak to. They have become great friends. Some days, we hunt from dawn until dusk."

"What do you hunt now that the aeternae is gone?" It still surprised him how he could speak of the beast that had once haunted him night and day without his heart thundering. It was now a distant, though horrible, memory.

"The aeternae is not the only monster of the ancient days to terrorize the people. You would be surprised how many there are roaming around the world. We caught the Nemian Lion's cousin—whose teeth are just as sharp—two months ago on the continent. There was also a manticore near Rome earlier in the year."

"You are a worldly-maiden. Is it everything you dreamed it would be?"

"Oh, yes. I love it, it is everything I had hoped. But tell me about yourself. What have you been doing these last months?"

"Training, mostly. It's a lot of hard work—a different kind of hard work from farming—but I enjoy it, and can't begin to tell you how blessed I am to have this opportunity. Also, fetching things—that's Serill's favorite job for me to do." He chuckled.

"Is he awful to you, this Serill?" Her eyes turned to slits.

"Nah, it's all in fun. Besides, I get back at him all the time. Just last week, he found a baby garter snake on his mattress. You should have seen his face."

Eliva laughed. It was the most beautiful sound.

"On my days off, I help my brother Sam and grandfather on the farm; or Bryn, if she needs it. Now that her training under the midwife Rosa is complete, she will be taking on more responsibilities and will get her own assistant."

"That is wonderful. I am so happy that you have found your calling. You have a good thing here. Strong roots." She squeezed his hand, then released it as though remembering herself.

For once, Talfryn didn't know what to say, and silence spread before them for a couple of minutes. She had that effect on him way too much.

"I will refill our cups," he offered, standing up.

"Talfryn." Eliva fidgeted with her goblet. "I have something to tell you."

"What is it?" Regaining his seat, he brought his face closer to hear her better over the din of celebrants.

Looking away, she bit her lower lip again, suddenly shy.

"Eliva?" Voice husky, his hand grazed her cheek. "You know you can tell me anything."

Her gaze fixed on his. "Well, it really isn't about telling, but..."

Her lips locked with his. The shock at her initiative didn't last more than half a heartbeat. Eliva's lips were warm and soft, everything he'd imagined them to be. Caressing her hair, her face, he breathed in her scent of cherries and fresh leaves. Everything else around them faded. All of his emotions spilled out of him as he deepened the kiss, pulling her closer to him. How much he'd missed her. How crazy she'd driven him during their time at the abbey. How she had come to care for others who needed help. By the time they came up for air, out of breath, it could have been hours or minutes.

Panting, he rested his forehead against hers. *Should I kiss her again? Is it too soon?* "I wish you weren't going back."

She shook her head, her hair tickling his face. "I am not going back."

Raising his head up, he stared at her. "Not to Diana? But you said you love the Hunt."

"I do. But"—she peered down at her hands—"I am not going back because something was…missing."

His forehead scrunched, trying to comprehend. "You'll return to Cataractonium, then, to your family?"

Another shake of the head. "There is little for me there apart from my mother, Thimble, Nalini, Circe, and Helius. There are so many dryads, they do not need me; and you know I never fit in there."

"Then…where will you go?" His heart lurched. *I will follow you anywhere. To the ends of the earth, if you'll have me.*

Eliva shrugged and looked around. "I was thinking of staying in this Derbyshire for a while. I hear the baron, whatever that is, is in need of a good huntsman—or huntswoman."

"The baron…" Talfryn smiled. "Sure, I could put in a good word. So, you mean it? You will stay?" Searching her face, he looked for any signs of a jest.

Her gaze returned to his, her green eyes so intense in the sunlight, adorable freckles and perfect lips slipping up into a genuine smile. His whole world lit up in that one gaze.

"The thing I was missing—the *person* I was missing"—she cupped his face, sliding her fingers along the light scruff of his cheeks—"was you, Talfryn. I had to leave to figure it out. The truth is, I love you."

He kissed her again. A thousand butterflies exploded in his stomach, each vying to get out. He wanted to kiss her for all of eternity.

"And I, you."

THE END

A WORD FROM THE AUTHOR

Thank you for taking the time to pick up *Delirious* and the rest of the Rise of the Charioteer series!

If you have a moment, I would really appreciate it if you would take a couple of minutes to leave a review on your favorite booksellers and social media sites.

- Amazon
- Goodreads
- Barnes & Noble

Reviews help authors find new readers and receive feedback about their works.

To receive alerts about the Rise of the Charioteer series and other series, sign up for my monthly newsletter at: https://susanlaspe.com

AUTHOR'S HISTORICAL NOTE

The actual title of the Sheriff of Nottingham during the time of this story was "Sheriff of Nottinghamshire, Derbyshire, and the Royal Forests." The office was used from 1068 until 1566, when it split into two separate offices: the Sheriff of Derbyshire and the Sheriff of Nottinghamshire. When going down a rabbit hole and looking at all of the sheriffs through the centuries, I came across the name of Gervase de Clifton (1313–1391) of Clifton Hall in Nottingham, who was sherif in 1345–thus how Padric got his surname. To my mind, Padric de Clifton's family haled from Nottinghamshire but his family moved to Derby when his father, Garrick, a relative of Gervase, became the captain at Derby sometime before the Bubonic Plague of 1348.

While researching a Welsh medieval abbey for this novel, I came across the Valle Crucis Abbey (Valley of the Cross), founded in 1201 by Prince Madog ap Gruffydd. According to historians, it is the best preserved abbey (although in ruins) in Wales after having been closed and abandoned in 1537 by royal decree during the Protestant Reformation. The abbey was quite wealthy, and in fact important guests were graced with dining on silver vessels and ale "flowing like a river." These could have been donated by a wealthy family to the abbey for such purposes.

Within the story, Abbot Caradoc's quote emphasized the abbey's wealth: *"It was so dreary when I arrived. But things changed quickly, so they did, thanks to my cunning...Don't you approve of the fine atmosphere and silver serving plates? That was all my idea."* Check out pictures of the abbey on the Visit Wales website:

https://cadw.gov.wales/visit/places-to-visit/valle-crucis-abbey

The hippodrome that I envisioned in Olympus is similar to the Hippodrome of Constantine in Istanbul, Turkey (Istanbul was Constantinople, now it's Istanbul...but before that, it was Byzantium, and then Nova Roma (New Rome)—talk about identity whiplash!) but on a smaller scale for my book's purposes. You can see it here:

https://visitturkey.in/place/hippodrome-of-constantinople/

ACKNOWLEDGMENTS

Well, friends, I can't believe it. We've come to the end of the series! A four book series was more of an endeavor (and adventure!) than I'd ever dreamed possible. But it wouldn't have been possible without you, dear reader, and the great people listed below:

For Mark, who sacrificed computer game time to read each of my books and gave me great feedback. I love you to Gallifrey and back!

For my beta readers and proofreaders, Kelsey Gietl, Rachael Johnston, Carla Varner, Christine Emnett, Mark Laspe, and Janice Arens. You guys are my outstanding crew. Thanks for sticking with me and cheering me on for the span of these four books! Padric, Talfryn, and Brynwen wouldn't be who they are without you.

To Sarah Everest for her impeccable editing skills and gleefully pointing out my overused words. (See, Sarah, I cut out "peered" a great deal in this one!) Thanks for finding all of my errors and laughing at Talfryn's antics!

And last but not least, to my Lord and Savior Jesus Christ, you are my anchor, my everything.

Veni, Sancte Spiritus

ABOUT THE AUTHOR

She lived, she wrote stories, she ate chocolate. But the most important part is that she ate all the chocolate.

But also...

Susan has loved watching television and movies, reading, writing, and art since her earliest memories. The push to create her own stories was influenced by Grimm's Fairy Tales and the Percy Jackson book series, as well as a love of history (one of her favorite subjects in school). Author of *Sorcerous, Treacherous,* and *Perilous* from the Rise of the Charioteer series, *Delirious* is her fourth published novel. When not working or writing, she can be found doing one of too many craft projects, scrounging the pantry for chocolate, or playing board games with her husband in St. Louis, Missouri.

facebook.com/Susanlaspeauthor
instagram.com/susanlaspe_author